PLATINUM DREAMS

by Kim Hudley

PART ONE

Southeast, Washington, DC

ONE

It was one o'clock in the afternoon, but Sharday Grant was still sleeping off the effects of the night before when her mother knocked loudly and entered her bedroom. "Not now, Ma. "Can't it wait?" Sharday grumbled.

"Come on, sleepyhead. Time to get up," Vickie Grant said as she headed over to the one window in the room. She paused in front of the vertical blinds she'd bought about six months earlier to replace the cheap plastic mini-blinds that still hung at most of her neighbors' windows. When she flipped open the blinds to let some sunlight into the tiny room, she forced herself to ignore the ugly metal bars covering the window and turned to smile at her daughter.

"Aw, Ma," Sharday groaned, frowning against the sunlight. "Why you do that?"

"Wake up, sleepyhead. I need to talk to you." Vickie nudged Sharday over a bit and sat on the edge of the bed. Unable to keep the excitement from her voice any longer, she shrieked, "It worked, baby! My plan finally worked!"

Sharday reluctantly opened her eyes and pushed the scarf that covered her micro braids higher up on forehead. "What you talking about, Ma? Which plan?" Her mother had concocted so many plans lately that it was hard to keep up. And anyway, she was still too sleepy to try to figure out what was going on.

"The big plan!" Vickie shouted gleefully. "Look, Sharday! I did it!" She bounced on the bed a couple of times and waved her left hand back in forth and front of her daughter's face.

"Wh-what's that?" Sharday stammered, squinting against the glare of the sunlight. She rubbed her eyes and could feel the grit scratching her eyeballs. "Where you get that from, Ma?" she asked slowly, sitting up and blinking to make sure she was seeing what she thought she saw.

"Bruce gave it to me last night!" Vickie leaned over and gave her daughter a quick hug before jumping up from the bed. "I'm getting married, Sharday!" she said excitedly, holding her left hand up and moving it slightly from side to side so that she could admire the way the sunlight made her engagement ring sparkle. "Can you believe it, baby? I'm finally getting married!"

"Oh my God! Oh my God! Oh my God!" Sharday was more than wide awake now. She eagerly climbed out of bed and grabbed her mother in a fierce hug. "Congratulations, Ma! Oh my God! Congratulations!"

Vickie hugged Sharday back just as fiercely and said, "Thank you, baby. Thank you so much." When they finally released each other, she looked into her daughter's eyes and added, "All my hard work finally paid off, huh?"

"No doubt," Sharday replied with a huge grin. "So, how'd it go down? Was y'all here when it happened?"

"Remember I told you Bruce was taking me out to dinner last night?" Vickie waited until Sharday nodded uncertainly before continuing. "Well, instead of taking me to Red Lobster or Black-Eyed Pea or one of the other restaurants we usually go to, he took me to this fancy Italian restaurant up on Wisconsin Avenue. I thought he was planning to tell me he got a promotion or something. You know how hard he works down at Metro. But before the waiter could even bring us our wine, Bruce walked around to my side of the table and got down on his knee."

Vickie paused to let what she was saying sink in. "Right there in that fancy restaurant with all them -- I mean, *those* -- rich white people watching him, Sharday," she emphasized. "Bruce kneeled down on the floor and asked me to be his wife!"

Still smiling, Sharday briefly shook her head in amazement. She looked at her mother carefully, taking in everything from the dainty red sandals on her feet to the matching red and white silk skirt set draped over her body to the trendy short haircut on her head and the nail tips polished in a French manicure on her fingers and toes. "God, Ma. You can do anything," she said in a voice filled with awe. "And it didn't even take you that long to do it."

Vickie laughed with delight. "And now me and you are going to celebrate our good news, baby. I've got some of that thick country bacon in the refrigerator, and I'm going to make us some cheese eggs and biscuits to go with it." She slipped her arm around Sharday's shoulders and steered her toward the bedroom door. "You go wash up while I get started on the food. I'll meet you in the kitchen."

Sharday went into the cubbyhole of a bathroom that separated her bedroom from her mother's. Vickie had covered the cracked linoleum on the floor with peach carpet. A see-through floral shower curtain and a framed picture of three birds where their towel rack used to be completed the remodeling job. Somewhat used to the changes by now, Sharday closed the door and headed straight for the mirror, immediately noticing that the pimple on her chin had almost doubled in size since the night before.

"Dammit," she muttered in frustration. The extra make-up she'd been wearing on the weekends was causing her skin to break out. She reached for the Clearasil and got to work, telling herself that an extra pimple here or there was more than worth it. A few minutes later, she was heading down the narrow, newly painted hallway to join her mother in the kitchen.

"So, how'd it go at the club last night?" Vickie asked, looking up at Sharday with a smile. She had finally come to terms with her daughter's nightclub performances. But it hadn't been easy. "I noticed you didn't get in until really late. Did your father show up again?"

"Nah, not this time," Sharday said. "But we had a good crowd last night. And the owner came up to us when the show was over and said he really think me and Donnell got what it take to make it.

"Oh, yeah?" Vickie said, making an effort to keep all emotion from her voice as she leaned over and slid the biscuits into the oven.

"And that ain't all," Sharday rushed on, oblivious to her mother's strained response. "Donnell told me last night when he was driving me home that he might be able to get us a gig at *The Cellar* on Thursday nights."

"On Thursdays?"

"For the summer," Sharday quickly added. "After I finish school for the year."

Vickie didn't immediately reply. One of her major goals in life was to get Sharday as far away from that little hoodlum, Donnell, as she could. But she was playing her cards close to the vest, afraid that if she came on too strongly she'd only push Sharday into his arms. "We'll see," she muttered at length.

"We'll see? What you mean by that, Ma?" Sharday whined. "Please don't tell me you trying to shut me down now."

"Who said anything about shutting you down?" Vickie asked irritably before she caught herself. "I said, 'we'll see,'" she continued in a much more agreeable tone. "We'll see whether Donnell manages to get the gig. And we'll see whether you still want to do it if and when he does."

"No doubt I wanna do it if he can work it out," Sharday said emphatically. She pulled plates and glasses from cabinets above the sink and asked her mother what she wanted to drink.

Vickie suggested they both have apple juice, then she turned back to their breakfast with a vengeance. She'd be damned if she was going to sit back and watch Donnell ruin her baby's life. He was nothing more than a criminal in the making. A boy from the projects with no future. Sharday could do much better than that, even if Vickie had to be the one to make it happen.

After the biscuits were buttered, they filled their plates and settled down at the black-lacquer and brass dining table set Vickie had recently bought second-hand. Sharday shoveled a forkful of food into her mouth and asked, "So when y'all planning to get married, Ma?" She swallowed after just a few chews and grinned. "Knowing you, I bet you wanna do it on Valentine's Day or something."

Vickie took a sip of apple juice, glanced down at her engagement ring, and cleared her throat. "Actually, Sharday, that's one of things I wanted to talk to you about." She put on the smile she'd practiced while lying in bed the night before and cheerfully said, "Believe it or not, we decided to get married in August!"

"Y'all decided to wait a whole year?" Sharday asked in surprise around another mouthful of food.

"No, silly," Vickie replied with a forced giggle. "We're getting married *this* August. A couple of months from now. And that means me and you are going to have a busy schedule this summer because we've got to–"

"What? How y'all gonna do that?" Sharday interrupted once she realized what her mother was saying. "I know Bruce ain't planning to move him and his precious daughter in here with us, so what you expect me to do for my last year of high school?"

Vickie cleared her throat again. "Well, I talked to Bruce about it last night and we decided that it would be better for you to transfer to the high school his daughter goes to over in Mitchellville where they live."

"Get real, Ma!" Sharday angrily pushed her chair away from the table and said, "I know you don't think I'm stupid enough to transfer to a new school for my last year. Plus, y'all can't just decide something like this without talking to me first."

"Calm down, Sharday," Vickie soothed. "You knew all along I was trying to get Bruce to marry me. You even helped me pull it off. Now, all we've got to do is–"

"But we was scheming for him to marry you some time next year!" Sharday shouted furiously, cutting her mother off. "I never agreed to nothing like this, and you know it, Ma! Y'all trying to ruin my life!" And with that, Sharday jumped up from the table and ran into her bedroom, slamming the door loudly behind her.

With tears of outrage streaming down her cheeks, Sharday rifled through her closet looking for something to wear. Her mother must've bumped her head and gone crazy, she fumed as she snatched a pair of low-rise jeans off a hanger, grabbed a pair of panties and a miniature top that looked like a sports bra from her dresser drawers.

And just where did that nerdy Bruce get off thinking he had some say over where she went to school for her senior year anyway? That's what she really wanted to know. She already had a father, thank you very much. Plus, she was almost eighteen and didn't need no clown like Bruce trying to step in now and start telling her what to do.

She stormed out of her room into the bathroom where she washed up in the sink and told her reflection in the mirror that she didn't have to go for this crap. She wasn't moving to no Mitchellville, and she wasn't going to no new school either. And wasn't nothing her mother or Bruce could do to make her.

She quickly got dressed, pulled her braids into a long, flowing ponytail that started at the top of her head, slung her backpack-style purse over her shoulder, and made a mad dash for the front door of the apartment.

"Sharday! Come finish talking to me, baby," Vickie called out just as Sharday put her hand on the doorknob.

She hesitated for a second, then without so much as a backward glance, she flipped the top lock over and barreled into the dingy-white, unadorned hallway. She hit the single flight of stairs leading to the ground floor at full speed. Seconds later, she pushed through the unlocked exterior door and ran down a winding pathway that connected her building to three more just like it.

She came to a stop in front of the last of the four buildings, leaned over and placed her hands on her thighs while she waited for her breathing to slow. An angry swipe at the tears that had once again collected in her eyes. A quick shake of her head to make her braids fall right after she stood, then she headed into the building.

Her girl, Tyesha, answered the door dressed in a spaghetti-strap tank top and cut-off jean shorts that were frayed at the edges. Her blonde-streaked weave was fierce, hanging practically down to the middle of her back. She had one of those slim, willowy bodies: long legs, narrow hips, and breasts so small she never had to wear a bra. With a body like that and her confident attitude, she pulled more than her fair share of players despite her average looks.

"I was just getting ready to call you, Day-Day!" Tyesha exclaimed, using the nickname Sharday was known by throughout the neighborhood. "You must've been reading my mind. What's up like that?" she asked playfully.

Sharday abruptly cut off the small talk, saying, "Girl, you ain't gonna believe the crap my mother trying to pull on me."

Tyesha got the point. She turned and led Sharday past a living room filled with dilapidated furniture into the bedroom she shared with her younger sister.

"Where Jolean at?" Sharday asked, referring to Tyesha's sister. She knew Tyesha's mother was at the weekend telemarketing job she worked to supplement her monthly welfare check. But she didn't want Jolean hearing her business and putting it out on the street before she got a chance to talk face-to-face with Donnell.

"Jolean went to her father's for the weekend." Tyesha picked up a cheap bottle of clear fingernail polish, the kind they sold at the dollar store. "So, what's going on between you and your mother?" she asked lightly. Sharday had a great relationship with her mother, so it couldn't be anything too bad.

When Sharday finished filling her in, Tyesha paused thoughtfully as she screwed the cap back on her nail polish. "Hmm, I sure wish my mother would get married to some man who had enough money to move us to the 'burbs."

"I don't wanna move to no Mitchellville," Sharday said sharply. "I told you what it was like those times me and my mother went over there to visit Bruce and his geeked-out daughter. Wasn't nothing happening on those streets. I mean no kind of action. It was like being in a ghost town or something."

"Sounds a lot better than hearing gunshots in the middle of the night and constantly running up on some crack head looking for her next trick."

"Come on, Tyesha! Think!" Sharday shouted in frustration. "Who I know out in Mitchellville, Maryland? All my friends is right here in DC. And what about Donnell? You think I wanna move out to the boonies and leave him here with all them low-life hoes that been sweating him for years? I don't think so!"

"What choice do you have?" Tyesha asked, thinking that if it was her, she'd be happy to leave this dump behind.

"I ain't going," Sharday said stubbornly, "and can't nobody make me."

* * * * *

Donnell's reaction to Sharday's news was totally different from Tyesha's. "Your mother tripping like shit, Day-Day, but don't even worry about it," he said. "I been thinking about getting my own place anyway. All this means is I gotta make my move sooner than I was planning."

He and Sharday were sitting on the plush brown sofa in his bedroom -- the largest of the four bedrooms in the apartment he shared with his mother and five siblings in Green Vistas, a sprawling low-income project at the bottom of the hill on Southern Avenue in southeast DC, less than a ten-minute walk from the buildings where Sharday and Tyesha lived.

"For real, Donnell?" Sharday asked him. "But how your mother and them gonna make it if you leave?" She knew Donnell had been paying the rent and utilities and buying food for his family for several years now. His mother had become addicted to crack cocaine back while he was in high school, so he'd dropped out and started hustling weed full-time to keep them from being set out on the streets.

"They'll be alright," he replied with a shrug. "The rent on this place ain't nothing but forty-three dollars a month. I can keep paying that after we move and plus drop some funds by here from time to time. Moms just probably be glad to finally get her bedroom back. And it really shouldn't be no problem long as she don't start cracking up all her money again."

"And you gonna be able to do it by August?" she asked uncertainly.

"Shit, I could do it by next week if I had to," he bragged. "Like I said, don't even worry about it. I got you."

"Oh my God, Donnell," she breathed with a sigh of relief. "You just don't know how much this means to me." She smiled at her handsome boyfriend with his muscular build and smooth caramel complexion. He always had her back. "I love you, Boo," she said, then she leaned toward him for a kiss.

Although he eagerly pulled her close and opened his mouth to receive her tongue, he was plotting all the while. It was time for him to show that old conniving witch, Vickie, what the deal was. He knew she didn't like him. Didn't think he was good enough for her daughter. But Sharday belonged to him now, and it was going to be that way until the day they put him six feet under. Vickie better fucking recognize!

He decided right then and there that he would step up his plans to get in the crack game. He'd already had a couple sit-downs with Boyd, the shot-caller that ran crack on the main parking lot in the Vistas. Now, all he had to do was take it to the next level. He would choose two or three of the little homies coming up behind him to take over his weed business so he wouldn't lose his clientele. And for his part, he would concentrate on making his name in the parking lot.

He squeezed one of Sharday's thighs and ended the kiss. "Day-Day, I got something I want you to listen to," he said. "It's that new track I told you I was working on." He got up and plucked a pre-rolled blunt from the drawer of the nearest night stand, handing it to Sharday before crossing the room to the huge cooler he always kept at the foot of his bed.

She lifted the blunt to her nose and sniffed the cigar paper that had been soaked in cognac and filled with marijuana. She and her friends had been smoking weed and drinking since junior high school. All of their parents did it, and so did everybody in the neighborhood who was considered cool, so it had never crossed their minds not to do it. Now smoking crack, that was another story. That was for losers because it destroyed your life. But a little weed and drinking never hurt anybody. They just made the good times more fun. "Mmm," she murmured. "Just what I needed."

"You want Arbor Mist or something else?" he asked as he grabbed a forty-ounce bottle of Heineken for himself.

She wanted to get her buzz on, so the thought of Arbor Mist -- a taste of wine mixed with a bunch of fruit juice -- made her shudder. "Give me something stronger," she said. "Like one of them lemonades. I could use one right about now."

He opened a bottle of Mike's Hard Lemonade and handed it to her, then he popped the cap on his forty and took a swig. A few steps to the far side of the room and he was standing in front of his studio, such as it was. A Mac desktop and laptop, keyboard, drum machine, mixing board, USB pad controller, 2 mics and headphones. Just the basics, but it did the job.

Actually, he would be glad to get a place of his own where he could spread out his equipment, update most of it, and really get serious about making his music. Not to mention the fact that he would no longer have to worry about his mother losing her mind over that crack again and trying to take his bedroom door off the hinges to bypass his two deadbolts so she could get a hold of his equipment and sell it.

Shrugging off thoughts of everything except his new song, he clicked on his CD player and pushed play. A haunting tune poured forth from the speakers set in each of the four corners of his bedroom, a cut that sampled Stevie Wonder's old-school number, *Pastime Paradise*.

"I need you to help me with the lyrics," Donnell said quickly, just before he began humming the melody he'd created. Partway through the song when everything except the strong beat fell away, he started rapping in a booming, rough-edged voice:

Uh huh, yeah, yeah,
Double D and Lady Day is kicking ass again,
Thought you caught us slipping, but we always win.
While other niggas be pretending when they on the mic,
we be slinging blazing lyrics day and night.

Learned our shit out on the streets so we always real

Keep them other niggas scrambling for a place to heal.
Fuck with us, get fucked up, and that's the way it be,
Never step to Lady Day and Double D.

The beat subsided and the music resumed. He started humming the melody again, but now he walked across the room and took the partially-smoked blunt Sharday held out to him.

He paused to inhale a mouthful of flavorful smoke and she picked up the humming where he'd left off. Before long, she was flying up and down the scales singing nonsense syllables in tune to the music, deviating from the melody often but flawlessly returning to it each time.

He nodded his head eagerly in encouragement and drank from his forty. She had a million dollar voice. No doubt about it. And that voice of hers plus his own skills would eventually get them a record deal.

"Oh my goodness, Boo, that joint bumping!" Sharday exclaimed after the music faded out. "How you come up with that? This your best one yet."

"That's what I think, too, Day-Day," he said, beaming proudly. "I'm gonna play it again."

As he headed back across the room to his studio, she sat there gazing at him with admiration. He was their manager, their promoter, their songwriter, and he supplied everything else they needed besides her voice. Of course it didn't hurt that she could sing better than most of the singers on the radio. Thousands of young girls growing up in the streets of America could sing but it would probably get them nowhere. Donnell was the one who was making all the difference for her. And she was so glad they had found each other. So as much as she loved her mother – and she really loved her mother a lot, she couldn't let her mother's dream of getting married come between her and Donnell and ruin her own dream of singing her way to the top of the charts.

TWO

It wasn't until Sunday night that Sharday slowed down long enough to give her mother a chance to resume their conversation about the forthcoming move to Mitchellville. She'd stayed out late with Donnell the night before, coming home to find that Vickie had fallen asleep on the sofa waiting for her, and then she crept back out of the apartment on Sunday morning while her mother was still in the shower.

Now, at a few minutes before ten on Sunday night, Vickie was sitting on their inexpensive black leather sofa waiting for her when she walked through the door. "I was wondering when you'd finally get yourself home," Vickie said, glancing pointedly at her watch. "Tomorrow is a school day, you know."

"I know, Ma." Realizing that it would be useless to try to put off the discussion any longer, Sharday slowly crossed the room and joined her mother on the sofa.

"Hopefully, you've had time to do some thinking?"

"What you mean by that?" Sharday asked, unsure where Vickie was heading.

"I mean that I would never do anything to harm you, Sharday. I've always got your needs and desires right at the forefront of my mind."

"Oh."

"Don't you understand what my marrying Bruce will do for us, baby?" When Sharday didn't respond, Vickie began ticking items off on her fingers. "No more scrimping and saving for each and every little thing we need, a nice big house in a fancy suburb instead of this cramped apartment in a desperately poor neighborhood, a college education for you, maybe even a used car when you graduate from high school, nice vacations to places we haven't dreamed of going. Baby, the list just goes on and on."

Sharday clamped down on the urge to say that she could care less about Bruce's money and the idea of going to college because she was going to be a star. She had already decided to keep Donnell's plan to get them an apartment a secret, so all she had to do was agree with whatever her mother said. It would be easier that way.

"Just imagine it, Sharday," Vickie continued. "We'll finally have a man around the house, and one who's willing to take care of us at that. I won't have to slave away as a secretary anymore because Bruce has already agreed that I can work part-time or even quit if I want to. And we'll both be in an environment where we can meet some positive people who know how to set goals and achieve them."

"Yeah, you probably right, Ma," Sharday said. And then, so it wouldn't seem like she was giving in too quickly, she added, "But I really don't wanna start all over at a new school for my last year. I won't know nobody at that school. And I probably won't even fit in with all them stuck-up rich kids."

"Don't worry about that, baby. We'll get you a whole new wardrobe before you start school in the fall. And Bruce's daughter can show you the ropes and introduce you around at school."

Sharday shrugged. "I guess I could give it a try."

"That's my girl." Vickie leaned over to give her daughter a warm hug. "You'll see," she said, "everything's going to work out just fine. And I'll help you adjust to our new situation. In fact, we'll both have to adjust to a new and better way of living. But me and you can do this, Sharday. And in the end, we'll be better off for it."

As Vickie chattered excitedly about all the advantages they would soon have, Sharday started feeling guilty about leading her mother on. But she managed to convince herself that one of the main reasons to keep Donnell's plan a secret was so that she wouldn't ruin her mother's wedding. She rationalized that the best thing she could do in this situation would be to help her mother plan everything and let her enjoy her wedding and honeymoon. Once the honeymoon was over though, Sharday would have no choice but to tell her mother that she wasn't planning to move to Bruce's place in Mitchellville.

THREE

The last two weeks of school flew by for Sharday. The temperature in DC was on the rise, the students were too antsy to sit still for long, and even the teachers didn't seem to want to be in class. Sharday and Tyesha were tight with a group of girls from the Vistas -- LaShawn, Elise, and Kayla -- and their little squad often skipped classes after lunch to smoke weed, drink and generally while away the afternoons hanging in the streets.

Before Sharday knew it, the last day of school had come and gone and she was knee-deep in her mother's wedding plans. Bruce was paying for everything, so Vickie had decided on a traditional ceremony followed by a lavish reception. And of course, everything had to be just perfect.

Sharday was under the impression that she'd already called every wedding-related business in the DC area, from caterers and florists, to formal wear shops and shoe stores. But just this morning, her mother presented her with a long list of companies that still needed to be contacted, and then she told Sharday that she was thinking about having Bruce rent a car for a few weeks so that she and Sharday could drive around to some of the shops before making their final decisions.

If it wasn't for Donnell, Sharday would've been stuck spending every minute of her free time on her mother's wedding. But Donnell had managed to score them the Thursday night gigs at *The Cellar*, and that gave Sharday the convenient excuse of having to spend most of her evenings practicing new material with him.

Now it was exactly two hours and twenty-eight minutes before their first show at *The Cellar* and Donnell was sitting in his car in front of Sharday's building, leaning on his horn every few seconds to make it clear that he was ready to go.

Sharday flicked her living room light switch on and off a couple times to signal that she was on her way. She had talked her mother out of coming tonight because she didn't want to be bothered with Bruce. But it hadn't been easy. And in the end, Vickie hadn't agreed until she and Bruce went to *The Cellar* to check it out for themselves last Thursday night. Sharday had been upset about the surprise visit until she learned that Vickie and Bruce had just gone in and sat down like regular customers without asking a bunch of questions. And now that Vickie was out running wedding errands and Sharday had the freedom to enjoy the first night of her new gig with Donnell and her friends, it was all worth it. She smiled as she smoothed down her dress and headed out the door.

Donnell scrambled from his car when he saw Sharday coming toward him. He took one look at the sexy but somehow innocent strapless red dress that hugged her generous hips while offering up her full breasts, and all he could think about was laying her across the back seat and climbing on top of her.

He snapped back to reality when Sharday smiled and said, "Hi, Boo. You ready to do this?"

"You know me. I'm always ready to make moves." As much as he wanted to pull her to him for a hug so that he could cop a feel, he'd long since learned not to get too close when she had on all that make-up she wore for the stage. He grabbed her hand and led her to the car instead, opening the passenger door and closing it behind her.

Sharday settled into Donnell's 2002 Chevrolet Impala and waited for him to climb in beside her. A lot of the drug dealers in DC had buckets -- older cars that didn't draw the attention a flashy new ride with nice rims would -- and she was just glad that Donnell's bucket had air and an AUX cord.

They were barely out of the parking space before she leaned over and clicked on the air. "What you got good on your phone?" she asked, turning on the radio and flipping through the stations.

"I got that new Future joint on my phone," he replied, referring to one of the current rappers. "Let's listen to that."

"Okay." She plugged his phone in and turned it up loud.

They were rolling across the Eleventh Street bridge that connected southeast DC to the rest of the city when Donnell lowered the volume on the music and said, "Think you can get away for a few hours Saturday afternoon?"

"Probably. Why?"

"I wanna get your opinion on some apartments. Depending on what you think, I might put a security deposit down on one of them."

She grinned at him. "You been out looking at apartments?" she asked delightedly. "I been handling my business like I said I would," he confirmed with a nod. "And I think I found a couple places you might like."

"Where they at?"

"One of them is in northeast off Benning Road, plus I found two in Maryland -- one in Oxon Hill and one in Landover."

"Sounds good to me," Sharday said agreeably. "What time you trying to go on Saturday?"

"Let's play it by ear. But right now, I'm thinking maybe one or two o'clock."

"I'll tell my mother we got a practice scheduled for Saturday afternoon," Sharday said, thinking aloud. "And that'll still leave me all morning to do wedding stuff with her."

Donnell turned the music back up without replying. He was sick to death of Vickie and that damn wedding of hers. But since he knew how attached Sharday was to her mother, he decided to keep his mouth shut. He got off the highway in downtown DC and headed up the hill toward F Street. Before long, he was double-parked in front of *The Cellar*.

"Let me just carry the equipment in and I'll come back and find a parking space," he said, then he climbed out of the car and headed for the trunk.

Sharday watched him lug his keyboard and the other items they would need tonight past the small crowd of people gathered in front of the club. He had on knee-length, black and white striped shorts, a tight-fitting, short-sleeved black shirt, black leather slip-on sandals with thick, wavy soles, and one of those tiny black caps that fit snugly on his head. He looked good – better than good, and Sharday noticed that two different chicks tried to holler at him as he walked by, but he spoke and kept on moving.

"That's right, Boo," Sharday murmured aloud to herself in the car. He belonged to her. He had never given her any reason to doubt that fact. And in a minute, if everything came together the way he was planning it, she would be off somewhere living with him in their very own apartment.

When Donnell came back to the car, he didn't even bother to search for a parking space on the street. He made a quick U-turn, drove down to the end of the block, and hooked a sharp right into a gravel-covered lot fronted with a big white sign stating that the charge was five dollars to park for the night.

Less than fifteen minutes later, he was introducing Sharday to the owner of *The Cellar*, a tall, wiry, Jamaican dude with a mouth full of huge off-white teeth who told Sharday to call him Clyde.

Clyde casually looked Sharday up and down. "Yeah, you'll do," he said. And then with a pointed look at Donnell, "If she's the same person who was singing on those songs you played for me."

"Oh, this is her," Donnell assured him. "Without a doubt. And she's gonna turn this joint out tonight. That much I can promise you."

"She better," Clyde said brusquely before he walked away.

"What's his problem?" Sharday asked as she watched Clyde swagger toward the rear of the club.

"Word on the streets is Clyde supposed to be some kind of kingpin or something," Donnell said. "Don't pay him no attention. He always be tripping like that. Long as he got our five bills at the end of the night it don't matter."

"If you say so," Sharday replied with a mental shrug. She was more than happy to let Donnell deal with the business end of things and she wasn't about to start second-guessing him now.

"Come on," Donnell said. "I gotta set everything up and get the deejay to do a mic-check." He grabbed her hand and led her to a raised, wooden platform at the front of the club. He carefully unpacked his equipment and arranged it just so, and he was still going back and forth with the deejay when Sharday spotted Tyesha heading toward them with Lee, merely one among the many other players currently strung out on Tyesha.

"What up, homies?" Sharday called out, glad for the distraction. Donnell was so particular when it came to their music that he could go on like this with the deejay forever.

"Hey, Day-Day. Hi, Donnell. Y'all remember Lee," Tyesha said.

Sharday nodded. "Of course. How you doing, Lee?"

"I'm alright," Lee replied at the same time Donnell looked up distractedly and said, "What up, Lee? Hey Tyesha." Donnell pointed to three tables which had been pushed together near the stage to form one long table. "That's us," he said. "Just take the reserved sign off."

"You still need me to be up here with you?" Sharday asked. When

Donnell shook his head, she eagerly descended the stage to join Tyesha and Lee.

She turned the reserved sign face down and took a seat near the middle of the table on the side facing the stage. Tyesha claimed the chair on her right.

"I'll get us some drinks," Lee said, still standing. Like Donnell, Lee was in his early twenties and would have no problem at the bar.

"Get me a gin and juice," Tyesha said. She was six months away from her eighteenth birthday and wouldn't have been able to get into the club if her name hadn't been prominently placed on the guest list.

"A bottle of water for me," Sharday said. "I got a show to do."

Lee had just stepped away from the table when Donnell's boys, Andre and Hakeem, showed up. They both had girlfriends -- Hakeem even had a woman and two kids at home. Still, more often than not the two men showed up together at Sharday's gigs with Donnell and proceeded to hit on every single woman in sight.

Sharday's girls from the Vista strolled up to the table not too long thereafter. Kayla had brought her long-standing boyfriend, John, who was also going into his final year at Ballou Senior High School in southeast DC. Elise and LaShawn were both dateless tonight, so they'd hitched a ride over with Kayla in John's beat-up Ford Escort.

Donnell never did come down to join them. Sharday noticed that he stayed up on stage dealing with the deejay the entire time. Twenty minutes before their show was scheduled to start, she got up and went to the bathroom to relieve herself and check her make-up and hair, then she joined Donnell in a spot slightly off the stage to the right of the deejay booth.

Clyde stepped up to the microphone and said a few words before introducing them as, "Sharday Grant and Donnell Dickerson, better known as Lady Day and Double D."

Sharday was surprised he managed to get their names right, given his rude behavior earlier. But now wasn't the time to get sidetracked. She watched Donnell walk on stage and take his place behind his keyboard, waited until he played the opening bars of *On The Run*, Jay-Z's classic song with his wife, Beyoncé. Only then did she walk onto the stage and start singing. Donnell liked to start their shows off with this cut because it gave him a chance to rap while also showcasing Sharday's spectacular voice, which was just as powerful as Queen Bey's.

After *On The Run*, they covered two more popular rap and R&B songs, with Sharday doing all the singing and Donnell handling the raps. Next, they performed their version of *Pastime Paradise*, which they'd ended up calling *Street Life Paradise*. And finally, they closed the show with an original rap number by Donnell called *Forever A Player*, which featured Sharday in a solo singing spot – a twist on the normal hip-hop format of an R&B song with a rap solo.

When they joined hands at the front of the stage to take a final bow before the small crowd that clapped long and loud, they were both dripping with sweat. While Donnell packed up his equipment, Sharday headed for the ladies' room to repair the damage to her make-up and allow her adrenaline rush to taper off.

A little while later, still flushed with the excitement of performing, she joined Donnell and their entourage at the reserved table where a fresh bottle of spring water awaited her. She quickly polished off the water and graciously accepted the compliments that flowed her way.

"What you drinking tonight?" Donnell asked, but before she could respond a waitress appeared with two bottles of Moet champagne nestled in sweating silver ice buckets.

"Courtesy of the owner," the waitress said, placing one bucket in front of Sharday and the other in front of Donnell.

"Oh, yeah?" Sharday said aloud to no one in particular. Apparently, this was Clyde's way of letting them know he liked their show.

"Tell Clyde we said 'thanks,'" Donnell replied matter-of-factly.

"And you can bring us two more just like that," Hakeem added. At twenty-six, he was a few years older than Donnell and Andre. He was also known in the neighborhood as an enforcer for Boyd's crack organization in the Vistas, although he currently lived in Landover with his two kids and their uppity mother who'd grown up in northwest DC and had a job at Nordstrom's, an exclusive department store.

"Make it three," Lee said, eager to let Tyesha know that he could hold his own.

Not one to be left out, Andre told the waitress that they could use some extra napkins.

Sharday's girls didn't utter a word while the waitress was at their table, and neither did John. They were all afraid to draw attention to themselves because they were under the legal drinking age.

Donnell slid one of the ice buckets across the table to Andre and said, "Here, nigga. Make yourself useful."

"I know that's right," Elise piped up now that the waitress had gone. "I'm trying to get my buzz on."

"Me, too," LaShawn agreed enthusiastically. "And after we finish this champagne, we need to go outside and smoke us some blunts."

"That's what I'm talking about," Andre said, still filling champagne glasses. He smoked wedd like it was going out of style. So even though he sold weed in the Vistas with Donnell, he usually smoked up most of his profits.

"Not me," Kayla said. "I'm taking a break tonight."

"Like we didn't already know that," Tyesha replied with a quick glance at Sharday. They all knew that John made a point of staying away from weed because he planned to join the Fire Department after graduating from high school. And for that reason, Kayla refrained from smoking whenever he was around.

"Whatever." Sharday picked up her glass of champagne and looked around the table. "Somebody make a toast."

"To Lady Day and Double D," Donnell immediately replied. "That should go without saying."

"I'll drink to that," Hakeem agreed, and they all lifted their glasses for the toast.

The waitress appeared with refills and topped off their glasses, leaving a bottle and a half of Moet on the table.

Hakeem picked up his newly filled glass of champagne and said, "I see somebody across the room I need to holler at," then he got up and walked away.

"We gonna hit them blunts or what?" Andre asked after Hakeem left, quickly draining his glass in two gulps.

"I'm with you," LaShawn said, standing.

"Me, too." Elise swallowed another mouthful of bubbly and stood up to join her.

"Anybody else coming?" Andre asked, looking at Tyesha and Lee.

When Tyesha briefly shook her head and said, "Maybe later," Andre,

LaShawn and Elise headed for the door.

Donnell drank some of his champagne and looked past Sharday to the other two couples still seated at the table. "What y'all think of that *Street Life Paradise* joint?" he asked.

"I thought it was fire," John said as Kayla, Tyesha and Lee voiced similar opinions.

"So did I," came a deep voice from behind them. Sharday's father approached the table and placed a manicured hand sporting a diamond-studded ring on her shoulder. "You did a good job up there tonight," he said.

"Daddy!" Sharday exclaimed. She jumped up to welcome her father who was as sharply dressed as always. Tonight he wore a tan, double-breasted suit, a pale blue shirt with a pale blue tie, and a multi-colored handkerchief on a pale blue background in his breast pocket. He was tall with a muscular build that was starting to soften slightly with age. And although he wasn't exactly handsome, he had so much charisma that women couldn't seem to resist him.

"I still got my stage face on," Sharday explained, squeezing both of her father's hands in her own instead of hugging him. "Did you see the whole show?"

"From the minute you stepped on the stage," her father confirmed. He slipped his arm around his daughter's shoulders and greeted Donnell, Tyesha, Kayla, and John by name. Turning to Lee, he extended his free hand and said, "I'm Frank Wallace, Sharday's father. Pleased to meet you."

Lee introduced himself and shook Frank's hand.

"Have a seat," Sharday said to her father. "Want some bubbly?"

"Sure. That would be nice." Frank walked around the table and took the seat directly across from Sharday's. "So *Street Life Paradise* is another one of your originals?" he asked Donnell, idly fingering the champagne glass Sharday placed in front of him.

"Yep," Donnell said. "Tonight was the first time we did it."

"Maybe you should add a sax solo to your next song," Frank suggested, as he routinely did about once a month or so. "I'd love to have a chance to be onstage with my daughter."

"Yeah, maybe I will," Donnell said vaguely. He liked Sharday's father -- Frank was a smooth old dude who still had a lot of style. But the last thing Donnell wanted was some washed-up saxophone player trying to get in on their act, even if it was Sharday's father.

"I be right back," Donnell said, rising from his seat. "I gotta go take care of some business with the owner."

As Donnell left the table, Sharday nudged Tyesha. "Don't y'all wanna go dance or something?" she whispered.

Tyesha was swift on the uptake, as always. "I feel like dancing," she immediately said to Lee. "And don't you like this song, too?" she asked Kayla, raising her eyebrows to indicate that Sharday needed some time with her father.

Once they were alone, Sharday looked at Frank and said, "Did you hear about Ma?"

He sipped his champagne. "What about her?"

"She getting married."

"What?" A look of confusion briefly flashed across Frank's face. "Did you say Vickie's getting married?"

"Unh huh. In August."

He laughed weakly and said, "Are you kidding me?"

"Nah, Daddy, I'm serious. Ma getting ready to marry this guy named Bruce who's some big shot over at Metro."

"I didn't even know she was dating," Frank murmured aloud. "And now she's rushing down the aisle to face the preacher?" He gulped the rest of his champagne and helped himself to a refill, wondering why Vickie had decided to get married after all these years.

Sharday watched her father curiously. She was surprised that the news of Vickie's wedding seemed to upset him. Her mother and father had stopped dealing on that level years ago, way back when she was in elementary school. So, why was her father acting all strange now that her mother was planning to hook up with somebody else?

FOUR

"Sharday," Vickie called out, knocking on the bathroom door. "Let's go, slowpoke. Bruce and April are waiting for us out front."

"Okay, Ma. I'm coming." Sharday took a final look at her face in the mirror before opening the door and clicking off the bathroom light. She joined her mother in the living room a few seconds later and said, "Let's do this."

"Maybe you should blot your lipstick," Vickie suggested, pulling a tissue from the expensive Dooney & Bourke purse she'd saved for months to buy.

"It's fine, Ma. Let's go."

Vickie handed her the tissue anyway. "Just take off a little," she urged. "For me?"

Sharday took the tissue and placed it between her lips, pressing down on it a couple of times. "Can we go now?" she asked impatiently, crumpling the tissue into a small wad in her palm. Vickie had harassed her all morning until she'd agreed to wear a boring pair of Gap khakis and a white button-down shirt instead of the skinny jeans and crop top she wanted to wear. Now her mother was regulating her make-up. Would it never stop?

"Thank you, baby." Vickie smiled and turned to open the front door.

Sharday followed her mother out of the apartment. She forced herself to lighten up when she saw Bruce standing beside his deep burgundy Lexus that was trimmed in gold. She had promised her mother that she would be on her best behavior today and she was determined to do just that.

Bruce was average-looking in every way. Unexceptional brown-skinned face devoid of facial hair, neither fat nor skinny, and although he wasn't tall, he couldn't really be considered short. He kissed Vickie quickly on the lips before turning to Sharday with a huge smile that seemed to be genuine. "Well, isn't my soon-to-be stepdaughter looking lovely today?" he said as he leaned over to embrace her.

"Hi, Bruce," she replied. "Good to see you again."

He winked at her. "We'll be seeing a lot more of each other soon, won't we?"

"Guess so," Sharday said pleasantly.

Bruce smiled again, then he opened the front and rear car doors on the side facing the curb.

As Vickie got herself situated in the front passenger seat, Sharday climbed into the back of the car and came face-to-face with Bruce's daughter who must've gotten her lighter complexion and more attractive facial features from her mother. "Hey, April," Sharday said in her friendliest voice. "What you been up to?"

"Hi, Sharday," April said in her proper, white-sounding voice. "Hello, Miss Vickie."

"Hello, April," Vickie replied. "How have you been doing, lately?"

"Fine, thank you."

Bruce got in on the driver's side and locked the doors. "Don't forget your seat belt, Sharday," he said before shifting into drive and pulling away from the curb.

Sharday buckled her seat belt and leaned back to better enjoy the luxurious ride.

"Not to point out the obvious," April said a few seconds later, "but we almost look like twins today."

Sharday took in April's freshly starched khakis, her pink button-down shirt that looked like it could've come from the Gap, the plain but expensive brown leather sandals. This girl was just too damn preppy for words. At least Sharday had some style about herself. She had left the bottom of her shirt unbuttoned and tied the ends into a knot before slipping on a trendy pair of criss-cross white sandals with wedge heels. April, on the other hand, being the nerd that she was, wore her shirt tucked into her pants and didn't even have enough fashion sense to polish her toenails.

"Yeah, I guess you right, April." Sharday said. "We do have on the same outfit more or less."

April nodded and turned to look out the window as they drove past the Vistas. She noticed that some of the buildings had boarded up windows and seemed to be abandoned. There were half-naked children running wild, groups of teens congregating between buildings, adults sitting in clusters on stoops and leaning out of windows, sickly looking women patrolling the corners. She stared in morbid fascination, marveling at the fact that all this activity was taking place on a Sunday afternoon less than a mile from the apartment building where Vickie and Sharday lived.

When her father turned the corner and left the Vistas behind, April wondered for the millionth time whether he knew what he was getting them into. Clearly, Vickie and Sharday came from a totally different world than the one they inhabited. Would it actually be possible to merge their two families into one big happy unit the way he envisioned?

"You girls sure are quiet back there," Vickie said, turning around to face Sharday and April in the back seat. "Given that you're getting ready to be stepsisters, I thought you'd have a lot to discuss."

Sharday spoke up. "We do, Ma," she said, "but right now we just chilling."

"Well, why don't we put on some music?" Bruce offered. "What station do you girls want to hear?"

"It don't matter," Sharday said at the same time April met her father's eyes in the rearview mirror and asked, "Can we hear WPGC on 95.5, Dad?"

"Sure, why not?" Bruce leaned over and punched several buttons on the dashboard.

Desiigner's *Panda* came on and April began singing along. She couldn't carry a tune to save her life, but she seemed to know most of the words.

Sharday looked at her in surprise. "You like rap?"

"Who doesn't?" April responded. "Everybody I know listens to at least some rap."

"Oh, yeah?" Sharday paused thoughtfully and then asked, "Well, who else do you like besides Desiigner?"

"I listen to a lot of rap," April said with her perfect diction. "I like Jay-Z, Lil' Wayne, Nicki Minaj, Drake, Kanye West. Just to name a few."

"For real?" Sharday leaned back in her seat and wondered what other surprises April had up her sleeve. Maybe the girl wasn't as geeked-out as she'd been thinking.

A little more than twenty minutes later Bruce turned off of Route One in Alexandria, Virginia and made a left into the parking lot of a place called *Maxie's*. They all climbed out of the car and headed into the fancy restaurant, where they were seated immediately because Bruce had thought to make a reservation ahead of time.

He took the liberty of ordering the all-you-can-eat champagne brunch buffet for each of them, asking the waiter to bring soft drinks for April and Sharday instead of champagne.

The buffet turned out to be several rows of long tables lined up in a room off to the side of dining area of the restaurant. It contained an amazing array of foods. There were a variety of salads arranged near melons, berries, grapes and other more exotic-looking fruits. Chilled shrimp was on display in clear bowls filled with ice, along with crawfish, clams, oysters, mussels and other seafood selections. Meats included roast beef, chicken, ham, bacon, sausage, and of all things, lamb. Rice dishes, grits with and without cheese, several types of pasta, as well as greens, beans, and potatoes of every sort were available. Desserts had been set in the center of one table flanked by baskets filled with biscuits, rolls, and various breads. There was even a station where customers could watch a chef prepare eggs, pancakes, waffles, and french toast on demand.

Sharday was so overwhelmed by the many choices on offer that she didn't know where to start. When Vickie announced that she had "a taste for an omelet," Sharday followed her to the chef's station and ordered blueberry pancakes topped with whipped cream. April and Bruce drifted off to other portions of the room and they all met up back at their table.

Following the protocol that Vickie had drilled into her head over and over again, Sharday spread her linen napkin on her lap and patiently waited for Bruce to say a blessing over their food. To her relief, he kept it short and sweet. Soon enough they were all doing some serious eating.

"How was church this morning?" Vickie asked Bruce and April between dainty bites of omelet.

"Wonderful," Bruce replied enthusiastically. "Pastor Barnett's sermon focused on Noah and the flood today. I personally thought he did a great job with the material."

"So did I," April agreed after a sip of orange soda. "Especially when he drew parallels between Noah's plight and that of modern Christians. He explained how, like Noah, we Christians often have to go against the tide of popular opinion and risk being ridiculed. But he also pointed out that the reward is everlasting salvation."

April was so freaking weird, Sharday thought as she bit into a slice of bacon. One minute the chick was going on and on about how much she loved rap music and the next minute she was talking about everlasting salvation.

"Sounds interesting," Vickie said before sipping from her crystal champagne flute while making a point not to extend her pinkie finger.

Sharday eyed the champagne in Vickie's glass and wished that April and Bruce would disappear. If they weren't here, she knew her mother would let her sneak in a few sips of champagne.

"And the choir was in excellent form this morning," Bruce was saying. He drained his own glass of champagne and signaled the waiter for refills.

"Has April told you about the choir at their church?" Vickie asked Sharday.

"Nah. What about it?"

"Well, we were thinking that you might be interested in eventually joining the choir," Bruce said with a quick glance at Vickie. "They're extremely good. And your mother says you're a very talented singer in your own right."

Sharday looked at her mother before turning to Bruce. "I'm kind of short on free time right now," she said. "Me and my boyfriend, Donnell, already got two steady gigs going."

The waiter appeared with champagne refills for Bruce and Vickie and fresh glasses of soda for Sharday and April. He inquired whether everything was to their satisfaction, and Bruce assured him it was.

When he left, Vickie said, "But that's only for the summer, Sharday. Once school starts back up and you drop the Thursday night thing at *The Cellar*, your schedule will be a lot lighter."

"How you figure that?" Sharday asked, feeling like she was under siege. "School always take up a lot of my time. Plus, me and Donnell still gonna be doing our regular Friday night gigs. And anyway," she tossed in with an irritated shake of her shoulders, "I don't know nothing about no gospel music."

Which is exactly why we want you to join the choir, Bruce thought. But aloud he said, "Oh, don't worry about that. Our choir director won't have any problem at all bringing you up to speed. I've seen her do it many times before."

Sharday looked at Bruce for a few long seconds before deciding to play along. Donnell had put down a deposit the day before on a nice one bedroom with den in the same complex in Landover where Hakeem lived. Since she knew without a doubt that she wouldn't have to make the move to Mitchellville, what would it hurt to pretend that she was down for whatever?

"Who knows?" she finally said. "Maybe I will end up joining the choir."

* * * * *

Sharday was curled up on one end of the sofa and Vickie was curled up on the other end. A partially eaten bowl of popcorn and two cans of soda lay forgotten on the coffee table in front of them. The only air conditioning unit in the entire apartment was going full blast in one of the living room windows.

Eyes glued to the television screen, Vickie and Sharday were both entranced. *Guardians of the Galaxy* was playing via DVD -- Bruce had rented it for them on the way back home from brunch.

Out of nowhere, the telephone began to ring and startled them both. They abruptly turned to look at each other, then Sharday erupted in laughter. "Oh my God, Ma," she said. "The phone scared the crap out of me."

Vickie put a hand to her chest and chuckled. "Me, too. Go see who's calling and I'll pause the movie." She reached for the remote control.

Sharday rushed to the kitchen to answer the phone. "Who this?" she said by way of a greeting.

"Day-Day?" a familiar voice asked.

"Andre? Is that you?"

"Yeah, it's me."

"Boy, what you doing calling me? Where Donnell at?"

Andre cleared his throat. "Uh, he the one who asked me to call you," he said lamely.

"For what? Where he at?"

"I hate to be the one to tell you this," Andre said in a much more composed voice, "but Donnell in jail."

"In jail?!"

"Yeah, Day-Day," he said somberly. "Donnell just called me and said he on lock down over in DC Jail. He said he got busted last night at about one o'clock in the morning."

Sharday glanced over her shoulder and saw that Vickie was sitting on the couch listening to her every word. She stepped farther into the kitchen and lowered her voice. "He got busted on the strip last night?" she whispered into the phone. "Who else was there? And where was you?"

"Uh, I wasn't out there," Andre said. "And I don't know who else was out there neither." The police had caught Donnell in the parking lot with twelve bags of crack, not out on the strip selling weed. But since Donnell had never told Sharday that was stepping up to the crack game, he'd made Andre promise not to tell her either.

"When they gonna let him out?" she whispered. Each time Donnell had gotten arrested before, the courts eventually released him into his mother's custody. Sharday just assumed the same thing would happen now.

"I don't know," Andre said. "But I do know he already got a lawyer. And he told me to tell you he gonna call you tomorrow."

"What they saying on the streets?" Sharday asked, wondering why Andre wasn't running his mouth nonstop like he usually did.

"Uh, I ain't been outside yet."

"Okay, Andre," she said reluctantly. "But make sure you call me back if you find out anything else."

"Alright, Day-Day. I'll hit you back later."

"Bye." Sharday hung up the phone and turned to find Vickie staring at her with a weird expression.

"Donnell's locked up?" Vickie asked in a hushed voice.

Sharday nodded.

"What for?"

"I'm not even sure, Ma." She sighed loudly and shook her head. "I don't feel like watching the rest of the movie now. I'm gonna go lay down for a while."

As Sharday walked dejectedly down the hallway toward her bedroom, Vickie leaned back and looked up at the ceiling. While she wasn't exactly happy that Donnell had gotten himself arrested and thrown in jail, she'd be a fool not to take advantage of what might be her one and only opportunity to pull Sharday from his clutches. But she would have to step very carefully.

Vickie closed her eyes and swallowed down the lump of guilt and regret that inevitably formed in her throat whenever she really stopped to think about the direction her daughter's life was taking. She knew Sharday had veered off into dangerous territory when she chose Donnell as her boyfriend, and Vickie felt a lot of the fault was hers for not making better choices in her own life.

For one thing, she'd made a big mistake in choosing Frank as her baby's father. A broke, wannabe musician who talked a good game but had no follow-through. He'd broken her heart and ruined their relationship with his empty promises. And it hadn't taken her very long to get fed up with watching him disappoint their daughter over and over again. So, she'd kicked him out of their lives.

But in hindsight, getting rid of Frank was just as big a mistake as hooking up with him in the first place. Because as rotten as he was – and he was truly rotten to the core, his daughter loved him with all her heart. So his absence left a huge void in Sharday's life, which in Vickie's opinion, ultimately led their daughter to latch onto Donnell and hold on tight.

In the beginning, Vickie had tried everything to get Sharday away from Donnell. Sensitive one-on-one talks, angry discussions and ultimatums, she'd even brought other more suitable boys around for Sharday to meet. But nothing had worked. And after a while, Vickie was forced to let it go because she didn't want to damage her close relationship with her daughter.

But now that Donnell was in jail, Vickie felt that she had a strong chance of being able to set Sharday back on the right track. And she probably wouldn't even have to work hard to do it. Because they were getting ready to move to a better neighborhood, and Sharday would be going to a better school where she would meet a better quality of boys. Plus, Sharday would have a new stepsister to bond with right from the beginning, and most importantly, she would have a new father figure in Bruce, who was a stable, successful, church-going man. Vickie opened her eyes and smiled, got up and began clearing off the coffee table and switching off the lights. Everything was going to be just fine for her and her daughter. All she had to do was hang on and wait for their new life to take effect.

FIVE

By the time Wednesday rolled around, Sharday was nearly out of her mind with worry about Donnell. She was so afraid of missing his call that she rarely left the apartment. But so far, he hadn't bothered to pick up a phone and dial her number.

Andre seemed to be pulling some kind of disappearing act, too. He never got back to her after that first call on Sunday, he wouldn't respond when she called him on his cell phone, and he had apparently stopped answering his home phone, too. Word on the streets had Andre still slinging weed on the strip, but every time Sharday convinced one of her girls to stop by there and talk to him, they came back saying he was nowhere in sight.

On Wednesday afternoon, Sharday found herself sitting in the living room under the air because it was almost too hot to breathe in her bedroom. To all appearances she was watching soap operas, but in reality she was worrying about what had happened to Donnell. She was extremely keyed up, nervous beyond belief. And every time the telephone rang, she ran for it as if her life were at stake.

At a few minutes after three, just as the theme music for *General Hospital* was coming on, she finally received the call she had been waiting for. "Person-to-person collect from Donnell Dickerson to Sharday Grant," the operator said. "Will you accept?"

"Yeah," Sharday eagerly replied, slightly out of breath from dashing to the kitchen. "Of course, I will."

"Go ahead, sir," the operator said, and then she disconnected and left them on the line.

"You still there, Day-Day?"

"Donnell," she said on a sigh of relief. "How you doing, Boo?"

"Considering where I'm at, I'm alright. But what about you, Day-Day? You been keeping your head up out there?"

"I just been trying my best to hang on. I miss you, Boo."

"Me, too."

"Well, what took you so long to call me?" she asked, her pent-up frustration and anxiety overflowing across the phone line. "I been hanging around this hot apartment waiting to hear from you for the last three days."

"Andre ain't get in touch with you like I asked him to?"

"Yeah, but I talked to him on Sunday and I ain't seen or heard another word from him since. Plus, he said you was gonna call me the next day. And the longer I didn't hear from you, the more scared I started to get."

Although Sharday couldn't see him, Donnell slowly shook his head in remorse. He was the one who'd told Andre to keep a low profile because he knew Andre had a tendency to talk too much and he didn't want Sharday finding out about the charges he'd caught.

"I ain't mean to scare you like that, Day-Day," he said apologetically. "But I been spending all my time trying to get a new lawyer. That damn public defender they gave me ain't gonna cut it. He don't even think he can get me out on bail."

"Why not? You always get out on bail."

"I don't know and it really don't matter," Donnell replied. "I got me a new lawyer who said it ain't no reason why I shouldn't be able to get bail." Actually, Boyd was the one who'd come through with a new lawyer for Donnell, but Donnell wasn't about to share that fact with Sharday.

"I know that's right. So when you supposed to be getting out?"

"Well, Day-Day," he stalled. "That's the catch to the whole thing. I really do think my new lawyer can get me up out of this joint. But he probably gonna need at least a week or two to make it all come together."

"A week or two?" she repeated in amazement. "Oh my God. You gonna be able to hold on that long?"

"I ain't got no choice," he said. He intentionally chose not to mention that he wasn't expecting any problems from the other inmates now that Boyd had hooked him up with a gang called *The Greater Southeast Crew* for protection. "But I need you to handle a few things for me in the meantime," he added.

"Well, you know you can count on me, Boo. Just tell me what you need me to do."

"It ain't gonna be exactly easy for you," he warned. "But what I really need you to do is make sure we don't lose our Thursday and Friday night gigs before I can get back out on the streets."

"Our Friday night gig really shouldn't be no problem. All I gotta do is let Mr. Weiss know what's up," she said, referring to the owner of *Club 202* who'd been working with them for more than a year now. "But Clyde ain't gonna be --"

Nah, Day-Day," Donnell interrupted her. "That ain't gonna work. You can't go around telling our business associates that I'm on lock down. I need you to do the shows by yourself this week. Just tell people I'm sick or something"

"How you expect me to do that?" she protested. "You the one with all the equipment and everything. Plus, I need you to do the background parts and the raps."

Donnell spent the last few minutes of his allotted phone time convincing Sharday that she could do their shows without him. He reminded her about the extra set of keys she had to the locks on his bedroom door, then he told her exactly which tracks to download onto his laptop and how to have the deejays play them so that his vocals would come through loud and clear.

Unable to think of a better alternative, Sharday reluctantly agreed. "I'll do my best, Boo," she eventually said, "but I can't promise you nothing more than that."

"That's all I'm asking, Day-Day," he said. "I gotta go."

"I love you, Boo."

"Me, too. Call you soon."

SIX

Sharday selected a yellow sequined dress with a relatively high neckline for her first solo gig at *The Cellar*. She was being accompanied by Vickie, Bruce and April, who said they were tagging along for moral support, and she didn't want to wear anything that would send Vickie into a tizzy.

Notwithstanding Sharday's good intentions, the yellow dress was still tapered enough to accentuate her womanly curves. Together with her stage make-up, it managed to create the impression that she was several years older than she actually was.

She and her mother had decided the night before that it would be best if they arrived no more than thirty minutes before show time so that Sharday could avoid a lengthy conversation with Clyde. Sure enough, as soon as they entered the club, Sharday spotted Clyde leaning against the bar watching the door. He met her eyes and immediately motioned for her to join him.

Sharday sent Vickie, Bruce and April to the reserved table near the stage, then she slowly walked across the club to face Clyde.

"Didn't think you'd show up without Donnell," Clyde said without preamble. "When's he getting out?"

"Wh-What you mean by that?" Sharday stammered.

"Don't play games with me," Clyde said rudely. "I know exactly where Donnell is and why he's there." Clyde glared at her and once again asked, "When's he getting out?"

"I ain't sure," Sharday said defiantly, raising her eyes to meet his without fear. "Probably in a week or two."

Clyde suppressed a grin of amusement. He enjoyed dealing with females who had a little spunk to them, just so long as they didn't get too carried away. "You prepared to sing alone?" he asked, brazenly looking her up and down.

"Yeah, I can do it," she said with a lot more confidence than she felt. "Won't be no problem at all."

"We'll see," he said menacingly, then he turned his back on her and ordered a drink from the bartender.

She made a quick stop at the reserved table to announce that the gig was still on. Next, she headed for the stage and removed the extra microphone that had been set up for Donnell. A brief consultation with the deejay as she handed over several CDs, a last minute check of her make-up in the bathroom, and there wasn't another minute to spare before show time.

Clyde simply introduced her as Lady Day, a talented singer who was making a repeat appearance. He made no reference whatsoever to Donnell or his absence, and he asked the crowd to put their hands together and give her a warm welcome.

At the sound of applause, Sharday turned and motioned for the deejay to start the first tape. When she heard the opening bars of Drake and Rihanna's *Take Care*, she gathered her courage, pasted on a smile, and promptly made her way to the stage.

The initial notes to escape from her throat were a little shaky, not as strong as she would have hoped. She squeezed her eyes shut and blocked out everything but the music. By the time she opened them again, her voice was flowing smoothly and easily projecting to the far reaches of the club.

She did four other songs in addition to the Drake and Rihanna number, including two of Donnell's originals, one being a song he had written solely for Sharday that had no rap solo. The deejay timed everything just right, seamlessly switching from one CD to another, and even managing to increase the volume on each pre-recorded track at just the right time so that Donnell's raps came through loud and clear.

After the last note of the final song, Sharday blew a kiss of gratitude over her shoulder to the deejay. She turned back to the audience for her final bow and found that Vickie, Bruce and April were giving her a rousing standing ovation. Also at the reserved table and joining in on the "standing o" were Tyesha and her date, Mark, a brother Tyesha had been dating on and off for the last two years but refused to admit she had special feelings for. The rest of the crowd remained seated, but they were clapping enthusiastically nonetheless.

Sharday grinned broadly and took an extended bow. She had pulled it off all by herself! And now she could tell Donnell she'd be able to handle their gigs on her own for a while. If nothing more, that should give him one less thing to have to worry about.

As was her custom after each show, she made a beeline for the ladies' room where she repaired her make-up and waited for her adrenaline surge to diminish. It wasn't long before she was ready to claim her place at the center of the reserved table.

"You did it, Sharday! Just as I knew you would!" Vickie exclaimed, rising from her chair as Sharday approached the table. "You were wonderful up there, baby! Absolutely wonderful!" She opened her arms and said, "Come give me a hug. I'm so proud of you."

"Thank you, Ma. But don't forget I still got on my stage make-up." Sharday put a hand on each of Vickie's shoulders and stepped in close to kiss her mother on the cheek.

Vickie wrapped her arms around Sharday's waist and hugged her daughter tight anyway. "Don't ever underestimate yourself again, baby," she whispered.

To Vickie's way of thinking, Sharday had just proved she didn't need Donnell to make it in the music business. But she knew that was a conversation her daughter wouldn't be ready for until some time in the future.

"Day-Day, you blew the roof off this joint tonight!" Tyesha said as Sharday took her seat. "You the man, girl, you the man!" she added playfully.

Sharday laughed. "Thanks, but why you always gotta be tripping?"

Mark spoke up then. "All jokes aside, Day-Day, your show was lit."

Before Sharday could respond, Bruce said, "I had no idea you were so talented, Sharday. Your performance was nothing short of outstanding." He grinned and nudged April, who was sitting next to him. "Looks like we'll have a future superstar in the family soon," he said to his daughter.

"Your voice is phenomenal," April agreed in an awestruck tone. "You're better than most of the artists in my CD collection."

"Thank you, thank you, and thank you again," Sharday said good-naturedly to the table at large. "But y'all better cut it out before I get a big head." She laughed and signaled for a waitress, ordering an ice-cold bottle of spring water.

"You know we won't be able to stay much longer, Sharday," Vickie said as the waitress walked away. "Tomorrow's a work day for me and Bruce."

"We can drop Sharday off," Tyesha volunteered.

"Sounds like a plan to me," Sharday quickly responded.

Vickie looked at Mark and asked whether he would mind giving Sharday a ride home.

"No problem, Miss Vickie," he replied. And then, with a smile, "After all, I'm going her way."

Sharday accepted her bottle of water from the waitress and began drinking greedily. "Just let me just finish this first, Ma," she said between gulps, "and then I can walk y'all out."

"Do you want me and Bruce to go with you to collect your money?" Vickie asked her.

"We'd be happy to do it," Bruce put in.

"Nah, that's okay." Sharday finished off the water with a huge swallow. "Clyde might be rude as all get out, but I don't think he the type to try to shaft me on my money.

"Are you sure about that, Sharday?" Vickie asked.

"Yeah, I'm sure."

"Well, . . . okay, then," Vickie said reluctantly. "I guess we'll be going."

After the necessary good-byes were exchanged, Sharday escorted Vickie, Bruce and April from the table. They were a few feet away from the front door of the club when Sharday's father, Frank, appeared out of nowhere.

"Don't tell me you're leaving already," Frank said, stopping directly in front of them and blocking their path. He smiled warmly at Sharday, took in Bruce and April with a single glance, then brought his eyes to rest on Vickie.

Sharday looked back and forth between her parents. She noticed that Vickie seemed to be more annoyed than anything else.

"Frank," Vickie said flatly. "I didn't expect to see you here tonight."

"I don't know why not," he replied pleasantly. "I make a point of coming to see *our daughter* in action as often as I can."

Vickie received Frank's message loud and clear: Regardless of what she might think of him on a personal level, because they shared a child she would never be totally rid of him. She smiled stiffly and said, "Allow me to introduce you to my fiancé, Bruce Campbell, and his daughter, April."

Frank extended a hand to Bruce and said, "Frank Wallace. Sharday's father and Vickie's ex, although I'm sure you've figured that out by now."

Bruce smiled. "Nice to meet you, Frank. But I don't recall Vickie mentioning that you and she were married."

"That's because we weren't," Vickie stated.

"In every way that mattered we were," Frank countered. He foreclosed further conversation on the topic by turning to April and shaking her hand. "It's a pleasure to meet you, April, " he said. "You must be . . . what? No more than a few years younger than Sharday?"

"A year younger actually," April replied. "I'm sixteen."

"I see," Frank said. He returned his attention to Vickie. "One big happy family, huh?"

"We'd like to think so," Vickie replied tightly.

Bruce cleared his throat and said, "We should be going now. It's getting late."

"Late?" Frank looked at his watch. "It's not even midnight yet."

"Some of us have to get up and go to work in the morning, you know," Vickie said sharply.

Sharday spoke up then, realizing that the situation was starting to get out of hand. "I'm not leaving, Daddy. I'm just walking them to the door. Meet me at the table up front in a few minutes."

"Okay, I'll do that," Frank replied, then he turned back to Vickie and said, "I'll give you a call some time next week."

Vickie looked at him blankly. "For what?"

"Because we need to discuss how your marriage is going to affect *our daughter*."

"Fine, Frank. If you really think that's necessary." Vickie kissed Sharday on the cheek and told her not to stay out too late, then she grabbed Bruce's arm and looked over at April. "Let's go," she said firmly.

Bruce and April said quick good-byes to Sharday and off they went with Vickie. It didn't escape Sharday's notice that not a one of them bothered to say goodbye to her father.

Sharday watched them leave. When the front door of the club closed behind them, she looked at Frank and said, "Why you go out your way to make Ma mad like that?"

"Is it my fault your mother's so sensitive about everything?" he asked. "I was just doing my job as a father. Trying to look out for you."

"Uh huh," she said. Any fool could see he was jealous over the fact that Vickie was going to marry Bruce. But what Sharday still couldn't figure out was why. "You coming to the table?" she asked him.

"Not right now," he replied. "You go on. I'll stop by a little later."

"Okay, Daddy." Sharday left him standing there and headed for the front of the club. She was pleasantly surprised to find a chilled bottle of Moet sitting in a silver ice bucket right in front of her seat.

"The waitress said the owner sent that to you," Tyesha informed her. "And Mark went to get me a drink." She pointed to the glass of soda she had been sipping from before and said, "Now that your mom and them are gone, I can finally start getting my buzz on."

Kayla, John, and LaShawn walked up to the table then with drinks in hand. They were immediately followed by Elise, who was clinging to a 9 to 5 type named Keith -- in his early twenties, of course -- that she had met the previous weekend.

"What took y'all so long to get here?" Sharday asked her girls, clearly upset. "I thought y'all was supposed to have my back."

"I can't believe y'all missed Day-Day's first solo gig," Tyesha chimed in.

LaShawn responded first. "Chill, y'all. We saw the show. We was just sitting in the back where we could order us some drinks without Miss Vickie giving us the evil eye."

"Day-Day, we gave you a standing o," Kayla said. "I thought you saw us."

"For real?" Sharday was appeased. "Nah," she said, "I can't see way back there from up on stage."

"Aw, you know you our girl," Elise added affectionately. "I don't even know why you trying to play us like that."

Sharday laughed. "Well, come on and sit down so we can get started on this bubbly." She reached for the bottle of champagne.

"That ain't gonna be enough for all of us," John said, taking a seat beside Kayla. "Somebody order us another bottle. I'll pay for it."

Elise whispered something to Keith. He signaled for a waitress and ordered two more bottles of Moet.

"So, you got it like that now, huh?" LaShawn asked John after the waitress left.

"It's called a summer job, LaShawn," he replied. "You should try it some time."

Everybody laughed.

"Okay, so you got yourself a little summer job," LaShawn said. "Big deal."

Mark returned with mixed drinks for him and Tyesha. He looked at the new arrivals and said, "They don't die, they multiply. What's up, y'all?"

Mark had been hanging around Tyesha long enough that everyone except Keith already knew him. Greetings were exchanged all around and Elise introduced him to Keith. Then the waitress returned with the extra bottles of champagne.

When everyone had a glass, Tyesha lifted hers and made a toast. "To you, Day-Day. Because you turned this club out tonight. Most people would've choked, being up there on stage alone for the first time. But not you. Like I said before, girl, 'you the man.'"

Amid chuckles here and there, they all touched glasses and drank. Sharday sipped her champagne and wondered whether now would be a good time to go see Clyde about her money. She wished Donnell was here to take care of this part of the business like he usually did. But he wasn't. And that meant she had to do what she had to do.

She took a big swallow of champagne for courage and excused herself from the table. She had taken no more than a few steps away when their waitress walked up and handed her an envelope. "This is from Clyde," the waitress said. "He told me to make sure I delivered it to you personally."

"Thank you." Sharday looked down at the envelope and saw "*Lady Day*" written across the front in huge block letters. She turned it over and read the hastily scrawled, "*See you next week*," on the back. Opening it carefully, she peeked at the two Benjamins and the 50 contained inside. She did a double-take and quickly counted again. Clyde had paid her six hundred dollars! A mere one hundred and fifty less than he'd given her and Donnell when they performed together the week before.

SEVEN

"This the last thing we gotta do, Tyesha," Sharday promised, handing her the typewritten invitation list for Vickie's wedding reception. "When I read the names from these cards," she held up a stack of RSVP's, "you check them off on that list."

"Girl, Miss Vickie must think you're a robot or something," Tyesha said.

Sharday chuckled. "Nah, she ain't even ask me to do this part. She been talking about doing it herself but don't never seem get around to it. So, I'm thinking we should just do it for her."

"Oh, so you're the slave driver," Tyesha joked. "Well, can I at least get another glass of Kool-Aid before you try to work me to death?"

Sharday chuckled again. "Girl, you a trip. But now that you mention it, I think I could use some more myself." She grabbed their empty glasses from the coffee table and headed for the kitchen. She gave them three ice cubes apiece and divided the last of the Mountain Berry Kool-Aid between them before putting the empty container in the sink. The telephone rang as she was returning to the living room.

"Here, Tyesha, quick!" she shouted. "Take these so I can get the phone!"

Tyesha jumped up from the sofa and hurried across the room to relieve Sharday of her load. She knew Sharday hadn't heard from Donnell since his one and only call almost two weeks ago. And for her girl's sake, she wished the lying nigga would get in touch.

"Hello?" Sharday said expectantly after snatching up the phone. She heard an operator's voice on the other end and smiled, nodding to Tyesha in confirmation.

Tyesha nodded back, then turned to make her way to the sofa. After placing their Kool-Aid glasses on coasters and reclaiming her seat, she reached for the remote control to the TV. Men weren't shit, she thought, flipping through channels. Not even Donnell, and she'd thought he was one of the better ones.

At the sound of the television, Sharday stepped into the kitchen and silently thanked Tyesha for giving her some privacy. She told the operator she would accept the call and waited for the click signaling that she and Donnell were on the line alone.

"Hi, Day-Day. It's me," Donnell said a few seconds later, and Sharday could hear the underlying depression that he was apparently trying to hide.

"Hey, Boo," she said reassuringly. "How you doing?"

"I'm alright," he replied unconvincingly.

"I miss you, Boo."

"Me, too, Day-Day. More than you know."

"Well, I got some good news about our gigs," she said cheerfully, waiting a beat before adding, "They been going alright, Donnell. For real, more than alright. Both of them."

"Yeah, Hakeem and Andre sent me word last weekend," he said, his spirits lifting as he momentarily pushed his own problems aside. "Matter of fact, I hear you been kicking ass on stage without me."

"What you mean without you?" she asked. "The only way I been pulling it off is by using *your* laptop with *your* raps. And anyway, how Andre and Hakeem know what I been up to?"

"They was at both shows," Donnell said. "You ain't see them?"

"Nah, they ain't even let me know they was there."

"Well, they sent me the news through Hakeem's girlfriend's cousin, who got a boyfriend on my block. From what I hear, you been holding your own."

"Only until you get out," Sharday said. "I like it a whole lot better when you up on stage with me."

Donnell didn't say anything, so Sharday asked him what was wrong.

"I don't know when I'm gonna get out of here, Day-Day," he finally said. "My new lawyer filed some papers to try to get me bail, but the judge said no without even giving us a chance to go to court. They say she a real bitch like that."

While Sharday was disappointed to hear that Donnell wouldn't be getting out on bail, she wasn't exactly surprised. By now, she already knew from the streets that he'd been arrested for selling crack cocaine, not weed. "Well, why the judge being so hard on you?" she asked. "You ain't never have no problems like this when you got locked up before."

"My lawyer said it's because I got a record behind me. Plus, I was already on probation when I caught this last charge."

"And it ain't nothing else behind all this?" Sharday asked, hoping he would volunteer the truth.

"Why you asking me that?" he said defensively, his voice rising slightly.

"I heard about the police catching you on the parking lot, Donnell," she said calmly. "Everybody talking about it. How you think I wasn't gonna find out? And why you ain't tell me yourself?"

He suppressed a sigh of defeat. He'd known all along there was a good chance she would find out. But he'd been holding on to the unrealistic hope that she would never have to know. "I'm sorry, Day-Day," he said. "I know I should've told you myself. But I just couldn't figure out how."

"You can tell me anything, Boo. I thought you knew." She sort of wanted to ask him why he made the switch from selling weed, which was basically harmless, to selling crack cocaine, which led to burglaries, prostitution, neglected kids, and all kinds of terrible things. But she was afraid she already knew the answer – he did it to make extra money so he could move them into an apartment and she wouldn't have to move to Mitchellville. Which made her feel like she was responsible for his being in jail.

He remained silent for what seemed to her a long time. Then he said, "The bail situation really ain't the worst part of it, Day-Day."

She felt a shiver of dread. "What you mean by that?"

"Ain't no need in hiding it now that you know the truth," he said, as if to convince himself. And then, after a pause, "My lawyer been talking to the government about my case. And it don't look like they gonna let me off with just probation again." Another brief pause. "They offering me a plea bargain but they want me to serve some time."

She could feel the tears forming in her eyes. "How much time?" she asked shakily.

"They talking four years right now, but my lawyer say he can probably get it knocked down to no more than two." What Donnell didn't add was that if he turned informer on Boyd he could escape doing any time at all. But what would his life be worth on the streets then?

"Oh my God, Donnell," she moaned. "Two whole years?"

"Hold on," he said abruptly. He put his hand over the telephone receiver, but she could still hear him tell somebody, "I said I be off in a minute, nigga. Now back the fuck up off me."

She immediately reigned in her emotions, realizing that the last thing he needed was for her to fall apart on him.

He came back to the phone and said, "Sorry about that, Day-Day. But I gotta get off here. I hate to lay all that on you and bounce. You gonna be okay?"

"I be alright, Boo," she said bravely. "They gonna let you have any visitors?"

"Yeah. I already put your name on the list."

"Then I be down there this weekend," she said. "I love you, Boo."

"Me, too, Day-Day. And I can't wait to see you."

Sharday hung up the phone and allowed the tears to flow freely down her cheeks. As she admitted to herself that they were gonna take Donnell away for two long years. And she was just as much responsible for it as he was. How would she make it out here alone until he came back? And what would he have to go through to survive being on lock down all that time?

EIGHT

It was exactly one week before Vickie's wedding, and Sharday and her girls had totally rearranged the front half of the tiny apartment she shared with her mother. They'd pushed the living room sofa against a far wall, lined up the dining room chairs on either side of it, and shoved the dining room table into a corner before loading it down with fried chicken, macaroni and tuna, potato salad, assorted chips and dips, plus crackers and cheese. A variety of liquor bottles and mixers lined the kitchen counters, while the refrigerator had been stuffed with cases of beer and soda. Last but not least, black market mixtape CDs with oldies from the '70s and '80s were stacked neatly beside the CD player on their miniature entertainment center.

All this had been done for Vickie's bachelorette party. She'd said she wanted an old-fashioned house party. Adding that it would be her "last and final blowout in the bowels of southeast." And Sharday was determined to give her mother what she wanted.

At five minutes before ten on Vickie's final Saturday night as a single woman, Sharday opened the front door of their apartment to admit the first of her mother's guests.

"Sharday!" exclaimed the big-breasted, brown-skinned woman. She wore a tight black minidress with matching stiletto heels, and her hair was pinned up in a mass of weave-enhanced curls. Opening her arms wide, she briefly enveloped Sharday in a perfume-scented hug.

"How you doing, Miss Cecilia," Sharday said with a smile when the woman released her. This was her mother's best friend from work -- or at least, she used to be. Once Vickie started taking a million and one evening classes to "improve" herself, she and Cecilia had slowly drifted apart.

"Well, look at you, young lady!" Cecilia said approvingly. "You filled out quite a bit since the last time I saw you, and those baggy clothes can't begin to hide it."

Sharday grinned. "I need to take a lesson from you, huh, Ms. Cecilia?

I see you still wearing the heck out of them minidresses."

Cecilia laughed. "Just trying to keep the brothers on their toes, Sharday," she said with a broad grin.

Sharday laughed, too, then she turned to call for her mother. "Ma!" she yelled out. "Miss Cecilia here!"

"Send her back!" Vickie shouted in reply.

"She in her bedroom, Miss Cecilia," Sharday said. "You know the way."

As Cecilia headed down the hallway towards Vickie's room, Sharday went to the kitchen and gathered up beers for herself and her girls. Her mother had said they could drink beer tonight, but not a drop of anything stronger, and they fully intended to take her up on the offer.

Sharday was approaching her own bedroom with two chilled cans in each hand when she caught a whiff of the unmistakable smells of incense and weed flowing forth from Vickie's closed door. She paused and raised her eyebrows in surprise. Her mother hadn't smoked weed in more than a year. She'd stopped smoking when she was improving herself, and Sharday knew that for a fact. Apparently, this was gonna be a blowout for Vickie in each and every sense of the word.

Smiling in amusement, Sharday stepped around the moving boxes that were stacked just inside her bedroom door and passed out beers to Tyesha, LaShawn, and Kayla. Elise had ditched them for the night to be with Keith, the guy with the office job who seemed to take up more and more of Elise's time as the summer wore on.

"I smell kush," LaShawn announced, using another of their slang terms for marijuana.

"So do I," Kayla said. "I thought it was my imagination."

Sharday swallowed a mouthful of beer. "Nah, that's my mother and her friend, Miss Cecilia. They probably back there blazing up," she said.

"Your mother's so unpredictable, Day-Day," Tyesha said. "I can't believe she's smoking again."

"Me neither," Sharday replied. "But she probably feel like this her last chance to do it before she get married."

"Well, we can blaze up, too," LaShawn said. "I got a blunt left over from last night. Y'all got any?"

"Girl, we can't smoke in here," Sharday said quickly. "You must be crazy. My mother would kill me."

"Miss Vickie still don't know you get high?" LaShawn asked in surprise. Then she shook her head and took a swig of her beer. She smoked weed with her mother all the time and couldn't relate to having to sneak around.

"Well, of course I told her I tried it before," Sharday said somewhat defensively. "It's just that I never really came out and said I do it all the time."

"Hmm, my mother knows I get high, but I can't smoke in our apartment either." This from Tyesha.

Kayla remained silent and no one expected her to do otherwise. It was common knowledge that Kayla's mother was usually too drunk to stay on top of what her kids were doing.

"Just hold up for a minute," Sharday told LaShawn. "I got some weed, too. And once the party get started, we can go outside and get our heads right."

"Why don't you stop being so pressed all the time?" Tyesha jokingly asked LaShawn.

Kayla laughed, but LaShawn looked at Tyesha and said, "Like you can talk."

Sharday heard a knock at the front door and glanced at her watch. "I gotta get that," she said. "Plus, it's time for me to turn on the music so we might as well go up front." She looked at Tyesha. "Do me a favor. Knock on my mother's door and let her know this party of hers about to jump off."

"No problem," Tyesha replied, finishing off her beer.

Sharday played hostess for the next half hour as the apartment gradually filled with her mother's guests. Cecilia was the only person Vickie had invited from her job. Everyone else who showed up either currently lived in the neighborhood or had lived there at some point in the past.

These were the people Vickie had spent her free time with before she embarked on her ambitious self-improvement plan that included classes with titles like, "*Dress for Success*," "*Maximize Your Potential*," "*Improve Your Everyday English*," "*Gourmet Cooking on a Shoestring Budget*." And once it became clear to her old friends that Vickie had let down her guard and reverted to her former ways for the night, they let it all hang out, too.

She and her friends were hand-dancing, doing the bump, the rock, the snake, and every other dance they could remember from decades past. Old-school music from artists such as the Commodores, Heat Wave, War, the Gap Band, the Ohio Players, and the Brothers Johnson filled the apartment. Vickie even kept an incense continually burning in her bedroom so that she and select buddies could tip back from time to time to reinforce their marijuana highs.

When *Flashlight* by Parliament/Funkadelic came on, Vickie let out a whoop and kicked off her shoes, heading for the center of the dance floor. "This is my jam!" she exclaimed loudly and proceeded to do the freak by herself in the middle of the floor as her guests formed a circle around her and chanted, "Go Vickie! Go Vickie!"

Sharday popped the top on a fresh can of beer and looked on in amazement. She hadn't seen her mother get down like this in a long time. And based on their recent outings with Bruce and April, Sharday was pretty certain that after the wedding she would never see her mother in this mode again.

NINE

Today was Vickie's big day and she was decked out in creamy off-white for the occasion. She had on an exquisitely tailored sheath that stopped at her knees, a matching cropped jacket liberally sprinkled with mother of pearl sequins, long satin gloves reaching slightly past her elbows, super sheer pantyhose and satin pumps, and a stylish semi-circular hat perched at just the right angle on her head.

"You look beautiful, Ma," Sharday whispered, handing her mother a bouquet of pale pink and cream roses.

"Thank you, baby," Vickie said with a slightly nervous smile, then she involuntarily tightened her grip on the bouquet as the organist played the opening bars of the Pointer Sisters' *We Are Family*.

On cue, Sharday and April stepped up to the door leading to the inner sanctum of the church and locked arms. They were dressed in identical pale pink sheaths with dyed-to-match pumps, pearl chokers, and teardrop pearl earrings. Sharday had even pulled her braids back into a modified French roll that echoed April's permed hairstyle.

Looking straight ahead and struggling to maintain a smile, Sharday slowly made her way down the aisle with April. After today, her life would never again be the same. She would have a new family, a new home, a new school in a totally new neighborhood. And while on the one hand she couldn't help being happy for her mother, what she really wanted more than anything was to wake up and be back in her old life.

Bruce was standing before the preacher at the front of the church. He wore an ivory tuxedo, a pale pink bow tie and matching cummerbund, patent leather ivory shoes, and a huge smile. He smiled at Sharday and April when they finished their synchronized walk and moved to either side of him, but he really beamed once Vickie stepped through the door of the sanctuary.

She was the woman with whom he planned to spend the rest of his life, and he felt deep within his soul that this time around he had picked someone who would make him happy. Although he'd never mentioned anything to Vickie one way or another, he suspected that she had made a conscious effort to improve her English and leave behind bad associations and habits to prepare herself for their relationship. And his unconfirmed suspicion that she'd gone to such lengths to be with him -- though he clearly didn't know the half of it -- endeared her to him even more.

Of course, he realized that Vickie was under the impression that he was rich. And he also knew that his annual salary of one hundred and forty three thousand dollars plus bonus left him far from wealthy, even when one took into account the generous child support payments he received from April's mother each month. But compared to most of the men Vickie had dated in the past, he was probably quite well-heeled. So, he was confident that he could provide her with the lifestyle she sought.

As Vickie walked unescorted down the aisle to take her place beside him, she was clearly nervous, but nevertheless radiating joy. Her father was seated in the front row on the bride's side, but Vickie had insisted she was way too old to have anybody give her away. "I'm a grown woman who makes her own decisions," she'd said. "So, I'm going to be the one to give myself away."

Now, Bruce eagerly stepped forward to meet her and took her hands into his own. "Forever and ever," he whispered huskily as he gazed into her eyes.

"Forever and ever," she whispered back, then she blinked several times to contain tears of happiness.

Bruce released Vickie's left hand but maintained his grip on her right as he turned and led her to the altar. Once in position, flanked on either side by their beloved daughters, they eagerly looked to the preacher to pronounce their traditional vows.

Pastor Barnett had overseen Bruce's spiritual progress for nearly a decade, but he knew that Vickie wasn't currently attached to a congregation of her own. For that reason, he had decided early on to take this opportunity to share a few words of biblical wisdom with the couple.

He spoke of how marriage was divinely designed to form a permanent bond between a man and a woman, briefly detailed the duties of husband as head of the family and wife as loving help meet, and wished the two of them a lasting and happy union before proceeding to the actual vows.

Bruce slipped a diamond-studded twenty-four karat gold wedding band on Vickie's ring finger at the appropriate break in the ceremony and said, "I do," in a resounding voice that was devoid of all traces of doubt.

Determined to follow suit when her turn came, Vickie managed to hold back her tears until Pastor Barnett officially pronounced them man and wife.

Bruce pulled a handkerchief from an interior pocket and gently wiped her cheeks before claiming her lips in a passionate kiss. Vickie responded enthusiastically, and almost a full minute passed before they both reached out to include Sharday and April in a four-way embrace.

* * * * *

The wedding reception was held at The Masonic Lodge in nearby Upper Marlboro, Maryland, one of the few decent places available on such short notice. The lodge was a relatively small but very tasteful meeting hall consisting of one large all-purpose room with hardwood floors and a profusion of windows, and a narrow hallway that ran the width of the structure at the rear and contained a small kitchen, two bathrooms, and two carpeted meeting rooms that had been appropriated as changing rooms for the bride and groom.

Vickie and Sharday had chosen pale pink table cloths and colorful floral centerpieces for all but the wedding party's table, which was covered in a heavy, lace-edged, ivory linen cloth and held a frosted crystal vase that had been filled with a stunning array of tropical flowers. Since the wedding party was so small, Vickie had opted to place them atop a make-shift platform in the middle of the area where the other guests were seated, instead of in the traditional location at the front of the room.

Champagne flowed freely among the adults in attendance as the catering staff served mixed greens with lump crab meat and vinaigrette dressing for the salad course, followed by a choice of prawn, cornish hen, and vegetarian entrees. For dessert the guests would be given slices of the triple-tiered, white-on-white wedding cake Vickie and Sharday had ordered several weeks earlier.

Bruce made a formal toast to celebrate his new marriage and new family before the eating started. But the guests didn't begin making their toasts until the main course was coming to an end. First to stand up was Bruce's older brother, Rob, who had flown in from Chicago for the wedding festivities. He was seated at a table with his own wife and kids, Bruce's parents who also lived in Chicago, and Bruce's younger sister, Felicia, who attended graduate school at American University in northwest DC.

"I would like to make a toast to my brother and my new sister-in-law, Vickie," Rob said once silence prevailed in the room. "I've watched from afar as my brother single-handedly raised my niece, April, from the time she was a toddler. And given my experience with these two terrors of my own," he pointed to his teenaged offspring, "all I can say is more power to you, bro'. You're a better man than me." The audience erupted in laughter.

"No, seriously," Rob continued a few seconds later. "Bruce is a good man, an honorable man. And I'm happy to see that he's found a good woman to stand by his side." He raised his glass and added, "To you, Vickie and Bruce, from me and our entire family. May you grow closer and draw strength from each other as you travel together through this journey called life."

Vickie's father, Leroy, stood up next. He and the rest of Vickie's immediate family had traveled by car from Philadelphia, which is where Vickie had left them when she fell in love with Frank Wallace and followed him back to his hometown of DC. Leroy cleared his throat and said, "First off, I'd like to welcome Bruce to the family. Vickie is my first-born, so I know her real good. And one thing I know for sure is that she wouldn't have married you today if she wasn't sure you was the right man for her. So, you and Vickie take care of each other. And look out for my grandbaby, Sharday, and my new granddaughter, April, too. And me and the family wish you all a long and happy life together."

Vickie's good friend, Cecilia, also made a toast. She stood on behalf of Vickie's former co-workers -- Vickie wouldn't be returning to work now that she was married -- and said that they would all miss Vickie but they were happy for her and wished her "nothing but the best." When Cecilia sat down, Bruce's boss, Matthew, one of a handful of white people there, made a few congratulatory remarks. He was followed by a member of the deacon board at Mitchellville Baptist Church, who ended by encouraging Vickie and Sharday to join their congregation.

Several long seconds passed after the deacon spoke, but just when it seemed that no further toasts were forthcoming, Tyesha stood up and smiled. She was seated at a table with her date, her mother and sister, Kayla and John, Elise and Keith, and LaShawn who was dateless as usual. Nobody else from southeast had been invited.

Tyesha's comments were short and to the point. She said that Sharday was her very best friend, that Vickie was like a second mother to her, and that on behalf of the old neighborhood she wished them and their new family the best of luck in the future.

Bruce claimed the spotlight then. "Vickie and I would like to thank each and every one of you for the warm wishes, and for joining us on this wonderful day of celebration. We look forward to seeing you all at our ten-year anniversary a decade from now. Same time, same place." He chuckled along with everyone else before adding, "And now, we're going to bring the formal part of the ceremony to a close by cutting the cake."

The caterers rolled the gorgeous wedding cake in to a round of impromptu applause. Bruce escorted Vickie to the rear of the room, where they cut the first slice together. They each picked up a piece and held it to the other's mouth, maintaining the pose for a few seconds to allow the photographer to take several shots before they fed one another. Their subsequent kiss drew whistles, catcalls, and hand-clapping from the assembled guests.

As the catering staff took over the task of slicing and distributing the dessert, the newlyweds began circulating, spending at least a couple of minutes at each table. Sharday and April were making a decent attempt at small talk and still eating their respective slices of cake when they noticed Vickie and Bruce beckoning them to the far side of the room.

"Wonder what they up to now," Sharday mumbled.

"They're at my mother's table," April said. "I guess they want to introduce you."

"Which one's your mother?" Sharday asked with interest. She had learned from Vickie that April's mother was supposed to be a hotshot lawyer who left Bruce and April because she wanted more time to focus on her career.

"The light-skinned one who's wearing the navy silk coat dress and has her hair pulled back in a chignon," April replied, rising from her seat.

Sharday followed April across the room. She didn't know what a chignon was, but she definitely wanted to meet the stylish woman April had identified as her mother. As Sharday got closer to the table, she saw that April's mother was literally dripping in ice. She had huge square diamond studs in her ears, a double-strand platinum chain with a heavy diamond pendant around her neck, several diamond rings on each hand, and a diamond-encrusted watch.

April went to stand by her mother's side, and Bruce slipped his arm around Sharday's shoulders. "This is my stepdaughter, Sharday," he said. "Sharday, meet April's mother, Cathy, and her husband, Terrence."

"How y'all doing?" Sharday said, leaning over to shake their hands.

"Nice to meet you, Sharday," Cathy said.

"It's a pleasure," Terrence added.

"Oh, well," Bruce said jovially, putting an end to any thoughts of a conversation. "Gotta keep moving. You know how it is."

"Of course, we do," Cathy said with an amused smile. "We've both been there and done that twice, too."

Sharday moved on with Vickie and Bruce, but April stayed behind. When Sharday saw that the next table was filled with Bruce's work colleagues, she said, "Uh, I think I'm gonna go see what Tyesha and them up to, if that's alright with y'all."

"By all means, Sharday," Bruce said agreeably, and it was clear to Sharday that he was floating on some kind of an emotional high.

Vickie smiled and affectionately squeezed her daughter's upper arm. "Go ahead, baby. And tell them we'll be around to say hello shortly."

Happy for the reprieve, Sharday turned and headed toward the neighborhood table. She paused halfway there and surreptitiously scanned the room for her father's face. Although he'd been one of the first people to return his RSVP card, he had yet to show up. As a matter of fact, Sharday hadn't seen or heard from him since that night he'd ticked Vickie off at *The Cellar*.

Shrugging off Frank's absence and assuming he would show up again once he came to grips with Vickie's new marriage, Sharday quickly made her way across the room. The neighborhood was represented in style. Elise had managed to tear herself away from Keith long enough to give her girls new hairdos. Sharday was sporting fresh braids, Tyesha's weave was gone only to be replaced by a fly short haircut that framed her face, Kayla's shoulder-length hair was blunt cut with a healthy shine, and LaShawn's customary gel twists were newly done and glistening with oil sheen. Elise had even given herself a burgundy bob-style weave.

Eager to fit in at what they considered to be a fancy wedding, each of her girls wore a simple sheath like her own with matching pumps. Elise's dress and shoes were a muted red, LaShawn's were light blue, and Tyesha had selected pastel green, while Kayla opted for yellow. John, Keith, and Tyesha's date, a brother named Sherwood, were all dressed in conservative suits and ties.

Tyesha's mother, Gloria, and her younger sister, Jolean, were representing, too. Jolean wore a pretty floral dress that her father had bought her, and Gloria had on a beige linen dress that Tyesha had helped her find in the clearance section of *Marshall's*. Sharday also knew from Tyesha that Gloria and Jolean had both gone to the beauty shop the day before for touch-ups and wet sets.

After claiming the one empty seat that had been left vacant just in case LaShawn came up with a date at the last minute, Sharday glanced around the table and grinned. "Y'all having fun yet?" she asked.

Gloria said, "Your mother had herself one beautiful wedding, Day-Day. Tell her I said thanks for inviting us."

"You can tell her yourself, Miss Gloria," Sharday said with a smile. "Her and Bruce supposed to be stopping by here to say hi to y'all."

"Why couldn't she pick a better deejay?" Jolean complained. "This one sucks."

Sharday laughed and said, "Nah, Jolean. He just chilling while we eat and stuff. Once my mother and Bruce get their first dance in, he gonna start playing some real music."

"Do you always have to be such a spoiled brat?" Tyesha said across the table to Jolean.

LaShawn took advantage of the moment by leaning towards Sharday and whispering, "Any chance of me getting some bubbly up in here?"

"I don't know," Sharday admitted, thinking that she wouldn't mind having a glass of champagne herself. "You might be able to pull it off once people start dancing and stuff."

"So, how you feel having a whole new family and everything, Day-Day?" Elise asked. "Don't it seem weird?"

"They not that bad," Sharday said, surprised to find herself defending Bruce and April. "Bruce is actually kind of nice and he been promising to get me and his daughter, April, a car to share once him and my mother get back from their honeymoon." She shrugged. "And me and April got something in common because she into rap."

"This is the best thing that ever happened to Day-Day," Tyesha said.

"I don't know about all that," Sharday said. She had finally accepted that she would have to move to Mitchellville, but calling this the best thing that ever happened to her was going way too far.

"Aw, stop trembling, Day-Day," John said. "This might be your one and only chance to get out of the ghetto."

Sharday bit back a rude reply about his fireman wanna-be status when she saw her mother and Bruce approaching the table. Vickie introduced Bruce to everyone except Tyesha, who'd previously met him at *The Cellar*, and then she thanked them all for coming.

"Well, I wanna thank you for inviting us, Vickie," Gloria said. "And I'm gonna make sure I take good care of Day-Day while you gone on your honeymoon."

"I really appreciate that, Gloria," Vickie replied. "And of course, Tyesha and Jolean are always welcome at our house."

"That goes without saying," Bruce confirmed.

Vickie and Bruce proceeded to the next table, and it wasn't long before they were standing in the center of the space at the front of the room that had been reserved for the dance floor. The deejay played *Stairway to Heaven*, an old-school joint by the O'Jays, and Bruce took Vickie into his arms for the first dance.

The deejay got down to business after that. He played old-school hits by Maze, the S.O.S. Band, Cameo, and the like, as well as newer non-rap songs by R&B artists such as Alicia Keys, Jeremih, Bryson Tiller, and Beyoncé. But in spite of the great music pouring into the room, few people besides Sharday's girls and their dates were dancing.

By now, Sharday was seated at the table with her relatives from Philly. She looked around the room in dismay, finding it hard to believe that Vickie and Bruce's wedding guests would rather stand around talking instead of getting out there on the dance floor. This so-called party was whack, nothing at all like Vickie's bachelorette party a week ago. It was probably an omen of how boring her life would be once she moved to Mitchellville.

"What's wrong, baby?" Sharday's grandmother asked her. "You looked right sad there for a minute."

"I'm alright, Grams," Sharday said unconvincingly.

"Don't worry, baby," her grandmother said sympathetically. "It's gonna be okay. Your mother would die before she did something that would hurt you."

Sharday smiled in an attempt to shake off her dark mood. "You probably right, Grams," she said with a cheerfulness she didn't feel. "I bet you I'm sitting up here worrying for nothing."

The deejay played *The Cupid Shuffle* and several of Sharday's cousins jumped up from the table to dance. "You coming, Sharday?" one of them asked. "Don't let me find out you don't know how to do the Cupid Shuffle," another one added.

"Puh-lease," Sharday said, quickly stepping up to the challenge. "In case y'all didn't know it, I practically invented the Cupid Shuffle."

Sharday and her cousins were joined on the dance floor by everyone from the neighborhood table with the exception of Gloria, and they ended up having so much fun that they stayed for three songs in a row. They were assembled near the open bar drinking sodas when Vickie motioned for Sharday to join her.

Sharday broke off from the group and followed Vickie to the bride's changing room. Neither of them spoke a word until the door was closed, and then Vickie hugged Sharday and said, "Oh, Sharday! This has been one of the happiest days of my life!"

Sharday couldn't help but laugh. Still holding onto her mother, she said, "I'm glad you enjoyed your wedding, Ma. You deserved it."

"Thank you, baby." Vickie released Sharday and grabbed a tissue to dab at her eyes. "Everything was perfect today," she said, "right down to the last detail."

"And now it's time for the best part!" Sharday added enthusiastically. "If that cruise ship turn out to be anything like them pictures we saw in those brochures, you gonna be having the time of your life for the next ten days."

"You'll know as soon as I do because I'm planning to call you at Gloria's the minute we step on the ship." Vickie pulled her new magenta walking suit and colorful silk blouse from a garment bag before turning back to Sharday. "Don't forget," she said. "I'm going to call you sometime between nine and ten o'clock tonight from the hotel room in Miami, and I'll call you at about one o'clock tomorrow afternoon once we board the ship. After that, I'll be calling you every morning at exactly nine o'clock, either from the ship or from whatever port we happen to be in."

"Okay, Ma," Sharday said, unzipping Vickie's dress. "I'll remember."

Vickie stepped out of her dress and sat down to peel off her pantyhose. "Now, I realize that Gloria is a lot more lenient than I am," she said. "So, while I want you to have a good time, I expect you not to overdo it."

Sharday merely nodded in response to that because she had every intention of packing as much fun as she could into her last week and a half in the neighborhood. She was going to visit Donnell every single day that they would allow him to have visitors, and she was also looking forward to hanging out with her girls as much as possible.

"I mean it, Sharday," Vickie said sternly as she pulled up her pants. "Be careful when you're out late at night. Keep your eyes and your ears open, and if anybody suggests anything you're uncomfortable with, I want you to catch a cab and go directly back to Gloria's." She reached for her blouse. "If worse comes to worse and you can't get a cab, just call over to Bruce's house and have his sister, Felicia, come pick you up."

"Come on, now, Ma," Sharday said reproachfully. "Ain't no way on Earth things could get bad enough for me to stay with Felicia and April in Mitchellville while you gone."

Vickie laid down the jacket she was about to slip on and met Sharday's eyes. "I'm only asking you to call Felicia if you find yourself in an emergency situation, Sharday. And even then, I would expect you to go back to Gloria's the following morning." She sighed. "I just want you to know that you have options, baby. The fact that I won't be sitting at home waiting for you each night doesn't mean that you have to put up with any and every situation you might find yourself in."

"I understand what you're saying, Ma," Sharday said, and she did. "I promise to call Felicia if I need to."

That seemed to satisfy Vickie, and Sharday busied herself packing away her mother's wedding outfit as Vickie finished dressing and repaired her make-up. Less than thirty minutes later, Vickie and Bruce were dashing for the limousine amid showers of confetti.

TEN

The heat and humidity in the small bedroom were oppressive, and the box fan in the window wasn't helping one bit. The night before, Sharday had helped Tyesha and Jolean push their twin beds together to form one large bed, and they'd agreed that Tyesha would sleep in the middle between Sharday and Jolean.

Last night the arrangement worked out just fine, mostly because they were all so tired after the wedding festivities that they fell asleep within minutes of climbing into bed. But tonight, Tyesha and Jolean were apparently lost in dreamland, while Sharday was too hot to even think about sleep.

She gently rolled onto her back and lifted her thin nightgown several times in a useless attempt to create a breeze. Hot or not, she was still happy to be here. All the air conditioning in the world wasn't worth being stuck in the boonies with April and Felicia.

She closed her eyes and thought back to her conversation with her mother earlier in the afternoon. Vickie had been beside herself with excitement, going on and on about how luxurious the cruise ship was in general, and how classy their stateroom with veranda was in particular. At the end of the conversation she'd mentioned the possibility of Bruce booking a three- or four-day cruise for "the family" over spring break.

Realizing that thoughts of the so-called family could keep her awake all night, Sharday decided to clear her mind and concentrate on getting some rest. Maybe counting sheep would help. Wasn't that what people usually did when they had trouble falling asleep?

Sharday was up to number sixty-four when Tyesha rolled over to face her and whispered, "Are you asleep, Day-Day?"

"Nah," Sharday whispered back, opening her eyes and abandoning the sheep.

"I was just wondering," Tyesha said, raising her voice a notch. "Is there anything special you want to do this week? Because I was thinking that we could hit the go-gos once or twice." She was referring to the nightly performances by local bands that played a home grown form of percussion-heavy music peculiar to DC. "And maybe next weekend I can get Mark or somebody to take us to *Six Flags* so we can check out that new roller coaster. We haven't been there all summer, you know."

"I wouldn't mind going to the go-gos," Sharday said. "But *Six Flags* probably won't work for me since I'm gonna be visiting Donnell on Saturday."

Tyesha thought Sharday's plan to visit Donnell every day the jail would let her for the next week and a half was ridiculous, way more than he deserved under the circumstances. "What does that have to do with anything?" she snapped. "We never hit *Six Flags* before 3 anyway."

"What? I'm supposed to be a mind reader now?" Sharday countered testily. "You ain't say what time you was planning to go."

Neither of them spoke for a few minutes after that, but then Tyesha said, "Did it bother you that your father didn't show up for the wedding yesterday?"

"Sort of," Sharday replied. "But I ain't taking it personal because he been tripping ever since he found out my mother was getting married."

"I can't even remember what my father looks like," Tyesha said sadly. "I was about two or three years old the last time I saw him. And my mother claims she doesn't have a single picture of him."

"And he ain't never tried to get in touch with you over all these years?" Sharday asked. She'd been wanting to ask Tyesha about her father for the longest, but somehow it never really seemed like the right time.

"Not that I know of," Tyesha said. "But even if he did, my mother probably wouldn't have told me. She can't stand his guts. All she ever used to say was that he was a no good nigga and that I was better off without him. So, after a while, I stopped asking about him."

"Maybe you should try to find him for yourself," Sharday offered. "The talk shows be helping people do stuff like that all the time."

"Maybe I should," Tyesha agreed. And then, after a few seconds, "You know, it probably wouldn't bother me as much as it does if Jolean wasn't so tight with her father. But every time I turn around, she's going to spend the weekend with him or talking to him on the phone or something." Tyesha sighed. "She just doesn't know how good she's got it."

Jolean spoke up then, surprising them both because they'd thought she was asleep. "If you only knew, Tyesha," she said. "You always think everything's so great for me. But trust me, it's not."

Tyesha wasn't buying it. "Yeah, right, Jolean," she said.

"But haven't you ever wondered how my father's wife and two new kids fit into the picture?" Jolean asked. "Don't you realize that woman tries to put her own kids before me every single chance she gets?"

Jolean paused for a few seconds as a picture of the skinny, buck-toothed stepmother she couldn't stand flashed through her mind. "But that's *my* father," she continued in a steely voice to cover up her thirteen-year-old pain. "I was his daughter long before he met that wench and I refuse to let her push me away. So, I call him all the time to keep up my bond with him. And I pretend to get along with his funky wife, and I play with my little brothers, and I do whatever it takes to make sure I don't get left out. And sometimes, I get my father alone and it's just like old times. But the rest of the time, it's hard work for me."

"Damn," Tyesha said. "I never really thought about it like that. Why didn't you say something? Maybe I could've helped you figure out how to deal with her."

Jolean never answered, so Sharday eventually said, "I can kind of understand why you never said nothing, Jolean. I mean, things ain't really all that great with me and father, but I never talk about it neither."

"That's because you know your problems with your father are just temporary," Tyesha said. "Sooner or later, he'll start showing up again and everything will go right back to normal."

"Nah, it's deeper than that," Sharday said. "For one thing, my father ain't never got not even one dollar to give me. And I know for a fact that when I was younger, my mother used to have to give him money just so he could take me places." Sharday thought back to how she herself would sometimes shake money out of her own piggy bank so that she and her father could go to the store for ice cream. But she didn't mention that because it was just too embarrassing.

"And for another thing," she said, "the only time I ever see him is when he come to my gigs. He always living off some woman so he ain't never got no place of his own to invite me to. And my mother stopped letting him come lay around our apartment years ago. So, even though it don't seem like it, we really ain't all that close. I mean, think about it. How close could we be when we only see each other at a crowded club once or twice a week?"

"Hmm, I have to admit that's messed up," Tyesha said. "But then again, I would still trade places with you or Jolean any day."

There was nothing left to say, so they each retreated into their private thoughts. Tyesha lay there wishing with all her heart for the father she couldn't remember, Sharday was wondering why her own father treated her like a casual friend instead of his only child, and Jolean was hoping, as she always did, that her father would one day divorce his wife.

ELEVEN

"*Stadium/Armory. Doors opening on the left*," the automated voice announced. Sharday stood and made her way to the nearest end of the subway car. When the doors opened, she was the first to disembark from the train.

She followed the sparse crowd up the escalator, slipped her fare card into the designated slot, and stepped through the turnstile. Within seconds, another much more steep escalator was delivering her from the depths of the underground subway station that looked like a space station from a science fiction movie.

Emerging into the blinding afternoon sun, she slipped on a pair of yellow-tinted shades and headed up 19th Street in northeast DC. A smile slowly crept across her face as she reflected back over the week. She was having the time of her life, visiting Donnell every few days, hanging out with her girls every evening, hitting the go-gos at night, staying up until the early hours of the morning with Tyesha and Jolean to talk about movies, music, clothes, neighborhood folks, and anything else of a frivolous nature that crossed their minds -- after that initial conversation about their fathers, they'd made a point of keeping their discussions on a light note.

But despite the fun and nearly unlimited freedom of the past week, Sharday couldn't help missing her mother. And in a way, their brief five or six minute telephone conversations every morning had only made her miss her mother even more. Because, with the exception of that one time when Sharday was twelve and went to summer camp in southern Maryland for eight days, she and Vickie hadn't ever been apart for more than a weekend.

Get used to it! she inwardly scolded herself, picking up her pace as she passed DC General Hospital. In less than a year she would be graduating and moving to a place of her own. So, the days of clinging to her mother's side were almost over anyway.

She cut through the parking lot on her left and walked down the small hill toward DC Jail, a sprawling tan-colored brick building. A group of twenty-something dudes were congregated on the pathway leading to the front door. One of them, a tall, skinny, dark-skinned brother with a head full of bushy hair that was leaning toward nappy, smiled at Sharday and said, "Hey, pretty lady."

"Hi," she said, not even slowing her roll.

"Oh, so it's like that, huh?" he asked as she passed by. "What a nigga gotta do to get you to stop?"

"I'm taken," she said over her shoulder, still walking.

"Well, your man slipping if he up in this joint. He sure can't do nothing for you now," the guy said, and he and his friends started laughing.

Whatever! Sharday thought but didn't bother to say aloud. She took the last few steps down the pathway and entered the slightly air-conditioned lobby. The mocking laughter behind her was immediately drowned out by the chaos in the interior of the building.

Almost everywhere she looked there were people. A woman in a short, tight jean dress was yelling into one of the pay phones, while a group of younger girls was crowded around the other phone squealing. Kids were darting here and there unsupervised, and females of varying ages -- with a few males sprinkled among them, had formed a line that reached almost to the door.

Sharday was so familiar with the scene by now that she didn't blink twice. She laid her purse on the graying conveyer belt and said hello to the guard before stepping through the metal detector, then she retrieved her purse and took her place at the back of the line.

A little more than twenty minutes later, she handed over her ID and told the corrections officer she was there to see Donnell Eugene Dickerson. He punched in something on his computer, wrote Donnell's name and inmate number on a slip of colored paper that he gave her when he returned the ID, and she made her way up the stuffy stairwell to the third floor.

Through a heavy black steel door, up to a plexiglass enclosed booth containing another guard, and over to a hard plastic chair with no cushioning. A long wait later and Donnell finally appeared in a bright orange jumpsuit on the other side of yet more thick plexiglass.

Sharday straightened up and eagerly grabbed the black telephone receiver. "Hi, Boo. How you doing today?" she asked as soon as he picked up the phone on his side.

"Better now that you here," Donnell said, putting his hand up to the plastic that stood between them.

She placed her hand opposite his and briefly puckered her lips to send him a kiss. "You miss me?" she whispered into the phone, knowing from experience that he wouldn't want anyone else to hear her asking him such a mushy question.

"And you know it," he said with a no-nonsense nod of his head.

"I miss you, too, Boo," she whispered with a lingering smile. And for a while, they simply sat there gazing at each other without saying anything.

When he reluctantly lowered his hand, she did the same and slouched down in the hard chair. "I ran into Andre at *The Cellar* last night," she said at length. "He told me he sent you some money he collected for you. You get it yet?"

"Yeah, I got it. It went through this morning."

"So, you alright for commissary now? You need me to add some more to it?"

"Nah, I'm straight. What Andre sent me should last for a good little while." After a short pause, he said, "Speaking of the gigs, Day-Day, what you planning on singing at *Club 202* tonight?"

"I'm definitely gonna do *Street Life Paradise*," she said, "because that's turning out to be one of your biggest hits." She grinned. "You would be surprised how popular that cut is now, Donnell. If I don't do it right up front, people usually start shouting for it."

He grinned back, despite himself. But then he quickly recovered his composure and said in the same neutral tone he'd been using all along, "Oh, yeah? What else you gonna sing?"

"I ain't sure yet. I was planning to figure that out on the way back home."

"I want you to go download some more tracks from out my desktop in my bedroom, so you can keep the shows fresh," he told her.

"Sounds good to me. Which ones you think I should get?"

He instructed her to pick out some of the recordings from their earlier shows, and he told her exactly where she would find them. Not too long after that, she saw the same corrections officer who had initially dropped Donnell off approaching to pick him back up.

She whispered to Donnell that she loved him, and he said, "Me, too,

Day-Day." She assured him she would be back the next visiting day, then she stood and watched as he was escorted through a gray metal door that closed with a resounding thud.

* * * * *

Sharday had her crew in tow when she arrived at *Club 202* that night. She and Tyesha were riding in a shiny, black Nissan Maxima with a brother named Slim that Tyesha had met on Tuesday night at the go-go. Kayla, John and LaShawn were directly behind them in John's beat-up Ford Escort. And Elise and Keith were pulling up the rear in Keith's sporty little Mitsubishi Eclipse.

When they turned into the small parking lot attached to the club, Sharday scooted over to the left side of the back seat and rolled down the window. "Hey, Abdou," she said, waving at the African parking attendant clothed in a navy blue uniform. "How you doing tonight?"

"Sharday!" he exclaimed, smiling brightly. "I'm great. How are you?"

"I'm fine." She pointed to the two cars behind her. "The Escort and the Mitsubishi is with me. Can you give them the hook-up?"

"No problem," Abdou quickly agreed, exiting the miniature guard booth to direct them to prime parking spaces on the front row of the lot.

Sharday and Donnell had first met Jerry Weiss, the owner of *Club 202*, at a city-wide talent contest the summer before. They didn't win first place, but the judges voted them a close second. And they were mingling backstage with the other contestants when Mr. Weiss walked up and offered them a spot on his Friday night line-up.

Donnell held out for what he felt was an acceptable salary, and they had been working for Mr. Weiss ever since. So, by now, Sharday knew all the other employees quite well. She greeted the two burly bouncers at the door by name and, in turn, they waved her little entourage into the club without fanfare.

Once she got her party settled at one of the tables on the balcony -- Mr. Weiss always banished his performers and their guests to the tiny upper level overlooking the rest of the club, she went back downstairs and headed for the deejay's station.

"Well, if ain't the lady with the golden voice," Deejay Smooth said by way of a greeting. He was an extremely handsome Mexican-American who'd grown up in DC and spoke the inner-city lingo without a Spanish accent.

"What up, Smooth?" Sharday replied with a smile.

"It's all about you, lady," he said. "What you got for me tonight?"

Sharday handed over the laptop and they discussed the order in which the songs were to be played, then they spent a few minutes making small talk. She was attempting to bring the conversation to a close when he said, "You didn't hear it from me, Sharday, but lately Mr. Weiss been making noises about you doing the shows without Donnell."

"But Donnell real sick right now," she protested, giving her standard excuse for Donnell's absence. "Mr. Weiss know that."

"I'm only telling you what I hear," Deejay Smooth said, raising his hands in a gesture of surrender. The consensus among the club's employees was that Donnell was probably in some kind of drug rehab program, but nobody had voiced this suspicion to Mr. Weiss and Smooth had enough sense not to mention it to Sharday now.

She sighed, wishing she could just tell everyone the truth about Donnell being on lockdown. Maybe then people would have some type of understanding for what he was going through. But since Donnell would go off if she told anyone here what was really up, she simply said, "Thanks for letting me know, Smooth. Ain't nothing I can do about it, but I'm still glad you told me."

She made a brief trip to the ladies' room after that. Although Mr. Weiss routinely scheduled at least two, and sometimes three, groups for his Friday night line-up, she and Donnell had always gone on first. That hadn't changed so far, so her show would start in just a few minutes.

After a quick check of her make-up, she headed for the stage. She did *Street Life Paradise*, knowing the audience wouldn't let her get away without it, and followed that up with another of Donnell's original cuts and then her version of Beyonce's *Sorry*.

With the show behind her, she stopped by the bar for a bottle of spring water before making her way to Mr. Weiss' tiny office at the rear of the club. There would be no Moet waiting at her table tonight, because Mr. Weiss didn't pamper his performers the way Clyde did. But this was still a good gig and Sharday intended to keep it.

She knocked on the closed door and waited for permission to enter, then she stepped into the office and put on her brightest smile. "Hi, Mr. Weiss. How you doing tonight?"

"As well as can be expected," he replied. "Have a seat, Sharday." He was a short, fat, Jewish man in his early fifties who'd owned *Club 202* for the last twenty years and had seen it all. "So, when can we expect Donnell back?" he asked, reaching into one of his desk drawers for an envelope.

"I'm not exactly sure, but it seem like he getting better," she lied. "Plus, I been thinking about trying to get somebody to step in for him for a little while until he get back on his feet." She'd come up with this plan just a few minutes ago at the bar after thinking back over her conversation with Deejay Smooth.

Mr. Weiss handed her the envelope and waited for her to count the two hundred-fifty dollars inside, which was exactly one-half of what he'd been paying her and Donnell together. "I'm sorry to hear that," he said. "I was hoping you would be able to give me a firm return date for him."

Jerry Weiss knew that his employees thought Donnell was in a drug rehabilitation program, but he would've bet his last dollar that Donnell had run afoul of the law and was temporarily hiding out in another town. He faced Sharday head-on and said, "I'm sorry, but I'm going to have to let you go, Sharday."

"Wh-what?" she stammered.

"It's clear Donnell's not coming back anytime soon," Jerry continued, "and my bottom line's beginning to suffer as a result." He shrugged. "This is purely a business decision, Sharday, so please don't take it personally. I enjoy your singing as much as any other discerning person would, but my customers like rap and Donnell was bringing them in on Friday nights in record numbers. That's not the case anymore, and just yesterday I auditioned an excellent rap group that should be able to get the youngsters back in here."

Sharday was simultaneously astonished, hurt, and confused. She didn't know what to say, so she sat there staring at him dumbly.

"Again, I'm really sorry to have to do this," Jerry said, standing and walking past her to open the door.

Still in a daze, Sharday got up and mutely followed him to the door.

She stuck out her hand to shake his when he extended it, and stumbled up to the balcony to find her friends.

"I'm ready to go, y'all," she said in a strangled voice as soon as she stepped up to the table.

"Girl, we just started getting our party on," LaShawn said, picking up a cocktail glass and draining it.

Tyesha took one look at Sharday and realized that something was seriously wrong. She stood up and said in a firm voice, "It's time to go. Now. Come on, Slim, take me and Sharday home."

Elise glanced up at Sharday and leaned over to whisper to Keith that it was time to go. "We right behind you," she said to Tyesha before turning to Kayla and John. "Come on, y'all. Let's go," she said, knowing that LaShawn would have no choice but to leave, too.

Sharday could feel the tears gathering in her eyes and knew she wouldn't be able to hold them back for long. "I meet y'all outside," she said in a shaky voice, then she turned and bolted for the stairs that would lead her to the front door.

PART TWO

Mitchellville, Maryland

TWELVE

Vickie and Bruce returned from their honeymoon the following Tuesday evening, and they stopped to pick up Sharday on the way home from the airport. Sharday came charging out of the bathroom the moment she heard her mother's voice float into the apartment. And as Bruce, Gloria, Tyesha, and Jolean looked on in amusement, Sharday and Vickie rushed toward each other with open arms and embraced as if they had been separated for a decade instead of a mere ten days.

When mother and daughter finally released one another, Vickie smiled at Gloria and said, "Thank you so much for taking care of my baby, Gloria. I wouldn't have been able to enjoy myself as much as I did if I hadn't known that this girl of mine was being looked out for." She affectionately slipped her arm around Sharday's shoulders.

"It wasn't no problem at all, Vickie," Gloria replied. "Matter of fact, we was happy to have Day-Day here."

Bruce spoke up then, forcing himself to ignore the impulse to wipe accumulated sweat from his forehead. It was so hot in this tiny apartment he could hardly breathe. "Well, we appreciate it, Gloria. And as a way of saying thanks . . . ," he revealed a colorful shopping bag he'd been hiding behind his back, "we brought presents for all."

They gave Jolean an exquisitely detailed, hand-carved wooden doll, while Gloria received a bottle of Jamaican rum, a T-shirt from Grand Cayman, and a gorgeous sarong-style skirt. For Tyesha, there was a bright red short set with *Made in Jamaica* embroidered in yellow, black and green on the hooded top.

Gloria and her daughters were thrilled with their gifts and they spent a few minutes marveling over them and thanking Bruce and Vickie. After hugs were finally exchanged all around, Sharday promised to call Tyesha later and Bruce hoisted her heavy duffel-style bag to his shoulder and led his wife and stepdaughter down to the air-conditioned comfort of his car.

Sharday was still high off the reunion with her mother, so at first, she willingly participated in a lively conversation about the week and a half she'd spent with Tyesha and the highlights of Vickie and Bruce's Caribbean cruise. But the closer they got to Mitchellville, the more subdued she became.

She eventually sank into silence, wondering whether she'd be able to pull off living with Bruce and April for the next year. Those two were just so different from everyone else she'd ever known. In the past, all she had to do was put on a good front when they came around and go right back to normal when they left. But now she would be stuck up under them twenty four and seven with no way out.

Too bad Donnell wasn't around to save her the way they planned, she thought sadly as Bruce turned into his driveway and rolled to a stop in front of the two-car garage that was attached to an imposing brick front home with thick white pillars on either side of the front door.

"We're here!" Vickie exclaimed.

"Welcome home," Bruce said warmly before climbing out of the car and walking around to the passenger's side to open Vickie and Sharday's doors.

On previous visits, Sharday had at least been able to admire the beauty of Bruce's home. But now that she knew she was here to stay, it was all she could do to grit her teeth and grudgingly follow her mother and stepfather up the curved walkway which separated a pretty flower garden from an expansive, well-manicured lawn that was bordered by shrubbery. They had almost reached the porch when April and her aunt, Felicia, came bounding out of the house to meet them.

"Dad! You're back!" April squealed with delight. She wrapped her arms around her father and squeezed him tightly, then she briefly hugged Vickie and Sharday, in turn.

Felicia followed suit by quickly embracing each of them, and when Bruce asked whether the delivery he was expecting had arrived, she nodded and smiled mysteriously.

"That's great!" Bruce said with a grin that stretched from one ear to the other. He grabbed Vickie's hand and said, "Come on, everybody. Follow me."

He led them into the house, down the long hallway which ended at the huge kitchen, and over to a door located near the imposing side-by-side refrigerator with water and ice dispensers on the front.

"This is my wedding gift to you, honey," he said to Vickie, opening the door and flicking on a light switch before gesturing for her to precede him into the garage. "I hope you enjoy it, and I hope you think of me every time you--"

The rest of his sentence was drowned out by the sound of Vickie's shrieking. "Oh, Bruce!" she shrilled. "It's beautiful! Absolutely beautiful!"

Sharday hurried past April and Felicia to join her mother and Bruce in the garage. "Oh my God, oh my God," she whispered, her mouth dropping open in surprise as she stared at a brand new silver Infiniti Q70 with a huge red bow affixed to the grill.

"Go ahead," Bruce encouraged Vickie. "Get in and see how you like it."

Vickie carefully opened the car door and climbed into the driver's seat, reverently running her hands over the steering wheel and dashboard.

"Start her up, honey," Bruce said. "Let's hear how she sounds." He hit a button on the wall beside him and the garage door slowly began to open.

Vickie wiped away the tears of joy that had begun spilling from her eyes before she closed the driver's side door and pressed the ignition. She fumbled around looking for the switch that would lower her window, then she held out a cell phone that she'd picked up from the front passenger's seat and said, "The person who dropped off the car must've left his phone."

Bruce chuckled. "Nope. That's for you, honey. I switched over to a family plan."

"Are you serious?" Vickie asked in astonishment. All she had was a pay-as-you-go phone that she used sparingly. When he nodded, she laughed nervously and said, "I . . . I . . . My goodness! I'm so overwhelmed I don't even know what to say!" She took a deep breath and briefly closed her eyes, looking up afterwards to meet his gaze head-on. "Thank you so much, Bruce," she said. "I really mean it." She wiped away newly gathered tears. "You're just too good to me, honey. How will I ever be able to repay you?"

"You do that simply by being you," he said earnestly, walking across the space that separated them and leaning over to give her a kiss. He straightened back up a few seconds later and grinned over his shoulder at Sharday, April and Felicia. "What do you guys say we take this baby for a spin?"

* * * * *

Later that night, after gifts from the Carribean had been distributed to Sharday, April and Felicia, and Felicia had returned to the apartment she shared with a fellow grad student, and everyone else had retreated to their respective rooms, Sharday stood just inside her own closed door trying to decide what changes she could make to render her bedroom more livable.

The first thing she would do is get rid of the weird painting hanging above the bed and replace it with her framed poster of all the hip-hop greats ranging from Kendrick Lamar and Lil Wayne, to Nicki Minaj and Remy Ma, to Tupac, Biggie, Trina and Aaliyah, to Jay-Z, T.I., Kanye West, and 50 Cent. After that, she would take those ridiculous floral drapes down from the windows, leaving only the beige vertical blinds that hung beneath, and strip the matching floral comforter from the bed. The quilt her grandmother had sent her from Philly last Christmas should fit nicely over her new double bed since it had always been a little too big for the twin she had before.

Of course, the Bluetooth speaker system, the 26-inch flat screen television with built-in DVD player, and the Apple computer and printer would stay exactly where Bruce or whomever he'd gotten to decorate the room had placed them. Sharday could even tolerate the braided, multi-colored rug that covered the beige carpet leading from her bed to a matching desk and chair.

But the rest of this crap has got to go, she thought with a decisive flip of her braids, marching across the room and pushing the chair from her desk over to one of the windows. She had already pulled both sets of drapes and their matching valances down, and she had just climbed up on the bed to reach for the Southwestern painting when her mother knocked on the door and entered her bedroom.

"Sharday!" Vickie whispered urgently, quickly closing the door behind her. "What on Earth are you doing, baby? Why did you take your curtains down? And what are you doing to that artwork?"

"What it look like, Ma?" Sharday said. "I'm getting rid of this crap." She lifted the painting off the hooks that secured it to the wall and turned around to face her mother.

"But that's a Salvador Dalí reprint," Vickie said. "And the curtains and spread are by Chris Madden."

"Who cares? They suck," Sharday said, stepping down from the bed and placing the painting on her desk. She snatched the comforter from the bed and piled it in a heap on the chair. "Tell Bruce to go get his money back. I rather use my own stuff in here."

"Oh, Sharday," Vickie said, dragging the words out and slowly shaking her head. "Why do you insist on making this transition so much more difficult than it has to be?"

"I'm just making myself at home," Sharday replied. "Ain't that what Bruce told me to do?" She briefly stepped inside her walk-in closet and reappeared half-lifting and half-dragging her hip-hop poster.

Vickie sighed audibly before moving across the room to assist her exasperating daughter. She helped Sharday hang the poster and spread the hand-crafted quilt over the bed, then she looked at Sharday and said, "Are you satisfied now?"

Sharday paused for a moment to take in the effect of the changes. "It'll do," she said with a nod. "At least, I can sleep in here now. And I can fix it up some more once I start unpacking my boxes from the apartment."

Vickie laughed, despite herself, and said, "You're something else, you know that? What am I going to do with you?"

"Well, I can't stop being me just because we moved in here with Bruce and April," Sharday replied defensively.

"I know that, baby. And I don't ever want you to be anyone other than yourself. As far as I'm concerned, you're wonderful just the way you are." Vickie sat down on the bed and patted the space beside her. "Come sit with me."

When Sharday took the indicated seat, Vickie turned to her and said, "Me and you can get through this, baby. We'll both have to adapt to a lot of changes over the next few months, but I promise I'll do everything within my power to make our new situation easier for you." She waved her arm to indicate Sharday's bedroom. "If you feel you need to redecorate in here, then you do that, baby. I'll even help you by getting one of Bruce's credit cards so we can go shopping for some new drapes and pick up whatever else you think you'll need."

"That's okay, Ma. This room really ain't so bad." And with that, Sharday unexpectedly burst into tears.

"My poor baby," Vickie murmured, reaching out for Sharday and rocking back and forth as she held her daughter closely. "Everything's going to be okay. I promise," she whispered soothingly. "What's the matter? You don't trust me to look out for you anymore?"

Sharday pulled away from her mother, sniffing and wiping at the salty water on her cheeks. "It ain't that, Ma. It's just, it's just . . . everything so messed up now!" she blurted, bending over and clutching her sides as a fresh wave of tears overtook her.

Vickie slipped her arms around Sharday's shoulders and said, "It's okay, baby. Just let it all out."

Sharday continued to cry for several minutes before moaning, "I got fired while y'all was gone, Ma. Mr. Weiss told me not to come back."

"What?" Vickie was bewildered. "But you've been with him for so long now."

Sharday sniffed and wiped her face with her T-shirt. "He said I couldn't pull in the crowds without Donnell," she whispered, finally meeting her mother's eyes. "He said he found another rap group that could do a better job than me."

"Oh, what does he know?" Vickie said sharply, her eyes flashing with anger. "You don't need him anyway."

"But I do need him, Ma. My gig at *The Cellar* only supposed to last until the end of the summer and then I ain't gonna have nothing."

"Well, we'll just have to get you another gig," Vickie said firmly, her mind racing all the while to come up with a plan. "That shouldn't be so hard to do," she added pensively, speaking aloud as her thoughts began to come together. "We can use Clyde for a reference since he's been so thrilled with your solo performances, and we can send out videos of you doing a number of songs without Donnell so you won't have to go around begging for auditions."

"Who knows?" Vickie continued confidently. "We might even be lucky enough to find you something that's not so far away from home now that we've moved." She smiled at Sharday then. "So, what do you think, baby? If you ask me, it's a pretty good plan."

Sharday had no interest at all in trying to score a solo gig without Donnell, but she was too drained to explain that to her mother. "I don't know, Ma," she said with a shrug. "Let me think about it for a while. Right now, I probably just need to get some sleep."

THIRTEEN

It was two o'clock on Saturday afternoon, and Sharday had set aside the next hour to write her first letter to Donnell. She hadn't been to see her Boo since Mr. Weiss fired her. Had skipped the last visit she could've made while she was still staying at Tyesha's because she wasn't quite ready to tell him. And now that she'd moved to Mitchellville, she no longer had a way to get over to the jail. So, she'd decided to break the bad news to him in writing, which would be a lot easier than telling him face-to-face, anyway.

She put on her Trey Songz playlist through her Bluetooth speaker system before she sat down and turned on her sleek Apple computer. After double-clicking on the icon for her word processing program and waiting for a blank document to appear on the screen, she used her mouse to insert the date without typing anything -- those computer classes she took in tenth and eleventh grade were finally coming in handy. That done, she paused for a few minutes as she tried to figure out the best way to begin the letter.

"Dear Donnell," she slowly typed, using the correct finger for each key, "I miss you so much and please believe me when I say my life is just not the same now that you are on lock down. I know that your life is not going too good either right now, and don't you wish we could have got that apartment in Landover like we wanted to? I sure do too boo, because my life is like some kind of Cosby Show or something right now."

Her hands briefly stilled as she thought about her first partial week in Mitchellville. "My mother is cooking dinner every day," she typed. "And my step father is making every body come to the table at 6:30 so we can eat together like a family as he put it. He was saying we have to share our life with each other and I kept thinking it was just like I'm living in a TV show. This week on Wednesday and Friday after we ate dinner because I had The Cellar on Thursday Bruce took us to some used car lots to look for a car for me and April to share, he said that starting next week we can only look for a car on Saturday and Sunday because the honey moon is over and he will have to do work in his office in the basement after dinner. Nothing is happening on the streets around here during the day or during the night and I am so bored all of the time. I only have one more week before school start and really really do not want to go. Are you missing me as much as I am missing you Donnell? I just wish I was with you in Landover right now."

She squeezed her eyes shut, opened them wide, then briefly shook her hands. "*Here is some really bad news that I have Donnell and I do not want to say it*," she continued reluctantly. But before she could decide exactly how to tell him about the situation at *Club 202*, she heard a knock at her bedroom door.

She saved and closed her unfinished document, while calling out, "Who is it?"

"It's me, baby," Vickie said from the hallway, determined not to try the doorknob until Sharday invited her in -- Bruce had recently convinced Vickie that Sharday was old enough to need privacy in her bedroom. "Are you ready to go to the mall?" Vickie asked when her daughter didn't immediately respond.

Sharday glanced at the clock on her computer screen and realized that the hour she had set aside had already passed. It was a few minutes after three o'clock. She quickly shut down the computer and pushed away from the desk. "It's open, Ma," she said. "Come on in."

Vickie turned the knob and entered. "I've got some good news, baby," she said with a smile as she closed the door behind her. "April still needs to pick up a few more items for school, so she's agreed to come to the mall with us. She also said she would pick out some outfits that will help you fit in at your new school."

"Great," Sharday murmured sarcastically. She was willing to go along to get along and all, but that did not include taking fashion advice from April. She stood and grabbed her purse from the bed, reaching inside for her make-up bag. "Just let me get ready. Okay, Ma?" she said. "I'll meet y'all downstairs in a few minutes."

"You look fine," Vickie said, staring at the make-up bag before meeting her daughter's eyes. "And anyway, you'll be trying on a lot of clothes and you don't want to get them smeared with make-up."

"Ma-a-a," Sharday whined impatiently. "Can't you just give me a few minutes to get myself together?"

"Okay, okay," Vickie said. "I'll wait for you downstairs." And with that, she turned and left.

FOURTEEN

"*IT IS NOW SIX O'CLOCK A.M.!*" the talking alarm clock on Sharday's night stand bleated, shattering the silence in her bedroom. "*PLEASE WAKE UP! PLEASE WAKE UP! PLEASE WAKE--*"

"Oh my God," Sharday groaned, leaning over to shut off the annoying voice. She fell back on the bed and wished she could just go back to sleep. Six in the morning was too early to even talk about getting up. But she and her mother were going to church with Bruce and April for the first time this morning and Vickie would kill her if she wasn't ready on time. So, she forced herself out of bed and stumbled across the room. Grabbed her robe and struggled with it before finally managing to get it on, only to realize that it was turned inside out. "Oh, whatever," she murmured irritably, stepping into her slippers before dragging herself down the hall to the bathroom she shared with April.

The smell of April's tangerine-scented shower gel slapped her in the face the moment she stepped into the bathroom. She also noticed that the mirror above the sink was still slightly fogged with steam. "Oh, crap," she whispered, suddenly wide awake. April had already showered and might even be dressed by now, while she was standing in the middle of a soggy bathroom with a jacked-up robe on.

She quickly piled her braids on top of her head and covered them with the bouffant-style plastic cap she'd brought from the apartment. Then she brushed her teeth and gargled, cleaned her face with Clearasil, and finished her shower in record time.

Back in her bedroom, she put on one of the boring church dresses Vickie had bought her at the mall the day before with white stockings and her new open-toed Kenneth Cole Reaction navy pumps, which were actually kind of cool. She pulled her braids up and wrapped a silk scarf around her head, added a few dabs of make-up and grabbed her purse. She was on her way to the kitchen when she met April at the top of the stairs.

"Oh! Good morning, Sharday!" April said brightly. "Miss Vickie sent me to get you for breakfast."

"Well, here I am," Sharday said with a shrug. And then, as an afterthought, "Good morning, April."

As she followed April down the steps, she noticed that the girl had on a plain black dress, off-black stockings, and a pair of boring black leather flats. Was April planning to go to church or to a funeral? And this was the person her mother expected her to start taking fashion tips from?

When they entered the kitchen to cheerful greetings from her mother and Bruce, Sharday glanced around for some sign of breakfast. All she saw was coffee for Bruce and Vickie, what looked like hot tea for her and April, and four tall glasses of orange juice surrounding a plate of toast and a platter of fresh fruit. Where was the country bacon or sausage patties? Not to mention the cheese eggs and biscuits?

At Sharday's dark expression, Vickie quickly spoke up. "This is just a little something to hold us over for a couple of hours, honey," she said reassuringly. "We're going to brunch after we leave church."

Bruce was looking up at Sharday with such a ridiculous grin on his face that she decided to sit down and get with program. But one taste of the tea and she found herself grimacing. "Ugh! What on Earth is that?" she asked her mother.

"It's herbal tea, Sharday," Vickie replied calmly. "It's good for you."

"That stuff is so nasty," Sharday said, wiping her tongue with her cloth napkin and frowning. "Can't I just have some regular tea?"

"It'll taste a lot better if you swirl one of those cinnamon sticks around in it first," April said. "I drink it all the time."

Sharday briefly shook her head and pushed the cup away. "Nah, that's alright. It ain't like I'm really into drinking tea or nothing."

"We'd better add a box of Lipton tea bags to the shopping list, honey," Bruce said to Vickie before turning to wink at Sharday. "And in the meantime," he cleared his throat, "I'll ask for a blessing so we can get started on breakfast."

* * * * *

They made it to church with plenty of time to spare because breakfast hadn't lasted more than twenty minutes. Bruce and Vickie held hands as they led the way to a pew near the front, smiling and waving at several people Sharday recognized from the wedding. April followed closely behind -- she also waved at a couple of the younger folks, and Sharday reluctantly pulled up the rear.

Malcolm Werther was seated in the second row of the choir stands behind the pulpit, and he felt a sharp jolt of emotion the moment he spotted Sharday walking down the center aisle of the church darting her eyes here and there suspiciously as if she expected a member of the congregation to jump up and assault her without warning. He leaned slightly to his left to get a better view of her and instantly fell in love.

She had full, pouty lips that made her mouth seem just a little too wide, a cute button nose, and beautiful almond-shaped brown eyes. No less than a hundred long braids sprouted up and over the top of the navy polka dot scarf she'd wrapped around her head. But despite her in-your-face hairstyle, she wore an elegant navy and white dress that subtly underscored her womanly figure and mid-heeled pumps that were totally appropriate for the occasion.

When she slumped down in her seat and stared straight ahead, he opened his hymnal and peered at her over the top of it. He hadn't been able to attend Bruce Campbell's recent wedding, but he'd heard enough after the fact from church members who'd attended to know that Mr. Campbell's new wife had a teenaged daughter. Obviously, this gorgeous creature was her.

Malcolm was so distracted during the service that he didn't absorb a word of Pastor Barnett's sermon and only half-participated with the choir. He spent the entire time surreptitiously watching Sharday, suppressing a smile each time she nodded off and her mother elbowed her awake, and wondering how he could arrange to meet her.

Too bad he wasn't close with April. Even though they lived only a few blocks away from each other and had played together as children, once they graduated to junior high they'd fallen into different social groups and hadn't exchanged more than a friendly greeting in years.

By the time the service was drawing to a close, Malcolm had settled on rushing down to the section where the Campbells were seated and pretending to mingle until he could wrangle an introduction from Bruce or April. But the last "Amen" had barely been said when the girl scooted past her mother and practically ran up the aisle toward the door, leaving Malcolm standing on the stage with his mouth hanging open.

He was still trying to decide how to proceed when he saw the new Mrs. Campbell making her way to the front of the church. He could hardly believe his luck when she stopped right in front of the stage and beckoned their choir director, Mrs. Jefferson, forward. She thanked Mrs. Jefferson for attending her wedding, said she truly enjoyed the choir's "outstanding performance," and then asked whether the choir had room for a new member.

"Well, we're always looking for new members," Gladys Jefferson said. "Have you sang with a choir before?"

"Oh, no," Vickie said with a chuckle. "I wasn't asking for myself. If there's one thing I'm not, it's a singer." She smiled at the rail-thin woman who looked to be about the same age she was, whom Bruce had told her was a widow, and said, "I was asking on behalf of my daughter. She has a wonderful singing voice and . . . and she recently expressed an interest in possibly joining your choir." Vickie knew she was stretching things a bit -- Sharday had only reluctantly agreed to consider joining the choir when pressed to do so. But Vickie was convinced that this would be a good way for her daughter to start meeting some new kids.

"Oh, that's right," Gladys said, tapping a finger against her forehead. "Now that you mention it, Bruce told me a few weeks ago that his soon-to-be stepdaughter had quite a voice on her." She smiled at Vickie and said, "So, where is she? Let's hear what she can do."

"I believe she stepped outside to get a breath of fresh air," Vickie replied without missing a beat, hoping the choir director hadn't seen Sharday beating a path out of the church like the place was on fire. "I'll go get her."

Vickie maneuvered through the lingering congregation members, stopping to tell Bruce that she'd be right back, and went in search of her daughter. She found Sharday on the sidewalk outside of the church leaning back against the fence and gazing up at the sky.

"Come back inside with me for a minute," she said, reaching for Sharday's hand.

"What for?" Sharday asked, allowing her mother to pull her forward. "Ain't y'all ready to go yet?"

"I want you to meet someone."

"Who?"

"Gladys Jefferson." And after a short pause, "She's the choir director."

"What?" Sharday stopped dead in her tracks.

"Shar-day," Vickie whispered urgently. "Please don't make a scene out here."

"But this my first time here," Sharday whispered back plaintively. "I ain't ready to meet no choir director yet."

"Oh, what can it hurt to meet her?" Vickie asked, pulling her daughter forward again.

Sharday groaned under her breath and followed her mother into the church, which by now had started to clear out. It wasn't long before she was shaking hands with Gladys Jefferson and being introduced to some guy named Malcolm Werther who was the back-up piano player.

"So, what would you like to sing for us today?" Gladys asked her. "You name it and Malcolm can play it. Anything from a traditional hymnal to contemporary gospel."

"Huh?" Sharday asked before glancing over at her mother.

"I told Mrs. Jefferson you were interested in the choir," Vickie said with a strained smile. "I guess she wants to hear you sing something."

"Right now?" Sharday asked her mother in disbelief.

Gladys cleared her throat and said, "Well, I can see you weren't expecting to audition today, Sharday. But would you mind singing just a few bars to give me an idea of your range?"

"Uh, . . . I need some time to practice first," Sharday said. "I really don't know no gospel numbers."

"Of course you do," Gladys cheerfully insisted. "Everybody knows at least one gospel song."

"Not me," Sharday said stubbornly, folding her arms beneath her breasts.

Vickie immediately recognized her error. She was pushing too hard, and if she kept this up her daughter would refuse to join the choir altogether. "I think Sharday's right," she said, lightly touching Gladys' arm. "It's only fair that she have some time to prepare."

Gladys took in Sharday's defensive stance. "Maybe so," she agreed.

Malcolm quickly seized the opportunity. "I'd be happy to help you select an audition song, Sharday," he offered.

She shook her head and said, "Um, thanks. But I don't think"

"I'll even supply the background vocals, if you want," Malcolm urged.

"You can sing, too?" she asked.

He nodded. "I sing first alto in the choir."

"Hmm," she said.

"Well, why don't you think about it and let me know," he suggested. "I'll give you my number." He tore a corner off a page of the sheet music propped on the piano and quickly printed his name and number.

Sharday reluctantly took the slip of paper and said, "Okay, I guess I could do that."

* * * * *

For brunch, Bruce took the family to a mom-and-pop diner in rural St. Mary's County, Maryland, which was almost an hour's ride from the church. The diner looked like it could stand a fresh coat of paint and the parking lot was mostly filled with pick-up trucks, but the food more than made up for the lack of atmosphere and they were served with a gracious smile by a stout, middle-aged white woman who identified herself as one of the owners.

They stuffed themselves shamelessly and Bruce waited until they had all finished eating before he broached the subject he had been wanting to discuss all along. He placed his napkin over his plate and said, "Our first Sunday together as a family. I hope everyone else is enjoying it as much as I am."

After Vickie said, "I know I am, honey," April forced herself to pleasantly say, "Me, too, Dad." The truth was that she wasn't exactly thrilled with her new family. Miss Vickie was almost too eager to please, and Sharday had such a bad attitude. But her father was happier than she'd seen him in years, so she would do whatever she could to try to make this work for him.

Almost as if to prove April's point, Sharday shrugged and said a nonchalant, "I can't complain."

"Glad to hear it," Bruce said with a chuckle. Then he smiled at April and Sharday and said, "Well, Vickie and I have been talking. And we both agreed that it's important for us to spend some time together each week as a family. To cement our bond."

"Ain't that why we been eating dinner together every night?" Sharday asked.

"Well, dinner is a start," Bruce said. "But during the week, I'm usually preoccupied with work. And once school starts back up, you girls will have homework and other school-related things to concentrate on."

Sharday doubted it. With Donnell in jail and her music career on hold now that she'd been fired from *Club 202*, school would be the least of her concerns. But she didn't tell Bruce that. She just looked at him and waited to see where he was heading with all this.

"What Vickie and I have in mind is something more," he said. "Some time we can spend together as a family without the normal pressures of the week. And we've decided the best way to do that is to make every Sunday family day."

"Isn't that a great idea?" Vickie asked at the same time Sharday was saying, "The whole day?"

"Pretty much," Bruce answered Sharday. She needed some structure in her life, and he was determined to be the one to provide it. "We'll go to the eight o'clock service at church each week, like we did today, and then we'll go somewhere for brunch. After that, we'll have a family activity. We'll go to a skating rink, a museum, an indoor swimming pool, maybe even a mall. Or sometimes, if we're feeling lazy, we might just decide to head home and play a couple of board games or watch a few movies. But whatever we do, we'll do it together. As a family."

"Will we be allowed to choose some of the activities?" April asked.

"Of course, you will, honey," Bruce said. "Otherwise, it wouldn't be any fun. And that's what this is all about. Doing something fun together each week."

"And when all this supposed to start?" Sharday asked.

Vickie spoke up then. "We're planning to start today, Sharday," she said. "Since we still have to find a car for you and April, we're going to spend the next few weeks searching the used car lots. But once that's taken care of, we'll start doing other activities."

"Oh," Sharday said. She didn't want any part of this so-called family day crap. But she wasn't about to say anything to mess up her chances of getting a car.

Bruce looked around the table at each of them and said, “So, we’re all in agreement, then? From now on, Sundays will be family day?”

Vickie and April quickly voiced their approval. Sharday forced herself to agree, too. But she was thinking that she couldn’t wait until she graduated from high school so she could get a job, move away from Mitchellville, and get back to her real life.

After Bruce paid for their brunch and tipped the waitress, they all trooped out to the car. They spent the next few hours scouring the used car lots in the area. April and Sharday spotted a number of cars they thought would be perfect, but Bruce and Vickie vetoed them each time, usually citing too many miles as the reason. Finally, they decided to call it a day and try again the next weekend.

Bruce turned down a side street to avoid making a U-turn on the main strip, and he was making a three-point turn in the middle of the shady, residential street when April said, “What about that car, Dad?” She pointed to a shiny blue Nissan Altima parked in a driveway adjoining a modest rancher. The front windshield of the car boasted a white For Sale sign, on which “*Air!! CD Player!! $ 5,000 or Best*” had been written with a coarse black marker.

“I wonder what kind of mileage they’ve put on it,” Bruce said, backing up and parking so they could get out and take a look.

As it turned out, the odometer registered less than sixty thousand miles and the interior of the Nissan was spotless. A tall, scruffy, pot-bellied white man who looked for all the world to be a redneck stepped through the front door of the house and headed toward them. He popped open the glove compartment and produced a full set of maintenance records, then he explained that his recently deceased mother-in-law had been the original owner of the vehicle and his wife could no longer bear to look at it.

Bruce took the car for a test drive before negotiating the price down to forty-two hundred dollars and leaving a two hundred and fifty dollar check as a deposit. “I’ll have my mechanic go over it one day this week,” he said. “And assuming everything checks out, you’ve got yourself a deal.”

“Well, then I guess I got myself a deal,” the white man drawled pleasantly, “’cause this car gon’ pass that inspection with flying colors.” He shook Bruce’s hand and said, “I look forward to doing business with ya.”

FIFTEEN

A general feeling of sadness had been building in Sharday all week, and by now, on the last Friday night before school started, she was beginning to slide into depression. Her movements were sluggish as she climbed out of the shower and trudged back to her bedroom to get dressed for her last performance at *The Cellar*. She selected a bright orange minidress with tiny white stars from her walk-in closet, hoping to improve her mood. It didn't work. Still took her much longer than normal to get dressed, style her braids, and apply her stage face. She had less than an hour and a half to spare when she finally headed across the hall to April's room.

"You're ready?" April asked, opening her door almost immediately after Sharday knocked.

"Uh huh." Sharday glanced at April's sleeveless white linen dress, boring pearls, and mid-heeled white sandals. Under normal circumstances, she probably would've suggested that April replace the pearls with a colorful scarf, add some eye shadow to match her lipstick and maybe even a bulky bracelet or two. But tonight, she didn't feel up to making the effort. "Let's go," she said flatly, then she turned and made her way to the stairs.

They shouted their good-byes to Bruce from the door leading to the basement, and he yelled back for them to have a good time. They made what was supposed to be a quick stop in the family room to tell Vickie they were leaving, but Vickie took one look at April's attire and offered to loan her a silver and jade necklace with matching bracelet and earrings. "Accessories make all the difference, you know?" she said to April.

When April ran upstairs to get the jewelry, Vickie turned her attention to Sharday. "Don't look so sad, baby," she said, slipping her arm around her daughter's shoulders and squeezing lightly. "We can fix this. All you have to do is give me the go ahead and I know I can have another singing job lined up for you in no time."

"I can't even think about that right now, Ma," Sharday said, still unconvinced that she could make it as a singer without Donnell. "Just let me get through tonight first. Then, maybe we'll see."

At the sound of April's footsteps pounding down the stairs, Vickie decided to give the subject a rest. Sharday would eventually come around. "Try to enjoy your show tonight, baby," she said, giving her daughter's shoulders a final squeeze. "Everything will fall into place when the timing's right."

"Okay, Ma. See you later." Sharday headed down the long hallway leading to the front door and met up with April on the front porch. The shiny blue Nissan Altima sitting in the driveway perked up her spirits a little, and depressed or not, being a teenager she wasn't about to forego a chance to drive. "We running late," she said to April, pulling her new set of car keys from the trendy white crocheted purse at her shoulder before heading for the driver's seat.

Sharday had learned to drive in Donnell's oversized bucket, so the much smaller Nissan was a breeze for her. She found herself zipping through the streets of their development, turning when April directed her to, and once she hit the highway she moved into the far left lane and firmly pressed her foot on the accelerator.

Although the trip to downtown DC was quick by any measure, show time was mere minutes away when they arrived at *The Cellar*. Sharday raced to the deejay booth at the front of the club to hand over her music, leaving April to find the reserved table on her own. There would be no pre-show hair and make-up check tonight. There was barely enough time for Sharday to catch her breath.

She hastily smoothed her minidress over her hips and returned the deejay's thumb-up before stepping onto the stage with a nervous smile. Everything was so rushed. She felt slightly off balance as a result. But the second she reached for the microphone her mood changed.

This would be her last club gig for a really long time. Why stand up here and blow it just because she felt sad and depressed? Forget that! She could sit around feeling sorry for herself later. Right now she needed to take a page from the hustler's script and go out in a total blaze of glory!

She gave that audience her all, throwing in every extra touch she could think of. Impromptu scatting here, exaggerated movements and gestures there, certain notes held longer than she'd ever held them before.

And with a boldness born of the knowledge that she had nothing to lose, she also chanted along on Donnell's rap sections in a husky, melodious voice.

The crowd immediately picked up on her vibe. "Woof, woof! Woof, woof!" they shouted intermittently with raised fists. They even rewarded her with a standing ovation when she brought the final song to a close.

Sharday was riding on a cloud of adrenaline when she grinned in exhilaration and took her final bow. She had let it all hang out for once and the audience had loved it. No matter what happened in the future with her music, she would always remember tonight.

She skipped the post-show bathroom trip and headed for the reserved table in search of the customary bottle of Moet. Clyde didn't disappoint her. The welcome sight of a glistening silver bucket beckoned her forward.

She grabbed the heavy bottle of Moet and filled a clean champagne flute, gulping from it greedily as her crew congratulated her on the exceptional performance. "Thank y'all so much," she said graciously, pouring herself a refill and drinking down half of that as she quickly glanced around the table. Tyesha and Mark, Kayla and John, LaShawn, Elise and Keith, April.

Sharday took her seat and finished off the glass of bubbly. "I'm doing this one by myself," she said, holding up the half-empty bottle. "Y'all on your own tonight."

"I know that's right," Tyesha said. "You deserve it, Day-Day. You're a rapper now," she added in a playful voice.

Sharday laughed along with everyone else at the table, then she refilled her glass and took a healthy swallow.

"And she serious, too," LaShawn said, noticing that Sharday hadn't released her grip on the Moet. "Y'all wanna order some more? I got ten dollars on a bottle." She lifted a cocktail glass to her lips and drained it.

"I got twenty," John said.

"Put me down for twenty, as well," April volunteered.

"You drink?" Sharday asked, turning to April in surprise. "I was planning on you driving us home." As a matter of fact, that was the only reason she had finally given in to her mother and agreed to bring April along.

"I've been known to drink a few beers or wine coolers with my friends on occasion," April said easily. "But since I'm the designated driver, I don't mind taking a pass on the champagne."

Sharday laughed in amazement. Apparently, her new stepsister was just full of surprises. "Well, don't let me spoil your fun. Go ahead and have a glass. Since you already used to drinking you probably won't even feel it that much."

Everyone else at the table anted up, and thanks to generous contributions from Mark and Keith, they had enough money to buy three more bottles of Moet. They were raising their glasses in a toast to Sharday at the very moment Frank Wallace stepped through the front door of the club.

Frank strolled over to the bar and ordered a double shot of Bacardi on the rocks with a splash of coke. He would've preferred Hennessy or Courvoisier, but his woman didn't get paid until tomorrow so he was a little short on funds tonight. Not that anyone would've guessed it from looking at him.

His nails were manicured, his diamond-studded jewelry gleamed, and he wore a custom-made charcoal suit with a pale yellow shirt and a deeper yellow tie and handkerchief. He was broke, but his appearance screamed money and class.

He handed the bartender an extra dollar -- true gentlemen always tipped, then he pocketed the change from his last twenty and picked up his drink. As he moved through the crowd, he wondered how Sharday would react to his sudden reappearance. Would she be happy to see him again? The way she usually was when he pulled a disappearing act to go on the road? Or would she be pissed off because she'd figured out that this time he had stayed away in anger at Vickie?

He swallowed a mouthful of cola-laced rum and assured himself that whatever Sharday's reaction, he could deal with it. After all was said and done, he was still her father. And if Vickie thought he was going to drop out of the picture and let that new husband of hers take his place, then she was living in a fantasy. He'd be damned if he'd let anybody take his daughter away from him.

He approached Sharday's chair from behind and placed a hand on her shoulder. "Surprise, baby," he said confidently in the deep voice that was his trademark. "It's me. Your one and only dear old dad."

Sharday's heartbeat accelerated the moment she saw that hand. She would've recognized it anywhere. As a matter of fact, she had been praying for the sight of it for months now. She took a deep breath and slowly stood to face her father. "Hi, Daddy. Long time no see," she said calmly, even as a partial grin of happiness forced its way onto her face.

Her reluctant half-smile told Frank everything he needed to know. He flashed his own pearly whites in relief, then he leaned over and kissed his daughter on the forehead while being careful not to get any make-up on his suit. "I've missed you so much, Sharday," he said, reaching out for one of her hands.

"I been right here where I always am, Daddy," she replied in the same calm voice. "Where you been at all this time?"

Frank sipped from his glass and shrugged. "You know how crazy my schedule can be sometimes," he said vaguely, making a point not to lie but hoping Sharday would assume he'd been on the road. He released her hand and turned to greet each of her friends by name, surprised to find her new stepsister seated among them.

April managed to smile and return the greeting, but her eyes were full of hostility. She clearly remembered how Frank had tried to upstage her father the last time they were here and she didn't appreciate it one bit. To avoid having to deal with him, she quickly excused herself to the bathroom.

Frank turned back to his daughter with a raised eyebrow, but Sharday was too preoccupied with her own thoughts to notice. The conversation she'd had with Tyesha and Jolean about fathers was on her mind, and the bottle of Moet she'd consumed told her that this would be a good time to get things on the right track for her and Frank. "Come take a walk with me, Daddy," she said. "I wanna talk to you for a minute."

Expecting Sharday to give him the scoop on her new stepfamily, Frank followed her to a secluded spot on the far side of the now-deserted stage. She caught him slightly off guard when she met his eyes and said, "I don't know if you remember or not, Daddy, but I ain't gonna be singing here no more after tonight. This was my last night."

He nodded slowly and nursed his drink as he mentally changed gears. "I do recall you saying this gig was only for the summer," he eventually said. "But *Club 202* will keep you busy enough during the school year."

"I had to let that go, too," she said flatly. "It wasn't working out." She'd eventually tell her father that she had gotten fired, but this certainly wasn't the right time to do it.

"There's no harm in taking a temporary break from singing, you know," he said agreeably. "In fact, it might not be a bad idea at all for you to buckle down and get your diploma under your belt first."

"You probably got a point, Daddy. But since I ain't gonna be doing no more gigs for a while, we need to set up another way to keep in touch. I got a car now, so maybe I can meet you somewhere some time."

"You have a car now?" he asked.

"Uh huh. Bruce bought me and April a Altima. And we got our own phone line, too, so you ain't even gotta worry about him or my mother answering the phone when you call me." She smiled and said, "Bruce don't know it but he making it real easy for us to stay in touch with each other."

Good ol' Bruce is trying to buy my daughter's affections, Frank thought as he swallowed the watery remnants of his drink. He pulled a small leather phonebook and an ultraslim ballpoint pen from his inner jacket pocket. "Write your new telephone number down for me," he said. "I'll call you this week so we can work something out."

She printed her new number clearly and added the new Mitchellville address, too, then she suggested they go back to the table and order some drinks.

Frank had too much pride to admit that he was financially tapped out, so he glanced down at his watch and said, "I wish I could, honey, but I should be going. I've got an early morning tomorrow."

"Okay, Daddy. But at least we got a chance to talk. That's the main thing."

"I agree completely," he said, leaning down to carefully kiss her on the forehead again. "I'll call you soon."

Sharday felt very pleased with herself as she watched Frank disappear into the crowd. The whole thing with her father had turned out to be a lot easier than she thought it would be. And maybe now they could finally start having a real relationship.

She returned to the reserved table to find that everyone except Kayla and Tyesha were missing. "Where everybody go?" she asked.

Tyesha looked up at her and said, "Mark went to the bathroom, Elise and Keith left a few minutes ago and Elise said she'll call you tomorrow, and you can probably guess where LaShawn is."

"Outside getting high," Sharday said without hesitation. "But where April go? And what about John?

Kayla spoke up then. “They on the dance floor.”

“You telling me April dancing?” Sharday asked. “Stop lying.”

“I ain’t lying,” Kayla said. “She kept sitting over there saying ‘that’s my song’ and acting like she was just dying to dance, so I told John to ask her and she practically broke her neck getting up out of that chair.”

Sharday shook her head. “I just can’t figure that girl out,” she said, taking her seat. “She the biggest church freak you ever wanna see, but she like rap music and she be drinking with her friends and now she out on the dance floor.”

“She’s cool,” Tyesha said. “She’s just a little different. That’s all.”

“Yeah, she a little different, all right,” Sharday said. And then, “But whatever. Right now, I’m trying to get me a drink.” She spotted a waitress heading in their direction and signaled for her.

“I was just coming to get you,” the waitress said with a smile. “Clyde wants to see you.”

“Oh, okay.” Sharday had been hoping that Clyde would just send her her money in an envelope like he’d been doing. But it made sense that he might want to say goodbye or something since this was her last night working for him.

As she followed the waitress toward the rear of the club, she spotted Donnell’s buddies, Hakeem and Andre, lurking near the bar. They didn’t seem to see her, so she didn’t bother to wave or anything. But she realized they would send Donnell word that she had done his raps tonight and she wondered how he would feel about it.

The waitress stopped a few seconds later and stepped aside to reveal Clyde sitting alone at a table at the back of the club. When he stood up, the waitress quickly moved away.

“Sit down,” he said brusquely.

Sharday did as she was told.

“The rapping was a nice touch,” he said, taking his seat again.

Sharday smiled and said, “Thank--”

“You should have been doing it all along,” he interrupted her. “As a matter of fact, I won’t accept anything less from now on.”

Sharday looked at him in confusion. The gig was over, so what was he talking about?

“Jerry Weiss is a damn fool,” Clyde said. “Wouldn’t recognize talent if he stepped in it."

"How you always know everything?" she blurted out in astonishment, suddenly realizing he somehow knew that Mr. Weiss had fired her.

At the look on her face, Clyde couldn't totally suppress his amusement. But he quickly replaced his tiny smile with a stern look and said, "Don't worry about that." And then, after a beat, "I'm switching you to Friday nights. Same salary. I was getting bored with my Friday night act anyway."

Sharday's heart began to pound in her chest. "Huh? You mean the gig ain't over?" she asked, a huge grin spreading across her face.

"Do we have a deal or not?" he demanded with mock impatience. He liked this girl -- he admired her courage, but it would never do to let her know that.

"Oh my God," Sharday said, still grinning from ear to ear and getting more excited by the moment. "Yeah! Oh my God. Thank you, Clyde. Yeah, of course we got a deal!"

"Good. Then I'll see you next Friday." He handed her an envelope containing her pay.

Sharday was so elated that she'd forgotten all about her money. She took the envelope and said, "Okay, Clyde, I'll see you next Friday. And thank you so much for letting me keep the job. I really mean it." She reached out to shake his hand.

SIXTEEN

When Sharday awoke at noon the next day, she was eager to get back to her letter to Donnell. The fact that she still had the gig at *The Cellar* more than made up for getting fired by Mr. Weiss. So, she no longer had a reason to avoid getting in touch with her Boo.

She slipped on her robe and went downstairs. Bruce was at work since it was Friday. But Vickie was in the family room watching a cooking show on cable, and she said that April was still asleep. "She's probably not used to staying out so late," Vickie said. "You didn't get her back here until two this morning."

"And I know she ain't used to staying on the dance floor like she did all night," Sharday said. "That's why she so tired."

"April? On the dance floor?"

"Yeah, Ma. I couldn't believe it either. But we was all so hyped about Clyde switching me to Fridays that we wanted to get our party on. And April hung with us song for song."

"Hmm," Vickie said with a smile. "You never know about people, do you?"

"You can say that again," Sharday said, thinking about how April drank several glasses of champagne last night and they didn't seem to go to her head.

A few minutes later, Sharday told her mother she was "going back up," then she grabbed a bowl of cereal and a glass of orange juice from the kitchen to take up with her. As she shoveled *Frosted Flakes* into her mouth, she turned on her computer and pulled up the letter. She read it over again as she finished off her cereal.

She gulped down her orange juice and pushed her dishes to the side. Then she deleted the last line that said, *"Here is some really bad news that I have Donnell and I do not want to say it."* In its place, she typed, *"Donnell I have some good news and plus some bad news too. Last night was suppose to be my last night at the Cellar but Clyde said that he was moving me to Friday so I could keep coming every week. That was so great for him to do and I am so happy that I will still have a gig during the school year because you won't believe this Donnell but Mr. Weiss had the nerve to fire me. He did it 2 weeks ago so last week and this week I only had one gig and I thought it wouldn't be no more gigs after last night. He said that I just wasn't pulling the crowds in no more and he said it was just business making him let me go. But who needs him any way because now Clyde got our back and since he already know what is going on with you I won't have to try to keep lying all the time like I did with Mr. Weiss. So I'm just glad we don't need him no more any way."*

Sharday paused for a minute before continuing. "Anyway, this is why I did not write to you already because I did not want to have to tell you about Mr. Weiss but now that's over. So, I want to tell you that I really miss you boo. And I can't wait until you get out so we can be together and I hope that your lawyer can get your time down so you won't be in there too long. And I got some more good news too, my step father Bruce bought me and April a Nissan Altima! I will come visit you next weekend after you get this letter. I want to come tomorrow but my mother said we need to go to the mall again since school start on Monday. And now Bruce and my mother are having family days on Sundays if you can believe it so they sucking up the whole weekend.

Sharday paused to shake her hands. Her fingers were beginning to cramp, so she would have to finish this letter and get off the computer. *"Boo I can't wait to see you next weekend. And I will wait for you to finish serving your time so we can be together again. I love you Donnell. And I hope you keep loving me too until you get out of there. Love Sharday.*

SEVENTEEN

Vickie, Sharday, and April were up and out of the house by ten o'clock the next morning. Vickie was driving her new car, with Sharday riding shotgun and April in the backseat.

"I called Lynn from the kitchen," April said as Vickie pulled out of the garage and clicked the remote to close the door. "She'll be on her front porch."

"Okay," Vickie said. "Just tell me how to get there."

"She lives right around the corner." April leaned forward and pointed. "Just make a left out of the driveway and another left at the end of the block. That's it. She's in the rancher with white trim at the end of the cul-de-sac."

"That sounds easy enough," Vickie said. And then, after she turned out of the driveway, she looked over at Sharday and said, "See, honey! After today, you'll already know two people at your new school."

"Unh huh." Sharday turned to look at the sprawling homes passing by. Each one of these houses was about the size of their whole apartment building back in the hood. They had pretty green lawns, two-car garages, more flowers and trees than she had ever seen in her life. And these were the people her mother was expecting her to fit in with?

Her shoulders involuntarily slumped when they stopped in front of a pretty white trimmed brick home with enough surrounding land to make up a whole city block and a short, skinny, light-skinned girl with long, wavy hair stepped down off the porch. The girl had on khaki shorts, a short-sleeved denim shirt that was tucked into the waistband of her shorts, a black leather belt, and a black pair of those expensive but plain sandals that April wore. This was hopeless, Sharday thought. These people were from another planet.

By the time they made it to Route 50, the highway that would take them to Annapolis Mall, Sharday had retreated into silence. Lynn's diction was just as proper as April's, and Vickie was using her new and improved

English skills, so Sharday felt like she was out of her element. The situation was extremely uncomfortable for her at first -- she wasn't used to feeling so self-conscious -- but then she convinced herself that the real reason she wasn't saying anything was because they were talking about her new high school and that was the last thing she wanted to think about this morning.

"Why can't y'all find something else to talk about?" she said in exasperation a few minutes later. "I really ain't trying to hear all that right now."

April and Lynn immediately stopped talking. Vickie said, "But this is for *your benefit*, baby. Don't you want to know what to expect on Monday morning?"

"I'll deal with it when I get there," Sharday said with an irritated shake of her head. "This my last free weekend. Can't I just enjoy it?" She leaned over and turned on the radio, flipping through stations until she found hip-hop on *WKYS*.

"Ooh, that's my song!" Lynn exclaimed as Rihanna's latest single flooded the car.

"Mine, too," Sharday said over her shoulder. She wasn't even surprised. Apparently, Lynn was a schizo just like April was.

They arrived at the mall about twenty minutes later and Vickie immediately steered them to an *AT&T* store. "Let's see what kind of deals they're offering," she said.

"But why you care, Ma?" Sharday asked. "You already got a cell."

"Because Bruce and I decided to add you and April to our monthly plan, too. You never know what kind of emergency might come up with the car."

"For real?" Sharday asked in surprise.

"All right!" April said at the same time. "I've been begging Dad for one all summer!"

Lynn reached into her black leather purse and pulled out a sleek black touch screen phone. She grinned at April and said, "I got mine last night."

April laughed. "And now, I'm getting one, too! Can you believe it?"

After they left the wireless store, they went to *Nordstrom's*. Lynn bought a cashmere twin set, Vickie bought lipstick and eyeshadow from a makeup counter, April picked out a classic trench coat that Sharday said was too boring, and Sharday picked out a pair of *Aeropostale* jeans and a *Nike* sweatsuit.

"Don't you need a trench coat, too, Sharday?" Vickie suggested.

Sharday shook her head and said, "Nah, not really. We got a car now."

When April and Lynn wanted to stop in the shoe department to look at ankle boots, Sharday said she'd rather get a pair of "Tims or Jordans." Vickie tried to interest Sharday in a cute pair of updated granny boots, but Sharday wouldn't budge. Vickie finally gave in and took her daughter to a shoe store that sold Timberland boots and Michael Jordan sneakers.

After they went to *Old Navy* at Sharday's insistence and *The Gap* at April and Lynn's suggestion, Vickie decided to call it a day. She wasn't exactly angry at Sharday; frustrated would be a more appropriate word. She had hoped her daughter would take a cue from April and Lynn's selections so she would be dressed like the other kids at her new school. But if it wasn't hip-hop oriented, Sharday clearly wasn't interested.

"All right, that's it," Vickie said wearily. "Time to head back home."

* * * * *

Later that evening, Sharday took her second shower of the day and headed for her closet. She selected a breezy floral miniskirt made of gauzy material, a form-fitting, sleeveless yellow top, and flat yellow sandals with long laces that she'd tie in a bow mid-calf. Tonight was special -- her final fling with her girls before school started back up -- and her gear had to be just right.

She clicked on her Bluetooth speaker system and sang along to her YouTube playlist as she got dressed. She and her girls were planning to go all out tonight. First, they would meet at a party in the Vistas, then they were going to the go-go, and finally, they would top it off with breakfast at *The International House of Pancakes, or* IHOP, as they called it. And despite Elise's moaning and groaning about how much she was going to miss Keith, they had decided that none of them would bring dates. Tonight was strictly ladies' night.

Sharday was putting on the abbreviated, non-gig version of her makeup when the telephone line she shared with April began to ring. Since April was spending the night at Lynn's, Sharday crossed her bedroom and picked up the phone, even as she saw the unfamiliar name and number on the caller ID. She was surprised to find that it was Andre calling.

"Boy, how you get my number?" she asked him. "And where you calling me from, anyway? This ain't your number."

"Tyesha gave it to me," he said. "And we got our number changed."

"I got caller ID now, Andre," she said. "This ain't your mother's name."

"It's in my cousin's name," he said irritably.

"Oh." In hood parlance, Andre had just told her that their phone had gotten cut off and they got it turned back on in somebody else's name. Probably some cousin that wasn't even old enough to have credit yet.

"But all that ain't important right now," Andre said. "Hold on a minute. I got Donnell on the line."

"For real?" Sharday squealed in delight. But Andre had already switched over to his other line. When he switched back, he checked to make sure that both she and Donnell were on the line before he said, "Okay, y'all got fifteen minutes," and then he noisily put down the phone.

"Oh my God Donnell," Sharday said breathlessly. "How you doing, Boo? I'm so glad you got Andre to call me."

"I"m hanging," Donnell said. "But what about you, Day Day? How come you ain't been to visit me?"

She hung her head, even though he couldn't see her. "I'm sorry," she said. And then, "But you know what, Boo? My mother and them been taking up all my time since we got here. I just sent you a letter yesterday telling you how they act like they trying to make us into the perfect family or something." There was no way she was telling him about Mr. Weiss over the phone.

He grimaced. If Vickie thought she could get rid of him that easy, she was out of her mind. "And you just gonna let them play us like that?" he asked Sharday. "After all we been through? You going out like that?"

"Come on, Boo," she said. "You know me better than that. I just been waiting for school to start so things could calm down. Starting next week, I'll be over there every Saturday. No matter what," she added in a voice laced with steel.

Donnell smiled inwardly. This was the Day Day he knew and loved. "Now, that's what I'm talking about," he said.

"And you know it. I ain't going nowhere."

"But what about *Club 202*? You ain't been there the last two weeks either."

"And how you know that?" she asked, realizing right after she said it that Andre and Hakeem must have told him.

"I got all kinds of eyes and ears out there."

"Uh huh. But Clyde switched me to Fridays. I put all that in the letter, too."

"But what you plan to--?"

Just then, Andre picked up the phone and said, "Y'all done? I gotta hang up now."

Sharday breathed a sigh of relief.

Donnell said, "Nah, man. Give us fifteen more minutes."

"I can't," Andre said. "My mother gonna kill me for running up her new phone bill like this."

"Aw, stop crying, man," Donnell said. "I told you I'm gonna pay for it."

"It don't matter. Y'all gotta get off here. These collect calls be costing way more than regular calls."

"Alright, nigga, damn!" Donnell said in exasperation. "Just give us a minute to say bye. Can you do that?"

When Andre put the phone down again, Sharday told Donnell that he didn't have to call her through Andre anymore. She quickly gave him her cell phone number and told him to call her collect on there once a week. "Even though my mother still making me bank some of my singing money, I should be able to afford that. Plus, I'll be there every weekend and we can write each other, too."

"I really ain't no writer," Donnell said.

And before Sharday could respond, Andre picked up again and put an end to the conversation.

Sharday smiled as she hung up the phone. She had really missed Donnell. It was so good to hear his voice. And it would be even better to see him again next weekend.

A few seconds of mindless happiness passed before she snapped out of it and looked down at her watch. She was gonna be late meeting her girls at the party if she didn't get a move on! Everybody was riding to the go-go with her, so it wasn't like they could leave her or anything. But she didn't want to miss out on even one minute of the fun tonight, so she hurried over to her dresser to finish putting on her makeup.

EIGHTEEN

The one thing everybody forgot to mention to Sharday was that only about half of the students at Mitchellville High were black. So, when April turned down the driveway leading to the student parking lot near the back of the building, and Sharday saw all those white faces mixed in with the black ones climbing from the buses lined up in front of the school, Sharday almost went into shock. She wanted to ask April what all these white kids were doing here. Wasn't Mitchellville supposed to be all rich blacks? But she couldn't seem to find her voice.

The student parking lot was also filled with a mixture of blacks and whites. There were even some foreign-looking types out there, too. And they were all walking together, climbing out of cars together, looking like the best of friends. What was this supposed to be? The *United Nation* or whatever?

It took April forever to park in the space she had chosen, and after she shut off the car, she sheepishly looked at Sharday and said, "I know. I need more practice parking."

"But . . . but . . ., " Sharday sputtered, "but I thought Mitchellville was all black."

"Most of it is," April said, noticing for the first time how shaken Sharday seemed. "But I thought you knew," she added gently. "The P.G. County School System was under a federal court order to desegregate for a long time. So all the schools are mixed."

Sharday shook her head mutely as she stared at the students streaming into the side doors of the school. Desegregate? Court order? What in the world had her mother gotten her into?

April's heart went out to her new stepsister. Judging from the neighborhood Sharday had come from, her old high school had probably been all black -- and low-income blacks, at that. She must really be freaking out right now. "It'll be okay," she said, leaning over to place a hand on Sharday's arm. "The white students here are really cool. Seriously. And most of them like hip hop just like we do. So, you've got more in common with them than you might think."

Tears of hopelessness and frustration had been gathering in Sharday's eyes, but at the touch of April's hand, she promptly checked her emotions. Because the one rule above all she had learned from living in the hood was that you never showed your weaknesses. She swallowed back the tears and forced herself to look at April head-on. Then she gave her trademark, nonchalant shrug and said, "Oh, I ain't worried or nothing. I'm just surprised, that's all."

April wasn't buying it, but she admired Sharday for trying to rise to the occasion. She casually removed her hand from Sharday's arm and looked at her watch. "Well, we'd better get going, then," she said lightly. "First day and all, you know?"

When April grabbed her book bag from the back seat and got out of the car, Sharday felt a strong urge to slide over to the driver's seat and take off. But she knew there was nowhere for her to go; she had no choice but to deal. So, she lifted her own backpack from the floor at her feet and reluctantly opened her door.

The morning ticked by so slowly that Sharday thought it would never end. Every single thing about this school was different from Ballou Senior High. The teachers seemed nice enough and they were going out of their way to make her feel welcome, but they didn't hook up their clothes to look fresh like her old teachers did, and they weren't down with the latest slang like her old teachers were.

Plus, the students here followed all the rules. They were loud in the hallways between classes as they hit their lockers and joked around, but by the time the bell rang, the halls were empty and the classroom doors were closed. They were quiet in class -- even the people on the back row. There were no wisecracks when the teacher asked them questions, no notes passed back and forth, and there was no cutting up by the students just because they felt like it.

The school building, itself, blew her mind, too. It was just as old as Ballou, but it was a lot brighter, more spacious, and it wasn't run down and raggedy. The only really weird thing was that her second period math class was held in one of the long line of trailers on the grass between the rear of the school and the football stadium! What kind of craziness was that?

By the time her lunch period finally rolled around, she was more homesick for southeast than she ever could have imagined. She stashed her backpack in her locker and headed for the nearest girls' bathroom. At her old school, all the smokers and potheads hung out in the bathrooms, but of course, this one was practically empty. And since she wasn't supposed to leave the school grounds during lunch, she was tempted to just close herself up in a stall until fifth period was over.

But she couldn't punk herself out like that, especially not on the first day of school. So, she took her time using the bathroom, washing her hands, lingering in front of the mirror. Then she straightened her shoulders and slowly headed downstairs to the cafeteria.

When she saw the lunch choices -- shredded barbecue pork or breaded veal cutlets, she wished she had followed April's lead and packed her own food. But she hadn't, so she settled on the shredded pork, grabbed a carton of milk and an orange, and stopped near the wall just beyond the cashiers to look for a place to sit.

At least the long white tables with matching benches were just like the ones at her old school. She knew exactly what to do. Since April had a different lunch period, Sharday would just claim the empty end of a table near the back as her own.

When she shifted her gaze to look for "her table," she was surprised to find that Lynn was waving to her from one side of the huge room and Malcolm, the guy from the church choir, was waving from the other. Both of them were sitting at mixed-race tables, but Lynn's was closer to the back. Plus, Sharday didn't want anything to do with anybody involved in the choir. She waved back at Malcolm and headed for Lynn.

The people at Lynn's table spent the whole time talking about their summer vacations to places Sharday had never been and the movies they had seen the weekend before. Sharday hadn't gone on a trip over the summer and she hadn't seen a movie that wasn't on cable or from the Redbox since Donnell had gotten locked up. After picking over her plate for a few minutes, she peeled and ate her orange, drank down her milk. She claimed she had to go to the bathroom about halfway into the period. And she knew she wouldn't be coming back to "the caf," as Lynn's friends called it, anytime soon.

Thanks to a senior assembly, the afternoon flew by pretty quickly for Sharday. The principal let the seniors go about twenty minutes early, so she had to wait in the car for April, who was only a junior. She didn't mind. She was just relieved to be done with school for the day.

When she finally pulled into the driveway at the house in Mitchellville -- the agreement was that April would drive in the mornings and Sharday would drive back, Vickie was waiting for them at the front door. Sharday hung back so that April could go into the house first, then she stepped through the doorway and into her mother's embrace. "Oh my God, Ma. It was a nightmare," she murmured into Vickie's shoulder.

Vickie rubbed her daughter's back and softly said, "This was only the first day, baby. It'll get better. I promise." She leaned back and looked into Sharday's eyes. "Come on," she said. "Let's go have a snack and you can tell me all about it."

"I ain't really hungry, Ma. I just wanna go lay down."

Vickie released Sharday and let her go. She waited about fifteen minutes before she went upstairs and knocked on her daughter's door. "Tell me what happened, baby. What was so bad about it?" she said after she closed the door behind herself and sat on the side of the bed.

Sharday propped herself up on her pillows and let everything off her chest. When she finally finished, she looked at her mother and said, "But all I gotta do is make it through the next nine months, Ma. After that, I ain't never gotta be bothered with none of them people again."

Vickie was sorry to hear that Sharday had felt so out of place on her first day, but it sounded like this new environment was everything she wanted for her daughter. She had never been able to give Sharday anything but the ghetto until now, and she was happy to finally have a chance to show her another way of life. "So, you're telling me you didn't see one single person you thought could eventually become a friend?" she asked.

Sharday groaned and flopped back against the pillows. "Didn't you hear everything I just said, Ma?" she whined.

"Not even one person?"

Sharday sighed before admitting that there were a few students in the assembly who looked like they might be kind of cool. "But I probably don't have nothing in common with them neither," she said. "And anyway, Ma, I ain't looking for no new friends. I already got enough."

Vickie was determined not to let Sharday sleepwalk her way through this next year. But she had plenty of time to teach her daughter how to adapt.

So, right now, all she said was, "I know it's hard, baby, but give it a chance. I’ll help you get through this."

NINETEEN

At a few minutes after five on Wednesday evening, Sharday was sitting at her desk trying to concentrate on the second chapter of her social studies textbook. Her new teachers gave out a lot more homework than she was used to. And with those family dinners at six thirty and a nine-thirty curfew on school days, she would hardly have any time during the week to spend with her girls.

When she realized that she had just read the same paragraph twice, she got up from her desk and turned on an old Tupac album from her playlist. It was still the first week of school, way too early to be stressing out like this. Maybe she should take the car after dinner and head to the hood for a quick visit.

She was warming to the idea of making a quick getaway when her cell rang, briefly startling her. She rushed across the room to get the phone from her purse and wasn't surprised to hear an operator at the other end.

"Collect call from Donnell Dickerson," the impersonal voice announced. "Will you accept the call?"

"Yeah," Sharday quickly agreed. And after the operator disconnected, she smiled and said, "Hi, Boo. You just what the doctor ordered."

"Same here, Day-Day," he said. "I just got your letter yesterday. I can't believe all the shit you going through over there. You holding up?"

"I'm trying," she said. "But I was just thinking about how I gotta find a way to free up some of my time. What's the use in having a car if you ain't never got time to go nowhere?"

"I can't believe you got a car now," he said in a neutral tone, even as he shook his head. He hated the idea of her cruising around town in a Nissan. She was bad – real bad, and a lot of brothers would be trying to push up on her. He could hardly bear to think about it.

"But it's like Bruce and my mother don't really expect us to use it during the week unless we going back and forth to school," she said in frustration. "They done gave us a strict nine-thirty curfew, we got them family dinners every night, and the homework I been getting each day is more than I used to have for a whole week." She sighed. "And now my mother and her new husband done got it stuck in their mind that I need to join the church choir. Can you believe it?"

By now, Donnell was fighting back a smile and nodding his head. Vickie probably thought she was taking Sharday away from him by keeping her out of the hood, but she was actually playing right into his hands. He needed Sharday to be sitting around at home thinking about him all the time, not out having too much fun to even remember him. "You probably don't wanna hear this, Day-Day," he said, "but that sound like a good idea to me, too."

"Oh, please, Donnell. Don't even try it. Singing with a bunch of church nerds just ain't in the plans for me."

"See, that's where you wrong," he said. "Think about it. Some of our best singers came from the black church. Whitney Houston, Marvin Gaye, Aretha Franklin, Toni Braxton, John

Legend . . . "

"But it's bad enough I gotta go to church every week now," she complained. "Ain't that enough?"

"Nah, Day-Day. I'm counting on you to hold this music thing down until I can get up out of here. And being in that choir gonna help you keep your edge. Just look at it like something you gotta do for your career."

"Well, when you put it like that, I guess it ain't nothing I can say." This meant she would have to call that guy named Malcolm from church so he could help her get a gospel song together, but she certainly wasn't going to mention it to Donnell.

"And I been thinking about the gig at *The Cellar*, too," he said. "You know how Clyde is. If you wanna keep it, you gonna have to start mixing up some different songs."

"I been doing that. Other than *Street Life Paradise*, I sing different songs every week."

"Well, I wrote a lot of songs that I never played for you and they all in my room," he said. "Plus, it's a lot of new stuff on the radio now that you can do."

"Yeah, they been playing a lot of hot tracks lately."

"Do you think your moms and them would let you keep my equipment while I'm gone?" he asked. "You could use it to record some of the new songs and mix your voice in as the lead singer. That way you can keep the act fresh. And I got a lot of old instrumentals you could pull some tracks from, too." What he also feared but didn't say was that if he left his equipment in his room at the Vistas, his mother would eventually end up selling it.

Sharday looked around her huge bedroom which was almost bigger than her old living room and dining room combined. "It shouldn't be no problem," she said. "I can keep it right in my room."

"Good. Hakeem and Andre'll bring it over one day next week."

"But you gonna have to tell me how to work everything again," she said quickly. "I seen you do it a million times but I ain't never really pay no attention to what you was doing."

"Don't worry about that, Day-Day. I'll tell you everything you need to know." One of his crew members clapped twice just then and he looked up at the clock above his head and nodded. He had ten minutes left, and they were punking a whole group of dudes just to get him that. It was now or never. He curved his bulky body around the pay phone and lowered his voice. "Day-Day, my lawyer finally got me a plea bargain," he said.

"Huh?"

"I ain't trying to let everybody know my business," he said in the same near whisper. "Niggas got a way of changing up on you sometimes, you know? But I talked to my lawyer and he said he got me a deal."

"How long?" she asked, unable to keep the dread from her voice.

"Twenty-two months. And plus, they gonna give--" he broke off when Sharday started crying.

"Twenty-two months," she moaned. "I know you said two years, but . . . but it's just too long!"

"I know, Day-Day. I know. And I'm sorry." He really felt bad. Sharday was going through a lot right now, thanks to that mother of hers. And instead of being there to save her from it like he said he would, here he was piling on more. He let her cry it out for a while, but his time was ticking away. Finally, he said, "But it really ain't as bad as it sound, Day-Day. We really only looking at about a year and a half because they gonna give me credit for the time I'm serving now."

Sharday sniffed hard and swiped at her tears, forcing herself to pull it together. Donnell didn't need her breaking down on him. He was the one facing the time, not her, and here she was making him feel worse. She cleared her throat and said, "Okay, Boo, a year and a half." It came out sounding a lot more shaky than she had intended, so she cleared her throat again and said in a much stronger voice, "We can do this, Boo. Don't forget I got a car now. And with me coming down the road to Lorton once a week, it probably won't be so bad."

His mouth dropped open in shock before he caught himself and quickly composed his features. DC Jail was just a holding space for people awaiting trial and people serving short time. DC wasn't a state, so it had no penitentiary. And in the past, most of the convicted inmates had been shipped out to the federal prison in nearby Lorton, Virginia. But the feds had closed Lorton down a few years back and Sharday knew that. Donnell had told her himself when one of his buddies got shipped out to a federal prison in Ohio. He was out of telephone time now, though, so all he said was, "Sorry, Day-Day, but we gonna have to pick this back up when I see you this weekend. I gotta go. My time up."

"Okay, Boo," she said. "I'm glad you called. And I love you."

"Me, too, Day-Day," he said, and then he was gone.

* * * * *

Vickie had made beef tips with mushroom sauce and rice, fresh spinach, and crescent rolls for dinner, and just like everything else she made these days, it looked and smelled delicious. After Bruce said the grace, they dug into the meal and each person spent a few minutes talking about their day. Bruce had made that an unbreakable rule from day one, saying it was the only way for them to stay involved in each other's lives.

Vickie spoke excitedly about some of the changes she wanted to make to the master bedroom and bath, Sharday and April each said a few words about school, and Bruce told them that he would be very busy with work for the next few months. He was the director of human resources at the Washington Metropolitan Area Transit Authority, commonly known as "Metro," and he said his department was gearing up to handle company-wide performance reviews and merit increases. He spent quite a while explaining the details of the process and why it was so important, and then he finally said it was time for general conversation.

They spent the next twenty minutes throwing out possible activities for future family days -- that was quickly becoming their favorite topic, and it wasn't until they were winding down that Sharday looked at her mother and said, "Oh, I meant to tell y'all. I decided to go on ahead and join the choir."

"Oh, Sharday! Baby, that's so wonderful!" Vickie exclaimed. "I knew you would eventually come around."

"Calm down, Ma," Sharday said. "It ain't like I'm really joining the church or nothing. It's just another gig. A way to keep my game tight until Donnell get out."

April and Bruce looked at Sharday in surprise, but Vickie's smile never wavered. This was a big concession on her daughter's part, and she wasn't going to do anything to blow it. She shrugged and said, "Whatever the reason, Sharday, I'm glad you decided to do it."

Vickie's casual tone brought Bruce back around. God had already touched Sharday's heart to join the choir and she had only been to church a few times. This was just her usual tough talk. Her actions were saying something else entirely. He smiled at her and said, "I'm glad, too, Sharday. And the Lord has a way of sneaking up on you, you know?"

Sharday shrugged and kept her mouth shut. She wasn't even trying to go there with Bruce.

April didn't know what to say, so she stood and started collecting the serving dishes since it was her week to clean the kitchen. Her father had told her about Sharday's background and the boyfriend who was in jail for selling drugs, but she was still stunned that Sharday could equate joining a gospel choir with a "gig" at a nightclub.

When April headed to the kitchen with her first load of dishes, Sharday said, "Well, I gotta go call that guy from the choir. I'm gonna need him for my audition." She looked at her mother and Bruce and then said, "And I was thinking that after that I might go visit my girl, Tyesha."

Bruce nodded. "Fine with me. As long as you meet your curfew."

"And that's nine thirty, Sharday," Vickie said. "Sharp."

Sharday quickly stood before they could they change their minds. "Nine thirty sharp," she said. "No problem. I got it."

TWENTY

Malcolm was so nervous and excited as he reached out for Mr. Campbell's doorbell that his hand trembled briefly. He was getting ready to see Sharday! After she blew him off in the cafeteria on Monday and skipped it altogether every day after that, he had started thinking she didn't want to be bothered with him. So, he was totally floored when she called yesterday and asked whether he would still be willing to practice with her.

Sharday was coming down the steps from her room when Malcolm rang the doorbell. She groaned and headed for the front door. She had planned to schedule something for one day next week, but Malcolm had sounded so gung ho when she called that she agreed to let him come at four o'clock today. Didn't want him to lose his enthusiasm. Plus, she might as well just get it over with.

Now, she arranged her face into a smile and said, "Hey, Malcolm," then she stepped back to let him into the foyer.

"Hi, Sharday," he said with a huge grin. "It's good to see you again."

She locked the door and said, "Come on back," then she led the way to the family room.

Malcolm was pulling a keyboard, an iPad, and some sheet music from his huge, black, leather bag when Vickie entered the room. He smiled at her and said, "Hi, Mrs. Campbell."

"Well, hello there, Malcolm!" Vickie quickly crossed the room to shake his hand. "It's so nice of you to help Sharday out like this," she said. "Thanks for coming."

He suppressed a giddy laugh, thinking that he should be the one thanking her for convincing Sharday to join the choir. "You're welcome," he said. "But I'm happy to do it."

Vickie smiled brightly and couldn't help comparing Malcolm's polite demeanor to Donnell's thuggish manner. This was exactly the type of young man she was hoping Sharday would eventually take up with. "Would you like something to drink?" she asked him.

"A glass of water would be nice if it's not too much trouble," he said.

Vickie assured him it would be no trouble at all and said she'd be back shortly.

Malcolm finished setting up his equipment and told Sharday that he'd selected a number of songs since he didn't know her range and style yet. "They play most of these on the radio," he said. "So, you've probably heard them before."

"I doubt it," Sharday said. "I ain't really into gospel."

He turned on his keyboard and said, "Well, I'll play the intro and first verse of a few of the songs and you can stop me if you hear something that sounds familiar."

Malcolm played the beginnings of three different songs, none of which Sharday had heard before, and he was starting on the fourth when Vickie came back and placed a carafe of ice water and two glasses on a mat on the coffee table.

Malcolm paused at the keyboard and said, "Thanks, Mrs. Campbell."

"Please, keep playing," Vickie urged him. "Don't let me disturb you." She lingered over the coffee table, pulling out coasters and pouring ice and water into the glasses. She was thrilled to see that Malcolm was so talented with his keyboard. And unlike Donnell, he also had a great singing voice. By the time she left the room, she had begun to formulate a new plan.

It wasn't until Malcolm had started playing the sixth song that Sharday finally said, "Oh, I know that one! They used to play it on the radio all the time!" She started singing along to his accompaniment, scatting playfully when she didn't know the words.

Malcolm listened intently. Sharday had an amazing range and near-perfect musical instincts. Mrs. Jefferson would have her singing solos in no time. He played the last few notes of the song with a flourish and said, "Wow! That was great!" He grinned at her. "That was *Take Me To The King.* A Tamela Mann song. Do you want to sing that one for your audition?"

"Yeah, why not?" she said with a shrug. "At least, all I gotta do is learn the words since I already know the melody." She reached for a glass of water and said, "Whew! I thought I wasn't gonna know none of them songs."

Malcolm laughed. "That would've been okay with me," he said. "I wouldn't mind teaching you a song from scratch." He picked up the other glass and emptied it with three huge gulps. He would never admit it to Sharday, but with he each passing song, he had found himself hoping that she wouldn't know any of them. That would've given him more one-on-one time with her before he had to share her with the rest of the choir.

Just then, Vickie came back into the room with a serving platter of peanut butter and jelly and ham and cheese sandwiches that she'd cut into neat little squares. She'd also added green grapes and strawberries to the platter. She set it down on the coffee table mat and said, “I thought you two might like a snack. Singing's hard work.”

“Thanks, Ma,” Sharday said.

Malcolm looked over at the platter and took in the assortment of goodies. Even though he wouldn't touch a bite until after he finished singing, it sure was nice of Mrs. Campbell to go to so much trouble. He smiled at her and said, “Thanks, Mrs. Campbell.”

“You're welcome,” Vickie said. And then she asked Malcolm, “So, what do you think of Sharday's voice? Isn't she amazing?”

Sharday couldn't have been more embarrassed. “Ma, please,” she whined. “He's in a choir. He probably knows a lot of good singers.”

“Not as good as you,” Malcolm said. “I can't think of a single person in the choir who even comes close.”

Sharday smiled despite herself and mumbled, “Thanks.”

Vickie smiled, too, and said, “Well, I'd better let you two get back to it. But if you need anything else, I'll be right in the kitchen,” then she turned and left.

Malcolm played *Take Me To the King* two more times with Sharday standing over his shoulder following the words on the sheet music before he looked at her and said, “Let's run through it one more time and I'll record it for you, okay?"

She nodded. "Okay."

He clicked on his voice memos and started over. When they finished, he sent the audio file to her phone, "You've pretty much got it now," he said. "If you use this to practice a couple of times, you should be ready by Sunday."

"I don't know," she said. "I think I'd rather wait until next Sunday."

"Okay, we can do that," he said easily. "And if you want, I can come practice with you a couple of days next week."

She inwardly cringed at the idea. She was planning to make a few after-dinner trips to southeast next week. So, she would need all her free time to do her homework and practice for *The Cellar*. "Uh, maybe you right," she said. "Let's just do it Sunday and get it over with."

Malcolm was disappointed that he wouldn't have the extra time with her, but he simply said, "Whatever you're comfortable with." He finished packing up his equipment and prolonged the visit a little longer by helping himself to some of the snacks Vickie had prepared for them. When he could put it off no longer, he told Sharday he had enjoyed practicing with her, lifted his bag to his shoulder, and followed her from the room.

As promised, Vickie was still in the kitchen. "Don't tell me you two are calling it quits already," she said, looking up from her seat at the table. "It's hardly been an hour yet."

"He brought a song I already knew," Sharday said at the same time Malcolm said, "Sharday's a quick study."

"Well, it sounded good from here," Vickie said enthusiastically. "You two make a great team." She stood and looked at Sharday. "Maybe Malcolm could help you learn the songs for the choir, too," she said pensively, as if she had just thought of it.

"I'd be happy to," Malcolm quickly interjected, but Sharday shook her head and said, "Nah, I'll be alright."

"Are you sure?" Malcolm asked her. "I don't mind."

Before Sharday could reply, Vickie looked at her and said, "Why don't you wait and see how it goes at choir rehearsal. You never know, Sharday. You might just find you need his help, after all."

Sharday suppressed a sigh of impatience. At this point, all she wanted to do was get Malcolm out of here. She looked at him and said, "Alright, I'll let you know."

Vickie smiled. She would turn things around for Sharday yet. She shook Malcolm's hand and thanked him for coming again, then she told him she looked forward to seeing him at church on Sunday.

TWENTY-ONE

Visiting hours at D.C. Jail started at eleven in the morning on Saturdays, so Sharday had worked out a deal with April. April would use the car after school on Fridays until Sharday needed it for *The Cellar*, Sharday would have it on Saturdays up to about four or five so she could visit Donnell and still have some extra time, and then April would have it the rest of the time on Saturdays until their curfew, which Vickie and Bruce had set for one in the morning. Thanks to church and family day, the car would mostly sit in the driveway on Sundays.

Now, at eleven thirty on Saturday morning, Sharday sat on the edge of a hard, plastic chair on the third floor of the jail waiting for the guards to bring Donnell out. More than a month had passed since the last time she'd seen him and she was growing more eager by the minute. When the grey metal door on the other side of the plexiglass finally opened and he stepped into view behind a correctional officer, she jumped to her feet and placed both hands on the thick plastic.

Donnell immediately quickened his pace, maintaining as much of a semblance of cool as possible as he hurried across the room to place his hands opposite hers. They stood that way without speaking for a few long minutes, but then he caught himself and pointed to her phone. "Pick up," he mouthed, then he reached for his own handset and sat down.

Sharday briefly rested her forehead against the plexiglass and closed her eyes, swallowing back the bittersweet tears that threatened to drown her. It was good to finally see Donnell again but this thick piece of plastic separating them was just too much. At least once he got to Lorton they could have contact visits. She suddenly smiled and opened her eyes. The strength to pick up the phone and sit back down was no longer lacking. "Oh my God, Boo," she said into the phone, "I ain't seen you in so long I almost started crying."

"I'm feeling you," he said, tapping his chest twice right over his heart.

"But, Day-Day, we gotta make the best of this, you know what I'm saying?"

"Yeah, I know you right, Boo," she admitted, slouching down in her chair. "So, how you doing? You looking good."

He ran his hand over the bald head he had gotten one of his crew members to touch up in the prison barbershop just that morning. "Sometimes a brother just gotta go with the flow," he said with a shrug.

She nodded. It looked good on him.

She told him about the audition song she had picked out for the church choir, but she made a point not to mention Malcolm. He said he had found a "bookworm" to write out the instructions for his equipment but didn't say anything about the judge approving his plea bargain the day before or his lawyer's prediction that he would be shipped north to either upstate New York or upstate Pennsylvania.

He felt guilty as he listened to her innocently go on about the songs she had performed the night before at *The Cellar*. He knew this was the time to tell her that he wouldn't be going to Lorton, but just couldn't bring himself to do it. Instead, he promised to start thinking up some rhymes for her to spit and steered the conversation to her life in Mitchellville. He was almost relieved when they heard his C.O.'s keys jangling on the other side of the door a few minutes later.

"Already?" she pouted prettily. "I can't believe it's over so quick."

"I know," he said. "But you be here next weekend, right?"

"Right," she said. And then she whispered, "I love you, Boo. And I miss you, too."

"Me too, Day-Day," he said, then he slowly hung up the phone and stood.

She didn't get up until the correctional officer had firmly closed the door behind him.

* * * * *

Sharday stopped by southeast on her way home to pick up Tyesha, who was going to spend the night in Mitchellville and go to church with the family the next morning.

"What the dealy-o?" Tyesha said playfully as she tossed her overnight bag in the back and climbed into the passenger's seat. "Girl, I can't wait to see your new house! I bet it's off the chain!"

"Stop tripping, Tyesha. It's just a house."

"Yeah, right," Tyesha said as she buckled her seat belt. "Like either one of us ever lived in a house before. And now you're living in an area known for having a lot of rich blacks?"

Sharday drove off. "Whatever," she said. "Lee still taking us to the go-go?"

"He's picking us up at nine, but he needs directions."

"Well, call him on my cellphone. It's in my purse and I get free minutes on weekends."

"He's probably not home," Tyesha said. "And anyway, I'm supposed to call him at eight."

"Alright then." Sharday leaned over and clicked on the radio.

"So, how was the visit?" Tyesha eventually asked.

Sharday sighed. "Hard. I just hate seeing him there. And I miss him so much I almost feel like I could die."

"That's messed up," Tyesha said with a shake of her head. She was still pissed at Donnell for lying to Sharday about what went down. She was even kind of pissed at him for getting caught up in the first place. But at the same time, she knew how much Sharday loved him, and she also knew how devoted Donnell had always been to Sharday. "Well, at least he got a good plea bargain," she said. "A year and a half's not that bad."

"I keep trying to tell myself that," Sharday said. "Maybe one day I'll believe it."

Tyesha shook her head again and neither of them said anything else for a while. But then, Tyesha decided it was time to lift the heavy mood. "Day-Day, you won't believe what Larry Green did yesterday," she said, referring to a crackhead who lived in the Vistas. Then she spent the rest of the ride telling Sharday funny stories about the crazy goings-on in the hood.

When Sharday turned into her new development, Tyesha abruptly stopped speaking and glanced around in awe. These houses looked like mansions! They were just that big and pretty! And they had so much yard around them it was almost like these people didn't have any neighbors! "Your new house is in here?" she asked Sharday in disbelief.

"Unh huh."

"I can't believe it!" Tyesha said excitedly, squirming in her seat.

"This place is all that, Day-Day! Ms. Vickie really hooked you up this time!"

"Not! Just wait until you see how boring it is."

"Who cares?" Tyesha shouted. "Girl, your moms got you living like royalty out here!"

"Who cares, Tyesha?" Sharday shot right back. "I ain't got nothing in common with these people around here. And I hate their half white school, and I hate missing out on all the fun in the hood." She pulled into the driveway of her new house and shut off the car.

"Y'all live in this one?" Tyesha asked in a hushed whisper. This house was straight out of a fairy tale. It was so tall with all those dark red bricks and those huge white columns.

Sharday ignored her and said, "Come on, Tyesha. They all probably waiting to give you the great big family welcome."

Tyesha grabbed her overnight bag and followed Sharday up the curved walkway past the pretty flowers and the perfectly-trimmed shrubs. How could Sharday hate living here? How could anybody?

Sharday told Tyesha to leave her bag at the foot of the steps in the foyer, then she led the way to the family room.

Tyesha followed Sharday to the back of the house, amazed by the elegant, color-coordinated furniture and accessories in the living room, the formal dining room with its fancy chandelier, the enormous eat-in kitchen with all the modern appliances. Even the family room looked better than her own living room, with its sumptuous green leather furniture and thick wooden tables. Vickie was sitting on the sofa watching one of those decorating shows and her husband was kicked back in the recliner reading some kind of manual or something. They looked like the perfect married couple.

"Look who's here, Ma," Sharday said as she stepped into the room.

Vickie smiled and said, "Hi, Tyesha. You remember my husband, Bruce, don't you?"

Tyesha nodded dumbly. Everything was so fabulous it was hard to take it all in. She could hardly think straight. "Hi, Ms. Vickie. Hi, Mr. Campbell," she managed.

"Hello, Tyesha. Welcome to our humble abode," Bruce said with a warm smile. "Make yourself at home. And please, call me Bruce."

"Okay, Mr. Bruce. Thank you," Tyesha said.

Vickie stood and gave the awestruck girl a warm hug, then she asked how Gloria and Jolean were doing.

At the mention of her family, Tyesha finally snapped out of her trance and smiled. "They're doing fine," she said. "My mother told me to tell you 'hi.' She said to tell you she appreciates you letting Sharday have me over for the night."

"Anytime," Vickie said.

Sharday spoke up then. "We going up to my room for a while," she said. "Come on, Tyesha."

"Will you two be around for dinner?" Vickie asked. "I was planning to order Chinese."

"We'll be here," Sharday said. Thank God her mother wasn't planning on showing off her new cooking skills. Tyesha was freaked out enough as it was. She grabbed Tyesha's arm and led her from the room.

When they got upstairs to Sharday's bedroom, Tyesha placed her bag at the foot of the bed and said, "It's so big in here. And you've got your own TV now, and a computer, too. And look at that stereo."

"Yeah, I gotta admit Bruce gave me the hookup in here," Sharday said.

Tyesha flopped down on the bed and said, "God, Day-Day! I just love it out here!" She grinned then. "You know what? We should blow Lee off and invite the girls over here to hang out."

"Nah, Tyesha. I wanna get out of here tonight."

"But I'll never be able to describe all this," Tyesha said. "And they won't believe me anyway. Plus, we go to the go-gos all the time. Let's do something different for a change."

Sharday resisted, but Tyesha eventually won her over. And when Sharday went downstairs to ask Vickie and Bruce whether she could have more company, Tyesha picked up the phone and immediately started making the arrangements.

"They said yeah," Sharday said when she came back, leaving off the fact that Vickie clearly wasn't too excited about the idea.

"Good," Tyesha said. "Kayla said John can drop her and LaShawn off, and Elise is getting a ride with Keith. They'll call for directions before they come. Plus, I called Lee and left him a message. I told him something came up and we won't be able to make it."

"But my mother and them could've said no," Sharday said.

"But I knew they wouldn't," Tyesha said.

When April knocked on the door a little while later to let Sharday know she was taking the car, Tyesha invited her to join them for the evening. "The rest of our friends are coming over, too," Tyesha said. "It's gonna be a lot of fun."

"I'd love to," April said, "but I've already got plans. I'm going to a movie with some of my friends and I probably won't be back until about ten."

"They'll still be here. You can join us then," Tyesha urged. She liked April, no matter what Sharday said about how weird she was.

After April agreed and left, Sharday waited until she heard April going down the steps before she turned to Tyesha and said, "Girl, why you do that?"

"Oh, give the girl a break, Day-Day," Tyesha said. "She's not that bad."

Sharday and Tyesha spent the rest of the afternoon up in Sharday's room. They listened to music, fooled around on the internet a bit, watched a few videos on BET. Sharday even convinced Vickie to let them bring their Chinese food up to her room and they ate in there, too.

When Sharday's girls from the Vistas arrived, they were just as impressed with her new house as Tyesha was. Kayla and LaShawn arrived at about a quarter to seven. Elise didn't show up until almost an hour later, but she brought Bootleg DVDs of the latest movies of Will Smith and Tyler Perry with her.

Bruce and Vickie agreed to turn over the family room so Sharday and her friends could watch their movies in there. And at Bruce's suggestion, Vickie even provided them with snacks -- popcorn, nachos and salsa, buffalo wings, miniature pizzas, sodas and juices.

Sharday's friends bypassed the leather furniture and sprawled comfortably on the floor in front of the television. Sharday put Tyler Perry's movie in the DVD player and joined her girls on the floor.

The opening credits were still playing when LaShawn said, "I got a good one," referring to a blunt. "Y'all wanna go outside before we watch the movie?"

"Girl, we can't do that around here," Sharday whispered in alarm. "These people be done called the police on us before we even took the first hit.'"

"But can't we do it in the backyard?" LaShawn asked. "Can't nobody see us back there."

"Except my mother if she look out her window," Sharday said. "Girl, you must be crazy."

"I don't want none anyway," Kayla said.

"Me neither," Elise said.

"Can't you give it a rest for one night?" Tyesha asked LaShawn. "Save it for tomorrow or something. It won't kill you."

LaShawn caught an attitude. "Why you gotta take it there, Tyesha? Acting like I'm pressed or something. You do it just as much as me."

"Not even close," Tyesha said. "None of us do."

"Whatever," LaShawn said. "You always gotta be tripping."

"Day-Day, pass me a pizza or some wings or something," Elise said. "I'm hungry."

Sharday looked at her and said, "Get it yourself, Elise. I ain't no maid."

"Well, excuse me, Miss Thing," Elise said. "But you the one who live here."

Kayla started laughing. "Dag, y'all," she said. "The way y'all arguing and stuff people would think we wasn't even friends."

Elise chuckled and said, "True that." She reached across Sharday to grab a pizza and a napkin.

"Yeah, but we go way back," LaShawn said. "Me and Kayla go back to elementary school."

"Me and Sharday, too," Tyesha said.

Elise said, "But all of us wouldn't be friends if it wasn't for me. I made friends with Kayla and with Tyesha in eighth grade history. And they ain't even know each other then."

"Stop tripping," LaShawn said. "Me and Day-Day kind of knew each other anyway because she used to come to my court to visit Donnell all the time."

"Remember that time Marvelle tried to punk me?" Sharday asked LaShawn, referring to the girl Donnell had dated before her.

"Yeah," LaShawn said. "She kept standing in front of his building calling you all kinds of hoes and stuff."

"And then I came outside and kicked her butt," Sharday said. "Even though she was older than me."

"And she thought she was so hard, too," LaShawn said.

Tyesha said, "Y'all remember the time Elise was beefing with that girl named Precious Hughes from southwest and she brought her whole crew over to the Vistas to jump Elise."

Elise started laughing and said, "Do we remember? Girl, please. I thought we was gonna get our butts kicked that day."

Kayla said, "Nah, you know the Vistas stick together when it come to stuff like that. They ran them girls out of there so fast I can't even remember what they looked like."

"Thank God," Sharday said with a laugh. "Some of them girls was kind of big."

"But they wouldn't have been the first big girls we dropped," Tyesha said.

And from there, Sharday and her friends were off and running. They spent the next hour and a half reminiscing about the earlier days of their friendship, from the people they'd fought, to the places they'd been, to the boys they'd dated. They were still talking when the movie ended.

"Dag, we missed the whole thing," Tyesha said. "Let's start it over."

Sharday was reaching for the remote to the DVD player when April came in and joined them. April said hello to everyone before she sat down next to Tyesha on the floor.

"So, how was the movie," Tyesha asked her. "What did y'all go see?"

"We saw the new Kevin Hart movie," April said. "I liked it."

Elise said, "Shoot, I'm starting to miss Keith. What time is it?"

"Time for you to have a good time and stop being so pressed about Keith," LaShawn said.

"Stop hating," Elise said. "You just mad because you ain't got no man."

"Beep, wrong," LaShawn said.

They had all been wanting to ask LaShawn about this for a long time, so Tyesha quickly seized the opportunity. "But now that Elise brought it up," Tyesha said, "I wanna know, too."

"Know what?" LaShawn asked defensively.

"Why you ain't got a man," Sharday said.

"Yeah," Kayla joined in. "I mean, it ain't like you ugly or nothing.

You got that natural beauty kind of thing going on."

"So, what's up like that?" Tyesha asked.

"Ain't nothing up like that," LaShawn said. She wondered what her friends would think if she told them the truth -- that she thought she might be gay. But, of course, she would never admit that to them. They might start tripping and not want to be friends with her anymore.

"So, why you don't never date nobody?" Sharday asked. "You gay or something?" she joked.

"Get real," LaShawn said. "I'm strictly dickly."

April spoke up then. "Maybe nobody ever asks her out," she said. "I know that's my problem."

"Really?" Tyesha said. "I don't see why not. You're cute enough. You probably just need to fix yourself up some."

"But her friends dress like that, too," Sharday said. "That probably ain't got nothing to do with it."

"Yeah, some of us just can't pull the guys like y'all do," LaShawn said. She was relieved to have an easy way out.

"Maybe it's because I always clam up whenever I'm around a boy I like," April said.

Elise nodded knowingly. "Yeah, that's probably it," she said. "You gotta show a guy you interested. If you don't, he just gonna move on to somebody else who do."

"But you can't act too interested," Tyesha added quickly. "That'll turn a guy off in a minute."

“Or make him try to just use you for sex,” Kayla said.

The conversation stayed on guys from that point on -- how to get them, how to keep them, how to dump them, how to tell if they were cheating on you, how to cheat on them without getting caught. By the time John and Keith showed back up at about midnight, the girls had talked through the entire movie again.

TWENTY-TWO

Sharday had set her alarm clock to go off thirty minutes earlier that Sunday, so it started screaming at five-thirty in the morning. She shut it off right after the first *"PLEASE WAKE UP!"*

"That clock is wild," Tyesha murmured, sitting up and rubbing her eyes. "That's what me and Jolean need."

"It's too loud," Sharday groaned. She yawned and looked up at Tyesha. "You wanna hit the bathroom first or lay back down while I take my shower? April usually be finished by now."

"I'll go first." Tyesha climbed out of bed and headed across the room for her robe and small bag of toiletries.

Sharday turned over on her side and snuggled her head into the pillow. But instead of dozing back off after Tyesha left, she found herself thinking about her forthcoming choir audition. She finally got up and played the recording Malcolm had left her. As it played in the background, she set out her underclothes, her fuschia and white church dress, off-black stockings, her black pumps.

She headed for the bathroom after Tyesha returned. The steam quickly lubricated her throat and she sang through *Take Me To The King* as she showered. She was still humming the song when she reentered her bedroom and found Tyesha putting on a sophisticated, striped, gray skirt suit. "Dag, girl," she said. "That suit is hot."

"*H & M,*" Tyesha said, referring to an international retail chain that sold cheap versions of the hottest clothes.

Once they finished getting dressed and putting on their makeup, they went downstairs for the pre-church snack Sharday had already warned Tyesha about. When Sharday picked up a Lipton tea bag, Tyesha opted for the herbal tea and followed April's lead by swirling a cinnamon stick around in her cup. "It's different," she said, not exactly liking it but enjoying the chance to try something new.

Bruce smiled. Vickie might be right about Sharday's other friends from southeast, but she was wrong about this one. This girl seemed like she could have a positive influence on Sharday.

"It's good once you get used to it," April told Tyesha.

Sharday laughed and said, "But it's the 'once you get used to it' part that kills you."

Vickie shot a warning glance at her daughter and said, "Shar-day."

"It was just a joke, Ma," Sharday said.

The rest of breakfast passed quickly. And although church was the usual boring affair by Sharday's standards, she noticed that Tyesha seemed to be really getting into it. Before Sharday knew it, the church was emptying and it was time for her to go down front and audition.

She headed toward the stage with Vickie. Tyesha, April and Bruce followed closely behind. She told Mrs. Jefferson what she was going to sing, Malcolm took his seat at the piano, and she proceeded to let it rip. By the time she finished, the remaining congregation members were clustered near the stage. They broke into applause and Mrs. Jefferson said, "Well, the Lord has certainly blessed us today! We'd love to have you as a member of our choir, Sharday!"

After the small crowd dispersed, Mrs. Jefferson told Sharday that rehearsals were on Tuesday evenings at six in the Sunday School room, and Sharday went back down to her mother, her stepfamily and Tyesha. Malcolm quickly took off his choir robe and joined them at the foot of the stage. "Wow, you were great!" he said to Sharday, grinning at her. "Tamela Mann would be proud!"

Sharday thanked him and introduced Tyesha. He shook Tyesha's hand and said hello to her and everyone else.

Tyesha smiled as she shook Malcolm's hand, taking in his expensive clothes and shoes and his good looks that Sharday had failed to mention. He had clear brown skin, short wavy hair and pretty hazel eyes. But more than that, he had class and it was clear that he was crazy about Sharday. Tyesha wished she could meet a guy like Malcolm, too. Somebody who clearly had a future ahead of him. Maybe if she kept coming out here, she would.

"You didn't tell me Malcolm was so fine," she whispered to Sharday after they had climbed into the backseat of Bruce's car with April.

"Compared to Donnell, he ain't," Sharday whispered back.

Tyesha looked at Sharday but didn't say anything. A year and a half was going to be a long time to wait for Donnell with a good catch like Malcolm lurking in the background.

Bruce spoke up then and suggested that Tyesha join them for brunch. "What do you think, honey?" he asked Vickie. "Family day doesn't officially start until after brunch anyway, right?"

Vickie agreed and asked Tyesha whether she needed to call Gloria for permission.

"Not really," Tyesha said. "She's at work right now."

Bruce took them to IHOP for brunch, where they each ordered a different kind of omelet. After they dropped Tyesha off, the family went to a skating rink in upper northwest DC and Sharday surprised herself by actually having a good time. She was reluctant to admit it, but April and Bruce were already starting to grow on her.

TWENTY-THREE

Sharday had forgotten all about rush hour, so thanks to bumper-to-bumper traffic on Mitchellville Road, she was fifteen minutes late for her first choir rehearsal. As she walked down the hall toward the Sunday School room, she could hear that they'd started without her. When she gently opened the closed door and stepped inside the room, everyone turned to look at her.

"Sorry," she mouthed with a shrug, trying to project a sense of confidence she didn't feel. She was nervous about trying to fit in with all these church people, but it would never do to show it.

Mrs. Jefferson smiled and said a quick, "Welcome," without faltering in her piano playing.

Malcolm waved and pointed to an empty chair on the second row.

Sharday shook her head and slipped into an empty seat on the back row instead.

"Well, hello, Sharday," Mrs. Jefferson said a few minutes later after she brought the song to an end. "I'm so happy you could join us." She stood and gestured for Sharday to come forward, then she looked at the choir members seated before her. "Everyone, this is Sharday Grant, our new member," she said. "Why don't we go around the room and introduce ourselves."

"Hi, Sharday. I'm Geraldine Swisher," said a heavyset, middle-aged woman on the closest end of the first row.

"My name is Cynthia Williams," said the pretty, petite, twenty-something woman seated beside her. "I'm the choir secretary."

There were thirty-three choir members, in all. Most of them were females, but there was a healthy sprinkling of males among them, too. And as far as Sharday could tell, they seemed to range in age from early teens to mid-fifties, at least.

When the introductions were done, Mrs. Jefferson directed Sharday to the same seat on the second row Malcolm had pointed to earlier and said,

"Why don't you sit here with the sopranos for now." She handed Sharday a thin, black notebook. "These are the songs we're currently singing," she said. "Right now, all I want you to do is listen and try to follow the words."

"Okay." Sharday nodded and flipped through the notebook. Not even one of the song titles was familiar. She spent the next forty minutes listening to a series of songs she'd never heard in her life. She knew she could sing and wouldn't have any problem fitting in on that level. But these people really meant what they were singing about God and Jesus. She could tell. And she knew she wouldn't be coming from that place. It wasn't that she didn't believe in God and Jesus, because she did. But she had only been going to church for about a month now. So, she didn't have the church background these people did. Even the teenagers were shouting "amen" and saying "hallelujah" between songs. And that made Sharday feel out of place. Not out of place enough to quit the choir, just out of place enough to feel like she wouldn't be able to fit in socially. Which seemed to be the theme of her whole life now that she was living in Mitchellville.

Finally, Mrs. Jefferson said, "All right, folks. That was great. We've got the Thanksgiving program coming up in two months and I've already picked out two new selections. We're going to do six songs in all, and as always, I'm open to suggestions. But get your requests in by the week after next, at the latest." She smiled and said, "Well, okay, then! Keep up the good work! And I'll see you next week!"

As everyone else began talking, Sharday stood and tried to make a quick escape. She had almost reached the door when Mrs. Jefferson called her back over and handed her a CD. "I made this for you to practice with at home," Mrs. Jefferson said. "I put the songs in the same order they're in in your notebook. And I sang the soprano part for each one."

"Thanks," Sharday said, slipping the CD into her purse.

"I think what I'd like to have you do is practice with us for two more weeks before you start joining us in the choir stands on Sunday mornings," Mrs. Jefferson said. "I don't expect you to know all the songs by then, but at some point, you're just going to have to plunge in."

"Okay," Sharday said.

"Oh, and I'll have to remember to bring a choir robe for you next week. I think a medium should do the trick, but I'll bring a large, too, just in case."

"Okay," Sharday said again. She was getting antsy to leave and hoped Mrs. Jefferson would wind this up and let her go.

"And just so you know," Mrs. Jefferson said, "whenever we have a special program coming up, I hold extra rehearsals on the Saturdays leading up to it."

Sharday quickly shook her head. No way was she going to miss her visits to Donnell just to come to some extra choir rehearsals. "I probably can't make it," she said. "My Saturdays already really booked up."

"Well, don't worry about that right now," Mrs. Jefferson said. "We'll work something out when the time comes."

"Okay, then." Sharday noticed that other people were already beginning to leave so she added, "I see you next week, Miss Jefferson, okay?"

Mrs. Jefferson nodded and said, "I'll see you then. And once again, Sharday, I'm happy to have you as a member of the choir."

Sharday said, "Thanks," and made a beeline for the door, only to be ambushed in the hallway by two teenaged girls who said they had been waiting for her. They reintroduced themselves as Simone and Ebony, then they chatted her up all the way down the hallway, down the steps to the first floor of the church, and out the front door. They seemed nice enough, but they were church girls, and Sharday knew she would never fit in with them.

Malcolm was waiting for her outside and offered her a ride home. When she told him she had driven, too, he said he'd walk her to the parking lot.

She said, "Okay," and started walking. She'd had enough of the choir and everybody in it for one night and she just wanted to get out of here. When Malcolm asked about practicing with her, she told him about the CD from Mrs. Jefferson and said she could handle it on her own. Before he could say anything else, she pointed to her car and said, "Okay, Malcolm, that's me. I'm out. See you next week."

* * * *

Sharday left her purse and notebook in the foyer and headed straight for the kitchen. She'd been given permission to skip the family dinner to go to choir rehearsal, so she was hungry. Plus, it was her week to do the dishes, anyway.

She could hear her mother and Bruce in the family room, so she stuck her head in to let them know she was back.

"So, how was rehearsal?" Vickie asked her.

"It was alright, Ma. But I tell you about it later. I'm starving."

Sharday heated up the plate of food her mother had left for her and quickly devoured it. She stuffed the dinner dishes into the dishwasher without rinsing them first and washed the few pots and pans. It wasn't long before she was in her bedroom watching a sitcom rerun and putting off doing the rest of her homework.

When she heard her mother call out to her and knock on the door a few minutes later, she shut off her television and said, "Come in."

Vickie walked in holding a stack of mail and closed the door behind her. "Hi, baby," she said. "So, how was it? Do you think you'll like it?"

"I don't know, Ma. I don't know nothing about no gospel music. I got a whole bunch of new songs I gotta learn now." She didn't even bother explaining to her mother that she didn't fit in with all those religious choir members because she knew her mother wouldn't understand. Just like her mother didn't understand about all those rich kids at school.

Vickie sat down on the bed beside Sharday. "Just tell Gladys you need some time to get up to speed, baby," she said. "I'm sure she'll understand that. And don't forget Malcolm said he would help you."

"Nah, Miss Jefferson gave me a CD to practice with. Plus, she said I ain't gotta sing for the first two weeks." Sharday shrugged then. "But, I don't know, Ma," she said. "They got a whole lot of songs."

"Just take it one step at a time, baby," Vickie said. "You can do this. Music is your thing."

"Hip hop, Ma. Not gospel."

"Music is music," Vickie said. "You'll see." She looked at Sharday closely then and said, "So, other than the choir, are you starting to feel more at home now? Is everything going okay?"

Sharday shrugged and said, "I'm alright, Ma. I still miss my friends and my old school and everything. But I guess I'll be alright."

"But you're not unhappy, are you?" Vickie asked anxiously. "I mean, isn't it getting better for you the longer we're here?"

Sharday looked at her mother. Living out here in the burbs and being married to Bruce was a dream come true for Vickie. Why ruin it for her mother? Especially when all she had to do was make it through one school year? And anyway, once she graduated and moved out on her own, her mother would need Bruce so she wouldn't be all alone. "Yeah, it's getting better, Ma," she said. Then she remembered the skating rink the weekend before and added, "And I guess Bruce and April starting to grow on me."

Vickie smiled with relief and said, "See, baby, I told you everything would be okay. And I promise it's only going to get better." She hesitated for a few seconds, debating the wisdom of what she was about to do, then she gave in and said, "Oh, I almost forgot." She flipped through the stack of mail in her hand and pulled out an envelope. "This came for you today," she said, handing it to Sharday. "It's from Donnell."

"Oh my God, Ma!" Sharday said, grabbing the envelope and looking at it closely. "Why you ain't give it to me earlier?"

"I forgot when you came in from school. I didn't remember until after you had already left for choir practice."

"You forgot? Oh my God, Ma! How you forget something like this?"

Vickie sighed and said, "I'm sorry, Sharday." And she really meant it. She had almost betrayed her daughter. And no matter how much she disapproved of Donnell, that would've been going way too far. Thank God, she had finally come to her senses. "Well, I'll give you some privacy so you can read it," she said. "I'll see you in the morning, baby." She leaned over and hugged her daughter hard before she got up and left.

Sharday waited until her mother had closed the door, then she ripped open the envelope and pulled out four handwritten sheets of paper. Only the first page was in Donnell's huge, lopsided handwriting, so she put the other pages on her nightstand and lay back on her bed to read Donnell's letter first.

Hi Day Day I was soo hapy to see you the otha day I wisht I cuda hugd and kist you. I told you I aint rilly no riter but I got to rite you about this becus I cudn say it in persun or on the phone. My lawyer got the ~~juje~~ juge to say yes to my plee bargin and thas all good but I aint gon be in Lorton becus they clozed it up. I dont no why you dont remimba that becus I tole you befor wen they sent Leon to Ohio but my lawyer said they probly gon send me to New York or maybe Pinsivana and thas not soo bad. I hope I git to see you a cupla more times befour I git sint out but if we dont we stil gon bee ok becus I love you and I no you love me. You my hart. Love Donnell.

Sharday was crying so hard by the time she finished the letter that she had to put a pillow up to her mouth so nobody would hear her. How could she have forgotten that Lorton was closed? And how in the world was she going to survive without seeing Donnell for a whole year and a half? Because her mother and Bruce would never let her go to all the way to New York or Pennsylvania to visit him.

She curled up in a ball and put the pillow over her head, then she cried like a baby for almost an hour straight. She could take a whole lot, but this was just too much. She wasn't strong enough to make it without Donnell.

She remembered how they had met at a party in the Vistas the summer before she went to eighth grade. He had asked her to dance as soon as she walked through the door and they spent the rest of the party on the front stoop getting to know each other. They had been boyfriend and girlfriend ever since without breaking up even once.

Donnell was the one she'd willingly given her virginity to after the junior prom in ninth grade. He was the one who knew things about her that her mother and Tyesha didn't even know. There was no way on Earth she could go for the next year and half without seeing his face. How was she going to make it through this?

TWENTY-FOUR

On Saturday morning, Sharday was the first person in the line that was already forming in the lobby of DC Jail. When the corrections officer waved her forward, she eagerly handed over her driver's license and asked to see Donnell.

"Sorry, but he's been shipped," the officer said after consulting his computer.

Sharday blinked in confusion. And then she wailed, "Oh, my God! Not already!" A flood of tears began to stream from her eyes as she whirled around and blindly ran from the lobby. She didn't stop running until she reached the car, where she fumbled unsuccessfully with her keys for a few minutes before she sank to the ground by the driver's door and began to sob.

She stayed there, covering her face with her hands and crying uncontrollably, until it suddenly began to rain. She raised her head to the sky in anguish and silently demanded that God send Donnell back. Was He trying to send her over the edge? Couldn't He see that she was going through more than enough already?

The rain only poured down harder in response, so she slowly stood and opened the car door. She climbed into the driver's seat and listened to the heavy droplets pounding on the hood. At least the sky was crying, too, she thought irrationally, then she lay her head on the steering wheel and began to sob aloud again.

The rain shower ended almost as quickly as it had begun, but it took Sharday another forty minutes to compose herself enough to be able to drive. She wished she could get high, but she didn't have any smoke. And since the mere thought of going to the strip in the Vistas where Donnell used to sling weed made her eyes fill with tears again, she reluctantly headed back to Mitchellville.

She arrived home so depressed that it was all she could do to make it up the steps to her room. Fortunately, Vickie and Bruce were still out shopping for the wallpaper and accent furniture Vickie would use to remodel the foyer. And although Sharday usually knocked on April's bedroom door and stuck her head in to say she was back with the car, today all she could manage was a knock in passing and a hoarse, "I'm back!" shouted from the hallway.

When she entered her bedroom, the first thing she saw was Donnell's equipment on the far wall. Hakeem and Andre had brought it by right before she started dressing for her gig at *The Cellar* the night before and she hadn't even had a chance to turn it on yet. Now, she closed her door and slowly crossed the room, drawn to his studio as a way to feel closer to him.

She lovingly ran her hand across his keyboard and turned on the other components Hakeem and Andre had set up on the sturdy, wooden bench that used to be in his room. She sat down on the floor and started going through his crates, where he had stored old-school vinyl and hundreds of CDs. As she sifted through his music, the memories began to overtake her.

Here was the very first song they had performed together in public, Mariah Carey and Old Dirty Bastard's *Fantasy*. There was the digitally remastered Minnie Ripperton CD, the one they had made love to the first time. And look, these were the last few copies of the single they had recorded and then sold from the trunk of his car because he said it was crucial to start a buzz on the streets. He was so smart when it came to the music business. And wasn't this the new song he was working on when he got snatched up from the parking lot?

She thought she had cried herself out, but she dissolved into tears again. So, when the telephone began to ring a few minutes later, she ignored it and decided to let April answer. The phone rang three times, and after a brief pause, it began to ring again. That meant it was for her and April had told the person to call right back.

She sniffed back her tears and crawled across the room to look at her caller ID. It was Tyesha, so she picked up and said, "I'll call you back," then she hung up and lay face-down on her bed.

Her cell phone rang within seconds and she ignored it, thinking it was Tyesha. But then she realized it could be Donnell. She dove for her purse and grabbed the phone. "Hello?" she whispered anxiously after she flipped it open.

"Girl, why'd you hang up on me like that?" Tyesha demanded.

"Mark's letting me use his car and I was gonna come by and pick you up. But now, I'm starting to have second thoughts."

"I ain't coming out today," Sharday said.

"You sick? You sound all stuffed up."

"Nah, I been crying," Sharday said, and then she told Tyesha what happened at the jail.

"He should've warned you," Tyesha said angrily. "What's wrong with Donnell? He's really slipping."

"But he in jail, Tyesha. It ain't like he got no control over nothing."

"I bet Andre and Hakeem knew. Why didn't he get them to tell you?"

"I doubt it," Sharday said. "Donnell ain't like that. He would've told them to tell me. Plus, he tried to warn me in his letter."

Tyesha rolled her eyes, but didn't say anything. Sharday was just too naïve when it came to Donnell. Finally, she said, "Well, you need to get out of there. I'm coming to get you, anyway."

Sharday resisted at first, but then she decided she would rather be out getting high. "Okay, but stop by the strip on your way," she said. "I want a dub," she added, telling Tyesha that she wanted a twenty dollar bag instead of a ten dollar one. "I got you when I see you."

"I don't have enough," Tyesha said. "But I can swing regular."

"That's cool," Sharday said, willing to take whatever she could get.

"Okay, see you in forty-five. Be near the door," Tyesha said before she ended the call.

Sharday closed her phone and lay on the bed wondering what Donnell was doing and where he was. She hadn't even asked where they had shipped him, but the guard probably wouldn't have told her anyway. This whole situation was just more than she could handle!

At that thought, she slowly sat up and swung her feet over the side of the bed. Maybe things wouldn't be so bad after all. Pennsylvania was kind of close -- her mom's people lived in Philly and that was less than two hours away. And New York really wasn't all that far either. People from DC drove to New York and vice-versa all the time.

All she had to do was say she was spending the weekend over Tyesha's every once in a while and make a one-day trip to New York or Pennsylvania. She could take a bus up there, visit Donnell for however long they would let her stay, and then get right back on the bus to DC. Her mother and Bruce would never even know.

And maybe the new prison would have contact visits like Lorton used to have. And maybe sometimes Tyesha could get one of her boyfriends to take them up there for the day and bring them back. Plus, once she graduated and moved out, she could visit Donnell every weekend if she wanted to. Who would be able to stop her?

By the time Tyesha showed up, Sharday was feeling a lot better. She had washed her face and put on more makeup. She had squirted some *Visine* in her eyes and changed her shirt before leaving a note for her mother and Bruce. She was ready to get her high on now, so she hopped in the car and said, "You got it? Where we going?"

"Elise didn't call you?" Tyesha asked, giving Sharday the dime bag before pulling off.

"Nah, what's up?" Sharday pulled a ten from her wallet and handed it over.

"I don't know. She just said she's gotta tell us something."

"Not today, Tyesha," Sharday said. "I don't wanna go to the Vistas today. Too many memories. Let's call and say something came up."

"She said it's important, Day-Day. Our girl needs us."

Sharday sucked her teeth and said, "Alright, but it better be important or I'm gonna be pissed." And then, "And I need you to stop by that gas station right before the highway so I can get a Phillie Blunt." She would've preferred the expensive cognac-soaked papers she used to buy in the hood, but she hadn't been able to find them in this area.

Sharday used her whole bag of weed to make one fat blunt out of the cigar and smoked some of it on the way to southeast. She and Tyesha smoked some more after Tyesha parked, and she was twisted by the time they climbed out of the car. "I can do this now," she said. "Let's go see what's up with our girl."

Elise, Kayla and LaShawn were waiting for Tyesha and Sharday on the raggedy bench just in front of Elise's building. A few of Elise's younger brothers and sisters were also out front playing.

"Let's go to the field, where we can have some privacy," Elise said, referring to the vacant, grass-covered lot across the street that used to house a low-income medical clinic but had since been razed.

"Unh unh, I got wheels today," Tyesha said. "Let's go sit in the car."

They trooped over to the small parking lot two courts away that Tyesha had parked in to spare Sharday the agony of going to the main parking lot. As soon as LaShawn climbed into the back seat with Kayla and Elise, she said, "I smell trees. Y'all got some more?"

"Yeah, I still got it," Sharday said. "But don't y'all wanna go for a ride instead of just sitting here? I got chip-ins for gas." She was feeling minimal pain thanks to the weed she'd smoked, but she still didn't want to stay in the Vistas if she didn't have to.

"I'm too high to be driving around," Tyesha said. But since she knew what Sharday was going through, she also added, "But I can make it to the hospital." Greater Southeast Hospital was less than a mile away, and because it was struggling financially, it had very few clients and there was a long, deserted side street next to it that Tyesha could park on.

"That'll work," Sharday said.

Once Tyesha pulled off, Elise said, "So, how you get Mark to let you use his car? I need to try some of your lines on Keith."

Tyesha laughed and said, "Girl, I didn't even have to ask. He offered. I guess I just got it like that."

"Well, I need to get me some of that, too," Elise said.

They all laughed, but then Sharday said, "Y'all know Tyesha got Mark whipped."

"You can say that again," LaShawn said.

"What you need to do," Kayla said to Tyesha, "is turn all them other brothers loose and give Mark a real chance."

Tyesha parked at the far end of the street and turned off the ignition. "What I need to do is focus on making a future for myself," she said. "Mark's alright, but he should've tried to go to college instead of taking the first job that came along. I want more than that out of life."

"Well, a hardworking man's good enough for me," Kayla said. "If John can get the job at the fire department, I'll be satisfied."

"Like they say," Tyesha said, "'to each his own.'"

"Here, LaShawn," Sharday said, handing over the rest of the blunt. "Light it, but don't hog it."

"I know how to share a blunt. Why you trying to carry me?" LaShawn said. Somebody always had something to say about how much she smoked and she was tired of hearing it.

"Aw, girl, stop being so touchy," Sharday said. "Just light the blunt."

"So, what's the big news?" Kayla asked Elise.

Tyesha turned to look at Elise and said, "Yeah, what's going on?"

"Well, ain't no need in beating around the bush," Elise said. And then she announced that she was pregnant.

LaShawn dropped the lit blunt and said, "Damn it!" At the same time, Sharday whispered, "Oh my God," Kayla said, "For real?" and Tyesha's face took on a look of horror but she didn't say anything.

"What Keith say?" Kayla asked.

"He don't know yet," Elise said. "Y'all the first ones I told."

LaShawn had picked up the blunt and hit it again. Now she said, "That's wild," and tried to pass the blunt over Elise to Kayla.

"Gimme some of that, too," Elise said. "I'm the main one who need it." She grabbed the blunt and greedily inhaled.

Tyesha's features immediately relaxed. "Any way you can come up with the money to get rid of it yourself?" she asked. "Why tell him if you don't have to? It'll just cause problems."

"Get rid of it?" Elise said after taking another hit from the blunt and extending it to Kayla. "Child, please! I'm keeping my baby!"

"Girl!" Kayla said, snatching the blunt. "Then why you smoking?"

"Stop tripping," Elise said. Both of her older sisters had smoked while they were pregnant and her nieces and nephews came out just fine. She looked at Tyesha and said, "But I do think I need to wait a while before I tell him. I wanna get closer to him first."

"If you still need to get closer to him, you don't need to be having a baby by him," Tyesha said. "And anyway, don't you wanna get away from all this?" She waved a hand around, encompassing the nearly abandoned hospital and the litter-filled woods across the street.

"Ain't nothing wrong with southeast," Elise said defensively. "I been happy here. And if Keith don't stick by me, I'll get my own apartment and me and my baby will be just fine."

"The only *apartment* you're going to get is right in the Vistas," Tyesha said. "Damn, Elise! Your grandmother raised your mother and your aunts and uncles there, your mother raised y'all there, and now your sisters are raising their babies there, too. Don't you wanna be the one to get out and stop the cycle?"

Elise glared at Tyesha and said, "Thank you very much, but I'm happy with my life, Tyesha. I don't wanna be like you. Somebody who ain't never satisfied with what they got and always trying to be somebody they ain't. I like living in the Vistas, if you don't mind. And plus, whether you know it or not, everybody can't be smart like you. You probably gonna get a scholarship or something but the rest of us normal people just gotta try to make it the best way we can." She started crying then.

"Aw, don't cry," Kayla said. She handed Sharday the blunt she had long since let go out and enveloped Elise in a hug. "It's gonna be alright," she murmured into Elise's shoulder.

"Please tell me you're at least planning to get your diploma," Tyesha said. She couldn't believe Elise was about to throw her life away like this.

"That's enough, Tyesha!" LaShawn said. "You done already made the girl cry!"

"Well, somebody's gotta keep it real!" Tyesha shot back.

Sharday finished off the blunt and lay her head back against the seat. Poor Elise. Tyesha was right -- welfare had changed and you couldn't live off it forever anymore. So, sooner or later, Elise was going to have to earn a living. But LaShawn had a good point, too. Since Elise had already decided she was keeping the baby, why make her feel bad about it? They were her girls. They should be supporting her. Sharday sighed heavily and closed her eyes, letting her mind drift away on the weed. Too many problems in reality. Better to just zone out.

TWENTY-FIVE

As the next few weeks slowly rolled by without a call or letter from Donnell, Sharday found that the only activities which brought her any joy were fooling around with his equipment and singing at *The Cellar*. And since her gig at *The Cellar* was limited to a brief interlude on Friday nights, she spent most of her free time playing with his equipment.

She still didn't know how to do much more than turn on the computer and play an album, an MP3 file, or CD -- his so-called "instructions" were just a basic description of the separate components and how they all worked when hooked together. And now that it was clear she wouldn't be able to figure things out on her own, she was going to follow Tyesha's advice and ask Malcolm to help her.

So today, instead of eating lunch in the car like she normally did, Sharday grabbed her insulated lunch bag from her locker and headed downstairs to the cafeteria. Malcolm was sitting at the same table she'd seen him at on the first day of school. She took a deep breath and headed toward him.

* * * * *

Malcolm Werther happened to look up and see Sharday coming toward him and his heart began to pound frantically in his chest. He hadn't seen her in the caf since that first time when she practically dissed him, and as always, she hadn't said more than a few words to him at choir rehearsal yesterday. Did he dare hope to have the pleasure of eating lunch with her today?

Malcolm unconsciously held his breath until Sharday walked right up to the table and stopped behind the person seated directly across from him, then he smiled broadly and said, "Hi, Sharday! Would you like to join us?"

She smiled back and said, "If y'all don't mind."

"Hey, move over and let her sit down," Malcolm said, gesturing for two of his friends to move apart so Sharday could sit opposite him.

"Thanks," Sharday said. She put her lunch bag on the table and sat down.

Malcolm introduced her to his friends. There were five other boys -- two black, two white, and one Asian. And there were four girls -- three blacks and one hispanic.

Sharday didn't bother trying to remember anybody's name. She simply said, "Hi, everybody," and started unpacking her lunch.

"What a surprise," Malcolm said to Sharday. "I haven't seen you in here since the first day of school."

"It's starting to get cold. Time to try something new," she replied before taking a bite of her ham and cheese sub.

He grinned. The cold weather was probably here to stay. Did that mean she was going to start eating with them every day?

Sharday didn't know why Malcolm was grinning at her, but she smiled back at him anyway because she couldn't afford to offend him. His friends were discussing Jack Black's latest movie, and when the hispanic girl seated next to Malcolm asked Sharday what she thought about it, Sharday shrugged and said, "I ain't seen it yet, but I heard it's funny."

"Well, what did you think of Denzel's last movie?" the girl asked.

Sharday shrugged again and said, "Didn't see that either. I ain't been to the movies in a minute."

"Sharday's a singer," Malcolm volunteered. "She probably spends most of her time practicing her vocals."

"You should know, Malcolm," the girl said sweetly. Then she turned back to Sharday and said, "So, do you play the keyboard, too, like Malcolm does? Almost everybody can sing to one extent or another. But it's the true musicians who are special."

Sharday's plan was to be friendly and pretty much keep her mouth shut until she could get Malcolm alone on the way out, but this girl was starting to work her nerves. "I just sing," she said in a tone that wasn't exactly pleasant, then she clamped down on the strong urge to ask whether the girl had a problem with that.

"Eww, yuck!" one of the white boys exclaimed just then. "This pie sucks!" He speared a piece of the pie with his fork and held it up. "This is a lethal weapon," he said. "They could use it to torture confessions from terrorists."

Everybody laughed and Malcolm and his friends started making jokes about how bad the food in the cafeteria was. But it wasn't long before the hispanic girl focused in on Sharday again. "Maybe we should organize a strike or something," she said. "What do you think, Sharday? Would you participate?"

"I doubt it," Sharday said. "I don't eat the food here, so it really ain't none of my business."

"That's just a cop out," the girl said.

"That's enough, Lorie," Malcolm said. "Leave her alone."

"What?" Lorie asked with mock innocence. "I'm just trying to get to know her." She looked at Sharday again and said, "So, what do you think? Should we strike or not?"

Sharday looked her straight in the eyes and said, "Like I said before, it really ain't none of my business."

"But it's your school, too," Lorie insisted. "And whether you eat here or not, you should have an opinion. Otherwise, you're just a waste of space."

One of the black girls gasped and the Asian boy said, "Lorie strikes again."

Sharday totally lost her cool. "Look, *bitch*," she said. "I done had enough of your shit. Now, I was trying to sit here and mind my business. But since you just dying to know what I think about everything, let me clear it up for you." She leaned across the table and pointed her finger mere inches from Lorie's face. "I *think* you better back up off me before I end up kicking your ass in here. Now, anymore questions?"

Malcolm was glad somebody had finally put Lorie in her place -- she could be a total witch at times. But everyone else at the table was staring at Sharday in astonishment, and Lorie was literally trembling with fear.

When Lorie didn't answer, Sharday said a menacing, "I didn't think so," and then she stuffed the remnants of her lunch in her bag and got up.

"Wait a minute, Sharday. You don't have to leave," Malcolm said.

"Trust me, I do," Sharday said. "Because I'm about ten seconds away from kicking your friend's ass." And with that, she threw her lunch bag over her shoulder and left.

Malcolm smiled as he watched Sharday walk away. Her in-your-face personality was like a breath of fresh air in his otherwise boring life, and the fact that she had a body to die for really added to her allure. He had to find a way to get closer to her!

Sharday was so angry as she marched out of the cafeteria that she rolled her eyes at everyone who made the mistake of glancing up at her. She hated this crappy school and every freaking one of these nerds in it. So, from now on, she was just going to stay to herself and concentrate on putting in her time. Because if she didn't, she was going to end up hurting one of these people.

She spoke only when spoken to for the rest of the day and the wall she put up around herself didn't encourage conversation. Although she hadn't exactly made any new friends so far, there were a few people that she considered acquaintances. But today, her demeanor left no question that she didn't want to be bothered with any of them.

It wasn't until she was driving April home and the school was out of sight that she finally loosened up. She and April were starting to develop a friendship, thanks to the large amount of time they spent together. So, she didn't hesitate to tell April what happened at lunch.

"What's the girl's name?" April asked when Sharday finished.

"Some chick name Lorie. I think she hispanic."

"Oh, don't worry about her," April said. "She can be an absolute pain when she wants to and everybody knows it. And anyway, it sounds like she had it coming."

"Yeah, that's exactly what I thought," Sharday said. Then she looked across the car at April and they both started giggling.

The laughter died down a few seconds later and April seized the moment by asking whether Sharday would mind if she started joining her on Fridays at *The Cellar*. "I had so much fun the last time we went without the parents," she said. What she didn't add was that she had been wanting to ask Sharday for weeks now, but somehow the timing never seemed quite right.

Sharday shrugged. "I don't see why not," she said. "My girls like you and you already showed us you can handle your own." She stopped at a red light and looked at April. "But I got one rule you gotta agree to first. You can't tell my mother or your father nothing you see. And I mean nothing, April. Especially if you think it's bad."

April quickly agreed. Sharday probably didn't realize it, but April had already figured out that Sharday and her friends smoked marijuana and she assumed that was what Sharday was referring to now. Weed wasn't that big of a deal. Although April hadn't tried it herself yet, she knew some people who smoked it and nothing terrible had happened to them. So, if Sharday wanted April to keep her little secret, she would. Especially if it meant that she'd be able to go *The Cellar* with Sharday from now on.

Sharday pulled into their driveway shortly after that and it wasn't long before she was sitting on her bed trying to figure out what she was going to do about Donnell's equipment. Asking Malcolm to help didn't seem like such a good idea now that she'd cursed out that chick at his table. So, who else could she get to help her?

The only person she could think of off the top of her head was Deejay Smooth from *Club 202*. But she really didn't want to ask him because she was still embarrassed about getting fired. She clicked on her television and lay back to watch *Judge Mathis*. She'd come up with somebody else soon. She just needed some time to think about it.

The telephone rang about twenty minutes later, just as *Judge Mathis* was going off. Sharday checked the caller ID and saw that it was Malcolm. She clicked off the television and quickly picked up the phone, fully prepared to defend herself. But to her surprise, Malcolm actually thanked her for tearing into Lorie.

"She's been pulling that kind of crap for years now and everybody always lets her get away with it," he said. "But she's finally met her match in you."

"Oh," Sharday said.

"So, I hope you won't let what happened keep you from joining us for lunch in the future. The rest of my friends feel the same way. They told me to tell you you're welcome anytime."

"Uh, thanks, but I think I'll just stick to the car from now on," Sharday said.

Malcolm sighed audibly. Lorie had ruined everything. "I'm sorry you feel that way," he said. "I was kind of hoping for a chance to get you know you better."

Sharday knew a perfect opportunity when she saw one, so she said, "Well, maybe you wouldn't mind doing me a favor then."

"I'd be happy to," Malcolm said eagerly, glad to have another chance.

"What do you need me to do?"

Sharday told him that a friend of hers had given her some studio equipment, but she didn't know how to use it. "Do you think you could help me figure out how to work it?" she asked. "I ain't really making no progress on my own."

"Well, I've never been in a recording studio before, but I'm a whiz at reading manuals," he said.

"But I ain't got no manuals."

"Not a problem," Malcolm said. "I can download everything we need from the internet. Are you near the equipment now?"

"Uh huh," she said.

"Great. If you can find the make and model number on each piece of equipment and read those to me, I can take it from there."

It took Sharday a while to find some of the model numbers, but she eventually managed to give Malcolm all the information he needed. By the time they ended the conversation a few minutes after that, they had agreed that Malcolm would come over on Saturday at two.

TWENTY-SIX

News travels fast among high school students. And by the next day, word had spread at Mitchellville High about what happened between Sharday and Lorie in the cafeteria. At first, Sharday thought she was imagining that the other kids were staring and giving her a little more space as she walked through the halls. But when one of the cool students, a girl named Ayanna who was in her math class, caught up with Sharday as she was crossing the grass between the portables and the main building and said, "I've been hearing some good things about you. Keep ya' head up, sister," Sharday finally put two and two together.

After that, a tiny corner of the chip she had been carrying around dropped from her shoulders. And although she stuck to the plan of keeping to herself, the school didn't seem so bad anymore. Maybe getting through this year wouldn't be so hard after all.

But as she was heading for her seat in sixth period English, her teacher called out to her and said that her counselor wanted to see her.

"Ooh, somebody's in trouble," one of the boys in the class whispered loudly. Several of the kids seated around him snickered.

"Whatever," Sharday murmured with a nonchalant shrug as she turned and headed for the teacher's desk to get a pass. She had long since realized that her fellow students were just on good behavior the first day of school, because the atmosphere had loosened up considerably since then. Of course, there were still a lot of nerds and geeks. In some ways, that was what Mitchellville High was all about. But there were also a number of cut-ups in each of her classes. Plus, the hallways no longer emptied right before each period started and quite a few students left the school grounds during their lunch periods, which was definitely against the rules.

As Sharday headed to the counselors' suite on the first floor near the principal's office, she concentrated on projecting cool. At Ballou, you only saw your counselor when you'd done something wrong. And thanks to her recent obsession with Donnell's equipment, she knew she was slipping on her homework. But she had already met her counselor once at the beginning of school for what he called a "get-to-know-you session." Hopefully, this would just be more of the same.

Her counselor was a youngish, white guy by the name of Jason Wheeler. He'd decorated his office with the usual public service announcements, but he'd also added framed posters of Lady Gaga, Beyonce, Usher and Justin Timberlake. He was trying his best to seem hip, but Sharday could tell that deep down he was just another nerd.

He waved her forward and gestured for her to sit down. As he engaged her in small talk, she began to relax. But then cleared his throat and said, "Now, for the reason I needed to see you today. We've decided to alter your schedule slightly, Sharday. Beginning tomorrow, we're placing you in alternative English."

She was stunned. This was the last thing she expected. "You mean you putting me in special ed, Mr. Wheeler?"

"No, no. Of course not," he said quickly. "We're placing you in alternative English, which differs from standard English mainly in that it emphasizes the development of writing skills."

"So, Miss Parsons said I can't write?" she asked, referring to her English teacher.

"Well, actually, I've been consulting with all of your teachers. Because you're a new student and all," he said. "And the teachers like you. Let me say that first. But the general consensus is that we can best serve you by helping you fine-tune your writing skills."

"I ain't never had no complaints about my writing before," she said. She'd gotten B's and C's in Ballou. But now, all of sudden, her writing wasn't good enough.

He leaned forward and smiled sympathetically. Alternative English would also help improve Sharday's oral language skills, but given her reaction, he didn't think now was the time to mention that. "This isn't a punishment, Sharday," he said gently. "Don't look at it that way. What we're trying to do here is prepare you for college, because your grades as they stand now are good enough to get you into a decent school. But it's going to be hard to succeed once you get there without very strong writing skills."

Sharday didn't say anything. She didn't give a damn about college because her future was in music. But lately, Bruce had been pressing her about college, too. He was always saying how he thought she'd enjoy going to a black school. And he'd even started ordering applications for her. So far, he'd gotten her some stuff from Howard and this school called Spellman. And he kept telling her that more brochures and stuff were on the way.

"So, have you decided which schools you'll be applying to?" Mr. Wheeler asked her. "The last time we met you were kind of vague."

She cast her eyes down. They already thought she was stupid. Did she really want to tell them she was planning on getting a record deal instead of going to college? She looked back up at Mr. Wheeler and said, "Uh, I been thinking about going to a black school." When he smiled and nodded encouragingly, she said, "But um, I ain't made no final decisions yet."

"Well, most of the deadlines will be coming up within the next two months, so you don't want to wait too long," he said. "But I've got some material that will help you narrow down your choices."

He stood and walked over to one of his file cabinets. "What I suggest you do," he said as he rifled through the drawers, "is select three or four schools and apply to those. And of course, you'll also want to apply to the University of Maryland just in case because they bend over backwards to accept students from Maryland."

He returned to his desk and sat down before handing her a stack of papers. "These articles should help you make some decisions. Some of them contain rankings, others talk about quality of life on the different campuses, there's even a listing of web sites."

"Okay. Thanks," she said.

"And maybe we should meet again in a couple of weeks to see how things are going," he said. "And in the meantime, if you haven't already you should start working on your essays. Ms. Adams -- she's your new English teacher, by the way, and she'll let you work on them for homework."

"Okay." Sharday knew about the essays that had to be submitted with college applications because Tyesha had already started working on hers.

"And I'm assuming you've already signed up for the SAT?" he asked.

She nodded, even though she hadn't. Tyesha was the only one of her friends who was taking the SAT.

"Good." He handed her a slip of paper and said, "Give this to Ms. Adams when you get to her class tomorrow, Sharday. The room number's written at the top."

Sharday took the paper and warily glanced down at it. Mr. Wheeler had just managed to ruin her best day here so far and leave her feeling, once again, like she really didn't belong.

"And here's your pass for Ms. Parsons." He checked his watch before scribbling the time and his signature on a pre-printed half-sheet of yellow paper. "Thanks for coming to see me today, Sharday," he said, standing and extending his hand. "I'll see you in a few weeks."

She stood and shook his hand before stumbling from his office, then she ducked into the nearest girls' bathroom and locked herself in a stall. She hadn't felt this out of place in her new life since that time April had brought Lynn to the mall with them. And right now, she felt so ashamed that she didn't think she'd ever be able to face her fellow students again.

Going back to Miss Parsons' class today was definitely out of the question, so Sharday slowly crumpled up her pass and dropped it in the toilet. She flipped down the commode cover and lined it with toilet paper, then she sat down heavily, placed her head in her hands and sighed. No matter what Mr. Wheeler said, she would be seen as special ed from now on. And once word got out, she was going to be the butt of everybody's jokes.

By the time the bell rang at the end of sixth period, her paranoia was in full effect. She tried to listen closely as varying cliques of chattering girls passed through the bathroom. But there were too many conversations going on at the same time to tell if anybody was talking about her yet.

When the bell rang for the beginning of seventh period and the bathroom quieted, she stayed on her make-shift seat. She was just a dumb girl from the ghetto; she couldn't measure up academically to these kids who were living in the lap of luxury. By this time tomorrow, everybody would know that.

Just then, one of the female teachers knocked on the bathroom door and called out, "Is anybody in there? Class started a few minutes ago!"

Sharday froze. She held her breath and willed herself not to move a muscle when the door opened briefly and then closed again. Of course, her nose started itching, but she ignored it. She counted to ten before exhaling silently and rubbing a finger back and forth across the bridge of her nose. She counted to ten again, and when she still didn't hear any footsteps, she peeked through the stall door and saw that the coast was clear.

She heaved a sigh of relief and slowly sat back down. Was she fooling herself about having a future in the music industry? Together, she and Donnell were better than most of the groups out there now, but the odds of getting a record deal were so slim. What would she do with her life if they didn't make it?

Singing was the only skill she had. She really didn't know how to do anything else. So, Bruce was probably right when he said she needed to go to college to have something to fall back on. But deep in her heart, she doubted whether she could make it through college.

She'd had a hard time making it to twelth grade. School had always been a struggle for her. Compared to somebody like Tyesha, Sharday had to study a lot harder just to get lower grades. And now that she was here at this jacked-up school, she could see that she'd be lucky to even get her diploma.

She shuddered involuntarily at the thought. Everybody needed a high school diploma these days. And her mother would never forgive her if she screwed up and didn't get one. Nah, that simply wasn't an option. Special ed or not, she'd have to do whatever it took to get that piece of paper.

And then what? she wondered. She thought about that question for a long time. She couldn't see cleaning offices, or working as a nursing assistant, or working in fast food, or being a telemarketer, or being a grocery store cashier, or doing most of the other things she'd seen people without a college diploma do.

As a matter of fact, she'd never even thought about her future on that level. Vickie had always talked about her going to college, but Sharday had assumed that she and Donnell would start doing a lot more gigs once she graduated, and that they'd be a little broke for a while but then everything would turn around when they got their record deal.

But now that Donnell was locked up, she needed to come up with some job ideas. And they couldn't be any penny-ante jobs either. She would have to make enough to pay for her own apartment and take care of herself.

She was still racking her brain for possibilities when the bell signaling the end of the school day rang. She was distracted on the ride home with April, and she spent the time before dinner trying to think of suitable jobs instead of practicing for her gig at *The Cellar* the next night. By the time six thirty rolled around, she had come up with the following options: a job at the Post Office, one of those entry-level government jobs like LaShawn's sister got and moved up on, a job as a salesperson at an expensive clothing store, or a job as a receptionist or a mail clerk or something in a big company like the one her mother used to work for.

Sharday felt a little better about herself as she headed downstairs to eat. She might not be going to college, but at least she had some plans for her future. Clearly, she wasn't as stupid as those people at Mitchellville High thought she was.

She was the last one to make it to the table, so she quickly took her seat and bowed her head. Bruce said a long prayer over the meal, they made small talk as they fixed their plates, and then it was time for each of them to say something about their day.

Sharday said she'd go last, and she told them the embarrassing truth when her turn came around. Why try to hide it from Bruce and April? They would eventually find out anyway. "I got put in special ed today," she said.

Bruce and April were shocked into silence, but Vickie's eyes flashed with anger and she said, "What? Special ed? That can't be right."

"Well, my counselor called it 'alternative English,'" Sharday said. "But it's basically special ed for people who don't know how to write."

April smiled with relief and said, "Oh! No, it's not Sharday. Special ed classes are called 'remedial.' The alternative classes are more like independent study. They're a lot smaller. So, you get one-on-one time with the teachers and they tailor the courses to meet your individual needs."

"Oh," Sharday said. And then, as April's words began to sink in, Sharday smiled, too.

"Now, that makes more sense," Vickie said. She looked at Sharday and added, "Because I know you're not special ed."

Bruce chuckled and said, "Whew! I thought we were going to have to go up there and set those people straight!" He said it as a joke, but he was partly serious. Sharday spoke southeast Ebonics, so it would've been all too easy for her new teachers to get sidetracked by her speech and miss her innate intelligence. Thankfully, they were trying to help her improve her language skills instead.

Sharday waited for the laughter to die down before she spoke up again. She hated to ruin dinner, but she needed to put everything on the table and get it over with. "And my counselor gave me some stuff on colleges, too," she began. "But--"

"Oh, really?" Vickie exclaimed at the same time Bruce said, "I was wondering when they would get around to that!"

"But I decided . . . " Sharday faltered briefly, and then she blurted, "But I don't really wanna go to college."

They were all stunned, even April, so Sharday started justifying. "I'm just not a school person," she said. "I'm having a hard enough time just getting my diploma as it is."

"What in the world are you talking about, Sharday?" Vickie said. "We've always planned for you to go to college. That special ed foolishness was just a misunderstanding. But I'm going to make an appointment to see your counselor anyway."

"Nah, Ma, that ain't it," Sharday said, but then she looked at her mother and backtracked. "I mean, yeah, okay. You right," she admitted. "That special ed stuff really had me tripping for a minute." She shrugged. "But I still don't wanna go to college no more. I'm just, I'm just tired of school."

"Come on now, baby," Vickie said. "Now, I know you're not going to jeopardize your entire future over a simple misunderstanding. You're not thinking straight right now. Just give yourself some time."

"Ma, I'm sorry. I know college real important to you, but it just ain't for me. I just wanna get me a job after I graduate so I can move out and hold my own until Donnell get out of jail. Then me and him can start focusing back on our music again."

"Donnell?" Vickie exclaimed. "Baby, he's in jail! You can't depend on him anymore! You've got to--"

"Calm down, honey," Bruce said to Vickie. "Let's talk this out." He looked at Sharday and said, "Are you saying you don't want to go off to college and leave Donnell behind while he's in jail? Because if that's what you're worried about, there are a lot of good schools right in this area. There's Howard, and Bowie State University, and American University where Felicia goes, and--"

"Nah, that ain't it, Bruce," Sharday said. "I just don't wanna go to college. I don't know how else to say it."

"You just don't want to go to college?" Vickie said. "Where is this coming from, Sharday? You've always wanted to go to college!"

"No, Ma. *You* always wanted me to go to college. I always wanted to be a singer and that's still what I wanna be."

Vickie looked deeply into her daughter's eyes, trying to figure out what was really going on. Was Sharday more traumatized by the sudden change in high schools than she had been letting on? Or maybe this was just another form of her depression over having Donnell snatched away so abruptly. Either way, Vickie had to find a way to get through to her child. Sharday was too young to realize it now, but if she didn't go to college, she would regret it for the rest of her life.

Vickie got up and walked around the table to stand beside her daughter. "Look, baby," she said, curving an arm around Sharday's shoulder. "I've always dreamed of you making it big in the music industry, too. Haven't I always been your number one supporter? But what are you going to do if -- and I hope this doesn't happen, but what if it doesn't work out? Without a college education, all you'll have to look forward to for the rest of your life is one dead-end job after another. And you don't want that, baby. Believe me, that's the last thing on Earth you want to do to yourself."

Sharday knew her mother was right, but she couldn't shake the belief that she wasn't college material. She averted her eyes from her mother's gaze and shrugged. "I don't know, Ma," she said. "I think the music thing is gonna work out for me. But I gotta spend these next few years paying my dues to make it happen. So, what can I say? Going to college just ain't in the plans for me."

Vickie was so infuriated with her daughter that she almost wanted to shake some sense into her. "Yes, it is, Sharday!" she insisted. "I don't know what's gotten into--"

"Well, I have a suggestion!" Bruce said, raising his voice to be heard over Vickie's shouting. "What about a compromise, like PG Community College? It's only a two-year commitment and it's a lot less intense. Not to mention the fact that Sharday would walk away with an associate's degree in something practical like computers or business. And who knows?" he said, making eye contact with Sharday. "You might even decide that it's not so bad after all and decide to transfer to a regular four-year university."

"Hmm, well, at least that would be a start," Vickie said as she turned the idea over in her mind.

Sharday looked down at the now cold food on her plate. Maybe this would be a way for her to try college without making a fool of herself by flunking out. "I don't know," she said, thinking aloud. "I don't think I wanna be stuck living at home and going to some community college. Plus, I don't wanna have to fool with that SAT."

April spoke up then. "But you don't need the SAT to go to PG," she said. "I know a couple of seniors who are planning to go there next year. And they said you don't even have to do an essay."

"And as long as you take a full courseload, your mother and I will help you pay for an apartment," Bruce said. "Of course, you'll have to find a roommate or two. And you might even have to pick up another gig or a part-time job to keep yourself in spending money. But you'll have a lot more free time in college. Except for around exam time."

Sharday was starting to feel kind of excited. This sounded like a no-lose situation. She could try a lightweight version of college and still move out on her own. And if things didn't work out, all she had to do was drop out and find a full-time job until Donnell came back. She glanced up at her mother and said, "Maybe I could give it a try."

Vickie smiled with gratitude and leaned down to hug her daughter. Thank God Sharday had finally come back to her senses. And thank God for Bruce and his brilliant suggestion. A community college was just what Sharday needed to rebuild her confidence before going on to a four-year university.

TWENTY-SEVEN

Sharday turned into the parking lot at Ruth's Chris Steak House and drove slowly around the building, looking for her father's car. When he called the afternoon before to invite her to lunch, he said he'd gotten a new one -- a white Lincoln Town Car. She didn't see it now, but she wasn't surprised since she was fifteen minutes early for their lunch date. She parked in a space near the entrance to wait for him.

Frank pulled into the parking lot ten minutes later, leaning to the side with his new diamond-encircled watch gleaming and his brimmed, navy hat cocked to the side. His woman had just gotten her settlement from an on-the-job injury she had a couple of years before, so his pockets were flush. They would be moving to a condo soon. Their ship had finally come in.

When his daughter beeped her horn, he waved and parked in a spot on the row behind her. He climbed out of the car wearing a million-dollar smile. He slipped on his new overcoat and sauntered over to give her a hug. "I'm glad you could make it, baby," he said. "I've missed you."

"I missed you too, Daddy."

He offered her his arm and said, "Next time I'll give you more notice."

"That's okay," she said. She beamed as she took his arm and headed for the restaurant. He had said 'next time.' Maybe things were finally going to change.

Frank had a reservation, so they were whisked to a table where he ordered for them both. "We'll take the Porterhouse for two with loaded baked potatoes and steak house salads," he said.

"And to drink, sir?" the waiter asked.

"A bottle of Moet for now," Frank said, "and iced tea and bottled spring water with the meal."

The waiter didn't even blink twice. He made a few notations on his notebook and said he'd be right back with the champagne.

Frank spent the first half of the meal asking Sharday questions about her new life in Mitchellville, trying to find out as much about Bruce as he could without directly asking. He spent the second half exaggerating his own circumstances. He said he'd finally closed a deal he'd been working on for a long time, so he was going to buy a condo soon and cut down on his traveling. Once he moved, he was going to start having her over a lot.

Sharday lapped it all up. She couldn't wait to start spending more time with her father. She gave him the number to her cell phone and told him that Clyde had switched her gig to Fridays. "But even if you do start coming again," she said, "that still ain't gonna be the only time we see each other, right?"

Frank agreed as he settled the bill and left a generous tip for the waiter. He slipped Sharday a crisp, fifty dollar bill as she climbed into her car, telling her to buy herself something on him, then he squeezed her hand and said he'd see her next week at *The Cellar*.

Sharday was too overwhelmed to speak. She couldn't ever remember him giving her money. She carefully folded the Grant and slipped it into her purse, looking up at her rearview mirror just in time to see Frank climb into the shiny, white Lincoln. He seemed like a totally different person. She had never seen him truly on top of his game before. So, this was what it felt like to have a real father.

She honked and waved as she pulled off ahead of him, happy that he was finally ready to step up to the plate. She had been in the third grade when her mother told him that he was no longer welcome at her house, that he needed to find somewhere to take Sharday when he wanted to see her. And by the time she graduated from elementary school, she was lucky if she even heard from her father on the phone every couple of months.

It wasn't until last summer, when he found out about the gig at *Club 202*, that Frank had started coming around on a somewhat regular basis again. But even then, he would disappear for weeks at a time and come back saying he had been on the road. And he never made an effort to see her outside of the club.

She smiled now as she clicked on her radio and headed for the beltway. To use her father's words, they were "entering a new phase." And she didn't think she was being naïve by believing in him, because he was clearly a changed man. You only had to be around him five minutes to see that. Maybe this is how he would have been all along if he'd had his finances in order.

She was floating on a natural high by the time she made it back to Mitchellville. So, when she bounced into the house and found Vickie waiting for her one of the living room sofas, she grinned and said, "Oh my God, Ma! It was great!"

"Well, come tell me about," Vickie said, forcing a smile as she patted the cushion next to her. She didn't trust Frank. He was a selfish, lazy bastard who only did what benefitted him. He'd walked out on Sharday years ago, and it wasn't until the girl started making a name for herself on the local music scene that he even started showing his face again. Once he reappeared, Sharday seemed to magically forget all the past hurts and disappointments he had caused her. But Vickie hadn't forgotten. She still remembered each and every one.

She listened as Sharday went on and on about how he had turned his life around. He had worked out some kind of business deal, he had a new car, he had a lot of money now and had given Sharday some, he was buying a new condo and was going to start having Sharday over all the time. Vickie nodded and smiled through it all, then she said, "Well, I'm glad Frank's finally getting his act together. So, what kind of work will he be doing? Does this deal involve music?"

Sharday shrugged and said, "Probably. He ain't get into the details or nothing, but I could tell it was something big. And knowing him, I know it got something to do with music."

"Oh, honey," Vickie said. "Well, did he at least say when or where he's planning to move?"

Sharday looked down at her watch. Vickie could be so negative sometimes when it came to Frank, and Sharday didn't want to go there today. "I don't think he know yet," she said. "I got the feeling his deal just came through." She was unable to suppress a grin as she added, "And he called me the same week. I'm telling you, Ma. He ain't the same no more."

"Well, hopefully, things will work out for him," Vickie said, taking pains to mask her rising anger. She just knew in her heart that that bastard, Frank, was setting her daughter up for yet another disappointment. But this time, she would find a way to make Sharday see it for herself in advance.

"They will," Sharday said with conviction. "You had to be there." She shrugged then and said, "But anyway, Ma, I need to go throw on some jeans or something before Malcolm get here. I done already pushed him back to three. The last thing I wanna do is have him down here waiting on me."

Sharday dashed upstairs and stuck her head in April's room to say she was back, then she headed to her own bedroom to strip off her dress and pull on baggy jeans and a hooded sweatshirt. She was sitting on the bed putting on a pair socks when her cell phone began to ring, so she pulled it from her purse and answered, "Hello."

"Hi, Day-Day. It's me."

"Donnell!" she exclaimed, dropping the sock she still held. She clapped her hand over her mouth for a few seconds, then she removed it and said in a much lower voice, "Oh my God, Boo. Where you at? How you been doing?" She turned on her Bluetooth speaker system and clicked on a station from the computer.

"I'm at Allen Brook Federal Correctional Institution," he said. "It's in New York State, but they say it's right before you get to Vermont. I would've been called. But I been waiting all this time for them to transfer my commissary so I could get a phone card."

"Oh my God," she said again. "So, how you been doing, Boo? How is it out there?"

He lowered his voice and said, "Too far." And then, "But kinda better, too. I mean, at least they ain't got roaches crawling everywhere you look. And plus, they give you a job so you can make some money." There was also an affiliate gang of The Greater Southeast Crew up there, called the Bronx Bangers, but he wasn't going to mention that to Sharday.

"For real?" she said. "So, you got a job and stuff now?"

"Nah, not yet. And I hear they don't be paying no more than like twenty-five cents a hour or something. But at least you can put it in your commissary and buy phone cards with it."

"Well, I can put some money in commissary for you," she offered. "Or you can start back calling me collect. I don't care."

He thought about that for a few seconds. He didn't really want her putting money in his commissary like she had to take care of him and shit. But the Bangers had a big phone card scheme going up in here and he wanted in on it. "Uh, maybe you could just put some money on my phone card sometimes," he said, even though he hated to. "I got a *AT&T* card, so you could do it from down there. But keep track and I'll hit you back once I get out of here."

"Aw, come on, Boo," she said. "It ain't even like that with us."

"Yeah, I know. You right, Day-Day," he said. "But keep track anyway. Sometimes, a man just wanna be a man."

She had just finished writing down his account number and p.i.n. when she heard the doorbell chime. She knew it was Malcolm -- her alarm clock read exactly three minutes after two, but she ignored the doorbell and kept talking, anyway. She briefly told Donnell about her lunch with Frank before moving on to the problems she was having with the equipment.

Donnell told her to go over to the studio and turn everything on, and then he started giving her step-by-step instructions. He didn't email or use Instagram; he didn't use his computer to do anything besides making music, and he had totally mastered all aspects of his recording software. She was learning the basics of the software program when somebody knocked on her door. "Damn, Boo," she whispered. "Somebody at my door. Hold on a minute, okay? I be right back."

She put the phone face down on her bed before she opened the door. She wasn't surprised to see her mother standing on the other side.

"Didn't you hear the doorbell?" Vickie asked her. "Malcolm's been waiting for at least fifteen minutes."

"I be down in minute," Sharday said. But at her mother's indignant look, she added, "Please, Ma. I ain't got no shoes on." She gestured down at her feet. "Tell him I be right down."

When Vickie left she closed the door and rushed back over to pick up her cell. "Sorry about that, Boo. That was my moms," she said.

"They gonna cut us off in a few minutes, Day-Day," he said urgently. "But I put some rhymes for you to spit at Clyde's on a recording and my new poetry teacher gonna be sending it to you. His name Greg Foster."

"You taking poetry out there?" she said.

"Yeah, but I tell you about it when I call you back Wednesday night."

"What time?" she asked, but all she heard was a click and a dial tone in response.

She slowly closed the phone and smiled as she put it in her purse. Wednesday was just a few days away. She looked down at her feet and stripped off the one sock she had put on earlier, then she quickly stepped into her bedroom shoes and rushed downstairs to Malcolm.

He was sitting on the sofa with Vickie, and he smiled and stood when Sharday entered the living room.

"God, I am so sorry, Malcolm," she said, ignoring her mother's glare. "I ain't mean to keep you down here waiting like this. But my best friend called and it was a emergency."

He shrugged off her apology. He would've waited an hour without complaint. "That's okay, Sharday," he said. "I didn't mind. And anyway, I had your mother to keep me company." He turned his smile in Vickie's direction.

Vickie smiled back. He was such a charming and well-mannered young man. And with his musical talents, he could replace Donnell for Sharday in so many ways. "It was my pleasure, Malcolm," she said sincerely.

"Well, let's go ahead and get started," Sharday said to Malcolm. "I done already wasted a lot of your time as it is."

"Yes, you two go on up," Vickie said, shooing them away. And then, because she was a mother, "But don't forget to leave the door open, Sharday. And I'll bring up a pitcher of water and some glasses a little later."

"Okay, Ma," Sharday said, turning to lead the way.

Malcolm grabbed his black, leather bag and followed Sharday up the stairs. He couldn't believe he was getting a chance to spend time in her bedroom! He'd assumed that she would move the equipment to the den! But she was giving him a glimpse of her inner life instead!

He glanced around at the pictures grouped here and there, the poster over her bed of the top hip-hop artists, the ongoing list of artists and songs sitting on her computer. Hopefully, he'd get a chance to take a better look after her mother came up with the water.

He followed her over to the make-shift studio, which was actually quite impressive in person, then he unzipped his bag and pulled out the pile of manuals he'd downloaded from the internet. He'd read them all, so he had a pretty good idea of how each piece of equipment worked. And with Sharday's newfound knowledge of the recording software, they were able to get everything up and running.

The drum machine and special effects machine were so much fun that they got stuck on those at first. But by the time Vickie came up with drinks and a snack they had turned their attention to the computer, which was where the music was really made. They distractedly promised to take a break, but they stayed huddled over the equipment for an extra hour instead. When they finally tore themselves away at five o'clock, they agreed to meet again the following Saturday.

TWENTY-EIGHT

Sharday's life began to take on a predictable pattern: an after-dinner trip to southeast on Mondays; choir rehearsals on Tuesdays; a call from Donnell at eight on Wednesdays; extra homework on Thursdays; the gig at *The Cellar* on Fridays; a call from Donnell followed by a studio session with Malcolm and more extra homework on Saturdays; church and family day on Sundays. But everything changed when report cards arrived in the mail two days before Thanksgiving.

Of course, April made the honor roll. She'd gotten four A's and two B pluses. But Sharday made three D's, two C's and a B minus, and Vickie wasted no time putting her on lockdown.

"Starting today, you're on punishment," Vickie said furiously. "You're not to leave this house once you get home from school except to go to choir rehearsals and *The Cellar* on Friday nights. And I want you back in here by eleven-thirty on Fridays from now on, too. And that equipment of Donnell's? You can forget about it. It's going down to the basement as soon as Bruce gets home from work."

"But I already been spending a lot more time on my homework lately, Ma," Sharday protested. "I don't even go out on Saturdays no more. That's how I brought my grades in social studies, math and English up."

"Then the extra time at home will help you bring up the rest of your grades," Vickie said. "You've got six classes, Sharday. And I expect you to do your best in all of them."

"Well, at least can Malcolm still come over on Saturdays?" Sharday asked. His visits had become one of the highlights of her week.

"Not until you get your grades up," Vickie said firmly. She still wanted to keep Sharday as connected to Malcolm as possible, but that couldn't take precedence over getting her daughter through high school. "And you can thank Bruce that I'm not taking away your phone privileges. But I'll snatch up that cell phone and that line you share with April so fast you won't know what hit you if I even suspect you're abusing them."

"Okay, okay, Ma," Sharday said quickly. "I hear you loud and clear." If Vickie took away her cell phone, she wouldn't be able to talk to Donnell anymore. And she would do anything to avoid that. Plus, those C's in math and social studies and that B minus in alternative English proved to her that she could make it at Mitchellville High. As a matter of fact, she wouldn't even have those three D's that were ticking her mother off so much if she hadn't gotten behind on her homework in the first place.

"I'll do better," she promised her mother. And now that she knew she could, she knew she would. She wanted to get her high school diploma. And now, she also wanted to go to PG Community so she would have something to fall back on.

Vickie and Sharday were closed up in Sharday's bedroom, and Vickie had been pacing back and forth in front of Sharday as she laid down the law. But now, Vickie sat down on the bed next to her daughter and sighed. "Baby, I know it's not easy to adjust to a whole new way of life," she said. "To be honest with you, I'm having a hard time adjusting, too."

"You are?" Sharday asked in surprise.

Vickie nodded. "Sometimes, I think I'm in over my head," she said slowly. "I don't have any friends anymore. And no matter how hard I try, I just can't seem to connect with any of the women I've met at church. You and April are almost grown and really don't need raising anymore. And Bruce spends his evenings and most of the day on Saturdays working." She met Sharday's gaze then and said, "There's only so much redecorating I can do. You know what I mean, baby?"

"Dag, Ma. I ain't even notice. I thought you was happy."

"I am in a lot of ways," Vickie said. "I've just got too much free time on my hands. So, I've decided to look for a part-time job after the holidays are over. It'll get me out of the house a few days a week and give me a chance to make some new friends."

"But can't you find something else to do since we don't need the money no more?" Sharday asked. "I thought you said you was sick of working."

"I was sick of working, but that was when I had to put in a full work day five days a week," Vickie said. "And anyway, Bruce already suggested that I get involved in charity work like a lot of the women around here do.

But I've been too poor all my life to start working for free now. Whether I need the money or not, I just can't do that."

"Yeah, I'm feeling that," Sharday said. "But at least you can always quit if you decide you don't like it."

"I'll like it once I get used to it again," Vickie said. She put an arm around her daughter and pulled her close. "You and me are like that, baby," she said. "Give us enough time and we can adjust to anything."

After Vickie left, April came by to check on Sharday. "Was it really bad?" she asked. "Are you on punishment for the rest of your life?"

Sharday chuckled and said, "Nah, not quite. But she shut me down until report cards come out again. You can believe that."

"Well, I've got some news that'll take your mind off of it for a few minutes," April said as she sat down on the bed.

"Oh yeah? What's that?"

"Calvin called me on my cell phone a few minutes ago," April said, referring to a cute guy she'd met at *The Cellar* the Friday before.

"What?" Sharday said, dragging the word out. "What he say?"

"Well, at first he was just making small talk and stuff, but then . . .," April let the sentence linger to build up suspense as she smiled at Sharday.

"But then what?" Sharday asked, playing along.

"Then he asked me out this weekend!" April exclaimed. "To dinner and a club! On Saturday!"

"Now, that's what I'm talking about!" Sharday said. She laughed and added, "Some of Tyesha's mojo must've rubbed off on you!"

April laughed, too. But then she said, "But I can't go this weekend, remember? I have to spend Thanksgiving with my mother."

"Damn," Sharday murmured. "That's messed up." She thought back to what April had said when she first mentioned that she always spent Thanksgiving with her mother and Christmas with her father. Apparently, Cathy was a workaholic who really didn't have time for April. So, whenever April went over to her house, Cathy always tried to buy April off by taking her shopping for a lot of expensive things she didn't want. April wasn't mad at Cathy. She'd had a good life with Bruce and she was glad her mother had given her up instead of trying to keep her, which probably would've made them all miserable.

"But I told him I could go next weekend and he said that would be great," April said now with a huge grin. "He said he'll see me at *The Cellar* next Friday, and then we'll hang out again on Saturday night, too."

"Cool!" Sharday said. That would give her time to check Calvin out and make sure he wasn't gaming April. The girl was just too wet behind the ears to be able to spot a fake for herself. But Sharday had been raised on the game, so she wouldn't have any problem figuring out where the brother was coming from.

TWENTY-NINE

Thanksgiving break was a drag for Sharday. Bruce and his sister, Felicia, ruined the holiday because they were depressed that April wasn't there. Frank came to the *The Cellar* the next night, but Sharday couldn't spend any time with him because she had to leave right after she finished singing so she could make it back home by her new curfew. She also missed a go-go "battle of the bands" on Saturday because she was on lockdown. And then, at brunch after church, Vickie and Bruce said they were "taking a pass" on family day because Sharday could better use her time studying.

Now, it was her lunch hour on Monday and she was sitting in the car feeling sorry for herself. She didn't exactly blame her mother for putting her on punishment -- three D's was definitely over the top, but in her opinion, taking away the studio was going too far. If it wasn't for that, the thought of the next few months wouldn't be so bad.

Malcolm approached the car as Sharday was unwrapping her sandwich. He'd missed spending time with her this past Saturday and he was crushed that her mother had canceled their studio sessions as a part of her punishment. Those few hours they spent huddled over that equipment were the only time he really got to talk to her because she always kept to herself during choir rehearsals and at church, and whenever she saw him in the hallways at school, the most she would do was give him a little wave. So, over the weekend, he'd come up with the idea of joining her for lunch until her mother took her off punishment. But since she could be so unpredictable, he was worried that she might not go for it.

"Mind if I join you?" he asked as casually as he could manage after she rolled down her window. "I'm starting to get sick of the caf, myself."

Sharday smiled at him and said, "I heard that," then she unlocked the passenger's door and gestured for him to get in. She had come to like Malcolm over the course of the last month. He wasn't exactly street smart, but he was sophisticated in his own way because he was a military brat who had traveled a lot and lived in Europe and Africa. Plus, he was just a nice guy.

After Malcolm climbed into the car and unpacked his lunch, Sharday leaned over to turn up the heat. "It's probably cold in here to you since you ain't used to it," she said.

"Whatever's comfortable for you is fine with me," Malcolm said.

They ate in silence for a few minutes, then Malcolm said, "So, how was your holiday?"

"Boring," she said. "And yours?"

"A trip," he said. "It always is. My uncle got tipsy and started a stupid argument with my father, my mother and my aunt tried to break it up but started arguing, too, and then my brother and I got in the middle of it and started arguing with my cousins.

Sharday laughed and said, "That is a trip."

Malcolm popped the top on his soda and said, "Can I ask you a question?"

"Uh huh," she said warily, hoping he wasn't going to ask why she was on lockdown. All she'd told him was that he wouldn't be able to come over for the next two months because her mother had put her on punishment.

"What's going on with you and Mrs. Jefferson?" he asked.

"What you mean?"

"Well, it's clear that she's just dying to put you in the spotlight. But every time she offers you a solo, you turn her down."

Sharday shrugged. "I ain't really into the choir like that," she said. "I mean, I like learning all the new stuff she teaching me. Like how to follow the melody off sheet music and how the different types of singers have to flow together and harmonize and stuff. But I ain't never been no church person and I can't stand singing so early in the morning." She shrugged again and said, "I'm just doing it until I graduate and move out."

Malcolm smiled at her and said, "That's one of the things I like about you, Sharday. You know exactly what you want."

She shrugged and took a sip of her juice. "I don't know about all that. I just try to keep it real."

"Oh, that reminds me," he said. "I've come up with a couple of melodies you might be able to use with one of those raps you wrote."

"Oh yeah? Which one?" she asked. She'd written down the raps Donnell had sent her via voice memo, and when Malcolm saw them and assumed she'd come up with them herself, she hadn't bothered to correct him.

"The one called, *The Realest Thoughts I Ever Thought*," he said, and then he started outlining the possibilities.

They were still discussing his ideas when the end-of-the-period bell rang. And although she declined his offer to walk her to her locker, she agreed when he suggested that they have lunch together again the next day.

THIRTY

A week before Christmas, Kayla called Sharday to tell her that Elise and Keith had broken up. "He mad because she won't have a abortion," Kayla said. "He said he love her and all that good shit but he ain't trying to have no baby right now. He said he too young to have a baby."

"Well, why didn't she wait before she told him?" Sharday said. "That's what we agreed on." Her alternative English teacher had been urging her to write short, complete sentences and to talk the same way to reinforce her writing skills. It had been hard at first, but it was finally starting to take effect.

"She claim her love came down and she couldn't help herself," Kayla said. "But when you see her, act like you don't know. She said she ain't telling you and Tyesha."

"Why not?"

Kayla hesitated for a second before saying, "You ain't gonna believe this, Day-Day. But Elise done let LaShawn convince her that y'all think y'all better than us."

"What?"

"I know," Kayla said with a heavy sigh. "I keep telling them to stop tripping, but they ain't trying to hear it. They say you think you too good to hang out with us now that you done moved out to Mitchellville. And they say Tyesha always thought she was better than everybody from the Vistas."

"But I still see them every week at *The Cellar* and the only reason they don't see me more than that is because I'm on punishment," Sharday said, forgetting all about short, complete sentences. "And Tyesha the same person she always been."

"Like I said, Day-Day, they ain't trying to hear all that right now. Elise so sick from that baby she can't think straight and she believe anything LaShawn say. And you know how LaShawn been bugging lately. Last time I saw that girl she was talking about slinging trees just to finance her own habit."

"Damn," Sharday said. She knew about Elise's constant morning sickness and LaShawn's stepped-up weed habit, but she had no idea they'd been hating on her and Tyesha. When she hung up from Kayla a few minutes later, she called Tyesha and swore her to secrecy before telling her what was going on.

"Oh, who cares what Elise and LaShawn think?" Tyesha said. "They're going nowhere fast and I ain't trying to go with them. Dropping out of high school in the twelfth grade. How stupid can they get?"

"Come on, Tyesha, those our girls," Sharday said. "We just gotta talk to them and make them see ain't nothing changed."

"But everything *is* changing now, Day-Day. Elise is gonna be a welfare mother and I don't know what LaShawn thinks she's gonna do with no diploma. But I'm going to college and so are you now. And at least Kayla will be a secretary with a fireman for a husband. So, the three of us are leaving the two of them behind in the Vistas no matter how you look at it. Now or later, what difference does it make?"

"Get real, Tyesha. We all came up together and we gonna be friends for life. They just got it a little twisted right now but it ain't nothing we can't fix. All we gotta do is call them on it."

"Well, you do what you think you need to do, Day-Day. But I don't have time to be chasing after them and begging them to be friends with me. I've got my college applications and essays to get through right now, and then my internship applications are coming up right after that. I just don't need the hassle anymore."

"Well, I'm gonna call them," Sharday said. She hung up the phone and dialed Elise, who was sleeping and couldn't come to the phone. Then one of LaShawn's little brothers put her on hold and came back a few minutes later to say, "Shawn said she ain't here."

Sharday slowly hung up the phone. Everything from her old life was falling apart and there was nothing she could do to stop it.

THIRTY-ONE

The next day, Sharday received a small brown box from Greg Foster, Donnell's poetry teacher. Vickie brought it up to her room after she got home from school, saying it had come by UPS earlier. And as soon as her mother left, Sharday rushed over to her desk to pry open the package.

Inside was an even smaller box wrapped with brightly-colored paper and a red bow, and she grinned with delight as she realized that Donnell had somehow managed to send her a Christmas gift. She slowly peeled off the paper, savoring the anticipation, and when she finally removed the lid from the square, white box beneath, she found a flash drive surrounded by a delicate silver bracelet.

She picked up the bracelet and looked at the slim faceplate. It said "*I ♥ You*," and her eyes watered as she carefully fastened it around it her wrist. No matter what else happened, she would always have Donnell. He was her destiny and she was his. And no amount of time apart would ever change that.

She got up and slipped the flash drive into her computer, then she turned the volume to low and sat really close to one to the speakers to listen. Donnell had sent her two new rhymes. The first one was hardcore, and it would have her saying a lot of stuff about how she was the kind of female who played the niggas and didn't take no shit. She liked it because it reminded her of Tyesha. So, she decided to call it "Female Pimp" when she wrote it down later.

On the second rhyme, Donnell came from a totally different place and it blew Sharday away. He kept saying the words, "I remember," and he rapped about growing up in the projects like it had been a blessing. He spoke of the joy of being the one to get the welfare check from the mailman, the thrill of exploring abandoned cars with childhood friends, the satisfaction of getting all the use from a pair of shoes, and so on. Sharday loved it! She was going to call it "Ghetto Heaven," and since Vickie was letting her use the studio a few hours each week now, she couldn't wait to find some music for it.

She was just getting ready to eject the flash drive when she heard an unfamiliar male voice say, "Okay, Donnell. I'll give you some privacy for a few minutes." And then she heard Donnell say, "Alright man, appreciate it. What up, Day-Day! That was my motherfucking nigga you just heard! My nigga, Greg! My poetry teacher!"

She quickly turned the volume down a little bit more. Donnell was sounding a lot harder now that he was in this new prison and it mostly seemed to come from his so-called "poetry class" -- a bunch of thug rapper wannabes led by a student from a nearby college. She didn't want her mother and them to hear how he sounded because they wouldn't understand. But she knew he was just acting like this to survive while he was behind bars. Once he got out, he would be able to relax his guard and get back to being himself again.

"He helping a brother make it through this shit," Donnell continued. "Done got me started writing down some of my rhymes up in this bitch. Said don’t worry about no spelling, since I can't have no phone up in here I gotta do what I gotta do. And he right!"

Donnell lowered his voice then and said, "But anyway, Day-Day, Merry Christmas. I know the gift ain't all that but I get you something better when I get out. I love you, babe."

Sharday was stunned. Donnell had written that he loved her in his one letter to her, but he had never actually said those words to her before. All he ever said was "Me, too." She turned up the volume some and played that part over and over again.

THIRTY-TWO

School was out for more than a week over the holidays, so Vickie and Bruce took pity on Sharday. They let her use the studio every day, and when Vickie's parents came down from Philly the weekend after Christmas, Sharday was allowed to take them sightseeing for Christmas lights and decorations with April. Then Vickie took Sharday and April shopping for New Year's Eve outfits and said that Sharday could stay out until two a.m. for just that one night.

"Malcolm's still going, right?" Vickie asked.

"Unh huh," Sharday confirmed. She and Malcolm were becoming good friends now, and during one of their daily lunches in the car, she had invited him to join her and April at *The Cellar* for Clyde's "New Year's Eve Extravaganza." Clyde had switched her from her regular Friday night spot to Thursday night, so she could be on the lineup. And he was having a catered buffet meal, hats and noisemakers, and champagne near the stroke of midnight.

"Well, Bruce and I are going out, too," Vickie said excitedly as she examined and rejected a red gown. April was closest to her, so she said, "Unzip me, please, April. I think I'll try the green one next." And then, "We're going on *The Dandy*," she said, referring to a luxury ship that offered dinner cruises on the Potomac River. "We'll be celebrating the end of Bruce's busy season at work, as well as the New Year. We've hardly had any time together these last few months."

They spent all afternoon shopping. Vickie ultimately chose a floor-length, black satin gown with deep Vs in the front and back and a slit up the right leg. Sharday picked a shiny, blue, strapless dress with a matching shawl, and then she and Vickie both insisted that April go with a pair of high-heeled purple pumps and a purple minidress that looked great on her.

At two o'clock in the afternoon on New Year's Eve, Vickie, Sharday and April met in the kitchen for facials and manicures. They tried to convince

Bruce to have a facial, too, but he firmly declined. So, they spent the next two hours pampering themselves and talking girl talk.

Bruce ordered Chinese food in for a pre-dinner meal and he served them and put away the leftovers so they wouldn't mess up their nails. When they all headed upstairs to dress, he quickly showered and put on a snazzy black suit, a white shirt and black bow tie, and black dress shoes before leaving "the women" to finished getting ready. Still, he had to call them down an hour and a half later when Malcolm arrived.

"We're coming," Vickie called back. She was the first to come down a few minutes later. April followed closely behind with Sharday pulling up the rear.

Bruce whistled and said, "Beautiful, beautiful, and beautiful! I am truly a blessed man!"

Malcolm laughed and said, "I am, too, Mr. Campbell. Two of them are going with me." He was dressed in all black -- suit, shirt, tie, shoes and coat. He handed Vickie and April a single, long-stemmed red rose each, then he gave Sharday a half dozen of the beautiful roses.

Vickie and April thanked Malcolm and gave him an air hug to avoid getting makeup on him. When Sharday did the same, he hugged her to him and she hugged him back. But then she caught herself and quickly pulled away, saying she had to put the roses in water. By the time she returned, she'd convinced herself that she and Malcolm were reacting to the excitement of the holiday and not to each other.

Vickie and Bruce watched from the doorway as Malcolm escorted Sharday and April to his parents' SUV, a navy Chevy Trailblazer, and Malcolm honked as he backed out of the driveway.

"It's nice riding up high like this," Sharday said after they pulled off, reminding herself to try to stick to her "good English" tonight.

Malcolm chuckled. "I'm so used to it, I'm not sure I know how to drive a car anymore," he said. His parents also had a Mercedes they'd bought right before his family moved back home from Germany, but they hardly ever let him drive that.

"I like it, too," April said from the backseat. "When Lynn uses her father's Navigator, it feels like we're queens on the throne."

Malcolm clicked on the radio and said, "Okay, ladies, it's New Year's Eve. Time for resolutions. Who wants to go first?"

"I will," April said. And then, with a laugh, "I resolve to keep dressing fly during the coming year and to get my weekly exercise on the dance floor at *The Cellar*." Her true resolution was to get a boyfriend before the new year ended, but that was a private goal. Calvin had only been out for sex, and thankfully, Sharday had warned her right from the beginning. But maybe she'd meet somebody else tonight.

Sharday and Malcolm laughed, too, but then Sharday got serious. "Well, I resolve to keep my grades up and get into college," she said. "And I resolve to be patient, too," she quickly added, thinking about the long wait ahead for Donnell.

Malcolm had Sharday in mind when he said, "I resolve to be persistent and never give up on the things that really matter." But just to be funny, he added, "Like kicking my brother's butt in every game we play on *PlayStation 4* this year."

They laughed and kept talking and it wasn't long before they arrived at *The Cellar*. They checked their coats and Malcolm went to the bar for drinks while Sharday led April to the table that had been reserved for her. Although Malcolm was under age, he appeared a few minutes later with a beer for himself, a glass of champagne for April, and the bottle of spring water that Sharday had asked for.

Kayla and John claimed their seats at the table just as the first act, a quartet of male R&B singers called *Prime Time* began their set. Tyesha walked up with Mark in tow shortly after that and Sharday's crew was complete. Elise and LaShawn hadn't shown up in a month now, so nobody was expecting them tonight.

When Mark ordered two bottles of Moet to get the party started, Sharday excused herself and headed for the deejay's booth. She was up next on stage, so after she handed over the thumb drive with the new tracks she'd made on the new software program she got for Christmas and spent a few minutes chatting, she made a beeline for the bathroom.

She fussed with her hair and make-up a little longer than normal. She even spent a few minutes singing the scales to warm up her voice. She tried to tell herself she was going to the extra effort because it was New Year's Eve, but deep down, she knew she wanted to impress Malcolm.

She walked on stage to applause after Clyde introduced her and the deejay started her playlist. The music was so clear that it almost sounded like a live band and she quickly found her zone. She belted out five songs in a row, ending with a medley that included *Street Life Paradise*. And when the audience called out for an encore, she signaled for the DJ to play her last track and sprang *The Realest Thoughts I Ever Thought* on them.

At Malcolm's suggestion, she had set the rhyme to Eve's *Life Is So Hard* featuring the legendary singer, Teena Marie. The music and background vocals were on the CD, but Sharday sang Teena Marie's hook live and then she spit the rap Donnell had written for her. The crowd went wild with applause and she fed off their energy. She was hyped when she finally left the stage to a standing ovation.

She made her usual post-performance trip to the bathroom, but she was still buzzing with excitement when she returned to the table.

"Absolutely fantastic!" Malcolm said as he stood to pull back her chair. "You were phenomenal, Sharday!"

She was thrilled, but before she could respond, Tyesha said, "Yep, Day-Day turns it out once again."

After Kayla, John and Mark voiced their compliments, Sharday thanked them all and poured herself a glass of the Moet Clyde had sent her. "What happened to April?" she asked the table at large as she passed the bottle of champagne to Malcolm.

Malcolm passed the bottle on to the next person, saying he'd stick with beer, and then Kayla said, "You know that girl can't stay off the dance floor. She left as soon as you finished and the deejay came on."

A few minutes later, Clyde approached the mic and announced that the buffet was open. He said the deejay would carry them through dinner, and that a hip-hop band called *The Franchise* would take them into the new year.

"Good, I'm starving," John said. "Let's go eat."

Sharday told them to go ahead without her. "I still need to unwind," she said.

Malcolm said he'd wait for her, and they were sitting at the table talking quietly when Clyde walked up and handed Sharday her pay envelope. "Good job up there tonight," he said. "Who's your friend?"

Sharday introduced Malcolm and Clyde. Malcolm said, "Nice to meet you," and extended his hand to shake, but Clyde glared at him and said, "Where'd you meet her?"

Malcolm pulled his hand back and stared at Clyde, so Sharday said, "I go to his school now, Clyde. Plus, I joined his church's choir."

"Is that right?" Clyde said, clearly waiting for a response from Malcolm.

Malcolm debated not answering, but this man didn't seem like anybody he wanted to tangle with. "Yes, it is," he finally said.

Clyde nodded imperceptibly. He liked Sharday and didn't want to see her get screwed over by some young thug now that Donnell was gone. But this proper little boy seemed harmless enough. He looked at Sharday and said, "Go get your sister," then he turned and walked away.

"What was that about?" Malcolm asked Sharday after Clyde left.

"Don't take it personal," she said. "Clyde's rude to everybody. That's just the way he is." She looked around for April, but didn't see her. "Malcolm, I need to go find April," she said. "Clyde didn't say that for nothing. Why don't you hit the buffet while I go look for her?"

Malcolm agreed and they split up. Sharday checked the dance floor first, then she checked the bar and scanned the buffet line. She finally found April sitting at a table with a guy named Russell. He was cute and he was only about twenty years old. But he was one of Clyde's boys, and word had it that he was an enforcer.

Sharday wished Russell a happy new year and said she needed to steal April away from him. Then she steered April toward the buffet line and whispered, "You don't wanna mess with him, April. Don't ask me how I know, but he's a gang banger."

April looked at Sharday with wide eyes and whispered, "Who, Russell? Are you sure?"

Sharday nodded. "Unh huh, he's off limits."

April was so shaken that her hands trembled as she picked up a plate and a set of utensils. Clearly, she was out of her league with the guys in here. First, she picked a "pussyhound," as Sharday had called Calvin, and now she'd almost taken up with a gang banger. It was fun to come hear Sharday sing and have a good time dancing and all, but from now on, April would leave the men in here alone.

By the time Sharday and April made it back to the table, *The Franchise* was just starting to perform and everyone except Malcolm had already finished eating. Sharday asked Mark to call their waiter over and order her another bottle of champagne. "Now that I'm finished singing, I'm ready to get my buzz on," she said. "It's time to celebrate!"

"Order two, Mark," April said. "I'll pay for the extra one." She was planning to catch a buzz, too, so she wanted to be sure there would be enough to go around.

"Okay," Mark said. "And Day-Day, you can come outside with me and Tyesha after you eat."

Sharday shook her head and said, "Nah, I'm sticking to champagne tonight. But thanks, anyway." Malcolm still didn't know she smoked and that's the way she wanted to keep it. She could only hope that he had no idea what she and Mark were talking about.

"Well, I wanna go," Kayla said, and Sharday looked over at John, afraid that the conversation was about to become more specific. But then John smiled at Kayla and said, "Do your thing, babe. It's New Year's Eve," and Sharday breathed a sigh of relief.

Mark finally caught the waiter's attention and ordered the champagne. Malcolm insisted on paying for both bottles, telling Sharday and April that this round was on him. And then Mark, Tyesha and Kayla left to go outside.

Malcolm nursed his beer as Sharday, April and John started in on the Moet. Sharday also finished her meal, but April pushed her plate aside and said she wasn't hungry. By the time they all got up to dance -- Sharday with Malcolm and April with John, it was clear that April was tipsy.

They danced to back-to-back fast songs together until *The Franchise* slowed it down to play an Eric Benét ballad. April and John headed back to the table, but Malcolm reached for Sharday and said, "Shall we?"

She nodded and stepped into his arms.

He held her close, inhaling her perfume and relishing the way it felt to have her pressed up against him. "Thank you for inviting me tonight," he murmured into her ear as they moved to the music.

"I'm glad you came," she murmured back. But as soon as the words left her mouth, she realized that she was enjoying this too much. There could never be anything between her and Malcolm. He would be scandalized if he ever found out who she really was. And anyway, she belonged to Donnell.

"So am I," Malcolm said, and then he pulled her a little closer.

She knew she should've resisted, but she didn't. She blamed it on the champagne at first, then she convinced herself that she was making a big deal out of nothing. They were dancing together, not making a commitment. Why not just take it for what it was?

When the song ended, they released each other and returned to the table. Mark, Tyesha and Kayla had come back by then, and it wasn't long before the waiter came around with hats, noise makers and complimentary glasses of champagne.

They all joined the bandleader as he led the countdown to midnight, and then they clinked their glasses together and shouted, "Happy New Year!" as *The Franchise* began to play *Auld Lang Syne*.

Sharday blew on her noisemaker and turned to her left to give April a hug. When she turned to her right to do the same with Malcolm, he leaned in to kiss her on the lips and she willingly kissed him back.

THIRTY-THREE

Frank called Sharday on her cell phone the next night and she didn't know whether she was happy or sad to hear from him. He had never tried to see her outside the club again after the time he took her to lunch. And even though he had shown up at *The Cellar* every Friday night for about five or six weeks, he pulled one of his disappearing acts after that and she hadn't seen or heard from him since. Vickie kept saying that Frank would never change and Sharday was starting to believe it.

After they wished each other a happy new year, Frank said, "Baby, I'm at *The Cellar* right now. Why aren't you here?"

"I'm at home, Daddy. Clyde had a big extravanga last night and I sang for that."

"Well, I'm sorry I missed it, Sharday," he said. "But I'm sure you did a great job, as usual." And then, "Look, honey, about these last few weeks . . ."

"I know, Daddy. On the road again, right?"

"Nope, not this time," he said. "I moved into that condo I was telling you about. And I've been busy trying to get everything unpacked so I could invite you over for dinner."

"Really?" she said. Her wariness was immediately replaced with excitement. Her father was actually coming through.

"How does this weekend sound?" he asked. "Would you like to come on Sunday?"

She sighed and said, "Dag, Daddy. I don't think I can make it on Sunday." Her mother and Bruce probably wouldn't let her miss family day. Plus, she wasn't sure she wanted to blow off her new family, who had her back now, just to have dinner with her father, who was likely to up and disappear again whenever he felt like it. "We go to church every week now," she said. "And then we usually go out and we don't get back home until some time after five."

"Well, why don't you come by then," Frank said. "I wasn't planning to have dinner until about six anyway. We'll just push it back to six thirty."

Sharday quickly agreed. She was in the basement because she had been working in the studio before Frank called. So, after she wrote down the directions to his new place and promised she would be there on Sunday, she ran upstairs to share the news with her mother.

As it turned out, Vickie and Bruce had already gone up to their bedroom. And since Sharday was too excited to wait until the next day, she ended up telling them both at the same time.

"Well, I think that's great," Bruce said. Sharday needed her father to be a real presence in her life, not some shadowy figure lurking in a nightclub.

"I do, too, baby," Vickie said. As much as she couldn't stand Frank, she knew Sharday loved him and needed to spend more time with him. So, she would keep her mouth shut and hope for the best for her daughter's sake. But deep in her heart, she was convinced that Frank would never change.

THIRTY-FOUR

Sharday was impressed when she drove up to the gated community in Wheaton, Maryland and punched in the three digit code Frank had given her. Wheaton was in Montgomery County, one of the richest counties in the country. And this development was sort of new, so it was probably expensive.

After Frank buzzed her in, she drove past a series of buildings with garden-style units and parked near the long, curved, high-rise at the far end of the parking lot. The doorman said "Frank and Belinda" were expecting her, and then he had her write her name and license plate number in the visitor's log before directing her to a set of elevators around the corner.

Frank's condo was on the twelfth floor. He opened the door before she knocked and welcomed her with a hug. "I'm glad you made it, baby," he said after he released her. "Come on in. Let me take your coat."

"Thank you, Daddy," she said, grinning from ear to ear. She waited for him to hang up her coat in the closet in the entryway and followed him into a huge living room that was separated from the dining room by a two-sided fireplace. Both rooms had sliding glass doors that led to a curved balcony.

A slightly-built, light-skinned woman with a short, reddish, wavy natural eased herself off the obviously new beige leather sofa and limped toward them. Frank introduced her as Belinda, his "old lady." And when Sharday went to shake hands, Belinda embraced her and said, "It's good to finally meet you after all these years, Sharday. Welcome to our new home."

"It's nice to meet you, too, Belinda," Sharday said, immediately deciding to use her "good English" for the evening. She had never even heard of Belinda, but since the woman lived with her father and had apparently been with him for years, Sharday wanted to make a good impression. "This is a beautiful condo," she said.

Belinda thanked Sharday and invited her to take a look around. "Give her a quick tour, Frank," she suggested, then she limped off to the kitchen to check on dinner.

Frank was proud to show off their new two bedroom with two full baths and a balcony that extended from the living room to the master bedroom. He played king of the castle as he slowly led his daughter through the unit and pointed out different features in each room. His name wasn't actually on the deed, but thankfully, Sharday didn't know that. So, he milked the situation for all it was worth.

Belinda served a pot roast with mashed potatoes and gravy, cabbage, cornbread muffins, and iced tea for dinner. The conversation flowed freely as they ate. And Belinda eventually told Sharday that she had a grown son who was "incarcerated" and that she used to be a repair technician for the electric company until the bucket truck she was working in one day broke and she fell.

Frank quickly cut Belinda off, afraid that she would mention her half a million dollar settlement agreement with the electric company. "Well, Sharday has a close friend who's in jail, too," he said. "How's Donnell doing by the way?" he asked Sharday.

Sharday said that Donnell was fine and that she talked to him twice a week. When Belinda stood a few minutes later to get the dessert, Sharday followed her into the kitchen to help.

"I've been after Frank to let me meet you for so long," Belinda said as she cut three generous slices from a homemade chocolate cake. "But I don't have to tell you how stubborn that man can be."

Sharday smiled and held out the first dessert plate. She didn't really know that side of her father, so there was nothing she could say.

Belinda shook her head in mock frustration and said, "And guess what he's saying now that I'm making noises about getting married."

"What?" Sharday asked, holding out another dessert plate.

Belinda put down the knife and pie spatula and puffed out her chest. In a deep voice that was supposed to be an imitation of Frank's, she said, "'You know I'm not the marrying type, Belinda. But if I was going to marry anybody, it would be you.'" She started laughing.

Sharday laughed, too, but she found the inside scoop on her father fascinating.

Belinda shook her head again and said, "Too much, right? But I can't lie, I love him anyway."

After dessert, Sharday said she had to get back home. It was already nine o'clock, and the next day would be the first one back at school after Winter Break.

"Well, I really enjoyed this," Belinda said. "Let's do it again soon."

"How about next weekend?" Frank suggested. He wanted to start having Sharday over every week now. She had talked about Bruce's so-called family days during dinner and it had really gotten under his skin. He was her father, not Bruce. How could there be a family day if he wasn't involved?

"Oh, that would be great," Belinda said. "If you can make it, Sharday, I'll get us some catfish."

Sharday was thrilled that they wanted to get closer to her. She grinned and said, "Of course, I'll be here." She wouldn't miss it for anything in the world.

THIRTY-FIVE

Sharday's punishment ended the first week in February when second quarter report cards came out. She had improved in every one of her classes, getting an A in alternative English, B's in math and social studies, and C's from the teachers who'd previously given her Ds. And now that she finally had her freedom back, she was having a blowout of a weekend.

Last night, she had stayed over at Tyesha's because Tyesha really didn't have a curfew. They went to *The Cellar* so she could do her gig, but after that, they got totally stoned and went to the go-gos. They slept in late this morning, finally waking up at about noon, and then Tyesha got a college boy she'd recently met to take them to a basketball game at the University of Maryland.

Now, it was almost six thirty and Sharday was back home. She had just taken a quick shower and she was putting on black stretch jeans, a bulky red sweater and black leather boots to go out with Malcolm. They were planning to catch a movie and hit *Friday's* for dinner and she was expecting him in about fifteen minutes. But she was still working on her boots when April knocked on her bedroom door.

April came in wearing low-rise jeans, a chocolate brown turtleneck with extra long sleeves, a brown suede belt and the brown Manolo Blahnik boots her mother had bought her for Christmas. She twirled around and said, "So, what do you think? Do I look fly?"

Sharday laughed and said, "Girl, you know you look hot. Cathy really hooked you up with those boots."

"You don't think they're too much?" April asked. This date was really important to her and she wanted to look just right. After that scare with the gang banger on New Year's Eve, she had gone out with a guy from church who ended up being way too straight for her now that she was used to hanging out with Sharday. But tonight, she was going out with one of the football players at school -- the type of guy who never even looked at her before

Sharday came into her life.

"If I did, I wouldn't have suggested them," Sharday said. She had helped April put this outfit together Tuesday night, right after Sherwood called and asked the girl on a date. "You look great, April. Just like I knew you would," she said. "Now, get out of here so I can finished getting dressed."

"Ooh, that's right," April said with a grin. "You're getting ready for your date with Malcolm."

"It's not a date, April. You know that." Sharday zipped up her last boot and stood.

"Oh, I forgot," April teased. "You're 'just friends,'" she said, making quotation marks with her fingers.

"That's right," Sharday said firmly as she walked over to the dresser and spritzed herself with perfume. She knew she had developed feelings for Malcolm, but as far as she was concerned, they were just friendship feelings. She was too in love with Donnell for them to be anything else.

"Well, I'll leave you to it then," April said as she reached for the door. "And thanks for hooking me up."

"No problem," Sharday said. "Have fun tonight. And don't forget to wear the silver jewelry we picked out."

Malcolm showed up a few minutes later wearing navy corduroys, a cream turtleneck, and his black leather jacket and driving gloves. He kissed Sharday on the cheek when she let him in to speak to Vickie and Bruce, and then he held her hand as he escorted her to his parents' SUV.

As he was pulling out of the driveway, he said, "Would you mind if we eat first and then go to the movies? A buddy of mine told me about this new Japanese Steakhouse in Laurel and I was hoping we could give it a try."

"But I'm not dressed for a fancy restaurant," she said. "I've got on jeans."

"It's a casual place with tables set up around the grills where they cook your food," he said. He stopped at a stop sign and turned to smile at her. "And anyway, you look great, Sharday," he said. "You wear jeans better than any other woman I know."

She smiled back and said, "Thank you, Malcolm."

"So, are you up for it?" he asked as he pulled off again.

"Yeah, let's do it," she said. The vibe between them was heating up too fast tonight. It was almost like New Year's Eve all over again. They still ate lunch together every day, and the mood was nothing like this. So, hopefully, sharing a meal at the restaurant would put them back on the right track.

After Malcolm turned onto Mitchellville Road and picked up speed, he said, "Now that you're off punishment, I can't wait to get back in the studio. I've been working on a new song. I want you to hear it."

He plugged his phone into the stereo and when the first few notes from his keyboard came through the speakers, he turned up the volume.

The song was an R&B ballad. And it reminded Sharday of something somebody like Anthony Hamilton or Eric Benét would sing. As for the lyrics, Malcolm was singing about a girl he kept calling "the bomb," and he was saying that she had blown his mind and he would do anything to keep her.

When the song went off, she turned to him in amazement and said, "You wrote that by yourself? The music and everything?"

"Yep. Do you like it?"

"Oh, my God, Malcolm. I love it," she said. She started grinning then and said, "Dag, I didn't know you had it going on like that! Why didn't you tell me you write songs? Do you have any more?"

"I haven't been doing it that long," he said. "This is my first one. I've got a few more in progress, but they still need a lot more work."

"Wow," she said.

"So, did it remind you of anybody you know?" he asked.

"What? The song?"

"I wrote it for you," he said quietly. "Couldn't you tell?"

She looked at him and said, "Oh, my God. For real, Malcolm?"

When he nodded, she said, "Can I hear it again?"

This time she really listened to the lyrics. According to him, she had exploded into his life exactly when he needed her even though he hadn't know he was lacking anything. She was unique -- from the way she thought to something so basic as the way she walked. And she was so special that God had blessed her with the voice of an angel.

She didn't say anything for a long while after the song ended. "It's beautiful, Malcolm," she finally said. "But I'm not the person you think I am."

"That's the person you are to me," he said.

"That's just because you don't really know me."

"I've been around you enough to have a pretty good idea of who you are," he said. "And all the rest is just details."

"I guess," she said, but she knew details like the fact that she was practically a pothead and had a boyfriend in federal prison were really important.

Neither of them said anything after that, and a few minutes later, Malcolm turned off Route One, the main strip in Laurel, Maryland, into the parking lot for the restaurant. After a brief wait in the lobby, the hostess led them to two seats at a circular table with a semi-circular grill in the middle.

The grill was full and the tall, thin Japanese chef behind it chopped and flipped the food with his metal spatula for a while before he laid three square plates along one arm, arranged a different meal on each with a flourish, and served three white women seated a few chairs down from Sharday.

When he came over to take Sharday and Malcolm's orders, she asked for the Tempura shrimp dish and he ordered the Teriyaki beef dish. A waitress brought the sodas they had ordered a few minutes earlier, and Malcolm started telling Sharday funny stories about the two years he and his family had spent in Kenya. She always enjoyed hearing about his "years abroad," as he called them, and she was relieved that the vibe between them was back to normal.

After dinner, they went to the movies at the Laurel Towne Center, less than a half-mile away from the restaurant. The next showing of the new Will Smith movie they had planned to see was sold out, so they ended up seeing a romantic comedy instead. And when Malcolm eventually slipped his arm around Sharday's shoulders and pulled her closer, she found herself willingly leaning in to rest her head on his shoulder.

THIRTY-SIX

By the time Spring Break rolled around a month and a half later, Sharday knew she was spending way too much time with Malcolm. Lunch in the car at school, choir rehearsal, church, *The Cellar* most Fridays, the studio every Saturday afternoon. And although she always stayed home on Saturday evenings to study, sometimes she even let him talk her into catching a late movie on Saturday night.

In theory, they were only friends because she'd told him about her "out-of-town boyfriend" who would be coming back to DC the following year. But in reality, they were growing closer by the day and Sharday was starting to feel guilty. Two phone calls a week from Donnell and the occasional recorded tracks with a message at the end couldn't begin to compare with the amount of time she was spending with Malcolm. So, she was determined to go see her Boo before her vacation from school ended.

On Monday, Bruce and April had gone on a four and a half day tour of several colleges. But Vickie felt it was too soon to take time off from her new part-time job as a sales assistant at an insurance company, and Sharday had stayed home with her mother. Then last night, on Friday, Bruce and Vickie left to spend the weekend at a bed and breakfast in West Virginia. April had made arrangements to stay at Lynn's for the weekend, and Sharday went home with Tyesha after her gig at *The Cellar*. Now, it was six in the morning on Saturday and Sharday and Tyesha were on a Greyhound bus headed for Allentown, New York.

Sharday was financing the trip with some of the money Bruce and Vickie had given her to spend while they were gone. She and Tyesha would arrive in Allentown with time to spare before her two o'clock, hour-long visit with Donnell, and they would be back in DC before midnight. Nobody but the three of them and April would ever know anything about it.

After the bus driver merged onto the interstate and picked up speed, Sharday and Tyesha tore into the egg and sausage biscuits they had gotten from Burger King. They were gulping down supersized cups of orange juice when Tyesha pointed to the exit for College Park, Maryland and said, "Look, Day-Day! That's me next year!"

"I know, Tyesha. I know," Sharday said. Tyesha would be going to the University of Maryland in College Park on a full scholarship and the girl was so hyped that she had already nagged Sharday into driving her over to the campus a couple of times.

"Aw, don't hate, Day-Day. Relate," Tyesha said.

Sharday started laughing and said, "Girl, you need to medicate."

Tyesha laughed, too. Then she said, "Yeah, I know I'm over the top. But you know how important college is to me."

"Yeah, and I'm starting to feel the same way," Sharday said. That's why she had been staying home on Saturday evenings to do homework.

Tyesha finished her orange juice and yawned. "I'm tired," she said. "You sleepy, too?"

They had only gotten a few hours of sleep the night before, but Sharday shook her head and said, "Nah, I'm too excited to sleep."

"Well, I just need a quick nap," Tyesha said, yawning again. "Wake me up in an hour, okay?"

Sharday agreed and slipped in the earbuds to the iPod she had gotten for Christmas. As Tyesha slept, Sharday listened to hip hop and let her mind wander from topic to topic. She thought about Donnell, the weekly dinners with her father and Belinda, Elise and LaShawn, Malcolm's spring break trip to St. Thomas with his family. The next thing she knew, Tyesha was waking her up as they crossed the state line into New York.

She wiped the drool from her face and made a quick trip to the bathroom. After she came back, Tyesha said, "Too bad we can't go to the city while we're up here. I wanna see the Statue of Liberty or the Empire State Building or something."

"We can do that another time," Sharday said. "After we graduate." She and Tyesha were planning to get an apartment together that was halfway between College Park and Largo, where PG Community was located.

"Yeah, and we'll probably be able to stay for the whole weekend by then," Tyesha said. She was still secretly hoping that Sharday would eventually drop Donnell for Malcolm, but of course she would stick by her girl unless and until that happened.

Allentown turned out to be hours away from the New Jersey/New York border, and Sharday and Tyesha both fell asleep again. This time, Sharday woke Tyesha up as they pulled into the bus depot. And after they went to the McDonald's across the street to freshen up in the bathroom and have lunch, they caught a taxi directly to Allen Brook federal prison.

Sharday left her backpack with Tyesha in the waiting room before she stepped through the diamond-patterned metal gate and followed a female C.O. through a thick steel door. A male C.O. was waiting inside the windowless inspection area and he examined Sharday's jacket and shoes, which she had to take off and hand over, while the female ran a metal detector over her and patted her down.

Once Sharday passed the test, the female guard escorted her through another steel door that led to the outside grounds of the facility. A number of inmates were driving riding lawnmowers, but Sharday mostly kept her eyes straight ahead as she followed the C.O. down a long, winding walkway to the prison.

Three more guards, two more metal gates, and two steel doors later, and Sharday was finally sitting across from Donnell at one of several long tables in a windowless visiting room. They had been allowed to kiss and hug when he first came out, and he reached for her hands after they sat down.

"Damn, Day-Day!" he said. "You looking good as a shit sitting up in here! I don't hardly never get no visitors!"

She made a point to use her "ghetto English" as she squeezed his hands and said, "Well, me and Tyesha probably be coming up here all the time after we move, Boo." But even as she spoke, all she could think about was how different he seemed now. He had told her he was pumping iron, but she hadn't expected him to be so beefed up already. And with the bald head and his new, gangsta way of speaking, he almost seemed like another person.

But then he started talking about the "vocab lists" his poetry teacher was giving him to help him with his rhymes, the literacy classes he was thinking about taking so he could be one of them "smart rappers" like Jay-Z and Kendrick Lamar, and the music-related contacts he was making in the yard. "Some of these niggas got some serious contacts in the industry," he told her in a hushed voice. "I can probably have us a deal in no time once I get out here."

Sharday smiled and gazed into his eyes, soaking up every word. This was her Boo. One of the most dedicated brothers she had ever met. And no matter what kind of situation you put him in, he would always find a way to come out on top. "I know you gonna make it happen for us, Boo," she said. "One way or another."

They talked for a while about how they couldn't wait until he got out of there, she told him about the rumor that LaShawn was "lacing down," which meant sprinkling crack cocaine on top of weed, and he told her that Hakeem had caught his third felony case and was facing the "three strikes and you out" law.

When a C.O. tapped Donnell on his shoulder and barked, "Five minutes," Sharday couldn't believe their time was already up. Tears rolled down her face as she stood and met him at the end of the table for their final hug and kiss. "I'm gonna miss you, Boo," she said, squeezing him tight.

"Me, too, Day-Day. I love you, babe," he whispered into her ear. And then he released her and left without a backward glance.

THIRTY-SEVEN

When school started back up on Monday, Sharday tried to put some space between herself and Malcolm. She started having lunch with Ayanna from math class and her cool crew of friends. But when it became clear that Ayanna and them were into hooking school, Sharday backed off. She wasn't into cutting class anymore.

By Friday of the following week, she found herself back to having lunch with Malcolm again. They were sitting in the car eating in a companionable silence when she abruptly said, "I smoke weed, Malcolm. A lot."

He finished chewing and swallowed, then he said, "Oh, yeah? Chang smokes bud, too."

Sharday shook her head impatiently. Chris Chang was Malcolm's best friend. He was at the table that day when she'd told Lorie off and she had seen him quite a few times with Malcolm since then. He was alright, but he was basically just a rich Asian boy from the burbs. "Malcolm, I've been smoking weed since I was thirteen years old," she said. "I used to get high at least three or four times a week before I moved out here. Probably more."

He looked at her and said, "Okay, Sharday. And?" She had been pulling away from him ever since spring break. First, she began having lunch with Ayanna instead of with him. And now, he didn't know what she was trying to do.

"And I'm not like most of the girls you know," she said defensively. "Like I told you before."

He continued to hold her gaze. "And?" he asked again softly.

She shrugged. "And I'm just not the person you think I am. I'm from the hood. The real hood. You might think you know me, but you really don't."

This wasn't the first time she'd told him that he didn't really know her, so he said, "Well, what do I need to know about you that I don't already know, Sharday?"

She shrugged again and said, "I don't know, Malcolm. Everything. It's like . . . like I ain't being the real me no more now that we done moved out here." She knew she was slipping into her ghetto English, but she didn't care. "I mean, I used to cuss all the time and stay high and cut school and . . . and just wild out whenever I felt like it. Basically, I used to do all the stuff people in the ghetto do."

"But I don't care about your past," he said.

"But that's who I really am," she said in frustration. "I grew up in the ghetto all my life. One little year of living in the burbs can't change all that."

Malcolm just looked at her. He couldn't believe she thought some weed-smoking and curse words were going to run him off. "Sharday, you know the kinds of things I've seen," he said. "Children dying of malnutrition, kids and women toting machine guns and using them, too. You and I both know that I'm not your typical suburban teen either."

"You just don't understand," she said. "Living on a military base ain't the same thing as really living something. You a lot more like these people out here in Mitchellville than I could ever be."

"And if I don't have a problem with that, why do you?" he asked. "I accept you for who you are."

"But you ain't never seen who I really am because I been hiding a lot of stuff from you. I mean, you just finding out that I get high. And you met Tyesha, but you don't know nothing about my other two best friends from the hood. One of them got pregnant and dropped out of school and the other one started smoking crack. But that's the kind of stuff you don't know about me."

"Then stop judging me on things I don't know," he said. "Put me to the test, Sharday. Stop hiding and let me in."

She didn't know what to say to that because the main thing he needed to know -- the truth about Donnell, she just couldn't bring herself to tell him. Fortunately, the bell for fifth period rang and saved her. "I gotta be on time for chemistry," she said, and then she quickly began stuffing the rest of her lunch back into her bag.

THIRTY-EIGHT

Over the next few weeks, Sharday tried to shock Malcolm with increasingly wild stories about the things she'd seen and done in the hood. She got high with her friends whenever he came to *The Cellar* on Friday nights. She even started dropping hood slang in their conversations. But no matter what she said or did, his feelings toward her never seemed to change.

For his part, Malcolm was glad that Sharday had made the decision to trust him. He felt a lot closer to her now that she had let him into her "real life," as she called it. And even though she still mentioned her out-of-town boyfriend, he could tell that she felt closer to him, too.

But when the first week of May rolled around and the rest of the seniors started buzzing about the prom, Malcolm dragged his feet about asking Sharday to go. What if she planned to take her boyfriend instead of going with him? There was no way on Earth he could watch her play up to another man for the entire night.

When he casually brought up the subject that weekend in the studio, she said, "I've been thinking about just skipping it."

He looked up in surprise. That was the last thing he expected her to say. "But why would you do that?" he asked. "The senior prom is a rite of passage."

"Because it won't be the same now," she said with a shrug. "I always planned to go to Ballou's prom. With all my friends." And with Donnell, she thought but didn't add.

He smiled, relieved that her boyfriend wasn't the issue. "Come on, Sharday," he said. "It'll be fun. I'll be there with you. And then we can meet up with your friends at one of the Ballou after-parties."

"I don't know," she said. "I need some time to think about it."

Later that night, she caught Vickie alone in the kitchen and said,

"Guess what, Ma? Malcolm asked me to go to the prom with him."

"Oh, baby, that's wonderful!" Vickie exclaimed. She rushed across the room and gave Sharday a hug. "I knew he would ask you! I just knew it!"

"Well, I didn't, Ma. And for real, I wasn't even planning to go."

"But baby, this is your one and only senior prom we're talking about," Vickie said. She placed her hands on her daughter's shoulders and said, "The prom is one of the very few occasions you'll never forget, baby. And you've worked so hard this year that you deserve to be there." She looked at Sharday knowingly then and added, "And if you let your loyalty to Donnell stop you from going, one day you'll end up resenting him for it. I can promise you that, baby."

THIRTY-NINE

In the end, not only did Sharday agree to go to the prom with Malcolm, but she also let him talk her into performing with him, too. Apparently, he had quite the reputation as a talented musician at school. And when the prom committee asked him to sing a few songs, he said the only way he'd do it was if she accompanied him.

Now, it was prom night and she stood at the foot of the steps in the foyer at home wearing an off-the-shoulder, lilac, Calvin Klein gown and high-heeled lilac sandals. As Malcolm fastened a purple, lilac and white corsage to her wrist, Vickie snapped half a roll of film as Bruce and April oohed and aahed. All three of them followed Sharday and Malcolm out to the white limousine, which they were sharing with Chris Chang and his girlfriend, Suzanne Kim, and then Vickie reloaded her camera and insisted that Chris and Suzanne get out of the car so she could get pictures of them, too.

Fifteen minutes and many pictures later, the chauffeur finally pulled off and honked as he turned out of the driveway.

"Sorry about that," Sharday said to Chris and Suzanne.

"Ha, you should've seen my mother," Suzanne said with a grin. "She was totally over the top."

Sharday chuckled and said, "Well, at least it's not just my mother." She accepted the wine glass of sparkling water Malcolm had poured for her and settled back into the luxurious leather seat. "This is nice," she said, stretching out her legs and looking up at the moon roof and the tiny white lights that ran along each side of the ceiling.

"I know," Suzanne said. "A girl could get used to this." She had on a strapless, burgundy satin gown that looked great on her petite frame, and now she slipped off her matching bolero jacket and placed it on the seat beside her.

"It's finally prom night!" Chris announced as he popped open a bottle of Korbel champagne. He filled glasses for himself and Suzanne, then he looked at Malcolm and Sharday and said, "You're sure?"

"Not yet," Sharday said. "But thanks."

Malcolm raised his glass of sparkling water and said, "We'll catch up later, dude."

"Well, let's have a toast," Chris said. "To senior year! And the fact that it's almost over!" "I know that's right," Sharday said at the same time Suzanne was saying, "You can say that again!"

"And to the prom," Malcolm said. "May this be a night to remember."

They all touched glasses and drank.

It wasn't long before the chauffeur turned off Mitchellville Road and pulled to a stop behind a line of limos in front of the Radisson Hotel. He hopped out of the car and hurried around to the sidewalk to open the rear doors. "I'll be in the parking lot out back," he said. "Just call me on my cell phone and I'll come right back around. You all still have my business cards, right?" He was a tall, slim, dark-skinned, black man. He made sure to get a nod from each of them before he smiled and said, "Okay, then! Enjoy the prom!"

Malcolm reached for Sharday's hand and Suzanne slipped her arm through Chris' extended elbow, then they followed the steady stream of teenagers up the sidewalk, past the doorman who said, "Welcome to the Radisson," and down a hallway beyond the reception desk to the ballroom.

The lights were off in the spacious room, but it was illuminated by twinkling stars, lighted planets, and a huge full moon that were all suspended from the ceiling. Additional lighting was provided by candles that had been placed inside the miniature stellar constellations that graced the tables surrounding the dance floor, and above the stage at the front of the room was a blinking banner that read, *The Sky Is The Limit For Us!*

The prom had started almost forty-five minutes earlier, so most of the seniors were already there. Malcolm, Chris and Suzanne seemed to know every student in the room, but Sharday barely knew all the names of the people in her classes. And by the time they made it across the room to take their official prom photos, she was already starting to feel out of place.

She smiled into the photographer's lens for the picture as Malcolm held her close. She carried on a pleasant conversation with Suzanne once they sat down and Malcolm and Chris went for drinks at the alcohol-free bar. But all the while, she just wanted the whole thing to be over so they could move on to the after-party with her friends.

Finally, ten o'clock rolled around and it was time for her and Malcolm to perform. They stood off to the side of the stage waiting for the emcees, a skinny black cheerleader and a beefy white wrestler, to introduce them.

"Everybody having a good time tonight?" the wrestler bellowed into his microphone. The crowd roared and he said, "So am I! And now we're getting ready to crank this party up a notch!"

"Wait a minute, wait a minute," the cheerleader said. "First, let's have a round of applause for the deejay before he goes on break." And then, after the cheers died down, "Okay! Now, our special guest tonight needs no introduction because we've been bumping to his music for the last three years. So, everybody, please welcome Malcolm Werther to the stage! He'll be joined by Sharday Grant, one of our new students."

Malcolm grabbed Sharday's hand and led her on stage to rapturous applause. As he sat down at his keyboard and she took her place behind the stand-alone microphone, some of the seniors began chanting, "Mal-colm, Mal-colm."

Sharday was beginning to feel really uncomfortable standing up there and her smile wavered slightly, but then Malcolm started playing and her professionalism kicked in. They sang three songs back to back -- one ballad and two up-tempo numbers that the students could dance to. And by the time they finished, everyone was chanting Sharday's name right along with Malcolm's.

Malcolm and Sharday grinned at each other and took a bow. Then, just as they had rehearsed, they pretended to leave the stage before coming back and singing a medley of Rihanna and Drake songs. The crowd erupted in wild applause when they finally took their last bow and left for good.

Backstage, Malcolm felt so dizzy with emotion that he embraced Sharday and held her close for a long time. He'd had no idea that singing with her one-on-one in public would seem so . . . so intimate. The private time they spent together in the studio was nothing by comparison. "Sharday, that was phenomenal," he said after he released her.

"I know," she admitted. She had felt the connection, too.

They were still standing there smiling at each other when a member of the prom committee, a white girl named Rachel Billows, walked up and said, "So, here you two are! Come on! Everybody's out there waiting for you!"

Sharday and Malcolm received a standing ovation when they followed Rachel back into the ballroom, and as they made their way back to the table, a number of students came up to offer their compliments.

Suzanne jumped up to give them both a hug before they sat down. "That was superb!" she said. "The whole school will be talking about this next week!" She grinned at Malcolm and said, "You went to a higher level tonight, Malcolm! Truly!" Then she turned to Sharday and said, "And you! I had no idea you could sing like that, Sharday! You blew away everybody in the room!"

Sharday smiled and said, "Thanks, Suzanne." She was floating on an adrenaline high, so when Chris suggested they all go out back to the limo for "some alcohol," she quickly agreed. "Now, that sounds like a plan," she said. "Count me in."

The four of them wandered the first floor of the hotel until they found an exit that led to the rear parking lot. But there were so many white limousines back there that they ended up having to call their chauffeur and ask him to flash the lights. Once they finally made it to their vehicle, Chris reached into the cooler he and Malcolm had stashed in the trunk and pulled out the bottle of Korbel he had opened earlier.

"Get a bottle of that Moet, too," Malcolm told him.

As Chris filled two glasses with Korbel, Malcolm poured two glasses of Moet.

"What, no beer tonight?" Sharday asked Malcolm in surprise. She had never seen him drink champagne before.

"Tonight is too important for beer," he said.

Chris toasted Malcolm and Sharday, Malcolm made a toast to an enchanted night, Suzanne gave a toast to the senior prom, and Sharday wished them all an exciting future. Sharday, Chris and Suzanne finished off the bottle of Moet, but Malcolm said he would wait until the after-party to have more. Then Chris produced a fat blunt and they all went around to the side of the building so that he could smoke it with Suzanne and Sharday.

By the time they made it back to the ballroom, the prom king and queen were wearing their crowns and the deejay was playing hip hop. They hit the dance floor and stayed there for more than an hour. But when the deejay switched to white rock and pop songs, Sharday said she needed a break.

Chris and Suzanne stayed on the dance floor for at least another thirty minutes, and it was well after one o'clock when they all climbed back into the limo and headed for their private after- party at the Holiday Inn in southwest DC with Tyesha, Mark, Kayla and John. They had reserved four adjoining rooms on the third floor -- one for each couple. And although Sharday had paid for Kayla and John's room with some of the money from her gig at *The Cellar*, nobody but the three of them and Tyesha and April were aware of it.

Sharday and her group made it to the hotel first. They took the two middle rooms and threw open the connecting doors, then they met up in Malcolm and Sharday's room to continue partying. While Malcolm set up the bluetooth speaker and put on a hip hop mix tape playlist, Chris pulled a bottle of champagne from the cooler, Suzanne helped him fill four glasses, and Sharday stuffed towels beneath the doorway leading to the hallway. By the time the Ballou crew arrived about twenty minutes later, Sharday and Suzanne had slipped off their shoes, Malcolm and Chris had taken off their jackets and ties, and Sharday was rolling a blunt.

Tyesha led her group in from the other adjoining room and said, "Okay, we're here! Let the party begin!" She wore a form-fitting black gown with a lace bodice, Kayla had on a butter yellow gown with rhinestone-covered straps and a generous A-line cut to hide the extra pounds she'd recently gained, and Mark and John pulled up the rear in their rented tuxedos.

Sharday grinned and said, "Right on time! Somebody give me some blunt paper. I just used the last one I had."

As Mark handed her a package of cognac-soaked blunt papers, she introduced Chris and Suzanne to everyone.

Mark and Chris dragged in the extra chairs from their adjoining rooms and everybody got comfortable before they took an inventory of their party supplies. Chris had three blunts, Sharday had enough weed for two more blunts, and Mark had a plastic baggie of weed and another package of blunt papers. Chris and Malcolm had two bottles of champagne left each, Tyesha and Mark had three bottles of Moet nestled in their small cooler, and Kayla and John had a huge blue and white thermos that they said John had filled with Freixenet champagne. Sharday and Tyesha knew that the thermos was actually filled with sparkling cider because Kayla was five weeks pregnant and couldn't drink anymore, but there was no reason for anybody else to know that.

Sharday lit her blunt and puffed on it a couple of times before passing it over Malcolm to Tyesha on her right. Chris lit one of his blunts and took a few tokes before handing it to Suzanne on his left. When Mark ripped open the second package of papers and started rolling another blunt, Kayla backed her chair away and turned to John, "Come on and dance," she said. "I ain't smoking tonight."

As Tyesha handed Sharday's blunt to Mark, Malcolm looked at Suzanne and said, "I'll hit that one next."

Sharday and Chris turned to Malcolm in surprise. "What, you're smoking now?" Sharday asked him at the same time Chris said, "Dude, you're kidding, right?"

"Just one hit," Malcolm said. "I want to know what it feels like." He took the joint from Suzanne's outstretched hand and inhaled hard, then he started choking and quickly passed it to Sharday.

Sharday put the blunt in the ashtray and started rubbing Malcolm's back.

Chris grabbed a bottle of water from the cooler and twisted off the cap. "Here, drink this," he said, handing it to Malcolm.

Malcolm finished coughing and drank some of the water, then he laughed and said, "I've been wanting to try that for a long time."

After Kayla and John headed off to their room early and Malcolm announced that he would have only one more glass of champagne for the night, Sharday, Chris, Suzanne, Mark and Tyesha proceeded to get totally ripped. Finally, Chris looked up through bloodshot eyes and said, "We've only got the limo for three and a half more hours. So, it's been fun, but Suzanne and I are out of here." He reached for her hand and said, "Right, SuziePooh?" Then he unsteadily rose to his feet.

Mark said, "That's what I'm talking about." Then he turned to Tyesha and said, "You ready to go back to the room, too, baby?"

Tyesha nodded and let him help her up from her seat before she looked at Sharday and said, "Room service at five o'clock sharp, right? I'll call Kayla and John."

"We'll be there," Sharday said.

Malcolm glanced up at Chris and said, "Are you in, dude?"

Chris shook his head doubtfully. "Um, I don't think we--"

Suzanne spoke up quickly then. "We'll just meet you back here at six," she told Malcolm, "when it's time to go back down to the limo."

Chris and Suzanne headed off in one direction and Mark and Tyesha headed off in the other. After they closed their connecting doors and slid their locks into place, Malcolm looked at Sharday and said, "I'd better lock ours, too. I'll be right back."

He closed and locked the doors leading to the other rooms, then he turned off most of the lights and put on a playlist of R&B ballads. "You feel like dancing?" he asked her when a Jill Scott song came on.

"Sure," she said.

He took her into his arms and caressed her back as they swayed to the music. And as he slowly moved his hands south, he leaned forward to claim her mouth for a kiss. He had hit that blunt to give him an extra edge and he had purposely limited his drinking so he could remember every minute of what was getting ready to happen. Because if Sharday would have him, he planned to give her his virginity tonight.

She slipped her tongue into his mouth and squeezed his behind. She was so high, she was having a great time, and she didn't want the fun to stop. And anyway, it was part of the ritual to get your groove on after the prom.

When Malcolm began maneuvering them closer to the bed, she willingly followed. Since this was a one-time shot and they both knew the score, she planned to enjoy it.

He partially unzipped her gown and freed her breasts from the strapless bra. She unbuttoned his shirt and ran her hands across the expanse of his chest. They slowly undressed each other and carefully arranged their clothes on separate chairs, then they pulled back the covers and lay down on the queen-sized bed.

He was an expert at foreplay, so he gradually brought her to an explosive climax with his hands and mouth. But then he ejaculated into his condom before he could fully enter her.

"God, this is so embarrassing!" he said in frustration. He rolled off of her and lay down on his back, pulling the cover up over his groin. "I know most guys blow it their first time, but I thought I would be different," he muttered.

She turned to look at him in disbelief. "You mean you're a virgin?" she asked. He had played her body like an instrument. To the point that she had literally cried out in ecstasy.

"Well . . . technically, yes," he admitted. "But I'm not totally inexperienced," he quickly added.

"Well, I can vouch for that," she said with a sexy smile as she rolled over to fully face him. "And I'm glad you told me, Malcolm. Because your first time is supposed to be special."

"It has been special," he said softly, smiling back at her.

"And it's not over yet," she told him, then she sat up and leaned over him to unroll the spent condom.

FORTY

By the following Monday, Sharday had become a celebrity at school. The students in her classes fawned over her shamelessly, and every time she stepped into the hallway between classes, a crowd quickly formed. But after a year of feeling almost invisible, the sudden popularity seemed weird to her. So, when lunch time finally rolled around, she practically bolted out to the parking lot for a break from it all.

Malcolm was standing next to the car talking to a group of students and she motioned for him to come over. "Let's just eat outside today," she told him, grabbing his arm and leading him toward the rear of the building. "Everybody's been pushing up on me all morning and I need some time to regroup."

"Okay," he said.

A number of students called out to them as she led him down the sidewalk that ran alongside the building, but they just waved and kept walking. It was spring and the weather was nice, so people were everywhere. But Sharday had discovered a couple of private hideaways at the beginning of the year when she used to eat outside all the time.

As she steered Malcolm toward a private spot near the portables, he said, "You won't believe this, Sharday, but now a ton of people want to hire us to sing at their parties. Graduation parties, birthday parties, fourth of July parties, and every other kind of party you can think of. I got so many calls last night that my mother ended up taking the landline off the hook."

She looked at him in surprise and said, "Really? What did you tell them?"

"That I would run it by you and get back to them. What else could I say?"

"Oh," she said. And then, "So, you think they're serious?"

He nodded. "Definitely. Some people were actually trying to reserve dates. And all of them wanted to talk money."

"Oh," she said again.

After they sat down on a secluded grassy hill where they were partially hidden by a clump of trees, he pulled her to him for a kiss and she gave him some tongue. They had shared something really special a couple of nights ago and it had changed things between them for now. But she knew she would eventually have to maneuver them back to their former friendship.

For his part, Malcolm was happy that his plan was already starting to work. He was in love with Sharday and he was determined to steal her away from her boyfriend. So, he had recently accepted a spot in Georgetown's freshman class to be close to her, turning down his first choice of Cornell and a number of other equally good universities in the process. But he knew he had a whole year before her boyfriend moved to town, and he would be a fool not to take advantage of the opportunity.

They sat very close together, thighs touching, as they ate in a companionable silence. She eventually turned to him and said, "So, do you wanna do it?"

"I think it would be fun," he said. "Don't you?"

She shrugged. "Maybe. But I've already got the gig at *The Cellar*. But then again, school will be over and I'll only be working part-time for the summer."

"So, we'll just pick and choose the jobs we want," he encouraged her. "And I'll handle all the details." If they did this, he could take the summer off without working, like his parents wanted him to do, but he wouldn't have to be totally dependent on them for money. And since they were still kind of pissed at him for picking a local university instead of going away to college, he wanted to try to get back in their good graces.

"Okay, let's do it," she said. She needed all the professional singing experience she could get. And the extra money -- however much it turned out to be, certainly wouldn't hurt. "But no graduation parties," she said as an afterthought. "We'll be having our own parties anyway."

FORTY-ONE

Mitchellville High's graduation ceremony was held on the third Friday in June at the U.S. Air Arena in nearby Landover, Maryland. The arena was a huge indoor facility with rows of seats extending upwards to dizzying heights. But today, those seats were roped off and hundreds of folding chairs had been set up on the expansive center floor to accommodate the graduates and their families.

The seniors were seated alphabetically according to last names at the front of the room, which put Sharday near the center of the third row. And now, as she sat there at ten thirty in the morning waiting for the speeches to end, she was so excited she could barely contain herself.

Her life was finally starting to turn back around! She was done with Mitchellville High! This last year of school had been harder than all her other years put together, but she had made it through. And not only that, but she was coming out with grades good enough to get into PG Community.

She grinned as she thought of the great weekend she was going to have. After a small brunch with her mother and Bruce, April, and Frank and Belinda, April was treating her to a pedicure, manicure and massage at a black-owned day spa in uptown DC. Later that night, she would do her gig at *The Cellar* before heading over to the graduation party Malcolm and Chris were having. And then the following evening, she was having a backyard barbeque of her own and most of her relatives from Philly were coming down.

She eagerly returned her attention to the stage when the last speaker finished talking and the principal stepped up to the podium. But the rest of the ceremony flew by in a blur for her. Within minutes, the first group of seniors stood on cue and the vice-principal, senior faculty advisor, and guest speaker lined up beside the principal. Then, she was receiving her diploma and flipping the tassel on her cap as she smiled down at Bruce, who was crouched at the foot of the stage recording everything with his digital camcorder. And it seemed she had just settled back into her seat when *Pomp and Circumstance* began to play and it was all over.

She felt dazed as she rose with her row and filed down the aisle to the rear of the arena. When she stepped through the doors leading to the enormous inner lobby, she was surprised to see that some of the female graduates were crying.

She couldn't relate at all. She was happy that she would never have to step foot in Mitchellville High again. And with that thought, her earlier excitement returned. The way she saw it was the same way the valedictorian had put it: The future was theirs for the taking; all they had to do was step up and embrace it. And she couldn't wait to embrace her future.

PART THREE

Lanham, Maryland

FORTY-TWO

Sharday and Tyesha moved into their own apartment the weekend before college registration started. They had found an affordable two bedroom in a decent neighborhood in Lanham, Maryland, which was close to both "PG" and "Maryland," their schools. And they would be within a mile of a subway station and on several major bus routes.

Bruce, Malcolm, and Malcolm's younger brother, Evan, moved the girls' furniture in, while Vickie and April helped them unpack the household items they had bought over the summer. They didn't have much, so the whole process took only a few hours. But once everything had been set up, the apartment looked cozy and inviting.

In the living area, they had an old sofa and coffee table from the basement of the house in Mitchellville, a torchiere lamp, a framed poster of a field of wildflowers, and an inexpensive mini-entertainment center that held Sharday's Bluetooth stereo and television. Their wooden dinette set had come from a thrift store, but they'd covered the table with a pretty floral tablecloth. And although Sharday's room was a little tight because she'd squeezed the studio in there with some of her bedroom furniture from home, the full bedroom set Tyesha had bought secondhand through the *Washington Post* fit comfortably in her room.

Bruce ordered in pizzas and buffalo wings, and they all settled down in the combination living and dining area to wait for the food.

"This is great," Malcolm said to Sharday, who was seated beside him at the dining room table. "I would love to have an apartment like this."

"Out of the question, young man!" Evan said in a deep voice, obviously mocking their father. "You're going to live in the dorms. We want you to have the *full college experience*," he managed to add before he burst out laughing.

Sharday, Tyesha and April started laughing, too, but Malcolm said, "Oh, grow up, Evan. I bet it won't be so funny in three years when it's your turn."

Bruce spoke up from his seat on the sofa. "Well, if it makes you feel any better, Malcolm," he said, "I lived on campus my first two years at Hampton and those were some of the best times of my life. I wouldn't trade them for anything."

"The important thing is that you're going to college," Vickie told Malcolm. "It doesn't matter where you live while you're doing it."

There was a knock at the door just then and Tyesha got up to answer it. "I know this can't be the pizzas already," she said as she put her eye to the peephole. Then she said, "Oh, it's Isaiah," and she quickly unlocked the door to admit April's new boyfriend.

Isaiah was a tall, handsome seventeen-year-old April had met at the mall back in July. He and his family had recently moved to the area from Delaware. And he would be a senior at Mitchellville High this year along with April.

Now, he entered the apartment wearing cornrows, a small diamond stud in each ear, and drooping jean shorts with a white tee. "Sorry, I'm so late," he said to the room at large as he smiled at April. "But the doctor's office was so crowded. And I had to get my booster shot."

"Uh huh," Sharday teased him. "You would show up now that all the work's done, wouldn't you?" She liked Isaiah. He was basically a good boy with a slight, hip-hop edge. And as far as she was concerned, that made him perfect for the new and improved April.

He laughed and said, "Go on, Sharday. I wouldn't do that to you and Tyesha." He said a quick "what's up" to Malcolm and Evan -- Malcolm was always around and he knew Evan from Sharday and Malcolm's private gigs, then he made his way over to the sofa where April, Bruce and Vickie were seated.

April beamed as Isaiah crossed the room. She still couldn't believe how great her life was now. She had become a fly girl with a hip boyfriend who was totally crazy for her. And she had a lot more friends because Sharday's popularity at school had spilled over onto her. She felt like she was living in color now, whereas she had been living in black and white before.

Over the course of the next hour, Sharday and Tyesha's move-in day turned into an impromptu party. The pizzas and buffalo wings arrived. Gloria and Jolean came over in a taxi and Gloria brought homemade spaghetti, a tossed salad with French dressing, and a huge glass pickle jar filled with iced tea. Even Frank and Belinda stopped by. They brought a potted palm tree and a rotisserie chicken with fixings from *Boston Market*. And now that Frank and Sharday had established a closer relationship, Vickie, Bruce, and April were slowly beginning to accept him and his girlfriend into the fold.

They were all sitting around listening to music and having a good time when Kayla and John showed up. Kayla and John had gotten married right after graduation. Now, John was working as a security guard and Kayla was on public assistance, and they were living in a small two-bedroom apartment on Malcolm X Avenue in southeast.

Kayla was wearing maternity clothes these days and she stayed hungry all the time. So, she hugged Sharday and Tyesha and gave them a wrapped gift, said a friendly "How y'all doing?" to everyone else, and then she headed straight for the food.

"Kayla, you getting too big too quick," Gloria said. "You better slow down some, else you won't never lose all that weight."

"I be trying, Miss Gloria," Kayla said as she spooned an extra serving of spaghetti onto her plate. "But it's like I just can't help myself."

"Girl, you know you always been greedy," Sharday joked. "Don't even try to blame it on the baby." She had finally learned to turn her ghetto speech on and off at will, depending on who she was talking to.

Kayla laughed and said, "Day-Day, I know you ain't talking."

"Ooh, look at these!" Tyesha said. She had opened John and Kayla's gift and she was holding up a set of red pasta pots with water draining lids.

"I just saw those on TV last night!" Jolean said.

"That's the perfect gift for college students," Belinda said from the living room. "Pasta's cheap and easy to make."

"That's true," Vickie said. "But if you use the right sauce, it can be a very sophisticated dish, too."

"Thanks Kayla and John," Sharday said with a big grin. "We'll use them every chance we get." She knew money was really tight for them, and that made her appreciate the gift even more. The party lasted for two more hours because everyone was having so much fun. But shortly after three, people started slowly trickling out. And by four o'clock, Sharday and Tyesha had the apartment all to themselves.

They were both bubbling over with excitement, so they spent quite a while running from room to room and making a bunch of silly comments that all included the words "our new apartment." After they finally calmed down, they pulled out the bottle of Moet and bag of weed they had bought just for the occasion. Then they put towels up to the front door, lit an incense and cracked a window, and proceeded to get totally twisted.

They were sitting on the sofa finishing off the last of the champagne when Sharday said, "Too bad Elise and LaShawn couldn't be here today. I can't help it, Tyesha. I still miss our girls."

Tyesha drained her glass and said, "It's time to move on, Day-Day. I feel sorry for them, but everybody can't make it out of the ghetto. That's just the way life works. And anyway, LaShawn's a crack hoe now, so she's not even the same person we used to know."

Sharday looked at Tyesha and shook her head. The girl could be so cold when it came to cutting people out of her life. Over the summer, she had gotten rid of every single guy she was dating, including Mark. And when Sharday called her on it, she said, "I was a girl from the ghetto, so I dated boys from the ghetto, Day-Day. But I'm getting ready to be a college student from the burbs soon and that's the kind of men I plan to start dealing with."

Now, Tyesha shook her head back at Sharday and said, "Girl, you need to stop being so sentimental all the time. Everything's working out just like it's supposed to. And once school starts next week, we'll be meeting plenty of new people."

FORTY-THREE

Sharday had already quit the choir and put her mother and Bruce on notice that she wouldn't be attending church every week anymore. So, on Sunday morning, she got up at the crack of dawn and caught the early bus to Allentown. Since she was making the trip alone this time, she stretched out across two seats and wedged her purse firmly behind her back. Then she turned on her iPod and selected a Lil' Wayne song.

It wasn't long before the bus was hurtling up the interstate and she was lost in thought about the coming school year. She was planning to register for a total of seven classes this semester. But since each class met only two or three times a week, she would have a lot more free time than she'd had in high school, even when she factored in her job.

She had taken a part-time position as a retail clerk at *Old Navy* in Annapolis Mall that started right after graduation. And over the summer, she had worked whenever the managers scheduled her for a total of twenty-five hours each week. But now that college was starting up, she would be working on the weekends only -- from noon to eight on Saturdays and Sundays, which meant that she would be able to hang out as long as she wanted on Friday and Saturday nights since she no longer had a curfew.

She couldn't resist a grin at the thought. She was finally in control of her own life! From now on, she could do whatever she wanted whenever she wanted to do it. She didn't have to get anybody's permission first. And thanks to her and April's plan to switch off on the car every other week, she would also have twenty-four hour access to a vehicle two weeks out of each month.

She was still smiling when the yawns overtook her -- she and Tyesha hadn't gone to bed the night before until after midnight. So, she switched from Lil' Wayne to *CrazySexyCool*, an old TLC album, and then she lowered the volume on her MP3 player and settled in for a nap.

As it turned out, she ended up sleeping on and off for the rest of the trip. And it wasn't until they were about twenty minutes away from Allentown that she finally got up and went to the bathroom to pull herself together. One big mac meal, one taxi ride, and a series of C.O.s later, and she was kissing and hugging Donnell.

He reached for her hands after they sat down and said, "Well, I'll be damned. You actually made it up this joint on a Sunday."

She smiled and said, "See, and you ain't even believe I was coming. Why you doubting me like that, Boo?"

"I know your moms probably went off and shit," he said. "But fuck that, Day-Day, you grown now. And sooner or later, she gonna have to accept that."

She shook her head and said, "Nah, Boo, it ain't even like that. Ma cool with me doing my own thing now." In reality, Vickie had pitched a fit when Sharday announced that she was quitting the choir and wouldn't be going to church regularly anymore. And Bruce was the one who finally managed to convince Vickie that once Sharday moved out, the only things they could demand were that she kept up her grades and always had her part of the rent money. But Sharday didn't mention any of that to Donnell because she knew he already didn't care too much for her mother.

To change the subject, she started telling him about the new apartment. And even though she tried her best to keep her voice matter of fact, it was obvious that she was thrilled to be living on her own with Tyesha.

Donnell felt threatened by all of the changes going on in her life. She was supposed to be living with him right now, not in some other apartment with Tyesha's stuck up ass. And all that college shit was a problem, too. What if she started thinking she was better than him? What if she met some college boy she thought had more to offer her?

He wished he could turn time back and do everything all over again. At the very least, he wished he could get her to just go back to Mitchellville and sit tight until he got out. But none of that was an option. So, he had to do the best he could under the circumstances. Because he would rather die than lose Sharday.

He brought her up to date on his literacy classes and told her that his poetry teacher said his rhymes were way better than they had been when he first joined the group. Then he told her that a couple of inmates with contacts in the industry had already started talking him up so their people would be expecting to hear from him when he got out. And just before she left, he said,

"Nine more months, Day-Day. That's all we got left now. I be outta this bitch before you know it."

On the bus ride back home, Sharday realized that she was going to have to break off her relationship with Malcolm altogether. She had planned to steer them back to a platonic friendship over the summer, but instead they had gotten even closer because of the private gigs they did and all the time they spent hanging out together. And now that they were sleeping together on the regular, going back to friends only status was definitely out of the question.

She sighed and lay her head back against the seat. It was going to be hard to walk away from Malcolm because she had already developed feelings for him. But Donnell would be coming home soon. And she was still in love with her Boo. So, it was time for her to finally let Malcolm go.

FORTY-FOUR

Sharday and Tyesha were having the time of their lives. They took advantage of their newfound freedom every chance they got. But even though they generally partied into the wee hours of the morning on Friday and Saturday nights, they both took their responsibilities toward work and school very seriously.

Tyesha was on a strict schedule during the week. She had scored an internship at the Department of Energy over the summer and had done so well at her job that they kept her on part-time during the school year. She was making a lot more money than she could have made working part-time anywhere else. But she had to be at work from two to six each weekday afternoon, which meant that she had to take all of her classes in the mornings.

Sharday's schedule was exactly the opposite. Mondays through Fridays were pretty laid back for her because none of her classes started before ten in the morning and she was generally home by two or three. But on Saturdays and Sundays, she had to put in her eight-hour shifts at *Old Navy*.

After the first few weeks, Sharday and Tyesha fell into a routine. Tyesha was usually up and gone to class on weekdays before Sharday even got out of bed. And by the time Sharday got home from class, Tyesha was already at her job. So, Sharday would watch her favorite soap opera or do something equally inane to unwind, and then she would spend the rest of the afternoon studying at her desk.

The huge amount of homework she'd had at Mitchellville High didn't even begin to compare with college. Each of her professors had handed out a packed syllabus on the first day of class and said it was up to the students to get the assignments done in time for quizzes, exams, and papers or projects. And Sharday was determined to stick to her list of exactly what she needed to do every week to stay on top of her studies.

At about seven in the evenings, which was when Tyesha got home, Sharday would close her books so they could have dinner. They mostly ate the food she got from Vickie on Sunday nights when the car was handed off. Otherwise, one of them would make a pot of spaghetti, a box of hamburger helper, or something else easy.

After dinner, Tyesha would study at the dining room table. And since Sharday still had to put out a lot more effort than Tyesha, who seemed to practically fly through her assignments, she frequently joined Tyesha. But sometimes, Sharday would work on her music or spend time with Malcolm -- she still hadn't found the strength to end her relationship with him. And if it was her week to have the car, she might even go visit her father and Belinda, or hang out in Mitchellville with her mother, Bruce and April.

But on Fridays, Sharday always gave herself a break. She stayed on campus for a few extra hours after her last class. And then, whether she went back to the apartment or somewhere else, she would goof off for the rest of the day. Later in the evening, she would do a mini-rehearsal for her gig before she and Tyesha started getting dressed to go out for the night. And once Malcolm, April, Isaiah, Kayla and John showed up, they would all go to *The Cellar* together.

After Sharday gave her performance, they would party at *The Cellar* until about midnight. The night was over for Kayla, John, April and Isaiah at that point, thanks to Kayla's advancing pregnancy and April's curfew. But Sharday, Malcolm and Tyesha would hit the college parties and come dragging back into the apartment at three or four in the morning. And then, Malcolm would spend the night and leave when Sharday went to work on Saturday morning.

On Saturday nights, Sharday and Tyesha would do it all over again, hitting the go-gos first and then moving on to the college parties. Malcolm initially joined them, but once he and Sharday finished the last of their private gigs, he started staying in on Saturday nights. He needed to be fresh for church on Sunday mornings since he was still singing in the choir. And according to him, there had been more than one Sunday morning when he could barely keep his eyes open at church.

While Sharday was at work on the weekends, Tyesha spent all her time on campus at Maryland. She said she wanted to be a part of normal college life, just like Malcolm's father wanted him to be. So, she studied in the library, sat around in the student union, went to the *Terps* games, and did whatever else the other students who lived on campus did.

She eventually began to meet a lot of new people and it wasn't long before some of the guys started asking her out. But so far, she had turned every one of them down. When Sharday asked her why, she said, "Day-Day, I don't want to get hooked up with some freshman or sophomore who's going to be a broke ass student just like I am for the next few years. I'm holding out for a senior. Somebody who's going to be out making serious cheddar next year."

Sharday thought that was a jacked-up way for Tyesha to approach relationships. But since her own personal life was so screwed, how could she say anything? She just shrugged and said, "I hope you know what you're doing." And she knew that applied to her own situation even more.

FORTY-FIVE

One Saturday morning in early October, Sharday and Malcolm were tangled up together in her bed when they were awakened by the sound of someone pounding on the front door of the apartment. Malcolm immediately panicked, jumping out of bed to gather his clothes.

Sharday was groggy -- it was eight in the morning and they hadn't gotten in until four the night before. And at the sight of Malcolm running around the room collecting his clothes, she started laughing.

"I'm glad you think it's funny," he said as he struggled into his pants. "But what if that's your mother?"

Sharday stopped laughing and quickly got up. "If I start whistling, hide in the closet," she told him as she put on her robe. "I'll be right back."

By the time she made it to the living room, Tyesha was already starting to unlock the door. "Tyesha!" she whispered loudly, rushing across the room to throw herself in front of the door. "Who is it? Is it my mother?"

"Get out of the way," Tyesha said. "It's Jolean. Something must be wrong."

"Oh, my God," Sharday said. And she moved so Tyesha could open the door.

Jolean stepped into the apartment, took one look at her big sister, and suddenly burst into tears. "I . . . I . . . ain't got nowhere to live now, Tyesha," she said.

Tyesha pulled Jolean into an embrace and rubbed her back. "Come here, girl," she said. "What in the world are you talking about?"

"Momma practically threw me out," Jolean sobbed. "She let Walter move in. And I told her I wasn't living there if he was gonna be there. And she told me to do whatever I had to do because he wasn't leaving."

"Oh, my God," Sharday said again. Walter was an older man Gloria had met on the subway a few months ago. Tyesha and Jolean hated him because he was an alcoholic who worked on and off as a day laborer and they both felt their mother could do better.

"What?" Tyesha asked Jolean, clearly angry. "When did all this happen?"

"Last night," Jolean said.

"Oh, hell no," Tyesha said. "I know Momma's not choosing some old drunk over her own daughter."

"But she is, Tyesha," Jolean said, and then she started crying again.

"Not for long," Tyesha said. "We're going over there right now so we can get this shit straightened out. Give me a minute to throw on some jeans." She turned to Sharday, who had the car for the week, and said, "You can take us, right, Day-Day? Come on. Hurry up and get dressed."

"Okay," Sharday said. "But I need to let Malcolm know what's up first."

"Shit, I forgot all about Malcolm!" Tyesha said. And then, "But tell him it's an emergency, Day-Day. And tell him I'll find a way to make it up to him."

Sharday shrugged and said, "You know how Malcolm is. I'm sure he'll understand."

Fifteen minutes later, Sharday, Malcolm, Tyesha and Jolean were heading out the front door. Malcolm gave Sharday a quick kiss in the parking lot before he walked off toward the used Honda Civic his parents had bought him. She waited until he started his car before she pulled off.

Tyesha had managed to hold her silence while Malcolm was around. But even as Sharday turned out of the parking lot, her anger spilled over again. "What the hell is wrong with Momma?" she asked aloud in frustration. "I mean, come on! This is Walter we're talking about. And she's willing to throw everything away for him?"

"I know!" Jolean said from the backseat. She'd found her courage again now that she had her big sister to back her up. "But all Momma kept saying was how she deserves to be happy, too. Right! Like Walter can make somebody happy. Most of the time he's so drunk he doesn't even know where he is!"

The closer they got to southeast, the more agitated Tyesha and Jolean became. And Sharday's attempts to calm them down didn't change the situation one bit. By the time she climbed out of the car and followed them up the sidewalk past her old building, she knew this confrontation was going to be nothing pretty.

Tyesha unlocked the front door of the apartment with her old key and they all trooped inside to find Gloria standing at the window waiting for them. She was fully dressed, her hands were propped on her hips, and it was clear that she was pissed.

"Girl, you done lost your damn mind?" Gloria demanded of Jolean. "Don't you ever leave out of this house while I'm sleep like that again without telling me you going."

"I did what I had to do," Jolean said sarcastically. "Just like you told me to."

Gloria cut her eyes at Jolean and said, "Girl, who the hell you think you talking to? You ain't but fourteen years old. Don't think you too old to get your ass whipped."

Tyesha spoke up then. "Well, I'm too old to get mine whipped, Momma. So, maybe I should be the one doing the talking."

"Nah, you the one that need to be minding your own business," Gloria said. "Trust me."

"Well, when you kick my little sister out so you can move some man in here it is my business," Tyesha said. "What are you thinking, Momma? How could you choose a no-good bum like Walter over your own daughter?"

"Everybody knows he's a drunk," Jolean put in. "He's probably back there trying sleep another one off right now."

Gloria went off then. "Who the hell y'all think y'all is to be coming up in *my damn house* questioning *my* decisions?" she shouted at Tyesha and Jolean. "If I say Walter can move in, then that's the end of it and ain't nobody got nothing to say about it!"

"I live here, too!" Jolean shouted back. "So, I do have something to say about it!"

"I'm your mother, you ain't mine!" Gloria said. "I'm the one who pay the bills around here and make the rules! You the one that follow the rules and keep your damn mouth shut!"

Tyesha was outraged. "I don't think so, Momma!" she yelled, straining forward.

Sharday reached out to grab her arm then and said, "Calm down, Tyesha."

"Nah, Day-Day! It's crazy for her to be moving some old bum in here while she's still got a teenage daughter to raise! And if nobody else has the guts to tell her, I do!"

"That's it!" Gloria shouted. "I'm a grown woman and I'll be damned if I'm gonna stand here and argue with y'all about what I can and can't do in my own house!" She pointed at Tyesha and said, "It's time for you to go home, little girl. Because you about to write a check with your mouth I know your ass can't cash." Then she pointed at Jolean and said, "And you, you better take your little ass back there to your bedroom and stay out of my way for the rest of the day."

Jolean stood her ground, even though she looked scared. "As long as Walter's living here, I'm not staying here," she said.

"Then get your shit and go!" Gloria said furiously. "If you too grown to do what I say, you don't need to be here no damn way!" And with that, she marched off to her bedroom and slammed the door behind her.

Jolean started crying then, but Tyesha said, "Don't cry. She's tripping. Let's just go pack up some of your stuff."

"Yeah, you know you're always welcome to come stay with us," Sharday added.

Jolean stayed with Sharday and Tyesha for the next week and caught the subway back and forth to school. But the following weekend, she moved in with her father and his family.

FORTY-SIX

By mid-October, Sharday, Tyesha and Malcolm had totally shut down their social lives to prepare for midterms. Malcolm spent the bulk of his time either meeting with his study group or doing research for his papers. And Sharday and Tyesha had begun studying at the dining room table until well past midnight every night.

Malcolm and Tyesha still went with Sharday to *The Cellar* on Friday nights, as did April and Isaiah -- Kayla and John had stopped going now that Kayla's due date was fast approaching. But as soon as the gig was over, Sharday, Malcolm and Tyesha would head back to the apartment to hit the books. And then on Saturday nights, Malcolm would study in his dorm room while Sharday and Tyesha stayed home to do the same thing.

Once midterms actually got underway, Tyesha and Malcolm seemed to go on cruise control, but Sharday panicked and ended up pulling back-to-back all-nighters. "I'm not like you two. I have to keep going over and over it," she told Tyesha and Malcolm when they said the sleep would do her a lot more good.

She was so exhausted by the time she handed in her last exam on a Thursday afternoon that she went home and climbed straight into bed. She didn't wake up that Friday morning until a quarter to ten, so she decided to skip her classes and lounge around in her pajamas. But at noon, she got dressed and caught the subway to campus. Vickie was supposed to pick her up for a late lunch and she didn't want her mother to know that she had blown off school for the day.

Fortunately, by the time Vickie called on her cell phone to say she was double-parked in front of the administration building, Sharday was sitting in a student lounge two buildings away watching a soap opera. "I'll be right out," she told her mother. Then she grabbed her jacket and the backpack she'd brought for effect and headed outside.

Vickie snapped her cell phone shut with a smile of satisfaction. She was happy to finally have some quality time with her daughter. She hadn't seen Sharday for more than a few rushed minutes here or there ever since the girl had started studying for her midterms. And although she was proud of Sharday for applying herself in college and trying to establish her independence, she missed having her at home so much the ache was almost physical.

Vickie's life felt empty and lacking in purpose now that Sharday had moved out. And it certainly didn't help that Metro's year-end performance reviews were rolling around again and Bruce's workload had picked up. Not to mention the fact that April had become so popular she always had something to do and someone to do it with.

Vickie found herself with too much time on her hands these days and no idea of how to fill it. She was only working two days a week, on Tuesdays and Thursdays. And even though she had made friends with a couple of the women on her job, they were both full-time employees who had younger children and little or no free time.

But now, she grinned and pushed all that to the back of her mind when she saw her daughter hurrying toward the car. "Well, hello there, stranger!" she said, enveloping Sharday in a warm hug after she got in. "Congratulations on making it through your first set of college exams, honey."

"Thanks, Ma." Sharday buckled her seat belt, then she playfully swiped her forehead with the back of one hand and said, "Whew! I'm glad that's over! I've never studied so hard in my life!"

Vickie laughed and pulled off. "I know it was hard on you, baby," she said. "But I'm really proud of you for buckling down like that. You're turning out to be a very mature young woman."

"Thanks again, Ma. But let's just hope my grades reflect all the hard work."

"Oh, I'm sure you did just fine, baby," Vickie said. "You always do when you put your mind to it."

Sharday shrugged uncertainly. She thought she'd done okay, but she couldn't really be sure until the exams came back. "So, what's been up with you lately, Ma?" she asked, changing the subject. "How's the job coming?"

"Pretty good. Enough to keep me busy, but not so much that it's stressful or anything." Vickie did overflow administrative work for the sales department of a large insurance company.

"Anything new with Arlene's son?" Sharday asked. "Is the girl's mother still making her have the abortion?" Arlene was one of Vickie's new coworker friends whose fourteen-year-old son had recently gotten his girlfriend pregnant.

"Actually, that ended up working itself out," Vickie said. "Tiffany had a miscarriage a couple of weeks ago, or at least that's what she told Billy. Arlene thinks she wasn't ever pregnant and made the whole thing up. But she says it serves Billy right. Maybe now he'll learn how to keep his, and I quote, 'little wing wing in his pants.'"

Sharday laughed and said, "You have to let me meet her one day, Ma. She sounds like a trip."

"Oh, Arlene's turned out to be a total character," Vickie said. She told Sharday that Arlene was always mocking their coworkers, then she tried to demonstrate how Arlene mocked their boss's southern drawl.

From there, Vickie and Sharday segued into funny stories about things that had happened to them in the past. And by the time they made it to *The Cheesecake Factory* in Georgetown, they were both in high spirits.

They continued to reminisce over the meal, but Sharday couldn't help noticing that her mother had finished off both of the appetizers she'd insisted on ordering, plus every bite of her oversized entrée. And now Vickie was talking about ordering dessert.

"I can't even finish this," Sharday said, nodding toward her half-eaten basket of shrimp and fries. The portions at *The Cheesecake Factory* were huge. "But you're really putting it away today, Ma. Since when did your appetite get so big?

Vickie quickly closed the dessert menu and put it down, realizing that she'd eaten way more than she'd meant to in front of her daughter. She knew she'd been filling the void in her life with food lately. She had the extra pounds to prove it. But Bruce and April hadn't noticed yet, and she wasn't ready to admit it to Sharday either. So, she forced herself to laugh lightly and say, "Oh, I skipped breakfast this morning. But now that you mention it, dessert probably would be overkill."

She signaled the waitress for the check before Sharday could respond and said, "Come on, honey, let's get out of here." And then, with a mischevious lift of her eyebrows, she added, "Let's do some shopping before we head back. I mean, we are in Georgetown, after all."

FORTY-SEVEN

Jolean had begun staying over at the apartment a lot now that Sharday and Tyesha's schedules were returning to normal. She couldn't get along with her stepmother and she refused to go back home because Walter was still there. So, she was spending three or four nights each week with Tyesha and Sharday.

She would get her father to drop her off in Lanham on Monday or Tuesday night, and then she would catch the subway back and forth to school for the rest of the week. Her father would pick her up on Friday evening on his way home from work -- she said the weekends were a lot easier for her because he was home. And she would do it all over again the next week.

Since Tyesha and Jolean were still feuding with their mother as Thanksgiving approached, Sharday asked Vickie if she could bring them to Mitchellville for dinner.

"Of course, you can, Sharday," Vickie said. "You know Tyesha and Jolean are always welcome here. And anyway, April will be at Cathy's, as usual," she said, referring to April's mother. "And Felicia's going home to Chicago this year. So, we can use the extra company."

A few days later, Vickie took it upon herself to invite Gloria to Thanksgiving dinner, too. She was sure Gloria and her girls could work things out if they had a chance to talk without the boyfriend around. And Bruce had agreed to take Walter out to the garage or to the basement before dinner.

But as it turned out, Gloria and Walter didn't show up until the turkey had been carved, the grace had been said, and the food was being passed around the dining room table. Vickie hadn't told anyone but Bruce that she'd invited them -- she'd told the girls that the two extra place settings were just to round the table out. So when the doorbell rang, she looked up and said, "Hmm, sounds like we have a surprise visitor."

"On Thanksgiving Day?" Sharday said as she scooped a serving of candied yams onto her plate. "Nah, they're probably at the wrong address."

"We'll see," Vickie said as she stood and headed for the front door.

Bruce smiled as he watched Vickie walk away from the table. He was proud of her for wanting to help Gloria make up with Tyesha and Jolean. Cathy would never do anything like this -- she was too wrapped up in herself to think about anyone else. But thankfully, this time around, God had led him to the right woman.

A little while later, Vickie reappeared at the entrance to the dining room and said, "Surprise, everybody! Look who's here!" Then she stepped aside to reveal Gloria and Walter.

Gloria was looking ghetto fabulous in a red dress with a rhinestone trimmed v-neck and a furry jacket, and beside her was an older, emaciated Walter in a black suit and white shirt that were too big for him. He was holding a huge disposable aluminum container that was covered with aluminum foil.

"What?" Sharday said, dragging the word out in disbelief.

Jolean was too stunned to do anything but stare with her mouth hanging open.

Tyesha was clearly caught off guard, too, but she turned to Sharday and said, "What are they doing here?"

"Oh, so y'all ain't know we was coming, huh?" Gloria said as she stepped into the room.

Bruce quickly stood and smiled. "Happy Thanksgiving, Walter and Gloria," he said as he walked around the table toward them. "I'm glad you two were able to join us. I was just starting to think you might not make it."

Gloria shifted gears and gave Bruce a genuine smile. "Well, Happy Thanksgiving to you," she said. "Long time no see." She hugged him briefly before pointing to Walter. "This my boyfriend, Walter, Bruce. And that's my famous banana pudding he holding."

When Bruce turned his attention to Walter, Gloria headed over to the table where Tyesha, Jolean and Sharday had been whispering among themselves.

Sharday promptly pasted a smile onto her face and said, "Hi, Miss Gloria. Happy Thanksgiving." She didn't know what on Earth her mother had been thinking to invite Gloria and Walter without telling anyone. But now that they were here, she was going to do her part to make it work. Bruce would be horrified to see Gloria light into Tyesha and Jolean the way she had back in the hood. Not to mention the fact that it would totally ruin the holiday.

Tyesha and Jolean halfheartedly followed Sharday's lead. "Hi, Momma," they both murmured, almost in unison.

Fortunately, Vickie stepped up then and said, "Tyesha and Jolean! I'm surprised at you two! Get up and give your mother a hug!"

Jolean cast an anxious glance at Tyesha, who gave her an almost imperceptible nod in return. They both slowly rose and made their way around the table.

Vickie pulled Walter forward and shot Sharday a pointed look. "You remember, Walter, don't you, Sharday?" she said, motioning for Sharday to get up.

Sharday stood and headed around the opposite side of the table to shake Walter's hand and wish him a happy holiday. Vickie made Tyesha and Jolean do the same after they finished giving their mother a perfunctory hug, and Sharday took her turn with Gloria before they all headed for their seats.

When Bruce came back from taking Gloria's banana pudding to the kitchen, he said another blessing over the dinner. This time, he drew the prayer out longer, asking God to bless the two mothers at the table and adding some of his views about the importance of family. After he finally brought it to a close and everyone had contributed an "Amen," he looked around the table with an exuberant grin and rubbed his hands together. "Alright, folks!" he said. "It's time to get down to some serious eating!"

Plates were piled with heaping servings of all the traditional dishes, wine was poured for everyone except Jolean, who received sparkling cider, and the conversation started off easily enough because everybody had something to say about how delicious the meal was. But as the talk progressed to the unseasonably warm weather, and then on to the forthcoming *Redskins* game, it became painfully apparent that Tyesha and Jolean weren't participating.

And before anyone else could call them on it, Gloria glared across the table at her daughters and said, "Oh, what? So, now y'all supposed to be giving me the silent treatment?"

Jolean stared down at her plate, but Tyesha looked up at her mother and said, "Not really, Momma. It's more like we just don't have anything to say to you."

"Oh, yeah?" Gloria said. "Well, I ain't seen you in two months, Miss Smart Ass. And the last time I seen your sister was when she came with her daddy to get her stuff. So I got quite a damn bit to say to both of y'all."

"Now, just a minute, Gloria--" Bruce began.

Vickie cut in over him and said, "Come on now, Gloria. I know you're upset, but that's no reason to start cursing them out." She leaned over to touch Gloria's arm and said, "Why don't you wait until after dinner and talk it out with the girls in private. Give them a chance to have their say. I know it's not easy to listen to your own daughters questioning your judgment --- and believe me, I've been there with Sharday too many times to mention, but I find things usually work out better when I give her a chance to get her thoughts off her chest."

Bruce immediately jumped on the bandwagon. "Actually, Gloria, I've found the same to be true with April," he said. "Especially when I'm planning to do something that will affect her life, too." The situation that immediately came to his mind was his decision to marry Vickie. But, of course, he was too tactful to bring that up.

Walter didn't say anything, but he thought Vickie and Bruce were probably onto something. Maybe his own sons wouldn't still hate him so much if he had taken the time to really talk to them back when he and his wife had gone through the divorce. He grabbed his wine glass and took a gulp, wishing it were something stronger.

Gloria frowned and shook her head. "Well, I'm sorry y'all but I ain't into all of them new ideas about how to raise children. Now don't get me wrong, I love these two brats of mine just as much as anybody else love they children. If not more." She cut her eyes at her daughters then and said, "But *I'm* the mother, so y'all don't get no say about how I run my life. And that's just the way it go."

"Ex-actly," Tyesha said sarcastically as she swallowed a mouthful of collard greens. "And you wonder why we're not talking now." She speared a piece of gravy-covered turkey and put it in her mouth. She was determined not to let her mother spoil her dinner and make her start pushing her food around her plate like Jolean was doing.

Gloria pointed a finger at Tyesha. "That smart mouth of yours gonna be the end of you, Tyesha. You just better be glad we in Bruce and Vickie's house right now. But don't press your luck."

Jolean spoke up then, surprising everyone. "Well, I'm happy to see you, Momma," she said. "I missed you." Her eyes began to well up.

"I been missing you, too, baby," Gloria said.

"Then why you have to mess it up by bringing him?" Jolean asked plaintively as she sniffed hard and swiped at her tears.

Jolean's crying accomplished what Tyesha's combativeness couldn't. It softened Gloria's heart toward her children. She sighed heavily and said, "Walter ain't messing nothing up, Jolean. He basically been quiet since we sat down." She included Tyesha in her gaze and said, "What y'all got against Walter? He ain't never done nothing to y'all."

Vickie interrupted before Tyesha or Jolean could respond and said, "Gloria, you don't want to have that conversation with your daughters in front of us. I'll set up some tray tables in the den and the three of you can eat in there."

"Don't you mean the four of us?" Gloria said. "Walter coming too."

Walter finally found his voice then. "I don't mind staying out here at the table, Glo," he said, pronouncing it *glow*. "Go back there and talk to your girls."

"I'll help you set everything up, Ma," Sharday immediately said, then she stood and headed around the table. Her mother was amazing! She was actually going to pull this thing with Tyesha and them off.

"You should've told me you were inviting Miss Gloria and them," she whispered to Vickie once they were alone in the hallway. "I almost fell out when you brought them in."

"I didn't want you to give it away to the girls," Vickie whispered back.

"But I can keep a secret, Ma," Sharday protested, raising her voice slightly as they entered the kitchen.

Vickie slipped an arm around her daughter's shoulders and said, "I know you can, baby, but . . . Well, to be honest, I thought you might try to talk me out of it."

Sharday couldn't resist a chuckle. "Well, you got that right, Ma," she said. "I never would've believed it would work out like this."

"See?" Vickie teased as they approached the closet in the den. "Sometimes, mother does know best."

Less than fifteen minutes later, Gloria and her daughters were tucked away in the den and dinner had resumed at the dining room table for everyone else. Walter was pretty quiet at first. But once he finished picking over his dinner, he pushed aside his plate and started in on the wine in earnest. And the more he drank, the more he talked.

It wasn't long before his conversation turned personal. He told them that he had two grown sons of his own and that he had retired last year after thirty-two years at the Department of Commerce. "Yep," he said proudly. "Started off as a messenger right out of high school and ended up as the manager of the whole mail room."

"Really, Walter?" Vickie said. "That's quite impressive." She was glad he was finally opening up, even if it took a few glasses of wine for him to do it. She wanted to get to know him so she could decide for herself whether Gloria was making a mistake.

"It sure is," Bruce agreed. "It's hard to climb the ladder to management without switching employers at least once. And I'm in human resources. So, I should know," he told Walter.

Sharday looked across the table at Walter and smiled, but she didn't say anything. She couldn't believe he was actually getting tipsy off some merlot wine -- and he'd only had about three or four glasses. Wasn't he supposed to be an alcoholic?

"Yep," Walter said again. "D.O.C. was good to me. Helped me and my ex put both my boys through college."

"You were married?" Vickie asked.

"Almost thirty years," Walter said, draining his glass and reaching for the nearest bottle of wine. "Some of the best years and some of the worst years of my life. But the divorce was pure hell. Wouldn't wish it on my worst enemy." He swigged from his wine glass.

"I'm divorced, too, Walter," Bruce said. "So, I know exactly what you mean. Even when you know it's the right thing to do, divorce is hard if children are involved. As a matter of fact, that's why my daughter April's not here with us now. I got full-time physical custody, but her mother walked away with every Thanksgiving and a few other concessions."

"Well, I wasn't married to Sharday's father, but I can still relate," Vickie said. "It's really tough to walk away from someone you have a child with."

"But y'all won. I didn't," Walter said. And by now, he was beginning to slightly slur his words. "When all was said and done, I ended up losing my boys."

"Well, now that they're grown hopefully you can make up for lost time," Vickie said sympathetically. And then, because she had noticed Walter's slurred speech, she stood and announced that it was time for dessert. "Come on, Sharday," she said, giving her daughter a special look. "Help me clear these dishes so we'll have enough room."

"Okay, Ma." Sharday stood and began collecting the wine bottles. "I'll start with these empty bottles," she said, even as she scooped up the last two bottles that weren't empty.

"Why don't you bring us some coffee, too, honey?" Bruce said to Vickie. "I know I could use a cup."

"Your wish is my command, dear," she said, flashing him a smile. "One pot of coffee coming up." She picked up the turkey platter and followed Sharday down the hallway.

When Sharday stepped into the kitchen, she was relieved to hear only normal conversation coming from the den. She couldn't actually make out what Tyesha and them were saying, but at least they weren't yelling and screaming and carrying on. She turned to smile at her mother and whispered, "Sounds like they're working it out, Ma. You did it again."

"I knew they could do it," Vickie whispered back as she placed the turkey on the kitchen counter. Then she held up a finger to Sharday and walked closer to the den, loudly clearing her throat. "Well, I'll check on Gloria and the girls," she said, raising her voice so they could hear her. "You go ahead and take care of those bottles."

"Okay, Ma," Sharday said just as loudly.

Vickie waited a few seconds before sticking her head through the doorway to the den. "Everything okay in here?" she asked with a smile. "We're getting ready to have dessert out in the dining room. Can I bring anyone something? We've got banana pudding, sweet potato pie, apple pie, and chocolate on chocolate cake. Oh, and ice cream, too," she added.

"Actually, I think we about ready to come on back out there with y'all," Gloria said. She looked at her daughters for confirmation and they both nodded.

"Great!" Vickie said. Maybe Gloria could convince Walter to drink some coffee and sober up. And then, "But take your time finishing up in here while Sharday and I get everything ready."

When Vickie turned back to Sharday, Sharday gave her two thumbs up and a big smile and said, "I'll start bringing some more of the food back here. Ma. I already pulled out the coffee and a filter for you."

"Thanks, honey," Vickie said.

By the time Gloria, Tyesha and Jolean brought their dishes into the kitchen a few minutes later, Sharday was on her third trip to the dining room and Vickie was programming the coffee maker.

Gloria put her dishes in the sink and walked over to stand next to Vickie. "Thanks," she whispered, then she reached out to lightly squeeze Vickie's upper arm.

Vickie smiled at her and murmured, "Any time, Gloria. And I mean that."

Sharday came back then with the mashed potatoes, the rolls, and the giblet gravy. "Grab that for me," she said to Tyesha, indicating the gravy boat which was teetering on the side of the bread platter. "Now, you and Jolean can help me clear the table."

After Sharday, Tyesha and Jolean left for the dining room, Gloria asked Vickie what she could do to help.

"Oh, you can just grab one of those pies or something and go on back out there with Walter," Vickie said. "As soon as the coffee's ready, me and the girls will be out with the rest of the desserts." She was curious about what had happened in the den, but it was more important to get Gloria back in the dining room with Walter.

Once Gloria had picked up her banana pudding and left the kitchen, Vickie pulled the three large covered bowls of ice cream – rum raisin, strawberry, and pistachio – from the freezer and set them on the kitchen table. The coffee maker started buzzing a few minutes later, and then the girls came back from the dining room with a stack of dirty dinner dishes and more of the food. "We should have plenty of room on the table now," Vickie said as she picked up the carafe of strong black coffee. She reached for a sweet potato pie with her other hand and said, "Let's go ahead and take out the desserts."

When Vickie and the girls returned to the dining room, they were surprised to find that Gloria was standing, Walter was struggling up from his chair, and Bruce was nowhere in sight.

"We not gonna stay for dessert, y'all," Gloria said. "We gonna head on back across town before it get too late." She really wanted to get Walter out of there because he was drunk. And even though she wasn't surprised, she couldn't help being embarrassed. Walter was a good man, but he was also a stone cold alcoholic. And that wine he drank had probably set off all the vodka that was already in his system.

"I'm sorry to hear that, Gloria, but I do understand," Vickie said.

Sharday nodded and Tyesha said, "Okay, Momma," but Jolean just looked at her mother and didn't say anything.

"I'll call y'all at the apartment later on tonight," Gloria said to Jolean.

Bruce came back wearing his leather jacket and carrying Gloria's fake fur -- Walter hadn't worn a coat. "I'm going to give them a lift home. Okay, honey?" he said to Vickie.

"I told him to call us a cab, but he said he rather take us hisself," Gloria added.

"I wouldn't have it any other way," Vickie said with a smile.

Gloria hugged Vickie and Sharday before moving on to embrace each of her daughters. She held onto Jolean the longest, rubbing her youngest daughter's back and murmuring words of comfort into her ear.

Vickie told Bruce she'd walk them out to the garage, and then she told Sharday, Tyesha and Jolean to go ahead with dessert because she was going to hold off until Bruce got back and have hers with him.

Sharday waited until the adults were well out of earshot before she asked Tyesha and Jolean how things had gone in the den. "So, is everything back to normal now?" she asked.

"Not really," Tyesha said. "Momma made it clear that Walter's staying, so Jolean still doesn't want to move back home."

"But at least we're not mad at each other anymore," Jolean said.

Tyesha looked at Sharday and said, "She admitted that he's an alcoholic, Day-Day, and we basically agreed to give him a chance anyway. I mean, it's not like we really have a choice at this point."

Sharday shrugged. "You never know. Maybe it won't be so bad." And then, after a brief pause, "I'm having the cake and the pistachio ice cream. What about y'all?"

They kept the conversation light after that. Tyesha chose apple pie and strawberry ice cream, while Jolean had a heaping bowl of banana pudding followed by a generous slice of cake -- she'd been too nervous to eat much of her dinner but she was hungry now.

Back in the kitchen, Vickie had fixed herself a plate of seconds and was happily chowing it down as she got a head start on cleaning up. Thank God for the fashionable, but forgiving, empire waist dresses she had recently discovered. They hid the extra pounds and still managed to look sophisticated. But she was determined to go on a diet as soon as the holidays were over. And she would probably start exercising, too. Bruce claimed he liked her with "some meat on her bones," as he put it, but she knew she was letting herself go.

By the time the girls finished dessert, Vickie had loaded and turned on the dishwasher and put most of the food away. Sharday and Tyesha made quick work of the pots and pans while Jolean finished clearing the table and Vickie put the rest of the leftovers in the refrigerator. It wasn't long before they were settling down at the kitchen table for a game of spades.

Spades was one of the most popular card games in the hood, so they were all good at it -- even Jolean. And this afternoon, the cards were falling her way. She and Tyesha were partners and they scored two hundred points in the first hand, which was a feat considering that the game only went to five hundred, and then they ran a "Boston" on Vickie and Sharday, which meant that they totally shut them down and automatically won the game.

"Yeah, now that's what I'm talking about!" Tyesha shouted, giving Jolean high fives with both hands.

"Oh, you know how we do!" Jolean shouted back in exhilaration. "That's just the way we flow!" Talking trash was as much a part of the game as actually playing cards. And by winning in only two rounds, she and Tyesha had earned the right to do it.

"Okay, okay, so y'all got lucky," Sharday said.

"Pure luck," Vickie agreed. She picked up the deck of cards and began to shuffle. "Let's play another one. And since I have no doubt that we'll be winning this time, I'll even deal first," she boasted.

The cards fell more evenly during the second game, so it took a lot longer. They inched forward fifty to seventy points each hand, occasionally falling back when somebody got overconfident or the cards didn't fall the right way. And they were deep into what could prove to be the final hand -- Vickie and Sharday had four hundred and thirty points and Tyesha and Jolean were right behind them with four hundred and ten -- when they heard the garage door opening.

"Bruce is back," Sharday announced.

"And as always, he's right on time!" Vickie said. She slammed the big joker down on the table and waited for everyone to play a card, then she followed that with the little joker and the two of spades, which was the "baby joker" in the hood. By then, she was the only one with any spades left. And she won the last book with a measly five of spades. "Now, that's how the pros do it!" she said.

"Speak the truth, Ma!" Sharday said, jumping up to give her mother two high fives. "And that wasn't luck, that was skill!"

"Not!" Tyesha said. "If getting all three jokers in one hand wasn't luck, I don't know what is!"

Just then, Bruce walked in through the garage door and said, "I'm back! And I've been thinking about dessert the whole way home!"

"Great idea, Bruce!" Sharday said. "Me and Ma just put a mean whipping on them in a game of spades, so some dessert would be right on time!"

"Yeah, but we tore them up in the first game!" Jolean said. "Gave them the two-hitter quitter and took them out in the second hand!"

"Sounds like a tie to me," Bruce said.

Sharday shrugged and said, "Then I guess we'll just have to beat them again to break it." She didn't have any other plans for the day, anyway. Malcolm was supposed to meet her at the apartment later tonight, but they were going to stay in because she had taken a coworker's eight a.m. to four p.m. shift tomorrow so that she could have Sunday off. She was going up to New York to visit Donnell on Sunday. But of course, Tyesha and April were the only ones who knew that.

"Well, bring it on then," Tyesha said now. "You know Jolean and I are known for cleaning up our leftovers." She was staying in tonight, too, because Jolean wasn't going back home to her father's until the following afternoon.

Vickie called for a dessert break before the final game. She sent Bruce to take off his jacket and wash his hands, she quickly agreed when Jolean asked to make a turkey sandwich, and then she recruited Sharday and Tyesha to help her wipe down the kitchen table and set everything out.

Sharday's cell phone rang as she was unwrapping one of the sweet potato pies and she pulled the phone from her hip to check the Caller ID. Holy

Cross Hospital? This had to be a wrong number. She flipped open her cell and put it to her ear. "Happy Thanksgiving," she said.

"Oh, Sharday. Thank God, you answered," a familiar voice said. "I hate to ruin your Thanksgiving, but I've got some bad news."

"Belinda? What's wrong?"

"I had to bring your father to the emergency room," Belinda said. "He kept having chest pains and we thought he might be having a heart attack."

"A heart attack?" Sharday was visibly shaken. "But . . . but . . . but . . . "

Vickie took the phone from Sharday and placed it to her own ear, even as she slipped her arm around her daughter's shoulders. "Hi, Belinda," she said. "It's Vickie. Is everything okay?"

"I'm not sure yet," Belinda said. "I had to bring Frank to the emergency room because of chest pains."

"Well, what are the doctors saying?" Vickie asked.

"Nothing, so far. They just took him back."

Vickie looked up as she heard Bruce reenter the kitchen. "Hold on for a minute, Belinda," she said, then she lowered the phone and told Bruce what was going on.

"Tell her we'll bring Sharday right over," Bruce said without hesitation. "Tyesha can take herself and Jolean back to the apartment in the Altima and we'll drop Sharday off there later."

While Vickie relayed the message, Bruce went to get their coats and Tyesha headed for the closet in the den, where she, Sharday and Jolean had stashed their purses. Within minutes, Vickie had ended the conversation and grabbed her handbag, and they were heading for the cars.

Sharday was silent on the way to hospital, which was out in Silver Spring, Maryland, just a few miles from Frank and Belinda's condo. She was worried about her father -- chest pains were serious at his age, despite what her mother and Bruce were saying about how they didn't always indicate a heart attack. She was afraid that Frank would be taken away from her just as she was really getting to know him.

When they finally arrived at the emergency room, Belinda said that the doctors were still running tests on Frank, but that Sharday had already been cleared to go back and see him. Sharday was too nervous to go by herself, so she asked her mother to go with her.

As Sharday and Vickie followed Belinda's directions to Frank's curtained-off area behind the heavy double doors, Frank was lying in the narrow hospital bed facing the consequences of his irresponsible lifestyle. He had no medical insurance, no job, no money of his own. He wouldn't even have a place to lay his head at night if it wasn't for Belinda.

He had never filed taxes and never had a job that didn't involve a club owner paying him in cash, so qualifying for some kind of disability or social security benefits was out of the question. And if he up and died right now, he wouldn't even have an insurance policy to leave behind to cover the cost of his funeral.

He realized he needed some more time to get his act together, so he started trying to bargain with God. His music career was obviously never going to take off and if he hadn't been so lazy, he would've moved on a long time ago. But if God would just give him one more chance and get him out of this hospital bed, he promised to do something productive with his life. He would get a real nine-to-five job with a steady paycheck and benefits, and he would start pulling his weight financially at the condo, and he would . . .

"Knock, knock, Mr. Wallace. Your daughter's here," one of the nurses said, and he immediately recognized her voice. This was the middle-aged, heavyset black woman who was totally under his spell.

When the nurse pulled back the curtain, Frank was surprised to see Vickie standing just behind Sharday. He played it off and quickly flashed a charming smile that included her, as well, before he reached out for his daughter. "Thanks for coming so quickly, honey," he said to Sharday. "You must actually care about your old man, after all."

The nurse smiled at Frank and backed away when Sharday rushed over to hug him, but Vickie stepped into the enclosure and pulled the curtain shut behind her. And as Frank looked over his daughter's shoulder at Vickie's expensive clothes and jewelry, consciously noting the air of affluence that seemed to surround her now, the solution to his problems became crystal clear: All he had to do was marry Belinda! Vickie's life had definitely changed for the better once she married Mr. Moneybags Bruce. And if it worked for her, it could work for him, too!

Belinda had recently come into plenty of money -- enough for her and him both. And she had been hounding him to marry her for more than a year now. Once they were legal, she would be happy to add him to her medical insurance and she would probably even help him start a business. And if they ever split up, he would be entitled to some of that money of hers.

He felt a sense of peace come over him as he released his daughter and smiled at her. And for the first time all day, the sharp pains on the left side of his chest lessened considerably. He shifted his legs and invited Sharday to have a seat on the bed, then he asked her and Vickie what they had eaten for the holiday dinner. He was still holding court when the nurse returned about ten minutes later and said the doctor wanted him to have an echocardiogram.

Although the nurse told Sharday and Vickie that the procedure would only take a few minutes, it was more than an hour later when one of the doctors finally came out to the waiting room with an update on Frank's condition.

The doctor was a short, brown-skinned man who wore a turban and had a thick Pakistani accent. He said that none of the tests had revealed anything unusual and that "the patient" reported his symptoms had disappeared. "My tentative diagnosis is dyspepsia," he said, "more commonly known as indigestion. I'm going to release the patient and recommend a visit to his regular physician."

Sharday had been holding her breath, but at the mention of the word indigestion, she exhaled with relief and smiled. Her father was going to be okay, after all. She would still have time to finish getting to know him.

FORTY-EIGHT

The month of December flew by in a blur of studying for Sharday, Tyesha, and Malcolm. They had all done well on midterms -- even Sharday made straight Bs. And they were determined to do equally well on final exams.

But finals could account for up to fifty percent of the grade in a course and could touch on anything covered throughout the entire semester. So, the pressure was really on, and Sharday wasn't the only one to succumb to it.

Tyesha ended up taking two days in a row off from work during finals week so she could use the extra time to study. Malcolm stayed up twenty-six hours straight finishing up his last English Lit paper. Neither of them said a word this time when Sharday once again fell back on all-nighters to pull her through.

Fortunately, winter break started as soon as exams were over. And that meant they each had enough time to sleep, do some partying, and still get their Christmas shopping done before the holiday rolled around the following Thursday.

Sharday exchanged gifts with Tyesha and Jolean on Christmas Eve before she left to spend the night in the new bed Vickie had bought for her old bedroom in Mitchellville. She gave Tyesha a designer sweater that she'd gotten for a really good price, and she gave Jolean a pair of *Old Navy* jeans she'd bought using her employee discount. Tyesha's gift for her was an expensive-looking silver necklace and earring set, while Jolean had gotten her a knock-off *Gucci* handbag.

On Christmas morning, Vickie awoke Sharday at a quarter after nine. "Merry Christmas, sleepyhead," she said as she leaned over to hug her daughter. "I'm so happy you're home for the holiday." And then, with a grin, "Now, come on and get your butt out of bed! Everybody else is already up and we're ready to open our gifts!"

Sharday pulled on her robe and stopped in the bathroom to wash her face and brush her teeth before she went down to the living room to join her mother, Bruce, and April. She told Bruce and April "Merry Christmas" and hugged each of them, then she took her place at the foot of the Christmas tree beside April. It was their job to dig out the gifts, which were mostly for them anyway.

Sharday got new clothes, pajamas, bedroom shoes, perfume, a white gold necklace with a cross pendant, and a Smart TV for her bedroom at the apartment. April received a comparable array of gifts, including a digital camera and a photo printer. Bruce gave Vickie one-carat diamond stud earrings and a fur-trimmed leather coat, while she gave him an original, signed copy of Ralph Ellison's *Invisible Man* and diamond cuff links. Sharday and April had put their money together and gotten a ten-disc DVD set called *Motown's Greatest Hits* for Bruce, and a gift certificate for a pedicure, manicure and half hour massage at a black-owned day spa for Vickie.

After everyone finished oohing and aahing over their gifts, they headed into the kitchen, where Vickie turned on Christmas music and they all pitched in to prepare a light breakfast of cheese omelets, sliced cantaloupe and strawberries, orange juice, and coffee and tea. They weren't having guests on the holiday this year, although Vickie's parents were flying down the following night. So, they hung out at the kitchen table talking for a while after breakfast, and then they eventually drifted upstairs to shower and get dressed.

When they met back up in the kitchen about an hour later, Bruce had on a pair of khakis and a chambray shirt, Vickie had changed into a long, gauzy, free flowing dress, and Sharday and April wore jeans and sweaters. They had agreed to go for a "festive but homey atmosphere," as Vickie had put it. And since they'd all gotten their fill of turkey and ham on Thanksgiving and the week that followed, they were having stuffed Cornish hens and filet mignon for dinner.

Of course, Vickie had pulled out all the stops, anyway, and spent the day before preparing most of the meal. So, even though there wasn't much to be done today, the dining room table was covered with dishes when they finally sat down at three o'clock to eat.

"I have something I want to say," Vickie announced after Bruce said grace and they were all fixing their plates. "As of New Year's Day, I'm going on the *South Beach* diet and I'm joining one of those new women-only gyms that everybody's talking about these days. I know I need to lose some weight," she admitted. "And I'm hoping to get back down to the size I was on my wedding day." She smiled then and said, "But that means that all bets are off from now until the end of the year. I get to eat whatever I want whenever I want. And nobody gets to say anything about it. Deal?" She looked around the table at each of them.

Bruce said, "Honey, I think you're fine as you are, but if that's what you want to do . . . ," and then he let the sentence trail off.

"Ditto for me," April said.

But Sharday smiled at her mother and said, "You've got a deal, Ma." She was relieved to hear that Vickie was going to take control of her weight before it got too far out of hand. As a matter of fact, she'd been planning to bring up the subject herself after the holidays were over.

"Great!" Vickie said. "Now, let's dig in!" And on that note, she split open her baked potato and added salt, butter and a huge dollop of sour cream to it.

They were all hungry because they'd skipped lunch and only had a light breakfast, so they wasted no time tucking into the food. Conversation was steady but they were mostly focused on the meal, eventually helping themselves to seconds -- and in Vickie's case, thirds, too.

Finally, Sharday pushed her chair back from the table and said, "It's getting late. I should probably head out." She had promised her father and Belinda that she would join them for dessert.

Vickie glanced down at her watch and said, "I guess you're right, honey. It's almost five o'clock."

Bruce said, "Well, tell Frank and Belinda we said 'Merry Christmas,' Sharday."

She smiled. "Will do, Bruce. And I'll see y'all in the morning."

"Yep, bright and early!" April joked. It was her week to use the car, but since she didn't have any plans for the day until later that night when Isaiah was coming by to pick her up for a party, she had agreed to let Sharday borrow the car today. She would pick it up from the apartment in the morning when they dropped Sharday's gifts off.

Sharday laughed and said, "I know that's right!" She stood and walked around the table to kiss and hug each of them. "I had a blast!" she said. "Enjoy the rest of the holiday!" Then she dashed upstairs to get her overnight bag and her gifts for Frank and Belinda before she slipped on her coat and left.

She was in a great mood as she started up the car and pulled off. Who knew just chilling at home with the family would turn out to be so much fun? And now, she was going to get a chance to spend some time with her father and Belinda, too.

There was hardly any traffic on the streets, so she made it over to Wheaton in good time. Belinda answered the phone and buzzed her in. And Frank was waiting for her when she reached the front door of their condo.

"Merry Christmas, honey," Frank said as he welcomed her with a hug. "I'm glad you came."

She smiled broadly. "So am I, Daddy. Merry Christmas."

He released her and helped her out of her coat, then he told her to go put her gifts under the tree and make herself comfortable.

She went into the living room and put her gifts down before claiming a seat on the sofa. She got right back up a few seconds later when Belinda limped in from the kitchen so that she could hug Belinda and wish her a Merry Christmas.

Oh, Sharday!" Belinda said, hugging her tightly. "Merry Christmas, honey! We're finally going to be family now!"

"Huh?" Sharday said. She released Belinda and leaned back to look at her.

Frank stepped through the doorway just then, but he held his silence.

"I'm going to be your real stepmother now!" Belinda said, her eyes sparkling with excitement. "Your father asked me to marry him today!"

"Oh, my God! Really?" Sharday said. She leaned forward to hug Belinda again. "I can't believe it! Congratulations!"

"Yep, we've finally decided to make it official," Frank said as he settled into the cushy leather armchair, crossing his legs in a gesture of true confidence. He was feeling a lot more secure in his position around here now that Belinda had accepted his proposal.

"Wow!" Sharday said as she sat down on the sofa next to Belinda. She was surprised, but she was genuinely happy that they were getting married. Being with Belinda had clearly changed Frank for the better. "So, when's the big day?" she asked.

"We're going to do it next week," Belinda said. "In Vegas. We want to start the New Year off as a married couple."

"Wow," Sharday said again. And then, "So, let me see the ring."

"Oh, I don't have one yet," Belinda said, still smiling happily. "We're just going to have matching wedding bands for now. And Frank will get me a nice stone a little later down the road."

Frank was embarrassed that Belinda didn't have an engagement ring, but he would've been even more embarrassed to have her flashing around a tiny diamond chip, which was about all he could afford right now. So, he played it off and said, "That way, she'll be able to pick out exactly what she wants. Not to mention that prices are really inflated right now and we'll get a much better deal if we wait until after the holidays."

Sharday shrugged. "Whatever works," she said with a smile.

Frank smoothly changed the subject by announcing that it was time for them to open the gifts, then he rose and headed across the room to the Christmas tree.

* * * * *

Sharday didn't make it home until nine thirty that night. She had already called Malcolm and moved their nine o'clock date back to ten -- which was kind of late, given that he couldn't spend the night because was staying at home until the dorms reopened for second semester. But since he no longer had a curfew, per se, he would probably be able to stay out until at least two.

She grabbed her overnight bag and her gifts from Frank and Belinda from the trunk and headed for the apartment. When she unlocked the front door and stepped inside, she found Tyesha stretched out on the sofa watching a movie in the dark.

"Merry Christmas," she said, clicking on the light. "So, how'd it go with your mother and them today? Where's Jolean?"

Tyesha sat up and said, "Merry Christmas, Day-Day. Jolean went home with her father for the weekend. He ended up having to come pick us up because we couldn't get a cab. You know how it is over in the hood on Christmas."

"Yeah, I know," Sharday said.

"And what can I say about my mother and Walter? It wasn't too bad, but it wasn't exactly good either."

"Well, come tell me about it while I roll a quick blunt," Sharday said. "I've got just enough time to light one up and take a quick shower before Malcolm gets here."

"Girl, please," Tyesha said with a laugh. "You know I already rolled one. Already took a few hits off it, too." She and Sharday had put their money together and bought a fifty dollar bag of weed from Andre so they would have enough to last them through winter break. They were pretty much getting high whenever they felt like it now that they were on vacation from school.

"Cool," Sharday said. "Whip it out while go put my stuff in my room."

By the time Sharday returned to the living room, Tyesha had lit an incense, put towels at the front door and cracked a window.

"So, what happened?" Sharday asked as she sat down on the sofa and lit the blunt.

"Well, in Walter's favor, I have to admit that he's really putting it down for my mother financially," Tyesha said. "She's got new furniture in the living room and in her bedroom, and they bought me and Jolean some really nice gifts. And quite a few of them, too."

Sharday passed her the blunt and said, "Sounds like a good Christmas to me."

"It was at first." Tyesha sucked in a mouthful of smoke and held it a few seconds before exhaling. "But Walter's sons were supposed to come by for dessert." She hit the blunt a couple more times and handed it back to Sharday. "And when it became clear that they weren't going to show up, Walter started getting drunk."

"Oh, yeah?" Sharday said, smoke seeping from her mouth and nose.

"Yep, and that's when I decided that it was time for me and Jolean to get out of there. But then we had the whole situation with not being able to get a cab. And while we were stuck waiting for Jolean's father to come get us, Walter proceeded to get falling down drunk."

"That's messed up," Sharday said as she gave Tyesha the last of the blunt. "But I'm not really surprised. I told you how he got blitzed off that wine on Thanksgiving."

Tyesha blew out a large plume of smoke and crushed the blunt in the ashtray. "I know," she said. "But what really made it bad was that my mother kept trying to pretend like nothing was wrong. Even when she had to take him back to the bedroom so he could sleep it off, she gave us some lame excuse about how he was so tired because he's been working a lot of overtime lately."

"Maybe it's all about the money for her," Sharday said.

Tyesha snorted with disgust and rolled her eyes. "Well, you know what, Day-Day? If she wants to pimp herself for a few dollars, then fine. As long as it doesn't affect me or my little sister, I really don't care anymore." And with that, she got up and said, "I'm going to get some soda. You want something?"

"Nah, I need to hop in the shower real quick," Sharday said as she got up, too. She would have to tell Tyesha about Frank and Belinda's marriage plans tomorrow. "If Malcolm gets here before I finish, just send him back," she said, then she headed down the hallway for her bedroom.

FORTY-NINE

Somehow, Sharday never found time to take a trip up to Allentown over winter break. She had planned to go see Donnell at least two or three times while she was off from school. But as it turned out, she ended up being too busy to get away even once for the full day that a visit to him would take.

First, her grandparents came down the day after Christmas. Then, Kayla had the baby that Saturday afternoon. And since nobody in Kayla's family was willing to help her -- her mother stayed too drunk and her sisters had children of their own -- Sharday and Tyesha went over every day the first week after she got out of the hospital. Then there was Frank and Belinda's last minute wedding reception that Sharday spent three days helping them plan. And all the while, she and Malcolm were putting in a lot of studio time learning how to use *Pro Tools,* a more sophisticated computer program for producing music that he had bought with some of his Christmas money.

So, Sharday had valid reasons for not going to see Donnell. But that still didn't stop her from feeling guilty. She knew she had let him down big over the holidays -- at a time when just one visit from her really would've made a difference. And she decided to make up for it by visiting him as much as possible during second semester.

When registration week started, she attempted to cram all her classes into four days each week so she would have Mondays off to make the weekly bus trips. But then, two of the Tuesday/Thursday classes she needed filled up before she could get in and she had to register for the Monday/Wednesday/Friday versions. And with her job on the weekends, that meant she would be tied down seven days a week.

In the end, though, none of that mattered. Because three and a half weeks into the semester, Donnell called and told her he was being released to a halfway house in Baltimore.

"Oh, my God, Boo!" she said, jumping up from her bed. "For real? Oh, my God!"

"Yeah, I can't believe that shit neither," he said. And although he didn't elaborate, he meant it. The warden and his staff usually kept known gang members like Donnell behind bars until the last possible minute. Donnell didn't know how he had managed to slip through the cracks but he wasn't about to bring it to anybody's attention.

"So, when they letting you out?" she asked in the ghetto English she always used around him.

"Next week," he said so low only she could hear him, then he waited to see how she would respond. The fact that she didn't come visit him over the holidays had him wondering whether she was screwing around on him now.

It took her a few seconds to absorb what he'd said, and then she burst into tears. "Oh, my God, Donnell," she sobbed, sinking down onto the bed. "I been praying for this day for so long. You just don't know, Boo. But I didn't think it would come until May."

Her response told him all he needed to know and he pretended to cough to cover the smile that briefly spread across his face. Then he said, "Me, too, Day-Day. But look, I gotta go now. I had to call in a debt just to get these fifteen minutes."

"Okay, Boo. I love you," she said. "And I'll see you next week."

"Me, too," he said again. And then he disconnected the call.

She hung up, quickly wiped her face, and rushed out to the living room to share the good news with Tyesha and Jolean.

"Day-Day, you are so lucky!" Jolean said. "We don't even have one boyfriend between us and here you are about to have two!"

"Huh?" Sharday said.

Tyesha rolled her eyes at the blank look on Sharday's face. "You do remember Malcolm, don't you?" she asked sarcastically. “Hello.” She still thought Sharday would be better off with Malcolm. So, it bothered her that one word from Donnell had made Sharday forget all about him.

Sharday shrugged uneasily and sat down on the arm of the sofa. She'd been in denial about her relationship with Malcolm for so long that she'd temporarily blocked it out. But Tyesha was right. Now that Donnell was coming back home, she was finally going to have to do something about Malcolm.

"Girl, we need to talk," Tyesha said, taking Sharday's obvious discomfort for confusion. She sent Jolean back to the bedroom to get her school clothes ready for the next day.

Sharday sighed heavily and moved down onto the actual sofa. "I really screwed things up this time, didn't I, Tyesha?" she said. She turned up both palms and lifted her shoulders. "I mean, how can I even begin to explain this to Malcolm? Especially after all this time?"

"Maybe Malcolm's not the one you should be explaining it to. He's not the one who's been gone for almost two years, you know. He's the one who's been right by your side the whole time."

Sharday exhaled heavily. "I know. And in a different world, I could really see myself being with him. But in this lifetime, I belong to Donnell, Tyesha. And that's just the way it is."

"But why? Just because he was your childhood sweetheart doesn't mean you have to be with him forever. Day-Day, things happened. And you met a better man in the process. Why can't you just be happy about it and move on?"

Sharday slowly shook her head. "See, you still don't get it. Donnell is my soulmate, Tyesha. We come from the same place. We see life the same way. Plus, our dreams are exactly the same and we've both got that burning drive to make it."

"I knew it!" Tyesha said. "I knew this was really about your dreams of making it big in the music industry with Donnell. But Malcolm's got superstar talent, too, Day-Day. And you can't deny that. And unlike Donnell, he'll also have a college degree to fall back on."

"But don't you see? That's part of the problem," Sharday said. "Me and Donnell connect on a way deeper level because we're like two sides of the same person. Malcolm's not like us. He comes from money. And he's traveled all around the world. Music is just a hobby for him because he's got other options. But it's the only way out for me and Donnell."

"They only way out of what, Day-Day?" Tyesha asked in frustration. "Girl, when are you going to wake up? You're not from the ghetto anymore. You're from a big, pretty house out in Mitchellville now. And you graduated from the same high school Malcolm graduated from. Your stepfather's got plenty of money and your mother's determined to see you have nothing but the best. For real, even your father has money now, too."

"But all that doesn't change who I really am way deep down inside,"

Sharday insisted. “Based on how I grew up all my life before Bruce and April and Mitchellville.” She shrugged then and said, "Look, I really don't know how to explain it. All I can tell you is that I know in my heart that Donnell's the man I'm meant to spend the rest of my life with. I guess you'll just have to take my word for it."

Tyesha didn't say anything at first. She didn't believe that everybody had a soulmate out there somewhere. To her, it was just a matter of deciding what kind of person you wanted to be with and refusing to settle for anything less. But Sharday wasn't like that. She believed in true love, and destiny, and all those other sentimental notions. And who was to say which one of them had it right? "Hmm, maybe I will," she finally said. "So, when are you planning to tell Malcolm."

"I'm going over there right now," Sharday said. "I've already put this off way too long as it is." Then she leaned over and picked up the phone to call him.

Forty minutes later, Sharday was sitting next to Malcolm on his dorm room bed. "I have something to tell you," she said slowly, looking down at the floor between her legs. This was turning out to be one of the hardest things she had ever done. "It's really, really, really terrible," she said, forcing herself to continue. "And I just know you're going to hate me for it, but--"

"Hate you?" he interrupted, quickly reaching for her hands. "Haven't we already been through this before, Sharday?" he asked her softly. "Don't you know by now that you can tell me anything?"

"But this is different, Malcolm. It's not--"

"Whatever it is, you can tell me," he said firmly.

She looked at him for a few seconds. Then she said, "I can't see you anymore," and she simultaneously pulled away her hands.

"What?" he said, staring at her dumbly. That was the last thing he had expected her to say.

She stood and subconsciously moved away from him, stopping only when she bumped into his desk. "My boyfriend's coming back next week," she explained. "And he doesn’t know anything about you. And he's expecting--"

"But what difference does it make what he's expecting?" Malcolm said as he got up and crossed the room to stand before her. She hadn't mentioned her boyfriend in so long that he'd practically forgotten all about him and thought she had, too. "What you had with him is over, Sharday," Malcolm said now, placing his hands on her shoulders. "He walked away from you and stayed away. And I stepped in to take his place."

"But it's not exactly like that, Malcolm. He's been in jail all this time. And--"

"And you haven't seen him since he left. So--"

"That's not true," she said quietly, looking down at the floor again.

He dropped his hands from her shoulders and stepped back. "What? What are you saying, Sharday?"

"I'm saying I've been going to see him the whole time," she said, still looking at the floor.

"But . . . but . . ." He backed away from her in horror until he was on the opposite side of the room. "But when?" he asked. "We're always together."

"Well, he was in DC Jail at first -- but that was before I met you. And back then, I used to visit him all the time," she said, looking everywhere but in Malcolm's face. "But after I moved to Mitchellville, they shipped him to a prison in upstate New York and I started visiting him there. And . . . well. . . " She took a deep breath and finally met Malcolm's gaze. "And I just never stopped going, Malcolm," she said simply. "Not even after we started getting closer."

Malcolm felt a pain in his gut that was so sharp he almost doubled over. She had been using him all this time! And he was so stupid he'd fallen in love with her while she was doing it! He turned away from her to hide his emotions. And when he spoke again, it was in a cold and sarcastic voice. "So, you were right all along," he said with a bitter laugh. "I never really knew you, after all, Sharday. I never would have guessed you were a no good, low down, two timing tramp."

She cringed. Those were very hard words coming from Malcolm. But it wasn't like she didn't deserve them.

"You can go now," he said in the same ugly voice. "If I never see you again, that will be too soon." And when he turned around to look at her, disgust was written all over his face.

"I'm so sorry, Malcolm," she said, and the tears began to flow down her cheeks. "I never meant for things to turn out this way. But"

"But you can't turn a whore into a housewife, right?" he said with contempt. "I know the rules, Sharday. And now, I know what happens when you try to break them. Looks like your work here is done. So, get out."

FIFTY

Sharday was truly dragging on Sunday night when she made it home from work. She'd been depressed ever since Malcolm kicked her out of his dorm room earlier in the week and started refusing to take her calls. And the fact that she hadn't heard back from Donnell was making it worse.

Fortunately, Tyesha had agreed to drop the car off in Mitchellville for her tonight, so all she had to do was make it up to the apartment and turn over the keys. And after that, she could head straight for bed, which was where she'd been spending most of her time lately.

She sighed heavily but kept moving. It was only a matter of minutes now. Before she knew it, she would by lying down in the dark with the covers pulled up to her chin. But when she finally unlocked the front door and stepped inside the apartment, she was surprised to see her mother sitting on the sofa next to Tyesha.

Vickie was looking good these days. She'd been following her "low-carb" diet to the letter and also going to the gym three times a week. And as a result, she'd already dropped enough pounds to fit back into some of her old clothes.

Sharday tried to perk up and force a smile. She hadn't told her mother about Donnell and Malcolm yet and she didn't want her asking what was wrong. "Hi, Ma," she managed with a strain. "I wasn't expect--"

"I am so disappointed in you, Sharday," Vickie said, standing as her daughter approached. "You made the wrong choice, baby. And now, it's too late to fix it. Why didn't you talk to me first?"

"Huh?" Sharday said. "What are you talking about, Ma?"

Tyesha quickly stood and said, "I'll give you two some privacy," and then she escaped to her room. This was one conversation she wanted absolutely nothing to do with.

After Tyesha left, Vickie sadly shook her head at her daughter. "Elaine told me everything, Sharday," she said, referring to Malcolm's mother. "Right after church this morning. How could you do that to Malcolm? What were you thinking?"

Sharday was stunned. "I . . . I . . . I didn't have a choice," she stammered as she sank down to the sofa.

Vickie sat down beside her. "Of course, you did, Sharday," she said. "But you made the wrong one. And now, Malcolm's gone for good."

Sharday disagreed, even as she remembered how he had told her he never wanted to see her again. "Stop being over-dramatic, Ma," she said. "He's right in his dorm room where he's always been. And he'll eventually calm down."

"You really don't know?" Vickie asked in surprise. "Baby, he enlisted in the Air Force last week," she said gently. "The day after you told him about Donnell. And they shipped him off to basic training yesterday."

"Oh, my God, Ma," Sharday said. And the tears began to trickle down her face. "I never thought he would ruin his life over this. I mean, . . . I mean, I knew he would be mad, but . . . but . . ." The tears were flowing faster and she sobbed. "He hates me now, Ma," she choked out. "You should've seen the way he looked at me. And . . . and I . . ." And then, she totally broke down.

Vickie immediately reached out to envelop her daughter in hug. "Oh, baby. Come here," she said. But as she rubbed Sharday's back, she wondered how everything had gone so wrong. A week ago, she would've laughed at the suggestion that Sharday would choose Donnell over Malcolm when the time came. She'd been convinced that the move from southeast, and the new lifestyle, and the choir, and Bruce and April, and college, and even Malcolm's constant presence had changed her daughter.

But of course, she hadn't known then about Sharday's frequent trips up to New York to visit Donnell. And she couldn't help thinking now that she would've been more on top of what was happening with her daughter if she hadn't been so preoccupied with trying to keep her own life from spiraling out of control.

Vickie exhaled heavily and rocked her daughter slightly from side to side. "It's going to be okay, baby," she murmured. "You'll see. Everything will work out just fine." And she silently vowed to do everything within her power to make sure it did.

FIFTY-ONE

All in all, another month passed by before Sharday was reunited with Donnell. He didn't make it to the halfway house until a week and a half after he said he would. And once he got there, he had to complete a two-week orientation program before they would allow him "street privileges."

But finally, on a Tuesday afternoon in early March, he met her outside in front of the apartment when she got home from class. She was traveling on foot because this was April's week to have the car, so she spotted him before he saw her.

"Donnell!" she cried out, breaking into a full run. "Oh, my God! Oh, my God, Boo!" she said and threw herself into his arms.

He slid her backpack off her shoulders and let it fall to the ground so he could hold her close. "We fucking finally made it through, Day-Day," he said as he buried his face in her neck. "And I ain't never gonna leave you again. I put that on everything."

They kissed deeply then. And when he reached down to cup her buttocks, she felt his bulging erection and her body responded appropriately. Almost as if on cue, they released each other wordlessly, he leaned over to pick up her backpack, and she quickly led him up to the apartment and directly back to her room.

She barely got the bedroom door closed before they were all over each other. They were kissing, caressing, undressing, and murmuring with pleasure all at the same time. And once they managed to get her jeans off, he pulled down her panties and sank to his knees in front of her.

"I missed the way you smell," he murmured as he pushed her back against the door and spread her legs. He put his face right up to the lips of her vagina and inhaled deeply. "A nigga been dreaming of doing that for so long," he murmured.

Once he brought her to a climax, he used one hand to keep her pulsating and the other to put on a condom. It wasn't long before he pulled her to the floor and submerged himself inside her.

He found his own explosive release within minutes. But he offered no apologies because they both knew it had been such a long time for him. Instead, he shuddered with pleasure and rolled onto his back, pulling her on top of him. "I missed you so much, Day-Day," he murmured. "And that shit ain't no lie."

"I missed you, too, Boo," she said. "But I finally got you back now."

"And that's the way it's gonna stay," he said.

They lay there holding each other for a while before he released her and sat up to take off his condom. She reached for her panties, but he stopped her. "Not yet, Day-Day," he said. "We ain't done."

She started laughing and said, "I know that's right!"

"A nigga ain't changed," he said. "I'm still the same."

"Well, let's take it to the bed then," she said, keeping it ghetto as she grinned and rose to her feet.

"Let me look at you for a minute first," he said, and he explored her naked body with his eyes. "Now, turn around for me, baby," he said in a husky voice. "Real slow."

She smiled at him. He hardly ever called her baby. "I can do even better than that, Boo," she said softly. She went over to the studio and put on a sexy R&B ballad, then she gave him a private dance.

About halfway through the song, he got up and led her over to the bed. They used their hands and mouths to bring each other almost to the brink of satisfaction. And this time when he claimed her, his former staying power was back in effect.

A long while later, he removed the spent condom and pulled her close.

She snuggled up next to him and said, "We still got that magic, Boo. I guess some things just never change." But even as she said it, she wondered whether their old magic would extend farther than the bed. Her mother had recently started saying that she didn't have anything in common with Donnell anymore and that it wouldn't take her long to realize it. And although she disagreed every time Vickie said it, the thought had now been planted in her mind.

But when Donnell started talking about his plans to get them a record deal, her doubts disappeared. He said he wanted to get their demo tape made as soon as possible because of the people he'd met "in the joint" who had contacts in the industry. We gotta move real quick, Day-Day," he told her. "While they still remember me. Because these motherfuckers got the juice to get our demo to the big dogs. And I know that for a fact."

"I came up with a tight ass name for us, too," he told her. He'd been plotting this out for more than a year now, so he'd had plenty of time to work out the details. "I want us to start going by '*Double D-Day*.' What you think?"

She grinned and said, "I'm down with it. Like you said, it's tight."

"Yeah," he said. "And we gonna step up our game, too. Make it sexier. I been working out so I'm all cut up now."

"I noticed," she said, raking her eyes over his upper body.

He stretched slightly to emphasize his pecs and biceps, but he kept talking. "So, now a nigga can take off his shirt on stage like all them other rappers be doing," he continued. "You know what I mean? And we gonna show off that sexy body you got, too. Low-cut tops, miniskirts, stilettos. You know how the baddest chicks do now. But we gonna keep our shit classy."

She nodded slowly and said, "Yeah, I know what you saying." Sexy was the buzzword in hip-hop nowadays, so he had a good point. They had to have the right image if they wanted to make it to the top.

"Sex sells," he said. "And we gonna give the people what they want. But we got some time to work on that part. The main thing we gotta worry about right now is getting the damn demo together."

He climbed out of bed and walked across the room to the studio. He was pleased to see her new decked out laptop. He said that was one less thing for him to worry about trying to get. Then he fiddled around with this and that to make sure everything was working before he came back to join her.

"And another thing," he said after he settled back in beside her. "I finally came up with a way to get the rest of my street privileges. I was talking to my counselor and he told me the gig at *The Cellar* would count as a job."

"For real?" she said. Right now, they were only letting him out of the halfway house from six in the morning to six in the evening. But once he got a job, he could come back out from eight to eleven Monday through Thursday, he could stay out all day on Sunday until eleven at night, and on Friday and Saturday, his curfew wouldn't be until midnight.

"Yeah," he said. "So, I'm gonna call that nigga Clyde tonight and tell him I want back in on the gig. I need them extra weekend privileges to work on the demo. We gotta make it hot enough to fly fucking lids off." And although he would never admit it to her, he was also looking around for a side hustle. He hated to go illegal again, but a regular job was out of the question and all the halfway house had to offer was bus tokens and breakfast and dinner. Right now, he had a box full of phone cards he could sell for money. And he had spent the morning over in the hood with Andre selling some of them. But once they ran out, he would need more than the money from Clyde to get by. Especially since his mother had asked him to start helping her out with money again when he'd stopped by there this morning.

"I'm so glad you back," Sharday said, turning to massage his chest. "I been holding it down like you asked me to and all, but now I can finally breathe again. Because I know you gonna make everything happen for us just like it's supposed to."

He opened his mouth to receive her tongue as she leaned forward to kiss him, but then he squeezed her behind, lightly tapped it, and broke contact. "Don't wanna start nothing I can't finish, Day-Day," he told her. "It's getting late and I gotta be back in by six."

He rolled over and sat on the side of the bed. " A lot of niggas just walk right out of the halfway house and don't never come back," he said over his shoulder. "And don't nothing happen to them neither unless they get caught up on another charge or something. But I don't want no stupid shit like that coming back to haunt me once we blow up. So, I'm just gonna finish my time and get it over with."

"Make sense to me," she said. When she glanced at the clock and saw that it was almost four o'clock, she realized that Jolean would be coming in from school soon. Plus, her mother had taken to stopping by on weekdays without calling first ever since she quit her job a couple of weeks ago. And Sharday definitely didn't want Vickie to catch her in bed with Donnell.

She sat up and swung her legs over the side of the bed, too. "Well, let me hit the bathroom and get dressed so I can walk you to the bus stop," she said. And then, she quickly stood and left the room.

FIFTY-TWO

Since Sharday and Donnell were planning for him to rejoin her onstage this week, they spent the next two afternoons rehearsing. But when Clyde still hadn't returned their calls by Thursday night, they settled on a new plan: Sharday would approach Clyde after the gig and tell him Donnell was ready to come back.

Now, on Friday night, Sharday took a long, hot, bubble bath before she got dressed for *The Cellar*. She was feeling great. She and Donnell had spent all afternoon snuggling up and making love. Plus, she knew tonight would be the last time she'd have to perform alone on stage. Not to mention that her music career had been on pause and Donnell was finally back to get it jump-started again.

She sighed contentedly and stretched out in the tub, letting the bubbles float over her. She fell asleep within minutes and didn't wake up until Tyesha knocked on the bathroom door a half hour later.

"Are you almost finished in there, Day-Day?" Tyesha asked through the closed door. "It's getting late. And I have to get ready before Scott gets here."

Sharday quickly leaned forward to pull the plug on the cold water. "Girl, I fell asleep," she said, raising her voice so Tyesha could hear her on the other side of the door. "Just give me a few minutes. I'll be right out."

She stood and washed between her legs and under her arms before turning on the shower to rinse off. She wrapped a towel around her body and hastily opened the door.

"About time," Tyesha said as she stepped into the bathroom. "But at least it's not all steamy in here."

"Aw, you know I wouldn't mess up your hair like that right before your big date," Sharday said, barely suppressing her laughter as she dashed down the hall to her room.

"I told you it's not like that!" Tyesha shouted just as Sharday entered her bedroom.

Sharday chuckled and reached for her lotion. It had been obvious for more than a month now that Tyesha was crazy about Scott -- even Jolean had noticed. And the fact that Tyesha was bringing him to *The Cellar* tonight said it all, because she'd been going solo every Friday night since the summer before first semester when she'd ditched all her old boyfriends.

But Tyesha kept insisting that she and Scott were just friends. He was leaving for graduate school in North Carolina in the fall and Tyesha said she didn't need the hassles of a long-distance relationship. "Who has the time or money for that?" she'd said. "And anyway, Scott doesn't actually qualify under my rule of only dating seniors because he's still going to be a student for the next two years."

On some level, Sharday almost wished she could be more like Tyesha. Tyesha had always been able to turn her feelings on and off at will where relationships were concerned. And Sharday had no doubt that when fall rolled around, Tyesha would cut Scott off without any hesitation and never look back.

But Sharday knew you couldn't experience true love if you weren't willing to put your emotions on the line. And the possibility of getting hurt or hurting somebody else was just a chance you had to take. Hopefully, Tyesha would figure that out one day. Hopefully, the right guy would eventually come along and touch her heart.

With that thought, Sharday turned her attention to getting dressed. She headed to her closet for her current favorite outfit -- black form-fitting but stretchy pants with a boot cut flare, the scoop-necked top she had bought to go with them, and spike-heeled black leather ankle boots. Tonight might be her last chance to wear this to *The Cellar* since Donnell wanted them to make the act more sexy. He wanted her to start showing more skin.

She was putting on her stage face when she heard a knock at the front door. She knew Tyesha wasn't ready, so she called out, "I'll get it," and headed up front.

"If it's Scott, can you stay out there with him for a few minutes?" Tyesha asked as Sharday passed by her room. "I'm almost ready."

Sharday agreed to play hostess for a while, but was relieved to find that April and Isaiah had arrived first instead. They weren't company. So, she left them on their own while she went back to her room to finish her makeup.

Sharday and Tyesha were still in their rooms getting ready when Scott arrived about five minutes later. April let him in and introduced herself and Isaiah. She'd heard about Scott, but this was her first time meeting him.

Now, as she watched him sit down on the sofa and cross his legs, she thought he was a huge improvement over the guys Tyesha had dated in the past. He was well spoken with a friendly demeanor, and she knew he was a senior at Maryland. And while he was cool enough to carry off the dreadlocks which almost reached his shoulders, he didn't give off the "street vibe" all of Tyesha's old boyfriends used to project.

April suppressed a melancholy sigh. Tyesha seemed to be moving forward while Sharday was mentally stuck in the ghetto. It truly pained April to know that Sharday had dumped Malcolm, with whom she was clearly in love, for a convict from the projects of southeast who didn't even have a high school diploma. Sharday had to be suffering from really low self-esteem to make a choice like that. And the only thing April knew to do was pray for her.

Just then, Tyesha entered the living room wearing a blue and white minidress, navy stockings, and navy suede heels that buckled at the ankle to emphasize her long, lean legs. "Hey, everybody!" she said, although she was looking directly at Scott. "Ready to have a good time tonight?"

They all said hello, but Scott stood and walked across the room to meet Tyesha. He embraced her in a brief hug, and he had just planted his lips on hers for a quick kiss when Sharday walked in.

"Get a room!" Sharday said with a laugh. And then, "Nah, I'm just kidding. Hi, Scott. Hey, April and Isaiah. Since everybody's here, I guess we're ready to go."

They arrived at *The Cellar* about forty-five minutes later and Sharday proceeded to bring down the house, as usual. She received a standing "o" and took an extended bow. And when she turned to leave the stage, she felt the pressure of holding down the gig on her own begin to slip from her shoulders.

She could hardly wait to tell Clyde the good news about Donnell, so she skipped her post-show trip to the ladies' room and stopped by the reserved table for a glass of champagne to boost her courage instead. She and Clyde had established a pretty good relationship over the past two years, but it was still hard to talk to him. He was just as blunt and abrupt as ever.

She polished off the glass of champagne in four quick swallows and announced that she would be back in a few minutes. She was rising from her seat when a new waitress appeared beside her and said that Clyde wanted to see her.

The waitress led her to a table near the bar -- Clyde routinely switched tables, so you never knew where he might be lurking in the club on a given night. And when the waitress stepped aside to reveal Sharday, Clyde stood and gestured for her to sit down.

"So, Donnell finally made it to a halfway house," Clyde said as soon as the waitress left. "And now, he's blowing up my phone trying to get his job back." He looked Sharday straight in the eyes then and said, "You think I should let him come back?"

The question caught Sharday off guard, but she managed to nod her head and say, "Yeah." And then, "I mean, yes, Clyde. I do. After all, I was just filling in for him until he got back."

Clyde continued to stare at her. He figured she was trying to do the right thing by taking Donnell back. But he also knew she had no idea what she was getting herself into. Jail always changed a man. He had seen it happen too many times to count. And almost ten times out of ten, the change was for the worst.

"I'll audition him a month from today," Clyde decided aloud. "At four in the afternoon." That would give her some time to change her mind. All she had to do was say the word and he would cancel the audition without a second thought.

"A month? But--"

"Final offer," he said. "Take it or leave it."

"We'll take it," she said quickly, knowing they didn't have a choice.

"And he'd better be on top of his game, too," Clyde threatened. "Because unlike you, I don't have a sentimental bone in my body." And with that, he handed over her pay envelope and stood. "I've got other business to take care of," he said, and then he turned and walked away.

FIFTY-THREE

All in all, Sharday was pretty happy with her life these days. Once Donnell got over his fury at Clyde for making him audition again and putting it off for a month, he and Sharday had settled into a comfortable routine. He came over every day during the week after she got out of class and they would make love or chill together, then they would spend several hours in the studio working on their demo tracks, and just before he left, they would spend about thirty minutes practicing for the audition.

But Vickie disapproved of her daughter's decision to let Donnell back into her life. And the fact that he was always at the apartment, which Vickie and Bruce were helping Sharday pay for, only angered Vickie more. She knew she couldn't exactly order Sharday to stop him from coming around, but maybe she could convince her that he was a bad influence.

Vickie told Sharday that Donnell would always be in and out of jail because crime was all he knew and he wasn't qualified to do anything else. She said he was a distraction from college and everything positive in Sharday's life. And she insisted he would eventually bring Sharday down if she didn't get away from him.

Sharday felt her mother's opinion of Donnell was way off base. For one thing, Donnell wasn't interfering with college at all because she studied every evening after he left to go back to the halfway house, she stayed in most Saturday nights to hit the books now that Tyesha was spending more time with Scott, and during midterms, she had even skipped the daily studio sessions to do class work at the dining room table and Donnell didn't have a problem with it.

Plus, now that Sharday had the privilege of watching Donnell get creative in the studio every day, she was beginning to realize he was a musical genius. He wasn't doomed to a life of crime just because he had dropped out of school. Look at R. Kelly, who had a reputation for being basically illiterate, but was still one of the best songwriters and producers in the business.

And anyway, Sharday had never stopped loving Donnell. So, she had made the only decision she could when she chose to stay with him. And although she still missed Malcolm, she knew she would eventually get over him.

But on the other hand, Donnell was so hard now that he had been in prison. So, she couldn't help remembering the way Malcolm always had a smile for her, how he was so quick to laugh and always looked on the bright side of things. Truth be told, Malcolm had been occupying her thoughts so much lately that most nights before she went to bed, she would pull out her prom picture and just stare at him. "Where are you now?" she would whisper in the darkness of her bedroom. "Do you miss me, too?"

FIFTY-FOUR

Two weeks after Donnell auditioned and reclaimed his job at *The Cellar*, Kayla and John threw a Saturday night dinner party at their apartment. The baby, little Kayjon, was now four months old. Kayla had found a job as a receptionist. And John had recently received a letter saying he made it onto the list to take DC Fire Department's June entrance examination. So, they were ready to celebrate and they had rounded up as much of the old crew as they could.

Sharday came with Donnell since he had finally been given full street privileges. Tyesha brought Scott, who had basically taken Mark's place. And April and Isaiah had long since become part of the crew, so they were invited, too.

Andre showed up with his so-called fiance, a chick named Nanette he had been living with for the past year who had three kids by three different fathers and her own place in the Vistas. Elise had claimed she was coming, but she'd backed out at the last minute because she was six months pregnant with her second child and too ashamed to face Tyesha and Sharday. And Hakeem was doing a twenty-year bid in a federal penitentiary in Ohio, while LaShawn was so cracked out her own family didn't even know how to get in touch with her.

John and Kayla had turned their dining room table sideways and added a card table and borrowed folding chairs. The arrangement took up most of their small living and dining room area, but at least they would all be able to eat together. After dinner, John could take down the card table to make more room for socializing.

Kayla served spaghetti and meatballs with Italian sausage, a tossed garden salad, garlic bread, and the Chianti wine Sharday and Tyesha had dropped off a few days earlier. For dessert, she would bring out the two Trader Joe cheesecakes April had sent by Sharday and Tyesha when they brought the wine.

Donnell took one look at the setup and said, "Damn! That wine tempting a nigga like shit! But I gotta have Kool-Aid or soda or something like that. They pissing me," he explained, referring to the random urine tests he received at the halfway house.

"We got some Sprite," Kayla said. She went to get him a can, thinking it was good thing she'd left the baby with one of her sisters for the night. Donnell cursed with every breath he took. Plus, he was so loud now he probably would have scared poor Kayjon out of her mind.

April stared down at her plate and suppressed a shudder of revulsion. Donnell was too uncouth for words. And the more she got to know him, the more she disliked him. What on Earth could Sharday possibly see in somebody like that? And how much longer would she be able to keep her true feelings about him from Sharday?

But although Kayla wasn't exactly looking forward to having Donnell around her baby, April was the only person at the table who truly didn't care for him. Tyesha had already accepted Sharday's decision to stay with him and welcomed him back into the fold. Isaiah and Scott were much too enthralled by his musical talents to see him objectively. Nanette liked him because he was Andre's best friend. And everyone else had grown up with him and was happy to have him back home -- especially Sharday, who saw him through star-filled eyes.

Once the meal got underway, Donnell took center stage. He bragged about how well the demo was coming along. He said before they knew it he and Sharday were going to "blow the fuck up" because he had met some "niggas" in jail who could help him get them a deal.

"Anybody we've heard of?" Isaiah asked, mesmerized by Donnell. He knew a lot of the top rappers had spent time in jail and it wouldn't have surprised him if Donnell had impressed some of them with his lyrical skills.

"Nah, these the kind of niggas who call the shots behind the scenes," Donnell said, knowing they would never guess he was talking about certified gang members. Most people had no idea how much influence gangs and drug crews had in certain parts of the hip-hop industry. But just to be safe, he changed the subject and started amusing them with stories of some of the wild things he had seen in prison.

When everyone had gotten their fill of spaghetti and salad, Kayla brought out the two cheesecakes. One was covered with a strawberry topping, while the other was plain. "Dessert time!" she announced.

"Let's blaze up first," Andre said. "I got blunts." He was still as much of a pothead as ever.

"Yeah, let's do that," Nanette said.

"Y'all gonna have to take that outside," John told them. "Kayla don't allow no smoking in here because of the baby. Plus, I can't afford to get no weed in my system right before I take my physical."

"Yeah, dog," Donnell said. "I can't be up under that shit neither. Be done messed around and screwed up my next urine." He looked at Andre then and said, "Nigga, you know that."

"Whatever, nigga," Andre said. "We ain't got no problem taking it outside. Anybody else game?"

Sharday said, "Nah, I'm cool," and Tyesha and Isaiah begged off, too.

Andre knew April didn't smoke, so he looked at Scott and said, "What about you, man? You coming?"

Scott chuckled. This wasn't the first time someone had assumed he smoked weed because he wore dreads. "Don't let the locks fool you, Andre," he said. "I'm basically a square."

While Andre and Nanette were outside getting high, the ladies cleared the dinner dishes and cleaned the kitchen. The guys put away the card table and arranged the folding chairs on either side of the sofa, then John turned on the radio and placed a board game called *Dirty Minds* on the coffee table.

Once Andre and Nanette returned, they all gathered in the living room to play the game over dessert. None of them had ever actually played *Dirty Minds* before, which had them trying to come up with totally innocent answers to seemingly filthy-minded clues. And they ended up having so much fun they played it twice in a row.

John tried to get a game of spades started after that, but the party broke up. Tyesha said she and Scott were planning to catch a movie with April and Isaiah. And Sharday said she had to drop Andre and Nanette off before taking Donnell back to Baltimore.

As John headed for the bedroom to get the coats, he found himself grinning in anticipation. He was looking forward to having his wife all to himself tonight. The baby had put a serious cramp in their love life and he was hoping to make up for lost time.

Kayla had also expected their friends to stay longer, but she wasn't mad at them either. The baby still kept her up almost every night. And now that she was working and could no longer take her daily nap, what she really needed more than anything else was a good night's sleep. Maybe tonight, she could finally get one.

FIFTY-FIVE

Sharday and Donnell had their first serious disagreement in late April when she told him she would have to skip all studio sessions for the next month so she could study for finals and write two papers.

"Ha, ha. Real funny," he said at first, thinking she was joking.

That wasn't the response she needed to hear, so she said, "I'm serious, Boo. It's crunch time now." And then she caught herself and switched to her ghetto lingo. "Them exams and papers be counting for up to half the grade," she said. "So, I really gotta hit the books now. This make or break time for me, Boo."

"Forget about college, Day-Day," he said. "You don't need that shit no more. We this close to finishing the demo." His thumb and forefinger were almost touching when he raised his hand. "And I be out of the halfway house in June."

"And exams be over by the end of May, so what's the problem?" she shot back. "You ain't take me through all this when I did it for midterms."

"For two short weeks!" he said. But then he quickly calmed down and started laying out his case. "Day-Day, them midterms was a long time ago. Way back when I was still trying to get back used to the studio. But right now we so damn close to the deal I can almost feel it. All we got left is one song! Please don't do this shit to me right now, okay?"

Sharday knew she needed this year of college to fall back on just in case, so she went on the offensive. "Donnell, you know how hard I been working all semester to keep my grades up!" she said. "And I can't believe you asking me to flush it all down the drain now that it's almost over!"

"And I can't believe you putting school ahead of our music!" he said. "Since when college start coming before everything else, Day-Day? Where this shit coming from?"

Sharday was shocked to hear fear in Donnell's voice when he asked where this was coming from. She looked at him closely then, and she could see fear in his eyes, too. She'd always known he wasn't exactly happy about her going to college, but it wasn't until this exact moment that she realized he felt threatened by it.

She sighed heavily and sat down on her bed, gesturing for him to come sit beside her. Now that she thought about it, she could see how he might be afraid college would change her feelings for him. As a matter of fact, her mother was hoping it eventually would.

But Sharday knew that would never happen, so she decided to try a different approach. "I just don't think you looking at the whole picture, Boo," she said, reaching for his hands after he sat down. "I mean, we still need this apartment. And you know my mother and Bruce ain't gonna keep paying if I flunk out. Plus, you can still come over and work in the studio like you did during midterms. That ain't gonna change. It's just that I gotta take a break from it for a minute so I can get through this. For both of us."

She smiled then and said, "It won't be that bad, Boo. It be over before you know it. And after that, you got me all to yourself for the whole summer. I promise."

Donnell didn't like it, but he knew she was right. He definitely couldn't afford to put her up in a place of her own. And he damn sure didn't want her moving back out there to Mitchellville with that mother of hers. Vickie couldn't stand his guts and would do anything she could to break them up.

But this whole situation just made him that much more determined to get Sharday out from under her mother's control. And he was going to do it by the end of the summer, too. Because when fall rolled around again, he didn't want to hear one damn word about college.

"Alright, Day-Day," he finally said. "Do what you gotta do." Then he got up and walked back over to the studio.

FIFTY-SIX

The week after Sharday finished her exams, Donnell kept her in the studio from eight in the morning to eight-thirty at night for four days straight. They took Friday off so they'd be fresh for *The Cellar*. And it was understood she had to work at *Old Navy* all day on Saturday and Sunday. But the next week, they were right back at it again.

This went on for three weeks in a row, with the exception of the one morning they took off to attend April's graduation from Mitchellville High. But finally, on the third Thursday evening at exactly forty-two minutes after six, Donnell announced that their demo was done. They had totally reworked the three tracks they laid down before finals started. And instead of adding only one more song, they had added two.

They now had two club bangers – tracks with strong bass lines and anthem-type lyrics about partying and living the high life; one of those deep songs Donnell had started writing after he got sent to federal prison -- this one was about the hopelessness of poverty; one cut for the ladies -- which featured Sharday singing a hook about feelings that wouldn't be denied and Donnell rapping about a player who had met the right woman but was having a hard time changing his ways; and to Sharday's surprise, one track for the gangsters that focused on pulling "heists," moving large quantities of "caine," and "riding" on other crews, which meant doing drive-by shootings.

"How you manage to come up with this?" Sharday had asked the first time she heard the hardcore cut. She knew for a fact Donnell had never experienced any of the things he was rapping about on that song, but it all sounded so real.

"Niggas in the joint like to brag," he said. "And I made it my business to listen. Because those the kind of true life stories the people wanna hear."

"Wow," she said. "That's deep." And since she trusted him totally when it came to their music, she started working on the hook for the track.

Donnell got out of the halfway house for good on the Friday morning after they finished the demo. Sharday went to pick him up, and the first thing they did was stop by a Post Office to express mail a copy of the demo to Greg Foster, Donnell's old poetry teacher in upstate New York. Greg had agreed to take the demo over to Allen Brook and play it for Donnell's contacts during poetry class. And since the class was now being held on Tuesday afternoons, they wanted to make sure he got it in time.

Of course, neither Sharday nor Donnell had ever used express mail before -- they were using it this time at Greg's suggestion. And they were both under the impression he'd get their package Monday. But at a few minutes after eleven on Saturday morning, Greg called on Donnell's pay-as-you-go cell phone and awoke them from a deep sleep.

"Who this?" Donnell growled into the phone after Sharday roused him. They had partied until six in the morning celebrating his freedom and their new demo. And since he was getting high again now that he didn't have to worry about weekly urine tests anymore, his brain was fuzzy and his mouth was dry.

"Donnell! My man!" Greg said excitedly, affecting the "hip guy" persona he always projected around his prison students. "It's me. Your boy, Greg."

"Greg?" Donnell said, slowly sitting up and nudging Sharday back awake. "You got the demo already?" he said loudly for Sharday's benefit. And then he swallowed hard to produce some saliva.

Sharday was feeling the aftereffects of too many drinks and blunts, too, but her eyes popped open and she croaked, "He got the demo?" Then she struggled to sit up so she could listen in.

Donnell turned the phone face forward so Sharday could hear too before he asked, "So, what you think, man? You like it?"

"Like it?" Greg shouted. "Man, I love it! Airtight rhymes that paint pictures like photographs! The best songstress to hit the scene since Beyoncé! And beats so hot they strike a chord in your soul! I see platinum in the future for you and your lady, Donnell! No joke! Maybe even double platinum!"

Sharday was grinning from ear to ear by the time Greg paused to catch a breath. But Donnell just grunted and said, "I hope Rambler and them see it the same way. I need them to make this thing happen."

"And if they can't or won't, somebody else will," Greg said firmly. He wasn't entirely convinced Rambler and his gang had the industry connections they professed to have. But he'd already had that conversation with Donnell a few times, so he promised to play the CD at the next class and call back on Tuesday night.

True to his word, Greg rang again at a quarter after eight on Tuesday night. "You won't believe this, man!" he said as soon as Donnell answered. "But you were right about Rambler all along!"

"What you mean?" Donnell asked, glancing at Sharday, who was, of course, listening in.

"I mean he's actually who he says he is, Donnell," Greg said. "And he told me to take your CD over to *Urban Legends Records* at midnight on Saturday. He said someone would be expecting me."

Sharday jumped off the bed and let out a whoop of joy. "Yes!" she started exclaiming over and over as she punched her fists in the air.

Donnell had almost dropped the phone when she bounced up unexpectedly, but now he shushed her and pressed the phone tightly to his ear. "I wanna take it over there myself," he said to Greg. "What he tell you to do?"

When Donnell hung up a few minutes later, he said, "We going to Jersey Saturday night, Day-Day." Then he turned to look at her and grinned. "You hear me, baby? I said we going to Jersey!"

It had been so long since she'd seen a genuine smile on his face that she swooped down on him for a kiss as she said, "I hear you, Boo!"

He grabbed her and pulled her down on top of him, and she couldn't help but laugh. But then she looked into his eyes and said, "You my hero, Donnell. I always knew you could do it." And she leaned forward to kiss him.

FIFTY-SEVEN

At six thirty on Saturday evening, Sharday and Donnell were seated in the back of the Altima she shared with April as it barreled up the highway towards Sedgewick, New Jersey. Since this was April's week for the car and she had insisted on driving them up, she was behind the wheel and Isaiah was beside her in the front passenger seat.

The radio was on, and April and Isaiah were carrying on a conversation, but Sharday and Donnell were each absorbed in their own thoughts.

Sharday was stretched out with her head resting against the rear window on the driver's side, her legs across Donnell's lap, and her feet touching the door behind Isaiah. Her eyes were closed and she was thinking about *Urban Legend Records*.

Based on what Donnell had told her and what she'd learned from the internet, this was a small, black-owned, independent record label that started out five years earlier with two R&B groups who never sold beyond gold. But a year and a half ago, the label head signed a hot young rapper named Young Baller and somehow managed to push his debut disc all the way to platinum, which had put *Urban Legend* on the map. Sharday was convinced that Double D-Day's unique combination of rap and R&B would be right up the label's alley.

For his part, Donnell was staring unseeingly out the window next to him as he mentally prepared for the night ahead. He had to be ready to pounce on even the slightest opportunity to talk up the demo and give that extra push that Greg wouldn't have been able to give. This might be their one and only shot at the top. And he was damned sure going to take full advantage of it.

When April crossed the Maryland state line into Delaware, Isaiah turned down the radio and shouted, "Yeah, we're in my home state now! Delaware for life!"

Sharday opened her eyes and Donnell turned to look at Isaiah.

Isaiah twisted around in his seat to grin at them both. "I sure wish we could make a quick detour to let my homies see us," he said. "Because once you two make it big, nobody's going to believe I was there from the beginning."

Sharday smiled. Isaiah was one of the few people who believed in Donnell as much as she did. "Don't even worry about it," she said. "You know you good for a shout out in the credits."

"Well, don't leave me out," April joked. "After all, I'm the group's first unofficial chauffeur. Right, Donnell?" She still couldn't help feeling he was bad news. But since she knew Sharday would never leave him now that he was going to pull this deal off, she was determined to establish a relationship with him.

Donnell grunted in amusement and agreed with April before he turned back to the window. He knew she was changing her mind about him now that he'd come through, but he wasn't mad at her. It was supposed to work like that. Results deserved respect.

Sharday closed her eyes again and her thoughts drifted. She was happy April and Donnell were finally starting to get along. And she was still hoping her mother would eventually come around. But the only thing on her mind right now was *Urban Legend Records*.

They arrived in Sedgewick two hours early at ten o'clock, just as they'd planned. It was a large suburban town about twenty miles away from the Jersey side of the New York/New Jersey border. And *Urban Legend* occupied a beige brick house in a residential area near the outskirts of town.

Isaiah was behind the wheel by now, and as he slowly drove past the house, they could see that most of the lights were on inside. A black Cadillac Escalade and a black Lincoln Navigator were parked on a paved area to the side of the house, while a mix of older and newer Nissans, Acuras and the like, as well as a huge black Ford Excursion, lined the curb out front.

"Drive around some," Donnell told Isaiah. "Let's see who live around this joint."

Isaiah drove through the quiet residential streets in the immediate vicinity, but they didn't see any people outside. The houses were modest and well-maintained, even though most of them had bars on the lower windows. The vehicles in front of the houses were nice enough but nothing too extravagant. Overall, it seemed to be a nice, respectable neighborhood.

But about five blocks away, they crossed some sort of invisible line. Here, there were smaller dilapidated houses mixed in with apartment buildings. Black and brown folks were out in full effect on the sidewalks and street corners on this hot summer night. And music blared from many of the cars and homes.

"Well, I guess we in the hood now," Sharday said.

"Not the rap hood, the real hood," Isaiah added, borrowing a line from a Jay-Z song.

"Yeah, and now a nigga feel right at home up in this joint," Donnell said. "Go on back to the label's house," he told Isaiah.

April said she was starting to get hungry again, so they made a brief trip to the drive-through of a McDonald's they had passed on the way through town. After that, they went straight back to *Urban Legend*, parked at the end of the block and turned off the headlights, and settled in to watch and wait.

They didn't see much over the course of the next hour and twenty minutes. Two young thug types in white tee shirts pulled up in a late model Lexus and went in. A delivery man double-parked his Ford hatchback with a blinking "*Chicken Shack*" sign on top and dropped off three bags of food. Two women in miniskirts and weaves came out and got into an older Acura Legend. Other than that, nothing happened.

At exactly five minutes to twelve, Donnell and Sharday got out of the car and headed down the block. They climbed the few steps leading to the front porch and admired the graffiti-style sign above the door bearing the studio's name and logo, then Donnell raised his left arm so they could both see his watch. He waited until the precise stroke of midnight before he reached out to ring the doorbell.

The door opened almost immediately and an imposing muscle-bound guy with really dark skin and a bald head looked at Donnell and said, "Greg Foster, right? You got the disc?"

Donnell said, "Yeah, I got it. But actually I'm Donnell Dickerson, the rapper from Double D-Day." He stepped back and nudged Sharday forward slightly. "And this Sharday Grant, the other half of the group," he said as he raised his hands waist high and subtly flashed the hand signal for this branch of the gang -- the letters "O" and "G" in sign language, which stood for *Original Gangsters*.

The muscle-bound guy clicked on the porch light to look for the signature triple-strand tattoo ring on Donnell's right ring finger. Once he spotted it, he turned off the light and said, "What up, my nigga?" to Donnell, and "How you doing, Miss Lady?" to Sharday. Then he looked at Donnell again and said, "Let me see if I can let you in."

He closed the door and left Donnell and Sharday cooling their heels on the porch for almost half an hour before he finally returned and said, "They gave you two first floor privileges. Come on in."

"I'm Pit," he said as Sharday and Donnell stepped through the doorway. He led them into the living room, which was quite chic with its mauve walls and black leather furniture, and then he told them to sit down as he laid a pack of premium blunt papers and a plastic baggie full of weed on the table.

"Roll one, dog," he told Donnell. "Y'all want something to drink? We got Ciroc, Henny, Courvosier, Patron, beer, champagne, wine. Pretty much everything."

Sharday chose champagne and Donnell asked for the Courvosier he'd taken to drinking lately. It wasn't long before Pit returned with the drinks and put fire to the blunt Donnell had rolled.

Sharday and Donnell took weak hits of the weed and nursed their drinks so they would be straight enough to handle their business. And just as Pit leaned forward to roll another blunt, a short, fat brother sporting a spinning, diamond-encrusted version of the label's logo on a thick platinum chain entered the living room. He was accompanied by a petite woman in skintight jeans, a halter top and high-heeled sandals.

Pit told Donnell and Sharday that they had "lucked out." "This Big Jeff, the beat master around here," he said. "And that's Candy, his assistant."

Sharday and Donnell recognized Big Jeff's name from Young Baller's CD. He had produced some of the best tracks on the album. So, they quickly stood to shake hands with him and Candy.

"Them joints you did for Young Baller was hot, man," Donnell said. "On the real."

"Thanks, money," Big Jeff said. "I appreciate that."

"Especially *Bring It On*," Sharday added, referring to the street anthem that had dominated the radio airwaves the summer before. "That joint had DC rocking."

"Oh, yeah. Definitely," Big Jeff said. "DC show us mad love every time we roll through. I ain't got nothing but love for the fans down there." He looked at Donnell then and said, "So, where the demo, money?"

Donnell handed over the demo and Big Jeff looked down at the label Sharday had placed on it with the new software she'd bought the day before. It was pretty primitive as far as labels went. No picture or graphics. Just the group's name followed by "D's Cell" and "Day's Cell" and their respective numbers.

At Big Jeff's signal, Pit led them all over to the closed door leading to the dining room. He opened the door and stepped back to let them enter, then he closed the door behind them before he left.

The dining room walls were stark white, the long shiny black table looked like it belonged in a boardroom, and the matching black console supported an array of electronics that included a high-end stereo and a plasma television. Although the stereo was off, faint strains of music and excited chatter drifted into the room from the open door behind the opposite end of the table. There was obviously a party going on somewhere in the house.

Big Jeff handed the demo to Candy and sank into a cushy leather armchair on one side of the table while motioning for Donnell and Sharday to take seats across from him.

Candy closed the door at the opposite end of the table before she put the CD into the stereo and picked up the remote. Then she plucked a pre-rolled blunt from one of the console drawers and lit it, handing it to Big Jeff as she sat down beside him.

Big Jeff slowly smoked the blunt all to himself as he listened to the demo. Every now and again, he'd say, "Run that back a few bars," and Candy would do as he asked. But other than that, he was totally silent.

Sharday and Donnell couldn't tell, but Big Jeff was actually quite impressed with them and their music. He knew these were the kind of hot young artists *Urban Legend* had to keep signing to become a real force in the business. The label could only go so far riding on Young Baller's coattails.

After the last song ended, he had Donnell and Sharday perform the hardcore track a cappella. When they finished, he nodded appreciatively and said, "Where y'all get the heat?" Which meant he wanted to know who supplied the music for the track.

Donnell saw his chance and took it. "From me," he said, patting his chest. "That whole demo is all us, Big Jeff. Beats, production, lyrics, everything." And then, in a more serious tone with one-on-one eye contact, "We the real thing, Big Jeff. We been doing this shit together for years and we got the track record to prove it. Two years at *Club 202*. The last two years at *The Cellar*. And we talking two of the hottest clubs on the DC scene."

"So, we got years and years' worth of original tracks," Sharday added, getting into the spirit. "And plus, we already got a following in DC."

Big Jeff nodded again and said, "I'm feeling it. But I gotta see what my partners think." He struggled up from his chair. "We'll be in touch in two weeks," he said. Then he shook hands with each of them and told Candy to walk them out.

FIFTY-EIGHT

The next two weeks were tense for Sharday and Donnell. She stuck to her weekend schedule at *Old Navy* instead of spreading her hours throughout the week and taking on the extra shift she had worked the summer before. He refrained from going back to selling weed or getting deeper into the gang even though his funds were low. They were both in wait mode, and they spent most of their time getting high and daydreaming about a future with *Urban Legend.*

But the two weeks passed and they heard nothing from the label. And after another week went by, they left messages at the number Candy had given them, but still got no response.

When Donnell finally asked Greg to talk to Rambler, Rambler sent word to be patient. "He said 'these things take time, so be easy,'" Greg reported back. "And that's all he would say about it."

By this time, Donnell had already drafted a couple of young homies in the Vistas to sell weed for him and he was getting his supply from a fellow ex-con in *The Greater Southeast Crew*. He took the lack of word from *Urban Legend* as a sign that they weren't really interested, despite what Rambler said. And he decided to submit the demo to other labels.

Sharday got on the internet to research names and addresses, but it didn't take her long to figure out that most labels wouldn't accept what they called "unsolicited songs." She and Donnell would have to get a manager or publisher if they wanted to submit to the major labels and many of the independents. And Donnell didn't want to give up that kind of control. So, in the end, they only sent the demo to a handful of independents.

"That shit wasn't nothing but something to do," Donnell told Sharday after they left the Post Office and climbed back into the Nissan. "Forget leaving our career up to some lame-ass independent labels we ain't never even heard of. A nigga ain't about to go out like that."

He turned to look at her then and said, "My word is bond, Day-Day.

And you know that. And I promise I'm gonna come up with a way to get our demo heard by the majors soon."

She sighed heavily and said, "I know you will, Boo. But I was really counting on *Urban Legend*. Even though I shoulda known they was just too damn good to be true. Don't nobody get signed that easy."

"That's why we can't let this get us down, Day-Day," he said. "It's the game, not us. We just gotta pay our dues like everybody else do. But we both know we gonna blow the dome off the industry sooner or later."

She sighed again and said, "Yeah, I know you right." Then she cranked up the air conditioner and pulled off.

FIFTY-NINE

Over the course of the next few weeks, Sharday tried to resume a normal life. She took on more hours at work, joined the aerobics class Vickie had recently begun teaching, and started hanging out more at the house in Mitchellville and at Frank and Belinda's condo again. She even talked Tyesha and Jolean into helping her baby-sit little Kayjon every now and then so Kayla and John could get a break.

But the summer was slipping by and nothing was happening with Sharday and Donnell's music career. So when early August turned into mid-August, Vickie used her one-on-one time with Sharday after aerobics class to ask about her daughter's plans for the next year of college.

They were sitting on the sofa in the combination office, lounge, and changing room Vickie shared with five other female fitness instructors. Vickie spent a lot of her free time at the gym these days and her small section of the room showed it. It was nicely decorated with a mini-fridge full of low-carb snacks and drinks, a miniature television/radio, family pictures, a small potted plant. She also kept a bag with extra workout clothes, back-up toiletries and an emergency outfit with shoes in her bottom desk drawer.

She credited the gym with totally turning her life around and she loved being there. She was looking and feeling better than she had in years, and her marriage was stronger for it. She'd found a new set of friends who shared her healthy lifestyle and diet. And now, she was actually getting paid for part of the time she spent staying fit. The only real trouble spot in her life was this situation with Sharday and Donnell.

She sipped from her bottled water and let Sharday vent for a while over the lack of response from *Urban Legend* and the other independent labels. That was her daughter's favorite conversation these days. Finally, she set her water down and said, "So, what are you planning to do about school now that summer's coming to an end?"

Sharday shrugged and popped a couple of Vickie's macadamia nuts in her mouth. They were naturally low-carb, which she wasn't really into, but they were starting to grow on her. "I'm not sure, Ma," she admitted. "To be honest, I'm still kind of hoping *Urban Legend* will come through. Plus, Donnell's working on a plan to go up to New York City and chase down the major labels. But on the other hand, something in the back of my mind keeps telling me to go ahead and get this extra year of college under my belt because it's going to take a lot longer to get signed than we expected."

"Well, you know Bruce and I support you one hundred percent in your music, honey," Vickie said. "But we've been talking about it, and we both think you need to go back to college since nothing's actually happening right now. You can always skip a day of classes here or there to take meetings with the labels once they start responding. But in the meantime, at least until things start taking off, you should be in school."

"And if I don't go back to college, I'm on my own financially, right, Ma?" Sharday said. She knew exactly where this conversation was going.

"Well, what else do you expect me to say, Sharday?" Vickie asked. "Bruce would be having this same discussion with April if she were the one in your situation, and you know it. The bottom line is--"

Vickie stopped speaking when they heard rapid footsteps approaching the closed door to the room. They looked at each other and said, "Karen," referring to a personal trainer whose last appointment for the day had just ended.

Sure enough, the door opened and a petite but muscular white woman with freckles and curly red hair rushed in wearing electric blue spandex pants and a matching top. "Hey, guys," she said to Vickie and Sharday as she picked up the garment bag which lay across her desk and headed straight for the shower room. "Sorry to be so anti," she added with an apologetic smile. "But I have an hour to change and make it into the city. And my brother will kill me if I'm late."

After Karen disappeared into the shower room, Vickie said, "As I was saying, honey--"

"Okay, okay, Ma," Sharday said. "I get the point. I'm going back to school." She wasn't exactly angry at her mother and Bruce. She could understand where they were coming from. But she was already stressed out and this conversation had only increased her burden. Because Donnell was picking her up in a few minutes. Which meant she would have to explain the situation to him.

"I've gotta go, Ma," she said as she grabbed her gym bag from the floor.

Vickie walked her daughter to the door and gave her a warm hug. "We're just trying to look out for you, baby," she said. "That's our job, you know?"

"I know, Ma. I'll see you tomorrow." Sharday released her mother and left.

Donnell was waiting out front for her in the hoopty he'd recently bought from the auto auction. He climbed out of his aging Mercury Cougar and opened the front passenger door for her, giving her a quick kiss before she climbed in.

"You wanna get something to eat, Day-Day?" he asked as he pulled off.

"Nah, Boo," she said. "I just wanna go home." She turned to look out the window on her side.

He blasted DJ Khaled's latest track and headed for the apartment. She was clearly upset and he could tell she needed some space. So, even though he was pretty sure her mother had pissed her off and he wanted to know what happened, he left her alone. He allowed his mind to drift back to the conversation he'd had with his own mother the day before.

He'd been holding on to hard feelings against his mother for years. He resented her for checking out on crack and leaving him to raise his younger siblings. Still hadn't forgiven her for making him the man of the house way before he was ready. But she'd been clean for more than three and a half years now, long enough for him to start believing she had finally kicked the habit for good. And on yesterday, after weeks of her trying to draw him out, he'd finally admitted how hard her addiction had been on him, how scared and alone he'd felt every single day while it was going on. His mother cried and cried, apologized over and over for everything she had put him through. And when it was all said and done, they walked away feeling closer to each other than they'd been in years.

But now, he was pulled away from his reverie as he parked in a space in front of the apartment building and Sharday placed a hand on his arm. "I got something to tell you, Boo," she said. And I already know you ain't gonna like it."

"Just tell me straight up," he said, turning to face her.

"Well," she said slowly. "I was talking things over with my mother. And, well . . . well, I decided I'm gonna go ahead and register for college at the end of the month."

"Is that right?" he said quietly. Vickie was definitely kicking where it hurt. But she was out of her damn mind if she thought he wouldn't retaliate. He would just step up his plans to go to New York. He had already made contact with a fellow gang member in the Bronx who was willing to put both him and Sharday up, so the news that he was coming alone wouldn't be a problem. And since the Cougar was reliable enough to get him up to New York and back home every week to do the gig at *The Cellar*, he could be ready to leave by Saturday morning coming.

"Don't even worry about it, Day-Day," he finally said. "I ain't gonna trip off no petty shit like that. Especially when I know you not the one in control right now. All I gotta do is go up to New York and handle my damn business. Like I shoulda done a long time ago. But that's alright. Because we about to flip the whole script on everybody." And with that, he confidently climbed out of the car and walked around to open her door.

SIXTY

Donnell made plans to leave for New York the Saturday morning before college registration week started. He finalized his living arrangements in the Bronx, hired Andre to keep an eye on his weed business, and got a bootleg mechanic to tune-up the Cougar. He also came up with a "blueprint" for shopping the demo.

First, he would focus on the two black-owned labels he thought they had the best chances with: Irv Gotti's *Murder Inc. Records,* which still had a few R&B singers but desperately needed a new rap star because its only platinum rapper, Ja Rule, had long since faded into obscurity after losing a long-running battle with 50 Cent; and Sean "P. Diddy" Combs' *Bad Boy Records* because Diddy had worked with rappers like the Notorious B.I.G., French Montana, and Jadakiss, as well as R&B singers like Mary J. Blige and Faith Evans. If those two labels didn't bite, Donnell would try 50 Cent's *G-Unit Records*, and maybe *Def Jam Recordings,* which had practically everybody, including 2-Chainz, YG, Big Sean, Joe Budden, Lil Durk, DJ Mustard, as well as Jhené Aiko, August Alsina, Alessia Cara and Teairra Mari. And after that, he planned to go after the majors like *Columbia*, *RCA*, *Atlantic* and *Warner Brother Records*.

But on the Wednesday evening before he was scheduled to leave, Candy called on his cell phone and said that Double D-Day had a two o'clock appointment at *Urban Legend* on Monday afternoon. "With Tank this time," she said, referring to the label head.

Donnell was shocked speechless for a few seconds. Then he said, "Do this mean we finally about to get our deal?"

"That's up to Tank," she replied.

"Alright," Donnell said. "Then tell him we be there on Monday." And as soon as he ended the call with Candy, he called Sharday.

"What?" Sharday screamed when he told her about the appointment. "Stop playing, Boo! Oh, my God! Oh, my God! Oh, my God!" She was in the living room with Tyesha and Jolean and they both wanted to know what was going on. She grinned at them and shouted, "We got a meeting at *Urban Legend*, y'all! With Tank Smith!"

As Tyesha and Jolean began babbling excitedly, Donnell said, "So, now you can forget about all that registration bullshit, Day-Day. Because we going back up the road again. And this time, we ain't leaving until we got our deal."

"Well, hopefully, they finally ready to make us a offer and we ain't gotta worry about all that," Sharday said.

"But just in case we do," he insisted, thinking back to his conversation with Candy.

Sharday laughed then. "You worry too much, Boo!" she said. "We got a meeting with Tank Smith on Monday! Things finally starting to go our way! Come on over here so we can celebrate!"

Her excitement proved too contagious for him to resist. So, he decided to go with the flow for now and worry about the details later. "I'm on my way, Day-Day," he said. "You want me to stop by the liquor store first?"

"And you know it!" she said. "We about to get our party on, Boo. And we gonna order some food once you get here, too."

After Sharday hung up from Donnell, she jumped for joy with Tyesha and Jolean for a few minutes before she picked up the phone again to spread the good news. Her first call was to the house in Mitchellville. And when Bruce answered, she asked him to put her on speaker and get Vickie and April because she had an "important family announcement."

Bruce said, "April's not here. But your mother's sitting right beside me. Hold on a second." As he put Sharday on speaker and hung up the handset, she could hear him whispering the words "family announcement" to her mother.

"Hi, honey," Vickie said. "What's going on?"

"*Urban Legend* called us back!" Sharday blurted, unable to hold in her glee any longer. "Can y'all believe it? We've got a meeting with Tank Smith -- the head of the whole label -- on Monday! Our deal is finally about to come through!"

"Congratulations, Sharday!" Bruce said. "I knew they would eventually call back!"

Vickie said, "That's great, baby. But did they actually say they're ready to sign on the dotted line?"

Sharday shrugged. "Well, Donnell got the call. So, I won't know exactly what they said until he gets here. But we've got a meeting with the label head, Ma! What else could that mean but a deal?"

"Given how they've strung you along for the whole summer, who knows what that means?" Vickie said.

"I hate to admit it, Sharday, but I have to agree with your mother," Bruce said.

"And Monday's the first day of registration," Vickie added.

Sharday refused to let them bring her down. "But Tank Smith wants a meeting with us!" she said. "I can see you two don't really get how significant that is, so I'll stop by tomorrow and we can talk about it. But right now, I have to spread the word around."

When Sharday hung up from her mother and Bruce, Tyesha said, "Let me guess. Miss Vickie wants you to blow off *Urban Legend* so you can register."

"What is she thinking?" Jolean asked.

Sharday rolled her eyes and said, "Who knows? But that's definitely not happening." Then she picked up the handset again to call Frank and Belinda. This time, she was careful to control her excitement and say only that she and Donnell had an appointment with the owner of *Urban Legend* on Monday afternoon.

Frank laughed in surprise and said, "Are you kidding me, Sharday? The owner of the label?" He was happy for his daughter, but he couldn't help feeling a little jealous, too. In all the years he'd pursued a music career, he'd never gotten an opportunity like this.

Belinda said, "Oh, honey. I'm so proud of you and Donnell.

And the next thing Sharday knew, she found herself saying, "But the only downside is that registration at PG starts next week. I mean, what if I skip registration and they still don't offer us a deal? I'll be out in the cold."

Frank recognized Vickie's bougie point of view as soon as he heard it, so he said, "College isn't going anywhere, honey. It'll always be there. But an opportunity like this might only come around once in a lifetime."

"Pursue your dreams while you have the chance to, Sharday," Belinda urged her. "Almost anybody can go to college, but talent like yours is given only to the chosen few."

Sharday grinned and raised a thumb up for Tyesha and Jolean's benefit. After she clicked off from her father and his fiancée, she tried April's cell but got no answer. She was dialing Kayla and John's apartment when Donnell buzzed in on the other line to say he was pulling into a parking space out front.

Sharday hung up the phone and met Donnell at the front door. She managed to restrain herself just long enough for him to put the drinks on the table before she flung her arms around his neck and shrieked, "You did it, Boo! Oh, my God! We finally on our way!"

He instantly got caught up in the moment. "It's all about our music now, Day-Day!" he said as he lifted her off the floor and twirled her around. Then he set her back down and kissed her.

Tyesha and Jolean shouted out their congratulations and headed for the dining room to join them. It wasn't long before Sharday, Tyesha and Jolean were drinking champagne, Donnell was putting a dent in his Courvosier, and they all were puffing trees.

Jolean had given up the pretense of being a straight-laced virgin in front of Tyesha and Sharday about a month earlier. She'd told them that she liked her blunts and champagne and had a nineteen-year old boyfriend named Rome, who was planning to go to school for his CDL license so he could drive tractor-trailers long distance. And since Tyesha and Sharday knew they had done as much and worse when they were her age, they didn't give her too much grief about it. Now, Sharday drained her champagne glass and said, "Hit me again, Jolean." She turned to look at Donnell then and said, "So, Boo. What I wanna know is . . . What did Candy actually say when you talked to her? Did she say they finally gonna give us our contract or what?"

"Well, she ain't exactly say we was gonna get a deal out the meeting," he admitted after exhaling a cloud of smoke. But when he saw how Sharday, Tyesha and Jolean were hanging on his every word, he added, "But that shit was pretty much understood, you know what I'm saying? They done had our demo for months now, we put it down live for her and Big Jeff while we was up there, and here she is hitting my cell saying Tank Smith want us to come back for a meeting with him. I mean, damn. How much clearer could it get?"

"That's what I'm talking about!" Tyesha said at the same time Jolean said, "I know that's right!"

Sharday didn't say anything because she was comparing Donnell's opinion to her mother's opinion. She had to admit Vickie was right about *Urban Legend* leaving them hanging all summer after saying they would hear something in two weeks. And although there was no way she would blow off this meeting with Tank, who was to say it wouldn't lead to more of the same?

Donnell noticed that Sharday hadn't responded, so he said, "Look at it like this, Day-Day. The fact that Tank Smith even trying to see us mean our demo the shit if it don't mean nothing else. So, if we get up there and he ain't trying to do business, to hell with him. We'll just go to New York and find somebody who is."

Sharday puffed on the blunt Tyesha had passed her and slowly nodded her head. She wanted to win big, which meant she had to risk big. And with the way hip hop was constantly changing, she knew they had to push the demo while it was hot. Plus, her world wouldn't end if her mother and Bruce cut her off financially. She had money in the bank and they would still have the gig at *The Cellar*. And if nothing came through by the end of the year, she could always go back to school in January.

She looked at Donnell and said, "You know what, Boo? You right. We done came this damn far and it's too late to turn back now. So, I'm down for New York, too, if that's what it take." Then she raised her glass for a toast and said, "To Double D-Day. Whatever it take."

"To Double D-Day," Tyesha and Jolean echoed, but Donnell said, "Double D-Day. Do or die."

SIXTY-ONE

By the time the weekend rolled around, Sharday was so upset over her mother's refusal to accept her decision about college that they were barely speaking. But on Saturday morning, Sharday got up at the crack of dawn and went over to the house in Mitchellville, anyway. Because April was leaving for Northwestern University today.

Sharday plastered a smile on her face as she let herself into the house and headed toward the kitchen, where she found Vickie and Bruce in the last stages of fixing a huge breakfast of bacon, sausage, country ham, scrambled eggs with cheese, grits, hash browns, toasted wheat bread, biscuits, blueberries and strawberries. Vickie was now on a low-carb "maintenance plan," as she called it, so she could eat as much bacon, sausage, ham and scrambled eggs with cheese as she wanted. She could even have a few strawberries.

"Good morning," Sharday said, giving them each a perfunctory kiss on the cheek. "Need some help? Where's April?"

"Good morning, Sharday," Bruce said. "Perfect timing, as always!"

Vickie said, "Good morning. April's upstairs. Would you let her know breakfast is ready?"

Sharday looked at her mother and said, "Why don't we call a temporary truce, Ma? This is April's last morning home."

"I have no intention of ruining her last morning here, Sharday," Vickie said. "But everyone knows where things stand between me and you, so there's no need to pretend."

Sharday said, "Then I guess we'll do it your way, Ma. As usual." And she left to go up to April's bedroom.

April opened her door before Sharday could knock and quickly pulled her into the room. "I was hoping they'd send you up to get me," she said. "I have to tell you something. But you need to sit down first."

"I'm too sleepy for all this drama," Sharday grumbled good-naturedly.

She knew April was just as sleep-deprived as she was because they'd partied together at *The Cellar* the night before.

April sat down on the bed beside her and said, "You won't believe this, Sharday, but I think -- Well, let's say, Lynn thinks . . . that Malcolm came home this morning."

"Huh?" Sharday's mouth dropped open and she felt a rush of excitement, which immediately cost her a wave of guilt. She hadn't thought about Malcolm in months, ever since Donnell had kept her in the studio all those weeks finishing the demo and everything that followed threw her life into a tailspin.

April started explaining. "Well, you know Lynn and her family left for Yale earlier this morning," she said. "And Lynn claims they saw Malcolm getting out of a taxi in front of his parents' house when they rode by. She called me from her cell a little while ago."

Sharday shrugged with a nonchalance she didn't feel and said, "And I'm supposed to do what?" She was probably the last person on earth Malcolm wanted to see. Plus, it wasn't like the situation had changed since the last time she saw him. If anything, she and Donnell were even closer now.

When April saw the pain in Sharday's eyes, she realized she'd made a mistake. "I don't know, Sharday," she said softly. "Now that I think about it, maybe I shouldn't have told you. But I guess I thought you would want to know."

"Yeah, you did the right thing," Sharday said. "It's just that--"

She stopped speaking because they heard Bruce calling them from the foot of the steps. When April got up to open the door and tell her father they were coming, Sharday took a few seconds to compose herself before she stood, too.

"Oh, I almost forgot!" April said as she rushed back across the room to her desk and picked up her old iPhone, which was she carried in a pink, pretty case. "This is for you," she said. "Take it to Jersey so we can keep in touch by iMessage. My mother bought me a new one for college."

"Wow. Thanks, April," Sharday said as she slipped the phone into her pocket. And then, as a joke, "And tell Cathy I said thanks, too."

April laughed and gave Sharday a quick hug. "I'm really going to miss you, Sharday," she said.

"Same here, April." Sharday hugged her back, and then she led the way downstairs.

Breakfast was pleasant mostly because Bruce played peacemaker between Vickie and Sharday. He'd been skeptical of Sharday's plans to stay up north with Donnell at first, too. But once she presented her case, he came around. She had the financial means to support herself through the end of the year and she was willing to go back to school if a deal hadn't materialized by then. So, he didn't see the harm in allowing her some time to focus on her music career. And given her talent and determination, he wouldn't be surprised if she was successful.

After they finished eating, Vickie announced she would clean up the kitchen later and they all piled into the Lexus to go to Reagan National. Bruce was flying to Illinois with April and coming back on Monday night. Vickie had originally been scheduled to go with them, but she cancelled her ticket after she found out about Sharday and Donnell's last minute meeting with Tank.

Now, after Bruce pulled out of the garage, April looked back at the house and continued staring at it until they turned a corner and she could no longer see it.

Bruce had been checking his daughter's reaction through the rearview mirror, so when she faced front again with tears in her eyes, he said, "You okay back there, baby? I don't know about you, but I felt very conflicted the first time I left home for Hampton. And I can still remember it clearly after all these years. On the one hand, I was sad to be leaving everybody behind and I was nervous because I didn't know exactly what to expect. But on the other hand, I was so excited to be going to college and I knew I was standing on the threshold of my future."

April smiled and wiped the tears threatening to spill down her face. Leave it to her father to know just what to say. "And that's exactly how I feel, Dad," she said. "I'm sad, but I'm happy, too." She also realized, but didn't add, that having to leave her boyfriend behind made her situation worse. Isaiah was staying home to go to Howard, and she was already starting to miss him.

Sharday nudged April affectionately and said, "Girl, your first semester will fly by so fast you won't know what happened. Plus, you'll be back for Thanksgiving. And after that, it's all about finals and then it's over."

Bruce chuckled and briefly met his daughter's eyes in the rearview mirror. "Actually, baby, if your experience is anything like mine was, " he said, "you'll be counting the days until it's time to come home for winter break, but then you'll be dying to get back to school long before its over."

April doubted it, but she forced a chuckle, anyway.

Vickie laughed and turned to look at Bruce. "Sounds like you were on an emotional roller coaster back then, honey," she said to him. "But it was all worth it, wasn't it? Look how great your life has turned out." And then, for Sharday's benefit, she pointedly added, "Now, that's what college will do for you."

Sharday refused to take the bait and politely asked Bruce if she could hear the radio instead. When he tuned in to a hip hop station and switched the music to the rear speakers, Sharday leaned back in her seat and flashed April a look of triumph.

Traffic was light this early on a Saturday morning, so they made it to the airport in good time. And since April had shipped her belongings by UPS a few days earlier, which meant she and Bruce only had one carry-on bag each, it wasn't long before they were all standing a few feet away from the security checkpoint saying their goodbyes.

Vickie and Bruce were acting overly-sentimental because this would be their first time apart overnight since they had gotten married. But April was feeling excited again, so she hugged Sharday hard and whispered for her to be strong. "You're doing the right thing," she said. "Don't let your mother talk you out of it. It's our turn now."

"I know that's right," Sharday whispered back. "And I'm expecting you to go up there and turn Northwestern out. Just like me and my girls taught you to."

April laughed and said, "Oh, you can count on that, Sharday. The timid little wallflower you met a couple of years ago no longer even exists."

When Vickie and Bruce finally managed to separate a few minutes later, Vickie embraced April and told her to enjoy her first semester at college. "We're so proud of you, honey, but we'll miss you dearly," she said. "So, e-mail and call us as often as you can. And it goes without saying that we'll do the same."

As Bruce hugged Sharday, he murmured into her ear, "Don't worry, I'll help to convince your mother once I get back." Then, in his normal speaking voice, he added, "In the meantime, good luck with *Urban Legend.*

And don't hesitate to call my lawyer if you need to. I've already put him on standby."

After Bruce and April left, Vickie and Sharday stood and watched their progress through the security checkpoint, down the long corridor, and around the corner out of sight.

On the way back to Mitchellville, Sharday and Vickie were mostly silent at first. Sharday naturally assumed Vickie needed some time to deal with Bruce's absence. But Vickie was taking advantage of the quiet time to finalize her last chance plan to give her daughter a shot at a college degree.

She truly believed what she'd said earlier about Bruce's life turning out so great because he'd gone to college. And she wasn't willing to let Sharday's chances of a future like that evaporate just because some unprofessional, unreliable label executive wanted her to come running to New Jersey on a moment's notice.

Now, as they approached Mitchellville Road, Vickie glanced at her daughter and said, "You know, Sharday, I've been thinking . . . Maybe I could register for you next week and---"

"No, thank you, Ma. I--"

"Wait a minute, Sharday. Hear me out," Vickie insisted. "But first, let me backtrack and say I realize I was wrong to expect you to postpone the meeting until you could register. Even though I only asked you to push it back by a few days. Which really shouldn't be a problem since they don't know the difference between two weeks and two months. Especially since they aren't actually offering you a contract. And--"

"Ma," Sharday whined in exasperation. "Where are you going with this?"

Vickie smiled apologetically and said, "Sorry." Then she began to lay out her plan. She would register at P.G. next week in Sharday's name while Sharday went to New Jersey with Donnell. But they would hold off paying tuition until the last possible moment. If things worked out with *Urban Legend*, Vickie would simply withdraw Sharday from the classes. But if this meeting with Tank Smith was just more smoke and mirrors, which was probably the case in Vickie's opinion, then at least Sharday wouldn't miss a whole semester of college because of it.

Sharday slowly shook her head and sighed loudly as her mother backed into the garage. "Why can't you just accept my choice and support me on it like everybody else, Ma?" she asked. "I've been dreaming about breaking into the music industry for as long as I can remember. And you've been right in my corner the whole time. But now that all the elements are finally starting to come together, you're switching up and trying to stuff college down my throat. Why are you changing on me like this?"

Vickie shut off the car and turned to look at her daughter. "Because I don't trust those people at *Urban Legend* anymore, Sharday," she said. "And it just kills me to think that they're going to make you miss registration week and a whole semester of college for nothing. Chances are all they're going to do is end up stringing you along for another two or three months."

"But this is so much bigger than *Urban Legend* now, Ma," Sharday said. "It's about me believing in our demo so much that I'm willing to make a commitment and put everything on the line for it. If Tank Smith offers us a deal after this meeting, that'll be great! But if he doesn't, we have to start making the rounds at the labels and paying our dues just like everybody else. If I really want this -- and we both know I do, I have to go up to New York with Donnell and make it happen. I can't just sit back in my cozy little environment and expect it to drop into my lap."

Vickie had heard it all before, but this time she was so struck by the passion in her daughter's voice that she started having second thoughts. Maybe she was wrong to discourage Sharday from pursuing her music now. After all, she fully believed her daughter had the talent to make it; She just disagreed with the timing. But she knew from her own life that sometimes a door of opportunity closed never to reopen again. What if this was Sharday's only shot, her only chance to make the sacrifices it would take to secure her place in the record business?

Vickie opened her car door and said, "Well, it's getting hot out here, honey. Why don't we go in so I can get started on the kitchen while you tell me your plans again. I need to get clear on the details."

It took Sharday a few seconds to realize that Vickie was changing her position. But once it sunk in, she grinned and quickly climbed out of the car. "Really, Ma?" she asked as she rushed to meet Vickie by the trunk. "So, you're finally with me on this?"

"Let's just say I'm willing to consider it," Vickie said.

Sharday knew a victory when she heard it. She grinned again and hugged her mother. "Thank you so much, Ma," she said. "And I promise you

you won't regret this. I mean it, Ma. Everything's going to work out for me and Donnell. I can feel it in my bones. And I promise I'm going to make you proud."

Vickie smiled and held her daughter tightly. She loved this girl so much she would die for her. "You already have, baby," she said.

SIXTY-TWO

Sharday and Donnell left for New Jersey early Monday morning. They arrived shortly after eleven o'clock and checked into a Holiday Inn she had booked over the internet at a deep discount. She'd made firm reservations for one night. And depending on how things went, they could add additional nights on an as-needed basis up to Friday morning, when they would have to head back home to do the gig at *The Cellar*.

The hotel room they received was decent enough. It had a king-sized bed, cable television, a table and two chairs, and it was clean. They sat at the table and ate KFC chicken while they watched music videos, then Donnell stretched out on the bed and Sharday headed to the bathroom for a shower.

They were both still hoping this meeting at *Urban Legend* would lead to a deal and they were determined to do everything they could to make that happen. But they were also determined not to get strung along. So, they'd agreed that if Tank hadn't put a contract on the table by Friday morning, they were heading for New York the following week. They would keep the lines of communication open with *Urban Legend*, but they would also court other labels.

Now, Sharday took extra time with her make-up and put on a denim miniskirt, a white wrap blouse with a deep V-neck, and navy and white striped sandals with see-through wedge heels. Donnell quickly showered and dressed in slouchy jean shorts, a jersey, and a pair of Nikes. They were out the door by a quarter after one, even though the label was only twenty minutes away.

By one forty-five, they were climbing the steps to the porch at *Urban Legend*. Pit wasn't on the door today. But Lorenzo, the guy who answered and let them in, was just as big and beefy as Pit. He led them to the living room and they could hear music and conversation coming from behind the closed dining room door. But he bypassed the dining room and took the long way around to the kitchen for Sharday's bottle of spring water and Donnell's shot of Courvoisier. And at exactly two o'clock, he took them upstairs to

Tank's office, which would have otherwise been the master bedroom.

Tank was a towering, heavyset brother in his late thirties who wore a conservative button down shirt and jeans, but was loaded with bling. A spinning *Urban Legend* medallion like Big Jeff's on a thicker platinum chain, a huge square of diamonds in each ear, an icy watch that threw shine every time he moved his arm and, of course, diamond rings. As Lorenzo left the room and closed the door, Tank introduced himself and his lawyer, Billy Brown, a shorter, muscular brother in an obviously expensive black suit and quite a few diamonds of his own.

"Billy grew up with me in Brooklyn," Tank told them. What he didn't add was that Billy barely scraped through law school at night and now had *Urban Legend* as his sole client.

Tank gestured toward the comfortable leather armchairs opposite his desk and invited Sharday and Donnell to sit down. He led them in a few minutes of small talk about their trip up the road, but then he looked at them and said, "So, tell me why I should sign Double D-Day."

As they launched into their pitch, pulling out all the stops, he leaned back and put his hands behind his head. They had no way of knowing he was already sold on their music. He'd finally gotten around to listening to their demo a few weeks ago. And the moment he heard it, he knew Big J. was right about their potential to be the label's next platinum act. After a couple calls down to DC and an incognito trip to *The Cellar* last Friday to watch their show, all he needed to see now was how he clicked with them.

He had to admit that, so far, he liked their style. And he could tell Billy was down with them, too. But he still made them jump through the hoops before he suggested moving the meeting down the hall to the studio.

Sharday and Donnell felt they'd passed the first test. "Now, you talking *our* language, Tank," Donnell said at the same time Sharday said, "Oh, we can't wait to show you how we flow in the studio."

They all stood then and Billy slipped off his suit jacket and draped it over his chair. "After you," he said, gesturing for Donnell and Sharday to follow Tank.

Tank led the way down the hall. He told the young woman in the office in the second bedroom to hold his calls and he pointed out the bathroom at the end of the hallway to Sharday and Donnell, then he opened the closed door leading to the studio.

The original third bedroom was a long narrow space that now served as an entryway to the actual studio, which was located in the newer addition that had been built onto the room. Inside the studio, two rows of rolling leather armchairs lined the wall to the left of the thick plexiglass door that led back out to the entryway. The wall to the right held a full-sized refrigerator and a wet bar area with a microwave. But the bulk of the room was reserved for Big Jeff's state-of-the-art professional equipment and two recording booths.

Big Jeff was behind the boards working on a beat and smoking a blunt when they walked in. He was relieved to see Donnell and Sharday heading toward him with Tank and Billy. Tank could be a real hard-ass sometimes. But Double D-Day was an important part of Big Jeff's plans to take *Urban Legend* to the next level, so he was glad Tank hadn't ruined it.

"Just what I need," he said. "Some fresh voices for my new track." He stood to bump fists with Donnell and shake Sharday's hand. After he gave them a quick tour of the studio, he told them he wanted to try laying the lyrics to *Gangsta 101* over his new beats. "But pull up a couple chairs and listen to it first," he said

Billy had already rolled two armchairs over, so Donnell followed his lead and got two more. They were all seated and Big Jeff was playing the track for them when Candy entered the studio and gave them a silent wave before pulling up another chair.

Sharday and Donnell turned to look at each other after the song ended, and each could tell the other thought it was hot. So, when Big Jeff asked them what they thought, they didn't hold back.

"Fire!" Donnell said.

"Hot to death!" Sharday agreed. "You think we can make *Gangsta 101* work with it?" she asked Donnell.

"Oh, no doubt," he said.

"Then let's make it happen," Tank said with a nod to Big Jeff.

Sharday and Donnell took some time to get familiar with the studio. They tried each recording booth and settled on the one to the left. They performed an a cappella excerpt of *Gangsta 101* twice before they were satisfied with the playback. Finally, they told Big Jeff that they were ready.

Since he had crafted his music with *Gangsta 101* specifically in mind, he told them to do the lyrics straight through on faith. "Just trust me on this," he said. "I'll count you two down."

The first time around, they did as he said. And when he played the recording back, everyone in the room could see that he was on to something.

The next few times around, Sharday tinkered with the timing of the hook and Donnell adjusted the flow of his rhyme. And once Big Jeff did his thing on the boards, they all knew they had a hit on their hands.

"Remix!" Big Jeff shouted. "I knew that shit would work!"

"So did I!" Candy said.

Donnell was totally pumped. "Yeah!" he shouted. "Told y'all we the real thing!"

"And Big Jeff, you be working them boards!" Sharday added.

"Cha-ching!" Billy said. "I see money in the bank."

"Enough to make all our pockets heavier," Tank agreed.

After high fives and more boasting all around, Tank said he was ready to go back to his office and "talk business." Big Jeff and Candy stayed put, because Big Jeff never got involved with artist contracts – it tended to complicate things in the studio. But Sharday, Donnell and Billy left with Tank.

This time, Tank stopped at the office in the second bedroom and introduced Sharday and Donnell to his assistant, Maya.

"I'm his assistant, the receptionist, the notary, plus some," said the tall, curvaceous, twenty-six year old woman with smooth brown skin and maroon, shoulder-length braids as she stepped around her desk to shake hands with Sharday and Donnell. She had on low-rise black jeans, bejeweled black sandals that showed off her hot pink toenails, and a cropped pink shirt that stopped just above her pierced navel.

"The rest of my staff from this office is in the field," Tank said as he gestured to the two cluttered desks behind Maya's.

"As usual," Maya teased him. "I'm the one who holds it down."

"True," Billy said with a chuckle.

"Can't argue with that," Tank said to Maya. "So, go ahead and do what you do. Run the shop. I'll buzz you if we need something."

Back in his office, Tank got straight to the point with Donnell and Sharday. "I don't believe in beating around the bush," he told them. "I think you two got serious talent. And based on what just happened in the studio, we all know *Urban Legend* is the label to bring that talent out. So, let's do this." He turned to look at Billy and said, "Make it happen, Billy B."

"That's what I'm here for," Billy said as he popped open his briefcase and pulled out a thick stack of papers. He stashed the briefcase under his chair and smiled at Donnell and Sharday. "We want Double D-Day to join the *Urban Legend* family," he said. "And we're willing to put fifty thousand dollars on the table to make that happen."

Sharday and Donnell turned to look at each other in astonishment. This was happening a lot more quickly than they had expected.

Billy wasn't sure what to make of their silence, so he said, "Now, fifty thousand might not sound like a lot to you two, especially given the outrageous advances the major labels tend to throw at new artists these days. But those labels all have a sink or swim mentality. If your first album doesn't recoup that huge advance they paid you, they drop you and your career with them is over."

"Yeah," Donnell said. "A lot of groups come out with one okay album that don't exactly blow up the charts and you don't never hear from them no more."

Billy nodded and said, "But we don't operate like that here at *Urban Legend*. We're a family. Which means once we sign a group, they're here to stay." He briefly raised the hefty contract he held on his lap. "And on the financial side, we're giving Double D-Day a larger percentage of the royalties and more points than new groups normally get. And of course, production credits."

Sharday spoke up then. "So, you basically saying we get our real money on the back end, right?" she asked, keeping it ghetto, but letting her intelligence come through.

"Now you've got me," Billy agreed as he handed the contract to Donnell. "And it's all right there in writing."

Donnell slowly flipped through the pages before passing them to Sharday. His survival instinct told him to sign on the dotted line and get the money before they changed their minds. But he prided himself on being a good businessman, and the first rule of business was not to sign anything without reading it first. Since there was no chance in hell he could read this whole contract -- it had to be at least fifty pages, he was expecting Sharday to do it. That year she spent in college would finally come in handy.

But within minutes, Sharday looked up and said, "I ain't gonna lie.

All this legal stuff is way over my head." And then, to Donnell specifically, "We gotta call the lawyer in on this, Boo. I can't handle it."

"The lawyer?" Tank asked in surprise.

Billy said, "You two already have representation?"

"Well--," Donnell began.

But Sharday interrupted him and said, "Believe it or not, we actually do. We ain't hire him until the last minute. I mean, right before we left," she emphasized. "But now, I'm glad we did."

Tank and Billy looked at each other. Then after a few seconds, Tank nodded at Billy almost imperceptibly. Of course, the contract was tilted mostly in *Urban Legend's* favor. What label's contract wasn't? But at least this one wasn't totally one-sided. And Tank had been so blown away by Donnell and Sharday's skills and professionalism in the studio that he was willing to negotiate to sign them, if he had to. Because every instinct he possessed was screaming that these two kids could be the next big thing in hop-hop.

Billy was fully prepared to press Sharday and Donnell to sign the contract without running it by their lawyer first, even though he knew it was against the ethical rules of every Bar Association in the country. But since Tank was the boss and he obviously wanted to play this one straight, Billy pulled a business card from his breast pocket and handed it to Sharday. "Have your lawyer call me directly," he said. "I'll expect to hear from him by the close of business tomorrow."

Sharday had been literally holding her breath, and now she was ecstatic that she hadn't blown the deal. "Oh, we gonna make sure he call you way before that," she said to Billy. And then, with a wide grin that included both him and Tank, "Thank y'all so much for being fair with us. And for believing in us enough to put a offer on the table."

Donnell was pleased about the contract, too, and he let some of his excitement come through in front of Tank and Billy. But he didn't truly let go until he and Sharday had made it back to the car and pulled off. "Yeah!" he shouted in triumph as he turned the corner. "We did that shit, Day-Day! We finally got our damn contract!"

Sharday bounced up and down in her seat and said, "Oh, my God, Boo! I can't hardly believe it! I feel like I'm dreaming or something! And I don't know what Billy talking about, but fifty grand sound great to me!"

It was enough money to get Sharday out from under Vickie's control, so Donnell was cool with it, too. "Oh, a nigga can definitely make some shit happen with fifty g's," he said. "And anyway, the main thing ain't the advance, it's the publishing credits, the points and royalties – all that shit Billy was talking about is what really count. You know how it go, Day-Day. Niggas be in bankruptcy or out on the corner slinging crack to make money while they songs at the top of the charts. Hell no! We ain't about to go out like that."

"Well, let's call the lawyer," Sharday said. She glanced down at her watch and saw that it was after seven o'clock. "If he ain't there, at least I can leave him a message." She flipped open her cell phone and pulled the business card Bruce had given her a few days ago from her purse. "Quentin Tarver, Attorney at Law," she read aloud before she started dialing.

"Attorney Tarver," he answered on the second ring. Quentin Tarver had spent seven years in the legal department at Metro before he opened his own law firm. And he saw this referral from Bruce as a potential opportunity to break into the lucrative field of entertainment law. Bruce had said only that there was a chance his stepdaughter might be calling this week about a possible record deal. But since Quentin was very ambitious, he had boned up on the music industry and rearranged his schedule so he could stay near the phone for the next few days, anyway.

"I'll be happy to go over the contract for you," he said now after Sharday identified herself and explained the situation. "Are you near a fax machine?"

"We're in the car right now," she said, "but the hotel offers fax services and we should be there in less than ten minutes." She had purposely switched to her best English the moment he answered the phone. They needed the lawyer to take them seriously and do his best for them. And by now, she'd slipped up in front of Donnell enough for him to know she had this so-called "proper language" in her.

For his part, Donnell thought she was playing the call just right. Of course, he had long since realized how much she'd changed while he was gone. And the way he saw it, this was the perfect time to put those "college girl" ways of hers to good use. With her book smarts and his street knowledge, nobody would be able to get over on them.

"Ask how much he charging," Donnell said to her.

When Sharday relayed the question to Quentin, he said, "My normal fee is two hundred an hour. But your stepfather is a very good friend of mine, Sharday, so I'll give you a flat fee price once I see the contract and get an idea of how much work will be involved."

Sharday knew Bruce wouldn't have recommended Quentin if he wasn't a good lawyer, and Donnell thought the money they would have to pay was worth it to make sure they got a fair deal. So, they formally hired Quentin and stopped by the hotel to fax the contract to him, then they went to the only *Red Lobster* in town to celebrate.

SIXTY-THREE

Quentin called Sharday and Donnell back at nine thirty the next morning, awaking them both from a deep sleep. They had made an early night of it after the restaurant, but then they ended up lying in bed talking until daybreak.

Now, as the telephone in their hotel room rang, Sharday reached out for it and said a groggy, "Hello." But once she realized it was Quentin Tarver, she instantly woke up. "Can you hold on for a minute, Attorney Tarver?" she asked him. "Or would you prefer for me to call you right back?"

He said, "I don't mind holding, Sharday. And please, call me Quentin." He was much too eager to get their business to let her hang up and call him back. He saw working for them as the first step of his transformation from middle-class personal injury lawyer to wealthy lawyer to the stars.

Sharday said, "Okay, Quentin. Thanks. I'll just be a few seconds." Then she put the phone down and leaned over to shake Donnell. "Wake up, Boo," she whispered urgently. "The lawyer's on the phone."

Donnell's eyes opened immediately. And as he sat up, he asked her whether Quentin had already read the contract.

"I guess so," she said. She picked up the bottle of water she'd left on the nightstand and took a huge swallow from it before passing it to Donnell. "You ready?" she asked after he'd wet his throat, too. At his nod, she picked the phone back up and held it so they both could hear.

"Thanks for holding, Quentin," she said into the handset. "I'm back, and I've got Donnell on the phone with me.

Quentin said good morning again and exchanged a few pleasantries with Sharday and Donnell, but then he got down to business. Over the past four days, he'd taken online courses in entertainment law through the DC Bar and the American Bar Association, he'd read everything he could find in hard copy and on the internet about the legal aspects of the urban music industry, and he'd called a former law school classmate who represented a couple of hip-hop groups in Chicago and put him on standby for emergency consultations. So, Quentin felt more than qualified for the job.

He told Sharday and Donnell the contract was "fair enough," mostly because *Urban Legend* was giving them an eighteen percent royalty rate, which was a few points more than usual for a new group. "But the recoupable costs and expenses are where the labels really kill their artists," he added. "So, the first thing we need to do is hammer those out and put a cap on them."

When Sharday said she wasn't sure exactly what he meant, he explained that "recoupables" could include everything from their advance, to recording costs, to promotional costs, to tour expenses, to housing, food and limo fees. "And this contract contains all that and then some," he said.

Quentin kept them on the phone for another forty-five minutes explaining the basics of the contract and pointing out areas where he saw room for improvement. Finally, he said, "So, what I propose is that I call *Urban Legend's* attorney and start the negotiations. We've got a decent contract to start with. So, it shouldn't be too hard to work out something that's fair."

Donnell had let Sharday do most of the talking so far, but now he took over. "Well, the main thing we ain't wanna do was sign a jacked contract, Quentin," he said. "But based on what you been saying, *Urban Legend* ain't even coming at us like that. So, we need you to keep it real when you talk to Billy. Know what I'm saying? They ain't trying to screw us and we ain't trying to be greedy. And since they the only label offering us a deal, we don't wanna do nothing to blow it."

"I understand completely," Quentin said. "So, I tell you what I'll do. I'll make contact with Billy Brown to get a feel for how much room we have to negotiate, and then I'll get back in touch with you and Sharday so we can decide how to proceed. And in the meantime, I'll also fax my letter of representation over to the hotel. Take a look at it, and we can talk about it when I call back."

"Alright," Donnell said. "That sound like a plan."

Sharday told Quentin they'd be waiting to hear from him, then she hung up the phone and slowly turned back to look at Donnell. Everything was finally coming together for them and she was too overwhelmed to speak. So, when the tears began rolling down her cheeks, she shrugged and buried her face in his chest.

Donnell laughed from deep within and wrapped his arms around her.

"It's our turn now, babe," he murmured. "All we gotta do is sit tight for a minute and let Quentin do his thing."

But as it turned out, Billy wasn't as open to negotiation as Quentin had predicted. Just because Tank wanted to play it straight didn't mean Billy wouldn't try to win. He had a ghetto mentality, and his motto was that the strong were put on this Earth to devour the weak. He dug his heels in right from the start, refusing to budge on any but the smallest of points. And all the while, he was searching for the slightest sign of weakness from Quentin.

Quentin had dealt with men like Billy before. He came across them all the time in his solo practice. They made you fight tooth and nail for every concession, but they respected you once you did. And since Quentin's polite corporate demeanor could easily give way to unbridled aggression, he usually fared well with Billy's kind.

On Quentin's advice, Sharday and Donnell stayed away from the label during the negotiations. They distracted themselves with music videos, weed and sex during the day. And each night, they drove into New York City to scope out landmarks like Jay-Z's *40/40 Club*, and even “Jacob the Jeweler's,” the jeweler to some of hip-hop's biggest stars.

Sharday also spent quite a bit of time sending and receiving iMessages on the iPhone April had given her. She held an ongoing electronic conversation with her mother at the gym and at home, where Bruce often joined in. Plus, Kayla had iMessage on her Mac at work, Frank and Belinda shared an iMac in their condo, April had her new iPhone, and although Tyesha didn't have a permanent desk at work, she and Jolean both had access to Sharday's Mac at the apartment.

Donnell wasn't into iMessage, so he relied on his cell phone to keep in touch with Andre and his other "associates" on a daily basis. He called his mother on Monday night to tell her about the contract, which was something he wouldn't have done even a month earlier. And whenever Sharday got too carried away with her texting, he escaped downstairs to the hotel's weight room.

But on Friday morning as they were packing to check out, Sharday and Donnell lost their nerve. They were afraid to leave New Jersey without signing the contract because of their experience with *Urban Legend* over the summer. They called Quentin, told him they wanted to sign the contract as it stood.

He tried to convince them it would be a mistake to give in so early, but they wouldn't listen. They knew from his own words that the label was being "fair enough." They had decided to take their chances. "Right now, we just need to get our foot in the door, dog," Donnell said.

"And we can always renegotiate an album or two down the road," Sharday added. "Other groups do it all the time."

Quentin realized there was nothing he could say to make them change their minds. So, although it went against everything he stood for, he agreed to call Billy and make the arrangements.

Three hours later, Sharday and Donnell were in Tank's office finalizing the deal. The mood was festive because all parties felt they had won. Sharday and Donnell were now signed recording artists, which was the only thing they cared about. Billy had stonewalled his way through another contract negotiation and emerged victorious. And Tank had just acquired a group he knew would make him millions on very favorable terms.

After all the documents had been signed and Billy faxed the paperwork to have the advance money wired to Quentin's client trust account, Tank popped open a bottle of Crystàl champagne for a toast. "Welcome to the *Urban Legend* family," he said to Sharday and Donnell. And then, as he touched glasses with them, "To platinum plaques and thick bankrolls."

"I'll drink to that!" Sharday said.

Billy raised his glass and said, "Hear, hear!"

"To history in the making!" Donnell said before they all drank.

Tank buzzed Maya to come join the celebration. "But go get the posse first," he told her. "And bring about three more bottles of Cris back with you."

Maya entered the room a few minutes later with the champagne, Lorenzo and another bouncer type she introduced as Jimmy, three young roughnecks named Flip, Owl and Nate, and two young women whose names Maya couldn't remember but who identified themselves as Zena and Desiree.

After drinks had been poured all around, Tank proposed another toast. They quickly went through all four bottles of champagne, which Sharday and Donnell didn't realize would ultimately be deducted from their royalties, and then Tank announced he was taking them into the city for lunch.

Maya returned to her office with instructions to call Big Jeff at home at three-thirty and tell him Double D-Day had signed. Lorenzo stayed behind to man his post at the front door. But everyone else followed Tank, Billy, Donnell and Sharday outside.

Tank's posse headed for the black Ford Excursion at the curb, while Sharday and Donnell were allowed the privilege of riding with Tank and Billy in Tank's black Navigator. They were impressed when they climbed into the rear of the customized SUV and saw the luxurious leather seats with suede piping, the label's corporate logo emblazoned in suede on the headrests, several 15-inch television monitors, a blu ray player and a PlayStation 3, and yet, they had expected nothing less.

But when Tank turned onto West Twenty-First Street in Manhattan and pulled to a stop in front of *40/40 Club*, Sharday and Donnell were both awestruck. They had just driven by here a few nights earlier and fantasized about the day they would be able to go inside.

"Jay-Z's spot," Donnell murmured in amazement.

Sharday swallowed hard and said, "Oh, my God, Tank. You taking us to *40/40*?" She looked down at her capri pants and Donnell's baggy jean shorts. "But we not even dressed right."

Tank motioned for a valet parking attendant and said, "We're cool for lunch. Don't forget, Jay made part of his fortune off urban gear." Tank had on jeans and everyone else with him was dressed casually, too. With the exception of Billy, of course, who almost always wore a suit.

40/40 proved to be all Sharday and Donnell had anticipated and more. The decor was flashy. The eclectic crowd was dressed in everything from hip-hop clothes to suits and fancy dresses. There were celebrities sprinkled here and there, including a group of B-list black actresses, two well-known rappers with their respective entourages, and a deejay who had made his reputation by producing the hottest mixtapes on the scene.

Tank sent Billy and the posse to the table to order appetizers and more Crystàl, then he led Sharday and Donnell over to meet Deejay Amayzing. He introduced them as Double D-Day, his new group, and he said they had a fresh rap and R&B flavor that would be perfect on a mixtape. Before he led them away a few minutes later, Deejay Amayzing had agreed to sit in on one of their studio sessions in the coming months.

Sharday and Donnell knew that a blazing track on a widely-circulated mixtape would give them instant street credibility and help boost the sales on their first album. So, they were floating on strengthened dreams of success as they sat down to have lunch with Tank, Billy, and the posse. They savored Jay-Z's upscale bar food but took it as a sign of things to come. They told Tank they would go home for the weekend and return on Monday to start working in the studio because they didn't want to waste any time.

Tank suggested they'd be much more comfortable staying in his guest house than in a hotel. And when he pointed out that the guest house included maid service, access to his personal chef and a leased Mercedes, they looked at each other and silently agreed to ignore Quentin's warning about recoupable expenses. Tank's offer was too good to refuse and they weren't about to turn it down. They would enjoy the good life now and worry about the consequences later.

By the time they made it back to Jersey and climbed into the Cougar to head home, Sharday and Donnell were totally hyped. They had a decent deal with a good label, more than twenty thousand dollars each in Quentin's bank account, an appointment with the premier mixtape deejay, and they would soon be living in the lap of luxury and driving around in a Mercedes. They were finally on the road to stardom, complete with all the perks.

Donnell pulled off and turned the corner, then he leaned on his horn for a long minute. "Yeah!" he shouted. "That's for all the haters, Day-Day! Niggas who ain't wanna recognize! We was born to win! And we gonna take this shit straight to the top!"

She laughed and reached over to blow the horn herself. "Straight to the top!" she echoed. "And it ain't gonna be nothing but the best now that we rolling with Tank! That's just how he roll, Boo. I can tell."

"And I'm all for that shit," Donnell said. "What difference do it make who gotta pay for it in the end? We gonna sell so many records, it ain't even gonna matter."

"I know that's right!" Sharday said. Then she pulled out her cell phone and said, "I gotta call my mother and them. And my father and Belinda waiting to hear from me, too."

"Call that nigga Clyde first and tell his bitch ass we ain't coming back," Donnell said. He still hadn't forgiven Clyde for making him audition after he came back from prison, and this would be his way of getting revenge.

But Sharday wouldn't hear of leaving Clyde hanging at the last minute. She pointed out that he had been there for them when Mr. Weiss fired her, and even when Donnell was in the halfway house and needed a job to get his full street privileges. She insisted that they owed it to Clyde to perform this one last time and tell him in person that they were moving on. And when Donnell still didn't seem convinced, she said, "You know what, Donnell? Don't even worry about it. I'll just go do it by myself."

"Alright, Day-Day, damn!" he said. "If it mean that much to you, I'll do it!"

She took one look at the irritated expression on his face and burst out laughing. He grudgingly cracked a smile, and she leaned over to kiss him on the cheek. "You always come through, Boo," she said. Then she unlocked her iPhone and started dialing.

Thanks to bumper-to-bumper rush hour traffic as they rode through Philly, they had to go straight to *The Cellar* without stopping by the apartment first once they made it back to DC. But Tyesha and Jolean met them at the club with a fresh change of clothes. And everybody else Sharday had invited was there, too. Vickie and Bruce, Frank and Belinda, Kayla and John, Andre and Nannette, Jolean's boyfriend, Rome, and even Isaiah.

Sharday put her all into the show as a final tribute to Clyde. And Donnell stepped up his game to meet hers because his professional pride would allow him to do no less. The audience responded in kind, ultimately rewarding them with an extended standing ovation.

Sharday forced herself to resist the urge to grab the mic and say a final farewell. This crowd had been good to her over the years, and she was feeling very sentimental. But she didn't want to say anything that would tip Clyde off before she had a chance to tell him face-to-face.

Of course, Donnell couldn't have cared less about Clyde's feelings. And since he knew this was the perfect opportunity to start a buzz on the streets, he leaned into his mic and told the audience to be on the lookout for Double D-Day's first album. "It be in stores next year," he said. "And I promise y'all it's gonna be hot. So, y'all definitely don't wanna sleep on it." Then he thanked everyone for supporting them and led a stunned Sharday away to renewed applause.

"Why you do that before I had a chance to tell Clyde?" she whispered as soon as they were offstage.

"Aw, fuck him," Donnell murmured back. "Now he know."

She was annoyed, but she held her tongue. Why hassle Donnell for being true to his nature? Did she really expect him to walk off that stage without taking the opportunity to promote their upcoming album first? She would just have to repair the damage with Clyde. And as soon as she got a glass of champagne under her belt, she was going to go find him.

But she was still receiving hugs from family and friends when Clyde walked up to the table and said, "Seems congratulations are in order. Let me be first to offer a toast."

He had already sent over the two customary bottles of Moet, but now a pair of waitresses stepped forward carrying two more bottles each and proceeded to fill a champagne flute for everyone at the table.

"To Sharday and Donnell," Clyde said as he raised his glass. "I knew they had talent from the beginning. Not at all surprised Tank Smith snatched them up before somebody else beat him to it."

Sharday gasped and Clyde looked at her with a raised eyebrow. His employees had tipped him off when Tank came in incognito, so he'd known all along what was up. "Much thanks for keeping the house packed on Friday nights," he said without missing a beat. "And much success with *Urban Legend*. Go up there and make DC proud."

They all drank to that, as well as to the other toasts that followed. And once the conversation began to flow, Clyde handed Donnell their final pay envelope and told Sharday to keep in touch, then he was gone.

After Clyde disappeared, Donnell hung around just long enough to have another glass of champagne and then he was ready to go, too. He told Sharday he had some business to take care of and he'd meet up with her later, but he told everyone else that the drive from Jersey had worn him out and he needed to get some sleep.

Andre and Nanette left with Donnell. And Kayla and John made their escape a few minutes later. But the rest of the group stayed behind for an impromptu celebration in Sharday's honor. Bruce ordered appetizers, Frank sprang for more champagne, Jolean and Rome even got up to dance a couple of times. They all had such a good time that it was after midnight before they finally left.

SIXTY-FOUR

The rest of the weekend seemed to fly by for Sharday and Donnell. Outside of their Saturday morning meeting with Quentin, followed by a trip to his bank and a shopping spree, they barely saw each other. She was still a momma's girl at heart, so she spent most of her time with Vickie because she didn't know when she would see her mother again. He used his last two days home to fully disengage from the weed business for the same reason -- he didn't know when he would be coming back.

Now, it was ten in the morning on Monday, and they were leaving for Jersey. Vickie, Bruce, Frank and Belinda had come by the apartment earlier for a farewell breakfast with Sharday. And the four of them were standing in front of the building waving as Donnell and Sharday pulled off.

Sharday waved back and said, "I'm really gonna miss them."

Donnell beeped his horn a couple of times but didn't say anything. He was glad to get Sharday away from that overbearing mother of hers. He had finally won the battle with Vickie, even though her little breakfast stunt had prevented him from sleeping over last night, and she was the last person in the world he would miss.

After he turned out of the parking lot, Sharday looked at him and grinned. "Oh, well, Boo," she said. "Let's get on up the road to our Benz and the good life." Then she started laughing.

"That's what I'm talking about!" he said. "I can't wait to get up that joint and start living large. And now that we gonna have access to all that top of the line equipment, we gonna make it our business to come up with some hits that blow everybody away."

"I know that's right!" She plugged in her phone to play Gucci Mane's latest single.

He glanced at her and turned the volume down. "I'm serious, Day-Day. The only thing I'm leaving behind is the projects and a life of crime. And I ain't never planning to go back to neither one. So, hell yeah, we gonna enjoy the Benz and the guesthouse and everything else Tank throw our way. But we gotta stay focused on our music the whole time. Because I can't afford for us to mess this up."

She heard what he meant just as loud as she heard what he said. But since she knew he was coming from a place of insecurity, she said, "Neither can I, Boo. It might not seem like it to you, but ain't nothing changed for me either. If my mother was to up and leave Bruce tomorrow, that would be the end of that. You feel me? I mean, I could probably depend on my father and Belinda for a few dollars here and there, but they ain't gonna pay my bills. And I damn sure ain't trying to go back to *Old Navy*."

She reached over to caress his thigh then. "Plus, my dreams still the same as yours, Boo. That ain't never gonna change."

He grabbed her hand and held onto it tightly, remembering how she had stood up to her mother about not going back to college. "I know you still down, Day-Day," he finally admitted. "I was just tripping for a minute."

"So, we done with this?" she asked.

When he nodded, she said, "Good." And in a more playful tone, "Now, if you don't mind . . . " Then she leaned over to turn the volume back up on the speakers. She was too pumped about everything awaiting them at the end of this trip to stay serious for long. And as Gucci's fresh bars flowed from the speakers, she couldn't help snapping her fingers and rapping along.

Donnell's mood immediately lightened, too. He merged onto the interstate and turned the music up even louder. He'd gotten them everything he'd always promised her and more. And now that he knew for sure where she stood, he had no doubt they would find a way to rise to the top.

They smoked a blunt as they drove through Delaware, had lunch at a quaint diner in Pennsylvania, and stopped just outside of Oakton, Tank's Town, to stretch their legs and freshen up. Half an hour later, Donnell rolled up to the imposing black gates in front of Tank's estate and lowered his window to announce their presence through a black steel box.

A friendly Latina voice responded. And after the woman identified herself as "Cristina, the house manager," she gave them directions to the guesthouse and the gates slowly opened.

"Check out the cameras," Sharday whispered once Donnell rolled his window back up. "Top of the poles beside the gates. Peeking through the shrubs."

"Smart," Donnell said, noticing that the tall shrubs also hid a spiked black iron fence. As he drove down the winding tree-lined driveway, he admired the rolling green lawn that extended as far as the eye could see. But when Tank's mansion and the bubbling fountain in front of it came into view, his mouth dropped open in awe. "What?" he murmured, dragging the word out.

Sharday took in the sprawling white mansion with its huge second-story balcony and said, "Oh, my God, Boo. He got his own white house."

Donnell turned to the right at the fork in the road, as Cristina had instructed, and they gawked in silence at the sparkling aquamarine pool and Jacuzzi surrounded by rock formations that spurted water, the basketball and tennis courts in the distance. Another right turn and they were on a narrower paved road that curved to the left and ended in front of a charming white rambler with forest green trim.

Sharday and Donnell looked at each other in amazement. This was way better than the little guest cottage they had been expecting. It looked just like a regular home. Like they could pick it up and plop it right down in one of the suburbs of DC.

"A golf cart?" Sharday asked, pointing to an open-air vehicle in one of the two parking spaces under the carport. "So, he got a golf course, too?"

"Guess so," Donnell said. "Wouldn't nothing surprise me at this point."

They parked next to the golf cart and climbed out of the Cougar. They were heading toward the front of the house when a voluptuous, pretty Latina in form-fitting, stretchy black capris and a tiny white top opened the side door and called for them to come in through the kitchen.

She told them she was Cristina, "the voice from the black box." And although she was dressed like a hoochie, she had a firm handshake and proved to be quite professional. "Welcome to your new home, Sharday and Donnell," she said once they finished making small talk about their drive up from DC. "Let's take a quick tour, and then I'll leave you two to unpack and get settled."

She started in the kitchen, which was fully stocked with food, drinks, dishes, pots, appliances, and even had a cozy breakfast nook that featured a window overlooking the back yard. The dining room held a whitewashed wooden table and a matching china cabinet filled with fancy dinnerware and silver-rimmed glasses. And the living room was chic but inviting with its chocolate suede furniture, huge green houseplants and plasma television.

The house was made in the shape of an "L." And as Cristina led them down the long hallway off the living room, she stopped to point out the bathroom and the bulging linen closet directly opposite it. There were two furnished bedrooms on the side with the bathroom. But the master bedroom took up the whole side next to the linen closet and had an enormous walk-in closet, its own full bath, and sliding glass doors that led to a deck with a hot tub.

"Tank spares no expense when it comes to 'Smith World,' as we like to call it," Cristina told them on the way back to the kitchen. "So, I know you two will be comfortable here."

"Oh, no doubt," Donnell said enthusiastically at the same time Sharday said, "Who wouldn't be?"

Cristina laughed. "I felt the same way when I moved here with my husband and my son a year and a half ago," she said. "We live in the guesthouse on the other side of the mansion – to the left at the fork in the road." She'd met Tank back when she was stripping and struggling to raise her son alone. But, of course, she wasn't going to tell them that.

"So, we neighbors now," Sharday said.

Cristina smiled. "Yep. At least until I hit the lottery and buy my own mansion."

"Ditto for us," Donnell said, and they all started laughing.

Back in the kitchen, Cristina ran down the details. They could reach the main house by pushing the pound key and dialing one on any phone in the house, a pair of maids would come by every Monday morning to give them the full treatment but they could call for spot cleaning as often as they needed it, and since the weekly shopping was done on Monday afternoons, they should feel free to leave a list of whatever they wanted the maids to pick up for them.

She handed them each a set of keys to the guesthouse and a magnetized card to open the front gates. Said the cards could be deactivated if they were lost or stolen. Then she told them Tank would be expecting them at the main house for dinner at six thirty but to call if they needed anything in the meantime.

She was on her way out the side door a few minutes later when she turned back and said, "Oh, I almost forgot! The Mercedes Tank ordered for you two won't be delivered until ten tomorrow morning. But in terms of coming over for dinner, we mostly use golf carts on the grounds when the weather's nice, anyway. The one in the carport is mine, but I'll have one of the gardeners bring one by in case you two want to try it."

Donnell said, "We adventurous." He was so determined to fit in he would even learn to play golf if he had to.

"Looks like it might actually be fun," Sharday said to Cristina as they watched her hop into the cart and crank it up.

"It's a blast once you get used to it," Cristina confirmed with a grin. She backed out of the carport and gave them a final wave, then she made a clunky U-turn and left.

Sharday stayed in the doorway long enough to make sure Cristina was gone for good before she flung the door closed and let out a whoop of joy. "Oh, my God, Boo!" she screamed. "This house is the bomb!"

Donnell had been leaning against the wall trying to get the upper hand over his own excitement. He was just a boy from the ghetto. And the knowledge that this would be his home with Sharday for the next month or two was totally overwhelming, almost unbelievable to him. He knew she'd already experienced this kind of lifestyle in Mitchellville, so he was trying to maintain at least some level of cool. But once she started jumping up and down with glee, he knew it was okay to let go.

They hugged each other and danced around the kitchen floor. They continued to wild out as they explored the house again on their own. It wasn't until they'd released some of their nervous energy through a quickie bout of sex in the master bathroom that they finally calmed down enough to go out to the car for their belongings.

Once they unpacked, Sharday called her parents and Tyesha, then she took some photos of the house to post on Instagram for everyone to see. Donnell had a quick conversation with his mother before he called Andre to brag about the house in detail. Finally, he and Sharday took a long, hot bubble bath in their whirlpool tub and got dressed for dinner.

At six fifteen on the dot, they climbed into the golf cart that had been left under the carport. It proved easy enough to use and they enjoyed the experience of putt-putting along at a leisurely pace. But when they turned into the curved driveway that led to the mansion and saw a number of limos, two Bentleys, a tricked out Hummer, a Maybach Benz, and a few regular, less expensive cars, they realized this wasn't going to be the private, get-to-know-Tank-better dinner they were expecting.

"Oh, my God," Sharday murmured in awe as she gaped at the Bentleys and the Maybach. She'd seen her fair share of limos and Hummers in the DC area, especially out in Mitchellville, but the closest she'd ever come to a Bentley or a Maybach was watching music videos.

"Damn, Day-Day," Donnell murmured back. "These niggas ain't playing."

"Who you think he got in there?" she asked, an excited grin slowly replacing her wide-eyed stare.

"I don't know. But we about to find out." Donnell parked behind an older model Nissan Maxima and came around to help her climb down from the golf cart.

They were nervous, yet thrilled at the same time, as they mounted the steps to the mansion. And from the moment they entered Tank's grand foyer with its two spiraling staircases leading to the upper level, they were totally swept away. The sparkling crystal chandeliers, the enormous rooms with impeccable furnishings, the fact that the barrel-chested butler stopped at the entryway to the parlor and announced them as the guests of honor.

Tank immediately stepped forward to welcome them and introduce them to "the *Urban Legend* family." Young Baller, the label's famous rapper, was there with a well-known black runway model, the members of both of the label's R&B groups were present, some with dates or spouses who were celebrities in their own right, and when Big Jeff introduced his fiancé, he said she was a chorus girl in a long-running play on Broadway.

Tank and Billy were apparently on their own for the night, while Big Jeff's assistant, Candy, had brought along one of her girlfriends and Maya, the office manager, was with her sister. The bouncers, Pit and Jimmy, were also there, but their matching black polo shirts and headsets made it clear they were on security duty.

There was a lot of bling in the room, but the dress code was more or less casual and the mood relaxed. So, even though dinner was a sit-down affair in the dining room with servers supervised by Cristina, conversation flowed freely among the guests and included anecdotes about casting calls, fashion shows, hip-hop and R&B tours, even adventures with the paparazzi.

After dinner, Tank moved the party to the pool area. Large chimineas with roaring fires had been placed here and there, while music floated through the air from unseen speakers. And as the maids began filling drink orders from the outdoor bar and blunts began making the rounds, Tank's "posse" descended on the party.

These were a bunch of well-dressed thugs who brought the noise and kept flashing gang signs. Most of them were older guys who had terrorized the streets of Brooklyn with Tank and Billy as kids. And it turned out that Flip, Nate and Owl, the three posse members Sharday and Donnell had met before, were actually the younger brothers of original posse members who'd lost their lives along the way. The posse members were followed a few minutes later by Lorenzo, another one of the bouncers from the label house, and a vanload of young women who were dressed like high-class prostitutes.

The music was cranked up louder and more drinks and drugs were consumed. The heated pool and Jacuzzi were put to good use after some of the posse stripped down to their swimming trunks and Cristina announced there was a supply of new suits and trunks in the cabana. The party didn't start breaking up until they'd all gathered around the fireplace in Tank's entertainment room for hot coffees and teas and a heated buffet of buffalo wings, miniature egg rolls, shrimp skewers, and various other finger foods.

By the time Sharday and Donnell finally made it back to the guesthouse, they were so wound up they just knew they would lie awake all night talking. But even as they slid toward each other in the huge bed, the exhaustion from the long day began to kick in. He yawned loudly. She did the same and raised her face for a quick kiss before she snuggled into the crook of his arm. Within moments, they were both fast asleep.

SIXTY-FIVE

It didn't take long for Sharday and Donnell to realize that Big Jeff was a true night person. He expected them in the studio by six every evening, including weekends, and he kept them there until three, four, sometimes even five in the morning.

For the first few weeks, their sessions were closed to everyone except Tank and Candy. Big Jeff took the time to show them how to operate his equipment, and he was surprised when Sharday caught on almost as quickly as Donnell. When he gave them one of his tracks to work with, they impressed both him and Tank by adding a rap and lyrics that turned it into a hot song in two days.

But what really sparked the magic in the studio was the disc Sharday and Donnell had recorded of their best original hits. Big Jeff listened to the CD and realized he'd stumbled upon raw, untapped creative talent in Donnell, which revved up his own creative energies. And every time he concocted a beat with Donnell, no matter what the tempo, Sharday was right on the spot with a tight hook and helpful suggestions.

Now that they'd found their rhythm, Big Jeff felt comfortable enough to loosen the reins. He opened up the studio sessions, allowing the label's other artists, its employees and Tank's posse to come check out Double D-Day. He also told Sharday and Donnell that they would be off by midnight on Fridays and all day on Saturdays until he let them know otherwise. "Don't want you two burning out on me," he said, having long since figured out they were fellow workaholics.

Up to this point, Sharday and Donnell had been limiting themselves to their private daily practice sessions at the guesthouse followed by long hours in the studio with Big Jeff and dead-to-the-world sleep, so they were both happy to have the break. They spent the first couple of weekends shopping, vegging out in front of the plasma, catching up on sleep, cruising around in the Mercedes. Doing all the things they'd been too busy to do before.

Sharday even fell back into the habit of iMessaging, texting, and sending out emails. And one by one, her family members and friends filled her in on all the news they'd been withholding because she'd seemed like she was under so much pressure before.

Vickie was thinking of going to school for her certification as a fitness instructor because Bruce's boss was making retirement noises and Bruce would be in line for the promotion; April's newfound fly-girl status was making her popular in college, especially with the male students, which was kind of exciting for her, but she was too in love with Isaiah to even think of going out with anybody else; Frank and Belinda had finally tied the knot and were still in the honeymoon phase, however Belinda could tell Frank was starting to feel restless because he'd been away from his music for so long.

Tyesha had so much going on she had to share it with Sharday in parts. Her initial messages were about a young black lawyer named Howard she'd recently met who was "making bank" at one of the big law firms in downtown DC and was generous enough with his funds to make up for the fact that he was too busy working all the time to take her out much. Then she wrote, *"And you won't believe this, Day-Day, but my mother's planning to 'take a page' from* ***your mother's Book*** *and* ***marry Walter!!!*** *He went to detox for a weekend and has been going to AA meetings ever since, but I know for a fact that he's still drinking!"* By the time Tyesha finally got around to writing that she was at her wit's end with Jolean, who was trying to stay out to all hours with Rome on school nights because her father wouldn't let her see him on weekends, Sharday had already received a number of texts from Jolean complaining about how strict Tyesha was being now that Sharday was in Jersey.

Kayla's messages were mostly about Kayjon, and she sent new pictures of the baby every chance she got. But she also told Sharday that John had failed the fire department exam by a few points and was planning to take the next one. And she said Elise had snagged a hustler who'd moved her and her kids into a house in nearby Oxon Hill, Maryland and installed a beauty salon in the basement for her.

While Sharday was mainly reaching out by text, Donnell stepped up his phone calls to Andre, who'd recently announced that Nanette was pregnant, and his other associates back at home. He also called his mother from time to time, continued sending her periodic money orders to help out with the family. It seemed to him that nothing was happening in DC but the same old tired ass crimes and cycles of poverty he had fought his way out of there to escape. So, he made up his mind to enjoy his time away as much as possible. Hell, maybe he could even figure out a way for him and Sharday to stay up here after they finished the album.

"I don't know about you, Day-Day," he said to her a few days later, "but a nigga ready to start hitting the clubs and shit up here on Saturday nights. I'm thinking about asking Owl and them where they be hanging on the weekends. You better bet they ain't sitting up in the house."

"I heard that," she immediately agreed. Now that she was all caught up on her sleep, she was ready to get her club on, too. "Candy keep talking about this new spot in Harlem that's supposed to be so hot. Wanna try that?"

"Let's see what the posse say first," he said. Although he wasn't letting on to Sharday yet, his plan was for them to fit in with the posse as a way of getting closer to Tank. Because if they could get Tank to see them as friends instead of just employees, he probably wouldn't want them to leave.

As Donnell suspected, the posse mostly hung out with Tank on the weekends. But to his surprise, Tank told him and Sharday that he wanted them to keep a low profile until they finished the album. "I'm kind of superstitious like that," Tank said. "So, no industry functions for now." Then he raised his eyebrows at them and grinned. "But that won't be too much of a problem because we mainly turn up at the clubs and at our own private parties, anyway. Like I said before, it's all about the family."

From that point on, Sharday and Donnell spent their weekends partying with Tank, the posse, and sometimes Billy, too. They were still on a strict work schedule during the week. So even though Tank and his crew kept it live at the label house every weekday, too, Sharday and Donnell stayed on the grind in the studio with Big Jeff. But on the Friday nights when they weren't too tired, they went down to the basement after their session to kick it with the posse. And from three or four on Saturday afternoons until the early morning hours on Sundays, they were swept up in the luxurious whirlwind that was Tank's life.

He took them to the best restaurants and the hottest nightspots, passing them off as posse members whenever they crossed paths in the city with other celebrities. And he always ended the Saturday night festivities with a private after-party at his mansion that included breakfast.

Donnell was totally in his element and loving every aspect of his new life by now. He'd found a creative mentor in Big Jeff and knew they were making great music, he was living in a classy house on his own with Sharday and they were riding around in a Mercedes, he fit right in with his fellow gang members, also known as the posse, and he enjoyed hanging out with them on the weekends. Plus, the more he spent time around Tank, the more he liked him. And he could tell the feeling was mutual.

Sharday didn't exactly see things the same way. Of course, she couldn't have been happier with Big Jeff's genius as a producer, the progress they were making in the studio, and their lavish new lifestyle courtesy of Tank. She also appreciated her growing friendships with Big Jeff, Tank, Candy, Billy, Maya, and Cristina. But if she never saw the posse again, she knew she wouldn't miss them.

These were the type of guys she'd grown up with, so it felt disloyal not to like them. But things got so out of control whenever they were around. Plus, they brought out the worst in Donnell, who always had to prove he was just as hard as they were when it came to drinking, smoking, cursing, and generally wilding out.

Apparently, her mother and Tyesha had been right about the move from southeast changing her more than she thought. A couple of years earlier, she would've blended right in with the posse and thought nothing of it. Whereas now, she hated to see them coming. But at least she still had her street smarts, because her instincts were screaming that she had to get along with the posse to get along at *Urban Legend.* So, she pushed down her personal feelings and went out of her way to fit in with them.

In the meantime, she, Donnell and Big Jeff were recording like crazy in the studio. They fed off each other creatively, and the album was coming together so quickly it was almost scary. They were using all five songs from the demo since it hadn't been widely circulated, plus the remix of *Gangsta 101*, so there were six songs up from the start. Young Baller had talked his way into making a guest appearance on one song and Tank had made the executive decision to let one of his R&B acts sing the chorus on another track. And then, as late October turned into early November and it became clear that Double D-Day needed only one or two more songs to round out their debut album, Tank announced that he was bringing in a couple of big name producers to do the last two songs.

"It won't be cheap," he told Sharday and Donnell as he sat in the studio smoking blunts with them, Big Jeff, Candy, and Billy on the first Friday afternoon in November. "But I'm willing to pay the price to do this right," he boasted through a cloud of smoke, not bothering to mention that it would ultimately come out of their royalties. "Because we definitely got a classic CD on our hands. And all we need now is a couple of industry insiders who get radio spins just on the strength of their name to get it out there."

Donnell and Sharday looked at each other in surprise, then Donnell turned back to Tank and said, "Damn, Tank, you really coming through for us! I mean, we knew you had our back and all! But we wasn't expecting you to go all out like this!"

For her part, Sharday was grinning from ear to ear. "Oh, my God. Thank you, Tank!" she said. But then she wondered how Big Jeff felt about Tank bringing in outside producers. It had to seem like a slap in the face to him after all the hard work he had put into their album. She slowly turned to look at him. And to her astonishment, he winked at her and nodded his head.

"We got big plans for you two," Big Jeff said. Sharday and Donnell didn't know it, but it was actually his idea to bring in the outside producers. He'd done some of the best work of his career for Double D-Day and he wanted to make sure his masterpiece got maximum exposure. A first single from one of the top producers to get it popping, promises of a track from another top producer when his remix of *Gangsta 101* came out as the second single, and right before it all jumped off, a track on a hot mixtape or two. The hip-hop heads would be feening for the album by the time it was released and everything would be in position to send his creation all the way.

"Matter of fact," Big Jeff said now, "Amayzing's coming to sit in with us on Monday night. He's putting out a new mixtape over the holidays. And we all know once he sees you two in action, Double D-Day will be on it." He smiled as he leaned forward to put fire to the blunt that had gone out on him. Thanks to Sharday and Donnell, he was finally going to earn his superstar producer reputation.

"I'm glad you telling us in advance so we can be ready for him," Donnell said, deciding right then and there that they would stay in all weekend to practice.

"Yep," Sharday said on a quick burst of laughter. The good news was coming so fast and furious she was getting giddy. She put out her blunt in the nearest ashtray.

"Probably won't be much money involved—" Tank started.

"But most new groups would pay Amayzing to get on one of his mixtapes if they could," Candy broke in. "For the exposure," she added. "He's not doing the trunk of the car thing anymore. He's got a distribution deal now."

Billy spoke up then. "I'll call Quentin over the weekend to give him the heads up." He would handle the negotiations himself since the label owned exclusive rights to Double D-Day. But Quentin would also be involved to a limited extent because Sharday and Donnell had to sign the contract, too.

Sharday smiled at Donnell in relief. She was too high to focus on the details right now, but Quentin would take of it for them.

"Well, let's break out the Cris and call it a night," Big Jeff said with a nod to Candy, who got up and headed for the refrigerators to get the champagne. "Rehearsals for the Amayzing audition start tomorrow and Sunday at noon sharp and run for as long as they need to," he told Donnell and Sharday. "We can't do none of our tracks from the album. Don't want our shit leaked before we release it. So, we've got a lot of work to do."

"That's the same thing I was thinking, Big J.," Donnell said. "About the rehearsals all weekend and about the leaks." He should be used to it by now, but it still freaked him out that when it came to their music, he and Big Jeff were always on the same page.

Sharday grinned and said, "Well, this definitely calls for some bubbly!" Then she hopped up to help Candy with the champagne. She was more than happy to give up her weekend for a chance to be on a Deejay Amayzing mixtape. He was one of the few deejays who had both an underground following and a mainstream following. And if she and Donnell could manage to get a track on his next CD, the success of their own CD would be virtually guaranteed. She felt a shiver of excitement run through her as she grabbed a bottle of Cristal from Candy and picked up two champagne flutes. Everything was falling right into place for her and Donnell. It seemed their dreams were finally about to come true.

SIXTY-SIX

Sharday and Donnell were so hot in the studio on Monday night that Deejay Amayzing was sold on them within less than an hour. He was a short, slightly built brother who compensated for his small stature with an overconfident swagger. And as they segued from Big Jeff's jazzed up version of *Street Life Paradise* into Donnell's rendition of the Fugees' *Ready Or Not*, Amayzing stood and started clapping.

"It's a deal!" he announced. "I heard all I need to hear! And I got the perfect track in mind, too." Amayzing laughed triumphantly and rubbed his hands together. "Yessir!" he said. "I'm about to blow the game up with another scoop of the year!" He looked at Tank and said, "I don't know how the hell you managed to keep a fierce group like this under wraps all this time, bruh. But make sure you got an airtight contract. Because if they come through once I get them in the studio, I'm putting them on blast!"

Sharday and Donnell spent the next few days working pretty much around the clock to create a hot single for Amayzing. They were the last group to be added to the mixtape and he held them to a tight time schedule, but they managed to turn the uptempo Latin-flavored beat he gave them into a club anthem with a catchy hook.

True to his word, Amayzing dropped his new CD three weeks later on the Thanksgiving weekend. And by the Monday after the holiday, the industry was all abuzz about the new group called Double D-Day.

Tank wasted no time capitalizing on their newfound popularity. He took them on a fantastic shopping spree and had his "stylist" pick out an edgy provocative wardrobe for Sharday that was heavy on miniskirts and stilleto heels, with an urban cool collection for Donnell which included an array of jeans and body hugging sweaters and shirts. Then he gave them each a diamond-covered *Urban Legend* pendant on a platinum chain to secure their loyalties before he sprang them onto the New York scene. He took them to all the hottest holiday parties, album releases, and movie premieres. Even celebrity charity events. He quickly fell into the habit of asking them to perform on the spot to back up his hype about them. And all the while, he was putting out feelers to the top producers around the country.

They were both happy to finally come out of hiding and start making a name for themselves. But they were under so much pressure now, especially since they were still working with Big Jeff in the studio to polish up the album. Donnell relieved his stress by smoking more, drinking more, hanging out more with the posse. And although Sharday's schedule was extra crowded, thanks to the hair appointments, manicures and the like that were part of her new routine, she was determined to hang just as much as Donnell did. Because she definitely didn't want to leave him on his own with the posse.

To cope, she pretty much stopped smoking weed and cut way back on her champagne. She even took cat naps during her beauty treatments whenever she could. Still, the late nights with Donnell and the posse were taking their toll. She found herself experimenting with the same over-the-counter caffeine pills Tyesha had criticized some of her fellow classmates at Maryland for taking. And two weeks later, when Candy caught her popping caffeine pills and said, "Girl, you need to leave that fake shit alone and get with the real thing," then pulled a bottle of amphetamines from her own purse, Sharday couldn't deny that she'd been taking more and more of the caffeine pills even as they worked less and less for her.

"But I don't know," she hesitated, looking up from the prescription bottle to meet Candy's eyes. Speed was a real drug. A long way from blunts and bubbly. But then again, she was so tired she could hardly see straight these days. And anyway, she would only do it long enough to get the album finished and go back home. "Well," she said slowly, "I guess it couldn't hurt to try it. You know what I mean?"

SIXTY-SEVEN

Amayzing's mixtape sold more than two hundred thousand copies in the first month of its release – a career high for him. And Double D-Day's single was so popular it lit up clubs all across the country over the Christmas and New Year holiday season. By mid-January, Tank had received tracks for them from producers on the East Coast, the Left Coast, in the Midwest and the Dirty South – everybody who was anybody in hip-hop wanted to work with them. And although they quickly selected London On Da Track from Atlanta and Vinylz from New York City for their last two songs, it was the end of February before the album was finally ready for production.

By this time, Sharday was taking amphetamines, also called uppers, during the day to stay awake and over-the-counter sleeping pills at night to help her sleep. She had even picked up Candy's habit of identifying the uppers by color – "the greens," "the purples" and so forth – depending upon what Candy had been able to cop. But her conscience was starting to bother her, because she knew her mother hadn't raised her to be a junkie. And now that she had finished her work in the studio for *Urban Legend*, she was eager to get back home and clean out her system.

When Donnell suggested they take Tank up on the offer to stay in Jersey until the album came out, she insisted they needed to go home instead. "Boo, this the only chance we gonna have to take a break," she said. "We got about two months before the first single drop and after that it's on. Radio station dates, magazine interviews, gigs at clubs and charity events up and down the East Coast. And now that we got a mixtape track blowing up the clubs, more people probably gonna wanna book us."

"Shit, ain't nothing waiting for me at home, Day-Day," Donnell said. They were sitting in the living room of the guest house, and he gestured around at the luxurious setting. "I ain't trying to leave all this to go back to living in the projects or hiding from your mother while I'm staying with you and Tyesha."

Sharday knew she needed to go home, so she wasn't trying to hear that. "But those ain't our only choices no more!" she snapped. "Damn, Boo! We got a lot of money in the bank and we need to use some of it to get a place of our own! We can't live off Tank forever, you know!"

Donnell didn't like her tone but he was happy to hear she was finally ready to cut the apron strings to her mother and move in with him. "Whoa, Day-Day. Calm down," he said. "We just talking this thing through to decide what to do with it. Like we always do."

"I'm sorry, Boo. But I'm just ready to go home," she said. It seemed the more pills she popped, the more easily her temper flared. Another reason she needed to quit.

"Anyway, what you gonna do about Tyesha?" he asked. "And what about your mother?"

She shrugged. "Now that we can pay our own bills, I won't have to answer to my mother. And Tyesha been saying for months that her new boyfriend, Howard, willing to pay my share of the rent so I can move with you and she can have the apartment to herself with Jolean. He a lawyer, you know."

"Yeah, you told me," Donnell said distractedly as he thought through the situation. He had dipped into his bank account once or twice without telling Sharday, but he still had most of his share of the money. And since he couldn't keep her away from DC forever and Tyesha wanted the whole apartment, they did need a spot of their own. "Alright, Day Day," he said. "Let's go back and set up a home base."

When they told Tank the next day, it was clear that he wasn't exactly pleased with their decision. He warned them to lay low in DC and stay out of trouble. He said he would have his contacts down there keeping an eye on them. "No leaks, no performances, no nothing," he said firmly. "Just rest and relaxation. I've got a lot of money invested in you two and I can't afford no screw-ups."

Tank had been on the hip-hop scene long enough to see plenty of new rap artists go back to slinging drugs and living a life of crime to make money until their music careers took off. Some of those rappers had made it through, but others were in jail or dead right now. And he didn't want Donnell taking that risk. Which was why he had invited them to stay up here in the first place. So, now he decided to call in a favor from Big Slim, a major player in the gang whose name carried weight all along the East Coast. He would ask Big Slim to tell the leaders of *The Southeast Crew* to protect Donnell from the heavy lifting in the gang but allow him to make a nice chunk of change anyway. And with that settled in his mind, he felt a little better about them going home. He told them he expected them to check in with Maya by phone twice each week, on Wednesdays and Sundays. And he said he needed them back in Jersey in six weeks, "and no later," to start promoting the album. "The guest house and the Mercedes will be waiting for you two when you get back," he enticed.

Sharday and Donnell left two days later, at ten the following Thursday morning. The drive back home in the Cougar was a big letdown after cruising around Jersey in a Mercedes for the last six months. But while Sharday quickly got over it because she was so happy to be going home, Donnell brooded. He promised himself he would rent a nice SUV to stunt in as soon as they got home. They were signed recording artists now. They couldn't be riding around in this pile of junk. Plus, he was going to hook back up with *The Southeast Crew* and get in on some kind of moneymaking scheme so he and Sharday could floss until they went back to Jersey. Because now that he'd gotten a taste of the good life, he'd be damned if he was going back to just scraping by.

Sharday was also making plans for the next six weeks. Donnell had agreed to get a one-bedroom in the same complex she lived in with Tyesha, and they had already set everything up over the phone. All they had to do was go to the rental office in the morning and finalize everything. She would spend the first week after they moved in purging her body of the drugs she'd been taking. And then, the following week, she would go back to her job at *Old Navy* on a full-time basis – she had already arranged that over the phone, too. The apartment was going to put a dent in her bank account, so she would need the extra money. But more importantly, she needed a new routine that didn't include amphetamines and sleeping pills.

They stopped in Philly for a light lunch and Sharday headed to the bathroom after the meal to pop a couple of uppers. She was starting to come down from the ones she'd taken earlier and she didn't want Donnell to see her crash. But at the same time, she didn't want him to see her totally speeding.

So, as soon as they got back into the car and pulled off, she lit up a blunt and took several long hits to slow down the effect of the pills, then she clicked on the radio and started rap-singing along to Migos' latest hit.

It was a good thing she was planning to quit drugging soon because there was no way she could hide her habit from Donnell now that they were going to be spending so much one on one time together again. Up in Jersey, it was a different story. He had been too busy and stressed out to pay close attention to what she was doing. But that wouldn't be the case anymore.

When they finally pulled to a stop in front of the apartment building a little over an hour later, she grinned and said, "Home, sweet home! I know it's a big step down from what we just left, Boo, but I can't lie! I ain't never been so happy to see this place in my life!" She gave him a quick kiss before pulling her purse from the back seat, then she hopped out of the car. When he got out and headed toward the trunk, she met him back there and grabbed his arm. "Come on, Boo," she said. "Let's go see everybody. We can deal with our bags later."

Donnell grunted and led her up to the apartment. Of course, her meddlesome ass mother had planned a "homecoming party" and was waiting for them upstairs. Under any other circumstances, he would have blown off the party and headed on over to the Vistas. But this time, Vickie had arranged for Tyesha's mother and new stepfather, Walter, to pick up his own mother and youngest sister and bring them over here.

When Sharday let them into the apartment, they were greeted by dead silence. "Wonder where everybody is?" she asked him as she clicked on the hallway light. "I thought we were supposed to be celebrating." She waited for him to lock the door before she led the way down the hallway, then she almost jumped out of her skin when she entered the dining area and everyone in the living room stood and shouted, "Surprise!"

"Oh, my God!" she screamed. "Y'all nearly gave me a heart attack!" She laughed with joy as she looked around the room and saw her mother and Bruce, her father and Belinda, Tyesha and Howard – who was more handsome in person than in the pictures Tyesha had sent, Jolean and Rome, Isaiah, Gloria and Walter, and even Donnell's mother and two of his sisters. She was still laughing when her mother rushed across the room and enveloped her in a fierce bear hug.

"My baby, my baby, my baby!" Vickie said as she squeezed her daughter tightly and swayed her from side to side. "Sharday, don't you ever go away from me for that long and forbid me to come see you again! I won't be responsible for my own actions!" It had taken every ounce of strength she possessed, plus Bruce's constant encouragement, to comply with Sharday's pleading requests for her not to come up to Jersey and "ruin things."

"Oh, my God! Oh, my God, Ma!" Sharday said as she held on to her mother. "I missed you more than you could ever believe!"

Donnell slid past them and made a beeline for his mother, his youngest sister, Ebony, and his next to the oldest sister, Lynette. He hadn't known Lynette was coming, but he was glad she was here. Matter of fact, he was surprised at how happy he was to see his mother and sisters. It felt good to have some of his own family in the mix for a change. "What up, peeps?" he said with a lopsided grin. "Y'all must've missed me, too." He leaned down to hug his mother and noticed that she had put on some weight, which meant she was still off crack. Then he hugged each of his sisters, but held on to Ebony just a little longer. She had always been his favorite – smart as hell and just as pretty as she wanted to be. And he was determined to help her escape the trap of having too many kids too early by too many different niggas that Lynette and most of the other girls in the projects fell into.

As Donnell stood there chuckling while his sisters teased him about being a big-shot rapper, Sharday made the rounds through her father and Belinda, Bruce, Jolean and Rome, and now she was standing before Tyesha and Howard. "Hey, Donnell," she called out to him. "Come here for a minute. I want you to meet Howard."

Gloria was standing next to Tyesha. Always one to put on a show, Gloria looked at Donnell with mock outrage and threw her hands on her hips. "And I know you gonna come over here and tell me and Walter congratulations on our new marriage," she said. "Don't try to act like you don't know nobody just because your mother and them here. I been knowing you so long it's almost like I changed your diapers."

Everybody laughed and Donnell took it good-naturedly. "I was gonna come over sooner or later, Ms. Gloria," he said as he headed over to her and Walter. "You know that."

After Donnell shook Walter's hand and briefly hugged Gloria and Tyesha, Sharday introduced him to Howard. Then she crossed the room to chat up his mother and sisters while he worked his way through her parents and stepparents, plus Jolean and Rome.

About fifteen minutes later, Vickie called everyone over to the dining room table. She'd spent the entire day before cooking up an array of appetizers and finger foods, and she was eager for everyone to try them. "A party's not a party without something to eat. So, why don't we say grace and dig in. Honey," she said, turning to Bruce. "Would you do the honors?"

Once Bruce had said grace and everyone chimed in with their "Amens," Vickie said that the guests of honor should go first. "Come on up here, Sharday. You, too, Donnell," she said, gesturing for him to come forward. Now that Sharday was determined to move in with him, Vickie had made up her mind to develop some sort of a relationship with him. "We're all so happy to have the two of you back home," she said. "And it goes without saying that we're proud. Our own celebrities in the making!"

Donnell suppressed a smirk and said, "Thanks," as he stepped up to take the plate Vickie handed him. He had been surprised when Vickie pulled him to her for a hug earlier and welcomed him back. But once he thought about it, he realized she couldn't help but give him his due now that he had gotten them a record deal and they had their first CD in the can. It was about damn time she recognized.

"So, tell us what it was like going to all those premieres and stuff!" Jolean called out to Sharday and Donnell. "Every time I turned around, Tyesha was telling me y'all met this person and y'all met that person!"

"Did y'all get to meet Jay-Z and Beyonce?" Ebony asked with awe.

Sharday and Donnell spent the next few hours entertaining everyone with stories about the people they'd met and the things they'd done up in New Jersey. Andre stopped by while the party was in full swing with a very pregnant Nanette, who was less than two months away from her due date. And Kayla came in shortly afterwards, saying that John was at work and Kayjon was still at the babysitter's. The party didn't break up until well into the evening. And by that time, Sharday had to pop another upper to maintain her energy level. Thankfully, Tyesha and Howard had left a half bottle of wine in the refrigerator, which she poured into a big plastic cup filled with ice that she sipped from every few minutes to keep herself from speeding too hard in front of her family and friends. She couldn't wait until she and Donnell moved into their own apartment so she could hide out and kick her drug habit. But in the meantime, she had no choice but to keep up this balancing act.

SIXTY-EIGHT

The next morning, Sharday, Donnell, Tyesha and Howard went to the rental office so that Sharday could take her name off the apartment and sign a new lease with Donnell, and Howard could co-sign for Tyesha. They finalized the paperwork in no time since everything had been arranged in advance. And once Donnell and Sharday left with the rental agent to choose from the two vacant one bedrooms with dens, Tyesha and Howard headed toward his car so he could drop her off at school on his way to work.

Sharday and Donnell turned down the first unit the agent showed them because it was too close to the rental office. They both liked the second floor apartment at the back of the complex much better. Since they had each forked over twenty-five hundred and fifty dollars back in the rental office, for a total of six months rent in advance, the rental agent handed them their keys on the spot and welcomed them to their new home before she left.

Sharday smiled at Donnell and said, "I know it don't begin to compare with Tank's guest house. But at least it's ours, Boo."

Donnell nodded at her and looked around the empty apartment. This was a big step up for him, even though she had to practically force him to take it. It was a long way from the projects he'd lived in all his life. And it was the first time he had his own place, the first time he ever had his name on a lease. Life was good. Shit, for real it was great. And he knew in six weeks, they would be right back up in Jersey living on Tank's estate. "We be alright," he said. "Now, we just need to get us some furniture." Then he nodded again and said, "I'm gonna go unload the trunk so we can go looking."

Sharday paced out the measurements of the living/dining area and the bedroom while Donnell brought their clothes in and set up the studio in the den. Since she still had her keys to Tyesha's apartment, they went over there to get his album crates and the few pieces of equipment he'd left behind, her desktop computer and other personal items, including clothes and shoes. He refused to take any of the furniture she'd gotten from the house in

Mitchellville, and she didn't feel right taking any of the things she and Tyesha had bought together. So, after three trips back and forth, they were done.

Once they finished bringing everything in, they had a late breakfast at a local diner and hit an upscale consignment shop in Annapolis that Vickie had recommended, where they got a good price on all their basic furniture, which would be delivered the following Wednesday. Then they stopped by a rental car company not too far from the apartment so Donnell could rent a black Lincoln Navigator for one week. They were supposed to go to *Wal-Mart* and the grocery store after that, but decided instead to make a trip to the drive-through liquor store and get food from the local carryout.

When they got back to the apartment, Sharday popped a couple of uppers and opened a bottle of champagne. She sipped from her glass and picked at her food while Donnell ate and had a few drinks; they smoked a blunt and put on one of the movies they had borrowed from Tyesha and Jolean. He eventually crashed on the living room floor, but she was speeding too much to even think about sleeping. She covered him with a jacket and went to the bedroom to start hanging up their clothes.

They spent most of the weekend shopping for the apartment and fixing it up. But on Saturday night, he escaped to reconnect with *The Greater Southeast Crew*, telling her he wanted to hook up with his associates, and she spent several hours on the phone chatting up everyone and explaining that she would be hibernating for the next week. "I need some time to lounge around in my pajamas, catch up on my sleep, and just relax," she told her mother, her father, Tyesha and Kayla. "I won't even be answering the phone, so don't bother trying to call me," she added when she spoke to April. "I'll just see you next weekend when you get back for Spring Break."

* * * * *

Kicking her drug habit turned out to be a lot harder than Sharday expected. She was irritable, sluggish and emotionally off-balance. When she tried to sleep, she had nightmares that people were chasing her and woke up sweating. When she awoke, she felt hungry but everything she ate made her feel nauseous. She was so miserable that all she wanted to do was head out the door in search of pills.

But she didn't have any connections for uppers -- all her contacts were for weed. And going to the drugstore for sleeping pills would mean that she'd still have to kick those later too. Plus, deep down she knew she really didn't want to go buy more pills -- because more than anything in the world she just wanted to be done with them. But until she could get to that point, she needed the agony she was feeling to cease.

But it wasn't ceasing. It was getting worse with each passing hour. And by the time the afternoon of the first day rolled around, she knew she wouldn't be able to do it alone. She needed some help.

Donnell had called home a couple of times to check in and she'd faked him out by pretending to be groggy from sleep each time, encouraged him to hang out and said she just wanted to be left alone. But now, she wished he were here. Maybe he would know what to do.

She picked up the phone to call him but found herself instinctively dialing her mother instead. "Oh my God, Ma," she groaned as soon as Vickie answered the phone. "I need you to come take me to the hospital. Now."

"What? What's wrong, Sharday?" Vickie asked urgently, standing up and turning off the family room television even as she waited for Sharday to answer.

"My stomach hurts, and I've got a headache, and I feel like I have to throw up. I'm just sick," Sharday moaned.

"It's going to take me some time to get there," Vickie said. "Where's Donnell? Do you think we should call an ambulance?"

"He's out. And I don't need an ambulance. I can wait 'til you get here." Sharday groaned in misery. "Just hurry up, Ma."

"Okay, Sharday. Hang on, honey. I'm on my way."

Sharday hung up the phone and began sobbing as she curled into the fetal position on the bed. What on earth had she been thinking, taking all those pills like that? And what on earth had made her think she could just come home and kick the habit cold turkey on her own? She was clearly in way over her head. And now her mother was going to find out that she was nothing more than a drug addict. A junkie! *Please God,* she found herself praying as she felt another sharp cramp in her stomach, *if you could just help me get through this and get off these pills, I promise I will never do drugs again -- not even trees.*

In the meantime, Vickie had hung up the phone and rushed upstairs to grab her purse, which contained her car keys. She didn't stop to put on lipstick or comb her hair. She didn't bother to look in a mirror because her appearance was the furthest thing from her mind. She simply snatched up her purse, kicked off her slippers and slid her feet into a pair of leather mules, then she ran downstairs to the garage. She was on her own because Bruce was still at the office. And as far as she could tell, she didn't have a moment to spare.

Vickie zipped through her development as quickly as she could and hit Mitchellville Road, where she accelerated her pace. By the time she turned onto the highway and pressed the gas pedal even harder, she was truly speeding. She somehow managed to make it to Sharday's new building without getting a speeding ticket, and she bounded up the steps to the apartment and knocked repeatedly at the front door. This child should've given her a spare key for emergencies, like she'd asked, but Donnell didn't want her having a key to his apartment, so here she was standing outside unable to get to her daughter when Sharday needed her most.

Vickie breathed out a huge sigh of irritation and dug around in her purse for her cell phone. She called Sharday once, twice, three times to no avail. Then it occurred to her to call the management company and have them send someone to open the door. She was just dialing the number when she heard the top lock click on the door.

"Sharday! Sharday, open the door, honey!" she called out.

"I'm trying, Ma," Sharday croaked. She had been asleep having nightmares while Vickie was knocking on the door. But the repeated phone calls finally woke her up and she had slowly made her way to the front door.

Now, once she opened the door and saw her mother's face, she burst into tears. "Aw, ma," she sobbed, throwing her arms around Vickie's neck. "I just can't do this by myself. I really messed up this time and I don't know how to fix it."

"What are you talking about, honey?" Vickie asked as she slowly moved Sharday back into the apartment so that she could close and lock the door. "I thought you needed to go to the hospital and I drove over here as quickly as I could. What exactly is going on here?"

Vickie tried to lean back from Sharday so she could look into her daughter's eyes, but Sharday held on tightly and wouldn't let go. "What's wrong, honey?" she said. "Let go." She unsuccessfully tried to remove Sharday's arms from around her neck. "Do you need to go to the hospital or not? What's going on here?"

Sharday continued to hold on tight. She knew she had to tell her mother what was wrong, but she didn't want to have to face her while doing it. "I've been taking drugs and I'm trying to quit now but it's too hard so I need help," she blurted out, still holding on to Vickie.

At the word "drugs," Vickie's knees almost buckled. Her daughter on drugs? Surely, she must've heard wrong. Of course, she knew Sharday smoked a little marijuana now and again. But marijuana wasn't addictive. Quitting was just a matter of making up your mind not to do it anymore. "What are you talking about, Sharday?" she asked, once again trying to lean back to look into her daughter's eyes. "Let go, honey. I can't move."

"I can't let go, Ma. Because I'm just so . . . I'm just so ashamed." And with that, Sharday began crying so hard that she couldn't help but release her mother as she doubled over and wrapped her arms around her own waist. "Oh, God, Ma. It just hurts so bad," she moaned as she crumpled down to the floor and curled into the fetal position. "It just hurts so bad."

Vickie was so frightened for her daughter that the tears began to trickle down her own face, even as she dropped to her knees to comfort Sharday. "Don't worry, baby," she said with a confidence she didn't actually feel. She cradled Sharday's head in her arms and murmured, "You and I can get through this. Together, there's nothing we can't handle."

She began to rock back and forth as she tried to figure out what to do. Clearly, Sharday was suffering from withdrawal symptoms, but from what drug? When she asked and Sharday said that she had been taking "pills -- uppers and sleeping pills," Vickie felt a surge of relief that they weren't dealing with a really hardcore drug like crack cocaine or heroin, but she still didn't know what to do. Back in the days when they lived in the Vistas a few phone calls would've been all it took to learn exactly how to handle this situation. Somebody was always just coming out of rehab, or going to NA meetings trying to stay clean. But she'd long since severed those ties, and try as she might she couldn't think of a single soul who might be able to help them right now.

"Come on, Sharday," she said decisively as she stood and pulled Sharday up with her. "You asked me to take you to the hospital and that's what I'm going to do. Right now, that's probably the best place for you."

"Nah, Ma!" Sharday jerked away in alarm and stumbled backwards until she felt the wall at her back. She turned to lean against the wall and doubled over again, holding her stomach. "I can't go to the hospital," she said weakly. "What if Tank finds out? He won't release our CD."

"Well, we've got to do something, Sharday!" Vickie said sharply, more out of fear and frustration than anger. She took a deep breath and lowered her voice, walked over to Sharday and began rubbing her back. "I'm sorry, honey. But I can't just stand here and watch you suffer like this. And I don't know what else to do."

Sharday pushed herself off the wall and leaned against her mother. "Just stay here with me, Ma. That's all I'm asking. Just don't leave me alone."

"Okay, honey," Vickie said with a sigh. She would've preferred to take her daughter to the hospital where she could get the drugs out of her system under the supervision of doctors and nurses who knew what to do if something went wrong. But if the hospital was out of the question, then of course she would stay here and help her baby. What choice did she have?

Vickie led Sharday back to the bedroom and got her settled in bed. She prayed over her daughter, held her and rocked her when she trembled, repeatedly wiped her face with a damp cloth, helped her sip cold water, went to the kitchen and made dry toast and hot tea when she started refusing the water. And the moment Sharday drifted off to sleep, Vickie beat a retreat to the living room, where she picked up the phone and called Bruce. She told him where she was and why, explained why they couldn't tell anyone, then had him research the withdrawal symptoms of the two drugs on the internet so that they could figure out what she needed to do to help Sharday.

Bruce managed to maintain his composure because he knew that was what Vickie needed from him right now. But that didn't stop his mind from careening from thought to thought while he searched the web. How could Sharday let this happen? He thought she was a lot more grounded than this. She'd grown up in a neighborhood full of drugs and made it through unscathed. Only to end up getting hooked now? But on the other hand, he could only imagine the pressures she'd probably had to deal with up there in New Jersey. Trying to prove herself as a new artist. At a label run by black folks at that. And trying to keep up with that ex-convict she insisted on calling a boyfriend. What a bad scene . . . But whatever the situation, he was going to do everything he could to help her. Because she was his daughter now, too, just like April, and he loved her.

Aloud, he said, "Honey, maybe it's not going to be as bad as we think. The withdrawal symptoms for the amphetamines can include confusion, apathy, irritability, depression, increased appetite, a need for sleep. With the sleeping pills, if they were non-prescription, we can expect nausea, sweating, and shaking. But if they were prescription sleeping pills, she might also have unusual dreams, anxiety, stomach and muscle cramps, and vomiting." He took a deep breath and said, "It's definitely going to be painful for her to experience and painful for us to watch, but at least we're not dealing with anything life threatening here."

Vickie was sobbing softly, but she felt a sense of relief too. "So, this is actually something she can do at home. And it sounds like all I need to do is keep doing what I'm doing. Do they say how long it's going to take?"

"Anywhere from a few days to a few weeks. It depends on how long she was taking the pills, which we both know couldn't have been any longer than six months."

"Hmm," Vickie said. "Well, once she wakes up, I'm going to bring her back home with me. She'll be able to rest better there. And I'll be able to take care of her better, too."

"What about Donnell?" Bruce asked. "And where is he, anyway?"

"Who knows and who cares?" Vickie said dismissively. "If he was any kind of man, he never would've let something like this happen to Sharday. For all we know, he could be taking the pills too and not even trying to quit! As a matter of fact, he's probably the one that got her started on them in the first place!"

"Calm down, honey. Let's not jump to any conclusions here," he said, suddenly realizing that the situation over there could turn very ugly very quickly if Donnell came home before Vickie and Sharday left. "But now that I'm thinking this through, I think it would be best for us to get Sharday out of there before Donnell comes back and tries to stop us. I'll come over and help you." He stood and reached for his suit jacket. "I'm leaving now, so start packing whatever she'll need for the next few days. But if Donnell gets there before I do, hide the suitcase and don't say anything to him about what we're planning to do. Just be polite to him and let me handle it when I get there."

"Polite! I don't think--," Vickie began, but Bruce cut her off. "I'm serious, Vickie!" he insisted. "We don't know what kind of drugs Donnell might be on himself or how they might affect him. So, I need you to make sure you don't do anything to provoke him before I get there."

Vickie nodded her head slowly. Donnell was a pretty big guy, and he'd always had a criminal mentality anyway. "Okay, Bruce. You're right," she said. "I'll control myself. I promise."

"Thank you. I'll be there as soon as I can, honey," Bruce said before he hung up and rushed out of his office.

Bruce made it to the apartment in record time because he was so afraid of what would happen if Donnell got there before he did. Fortunately, Donnell hadn't returned by the time Bruce arrived. Bruce quickly lifted Sharday in his arms and carried her out of the apartment. Vickie followed behind him with the single suitcase she'd packed for Sharday, her purse and Sharday's purse, and she only paused at the front door long enough to pull Sharday's keys from a side purse pocket and lock the door. Less than fifteen minutes after Bruce had gotten there, they were well on their way to Mitchellville.

SIXTY-NINE

Back at the house in Mitchellville, Sharday gave herself over totally to her mother's ministrations. Vickie got her daughter bathed and into a pair of fresh pajamas and tucked into the bed in her old bedroom. She sent Bruce out for a baby monitor and they set it up in Sharday's room so that they could hear her every sound. They also prayed over Sharday frequently, and when Bruce suggested they bring a television into the room and leave it turned on to *The Word Network*, Vickie quickly agreed and helped him get it set up.

Sharday slept on and off for three days straight, only getting out of the bed with Vickie's assistance to use the bathroom from time to time and to be bathed each day. She sipped the cold water and hot tea her mother brought her, ate the warm chicken noodle soup and nibbled on the dry toast her mother fed her, and felt strengthened by her mother's constant presence.

For her part, Vickie spent most of every day at Sharday's bedside. She'd quickly made arrangements for colleagues to fill in for her at work, so from the time she awoke in the mornings until Bruce came home in the evenings, she was focused primarily on Sharday. Once Bruce came home, Vickie would rely on the baby monitor while she cooked dinner and they ate together. But as soon as the meal was over, they would both head up to Sharday's room so that Bruce could spend some time visiting with and praying over Sharday, and then Vickie would take over for the rest of the evening until it was time for her to join Bruce in their bedroom for the night.

This was the routine they had fallen into, and Vickie and Bruce were prepared to continue with it for as long as necessary. Vickie had already commandeered Sharday's cell phone and turned that off. And then she'd called Tyesha, Frank, April, and even Donnell, to explain that Sharday was suffering from an extreme case of exhaustion and would be staying in Mitchellville for a week or two so that Vickie could pamper her back to good health. Frank immediately agreed to give Sharday some space, saying he'd wait for her to call him when she was feeling up to it. April quickly agreed too, because she was coming home for Spring Break the following week and would see Sharday then. Tyesha gave Vickie a little pushback by repeatedly offering to come over each day and help take care of Sharday, but when Vickie insisted that it was more important for Tyesha to focus on her job and keeping her grades up, Tyesha finally relented.

However, Donnell flat out refused to cooperate. "Well, she can get all the rest she need right here at home in her own bed," he said.

Vickie tried to persuade him that Sharday needed her mother at a time like this, but Donnell disagreed. "She a grown woman and you the only one who don't seem to know it," he said. "If you ask me, it's time for you to cut the apron strings and give her a chance to come into her own."

"Well, nobody asked you," Vickie snapped, stung by the implication that she was holding Sharday back. Then she took a deep breath and said, "Look, she's here now and this is where she's going to stay until she's better. And that's just the way it's going to be."

"Yeah, right," he said with a dismissive snort. "Let me speak to Sharday."

"She can't come to the phone right now. She's sleeping. And anyway, I—"

Donnell cut her off. "Well, tell her to call me as soon as she wake up."

"As. I. Was. Saying," Vickie said firmly. "Sharday's too exhausted for the telephone right now. I'll tell her to call you when she's stronger. In about a week or so."

"How she gonna be too tired to open her mouth and talk on the phone?" he demanded. "Look Miss Vickie, I don't know what kind of bullsh—"

"Okay, that's enough!" Vickie shouted. "You will not disrespect me! If it weren't for you, Sharday wouldn't be in this position in the first place! You created this situation, now you deal with it!" And with that she hung up the phone.

But Vickie should've known Donnell wouldn't go away that easily. He called two hours later and she didn't answer. He called two hours after that and Bruce picked up the phone to talk to him. They talked for exactly eighteen minutes – Vickie timed it, and when Bruce hung up the phone he said that he didn't believe Donnell was responsible for Sharday's drug use.

In fact, as far as Bruce could tell, Donnell didn't seem to have any idea of what was going on. That's why Donnell was so irate, Bruce said, because he felt Vickie was once again trying to come between him and Sharday. He just couldn't believe that Sharday was so tired that she had to leave their apartment to get some rest and now she couldn't even come to the phone to talk to him.

Vickie wasn't convinced. She told Bruce that he was free to fall for Donnell's "innocent act" if he wanted, but she wasn't going to. And she immediately vetoed Bruce's suggestion that they candidly discuss Sharday's addiction and their efforts to help her overcome it with Donnell.

Donnell called three to four times per day for the next two days, and each time, Vickie either ignored the call or picked up the phone and said, "She's still sleeping," before hanging right back up. Sharday was getting better with each passing day, and there was no way Vickie was going to let Donnell back into the picture until her daughter had fully recovered. Her plan was to simply keep putting Donnell off, and so far, it was working.

But at 10:30 in the morning on Sharday's fourth day in Mitchellville – the very first morning that Sharday had felt well enough to change out of her pajamas and join Vickie at the kitchen table for a late breakfast of bacon, boiled eggs, toast and tea – Donnell showed up at the house looking for Sharday.

Vickie was surprised when the doorbell rang because she wasn't expecting anyone. And when she looked out the peephole and saw Donnell standing on the front porch, she almost had a heart attack. Her heart began racing a mile a minute as she tried to figure out how to get rid of him without letting Sharday know he was there. She decided to call the private security company that patrolled their community and have him removed. She didn't want him arrested – Sharday would never forgive her for that. She just wanted them to remove him from the community and warn him that the police would be called if he returned.

She went to the kitchen and said, "I think it's somebody trying to sell something. Let's just ignore them." And then, "I'll be right back, honey."

Vickie dashed upstairs to call the security company in private. She had just hung up the phone with them when Donnell began ringing the doorbell over and over. She ran downstairs, unsure of exactly what to do. And before she could come up with a plan, Donnell started yelling, "Day-Day! Day-Day you in there?" over and over at the top of his lungs.

Vickie stood in front of the door, looking back and forth from the door to the hallway that led to the kitchen. She realized that the only thing she could really do was hope the security guards came before Sharday heard Donnell yelling for her.

After a few seconds, Vickie heard heavy footsteps on the porch. She ran to look out the peephole and saw Donnell stomping down the stairs. Was he leaving? Maybe he thought they weren't home. Hopefully, he'd be gone before security even got there.

Vickie heaved a sigh of relief and headed toward the kitchen. But little did she know that Donnell was the house where the kitchen was located and both Vickie and Sharday could clearly hear him repeatedly yelling, "Day-Day! Day-Day you in there?"

"Donnell," Sharday murmured as she stood and quickly moved to the nearest window. Vickie followed, and she had just stepped up to the window beside Sharday in time to see the security guards rounding the corner to approach Donnell.

SEVENTY

Sharday watched in shock as two male security guards – one short and fat; the other taller with a muscular build -- walked slowly toward Donnell with their arms outstretched. Their mouths were moving, but she couldn't hear what they were saying. And all the while, Donnell just kept yelling her name over and over.

Sharday tried to unlock the window so that she could open it and call out to the guards and Donnell, but she was still struggling with the lock when, to her horror, the taller security guard shouted something to the shorter one and they both rushed Donnell.

"Oh my God! Donnell!" she screamed and began banging on the window. But Donnell was on the ground trying to fight the guards off, and they were struggling to subdue him, and none of them seemed to hear her.

Vickie pulled Sharday away from the window and said, "Stop, honey. You're going to break the glass."

Sharday was still weaker than normal, but the adrenaline surging through her body made her strong enough to pull away from Vickie. She ran toward the rear door that led from the kitchen to the back yard and began fumbling with the locks. "Help me open this, Ma!" she shouted. "We've got to help Donnell!"

Vickie walked swiftly across the kitchen and unlocked the door. Sharday bolted out of the door shouting for the security guards to leave Donnell alone, and Vickie followed her. This situation was quickly spinning out of control, and since she was the one who had set it in motion, she would have to be the one to bring it to an end.

"Let him go!" Sharday shouted at the security guards as she rushed toward Donnell. "Get off of him!" By this time, the guards had hauled Donnell to his feet and each of them was firmly holding onto one of his arms as he struggled to free himself.

"I'm going to have to ask you to stand back, ma'am," the taller guard said. "Please don't approach the suspect."

"Suspect?" Sharday shouted. "He ain't no suspect! This is my boyfriend!"

"Your boyfriend," the guard repeated. "But we received a call—"

Vickie stepped up then and cut him off. "I'm sorry, but there seems to be some sort of mix-up here," she said smoothly. "This young man is not an intruder. He's my daughter's boyfriend, as she said." She smiled at one guard first and then the other. "This is a family matter. If you know what I mean. And we would greatly appreciate it if you would just release him to us." She smiled again and said, "I'd be happy to call your supervisor and inform him or her of what a great job you've both done here. But please, just leave this to us to handle now."

The guards looked at each other, and then the taller one said, "Well, we're still going to have to write this up. We always have to complete an incident report every time we get a call."

"Understood," Vickie said. "And if you need my husband or I to sign off on anything, we'd be happy to do so."

"That won't be necessary, ma'am," he replied. And then he turned to Donnell and said, "We're going to let you off with a warning this time. But if we have to come back, we're turning you over to the police."

Donnell broke free now the guards had relaxed their grip and said, "Whatever, nigga. Just be glad I ain't suing y'all ass for tackling me like that. I wasn't breaking no law."

Sharday rushed over to Donnell and hugged him, while Vickie assured the guards that there would be no lawsuits and sent them on their way.

Vickie hated the idea of having Donnell in her house, but there was no way around it. So, she invited him in to talk things out.

"Nah, ain't no need for all that," he said. "I'll just wait out here for Day-Day to get her stuff so we can go."

"Sharday's not going anywhere," Vickie said. "She might be strong enough to leave in another week or so. But not right now."

Donnell pointed to Sharday and said, "She look just fine to me. And I ain't leaving here without her. She live with me now, not you. Just accept it so we can all move on."

"Well, appearances can be deceptive," Vickie said. "And I'm telling you that Sharday has just begun to recover from the—"

"Okay, okay!" Sharday quickly interrupted. The last thing on earth she wanted was for Donnell to find out about her drug addiction like this. She still wasn't sure whether she wanted him to know at all. But if he did find out, it wasn't going to be from her mother.

She turned to Donnell and said, "Why don't you wait for me in the car while I go get my stuff, boo?"

"But Sharday—" Vickie protested.

"Ma, please!" Sharday said. "We can talk about it in the house. Okay. Please?"

Vickie stared at Sharday for a long moment before she turned and headed back to the house. She couldn't really fault Sharday for not wanting to discuss her private business in the back yard. But there was no way Sharday was ready to go back to that apartment with Donnell yet.

Sharday kissed Donnell and watched him walk back around the house before she turned to join her mother inside. She had barely gotten back in the kitchen door when Vickie started in on her about how she still wasn't strong enough to go back to the apartment with Donnell.

"I'll be fine, Ma," she said. "You've already gotten me through the worst of it. All I have to do now is rest. And like Donnell said, I can do that back at the apartment."

Vickie couldn't have disagreed more. But she knew she couldn't force Sharday to stay, so she tried to reason with her. "Detoxing is only the first step, honey. And yes, we've done that. But now we've got to get to the root of what really caused you to take the pills in the first place so that we can make sure you won't do it again. And—"

Sharday interrupted because she could hear the fear in her mother's voice. "Stop worrying, Ma," she said. "I'm fine now. Thanks to you. And okay, maybe we've still got some work to do. But there's no reason I can't do it while I'm staying in the apartment."

Vickie shook her head. "I don't think so, honey. You need to tackle the mental part of it *before* you go back to the environment where the temptation is. Because if you don't, you could end up right back where you were. And I know you don't want that."

"Oh my God, Ma," Sharday said as it finally dawned on her what her mother was trying to say. "You must think Donnell is taking the pills too, right? And that's why you don't want me to go back?"

When Vickie confirmed her belief that Donnell was at the heart of Sharday's drug problem, Sharday sat her mother down at the kitchen table and explained everything to her. She told her about the caffeine pills, and how that escalated to the uppers, and how she began using the champagne to help control the effects of the pills, and how Donnell never knew anything about any of it, and how she still wasn't sure she even wanted him to know.

Vickie shook her head slowly, astonished that she had been so far off base. Her instincts were usually right on point. But not this time. She cringed when she thought back to how Bruce had tried to convince her that Donnell wasn't responsible for Sharday's addiction. And the fact that she had almost gotten Donnell arrested today only made her feel worse. Clearly, he wasn't the total monster that she had always believed him to be. She still didn't think he was right for her daughter, but maybe it was time for her to back off some.

"Well, maybe you can do the rest of the work from the apartment," she conceded. "But you've got to stay on bed rest for at least another week, Sharday. And I'm going to be coming over and calling to make sure you do. And you need to go to church every Sunday, too. Because you're going to need the Lord's help to really kick this thing. And maybe you should consider going to some of those Narcotics Anonymous meetings. Or we could probably get you some counseling if you don't want to do that. And—"

Sharday started laughing. "Okay, okay, Ma," she said, relieved that her mother had finally come around. And then, with a sigh, "But I need to get my stuff packed because I'm starting to feel tired. And Donnell's outside in the car waiting for me."

"I'll pack for you, honey," Vickie said as she stood. "Here, put your feet up." She lifted Sharday's feet to a chair. "And let me get you a cup of tea to drink while you're waiting." She walked across the kitchen to fix the tea. She would miss Sharday. She had gotten used to having her around and taking care of her. And she definitely hated to see her daughter leave this early on in the process. But they would find a way to make it work. Just like they always did. Because together, they could get through anything.

SEVENTY-ONE

True to her word, Sharday went home and lounged around the apartment in her pajamas for the next week and a half. She talked on the phone and played around on the computer a little bit. She also spent a lot of time lying in bed or on the sofa watching television. Although she mostly watched movies, she had gotten hooked on two of the Christian shows that repeatedly played on the TV in her bedroom in Mitchellville.

Holy Hip-Hop played rap and hip-hop songs that sounded just like the songs from the radio, except the lyrics were all about serving God and following Jesus. And *Enjoying Everyday Life* featured an older white woman, named Joyce Meyer, who always preached about how to make your life better by following the teachings of the Bible.

Sharday watched both of these shows each day because they helped her feel closer to God and more sure of herself. But she did it while Donnell wasn't around because she just didn't want him to know about it. She also pulled out the white gold necklace and cross pendant she had received for Christmas the year before and began wearing them under her shirt every day for the same reason.

Vickie visited Sharday at the apartment each and every day. She'd gone back to work, but she'd rearranged her schedule so that most of her clients came in the mornings, and the few who couldn't do mornings came later in the evenings. That gave her every afternoon to spend with her daughter. She cooked food and stored it in the freezer and fridge, she hung out and watched television with Sharday, she also prayed with her daughter and sometimes they reviewed Bible verses Bruce had selected the night before. But more than anything else, Vickie spent a lot of time talking with her daughter. She helped Sharday realize that the biggest mistakes she'd made was putting her desire to keep track of Donnell ahead of her duty to take care of herself.

"That's a classic mistake many women make," Vickie told her

daughter. "Letting everything else go while they run behind some man. But that's not the way it's supposed to work, honey. And anyway, if you can't trust him when you're not around him, then he's not the one for you. Because you'll never be able to monitor another person's behavior 24 hours day. It's simply impossible."

Sharday explained that she wasn't worried about Donnell cheating on her because he had never given her any reason to believe that he would be unfaithful. As a matter of fact, he had always made it clear that he loved her and wanted to be with her, and she had no doubt about that. The problem was that she didn't trust him to control his own behavior when she wasn't around. He had a way of going with the flow and getting wild when everyone else got wild. So, she found herself trying to save him from himself.

"Same thing, different words," Vickie said. "The bottom line is that it is not your responsibility to control Donnell's behavior. Honey, you couldn't even if you wanted to. There's just no way you can spend every minute of every day around him. And even if you could, you would end up destroying yourself in the process because there would be no time left over to focus on you. Look at what you've just gone through, honey. That's the result of focusing too much on Donnell and not enough on you."

Even as Vickie was speaking, Sharday knew that her mother was right. Donnell was a grown man with the responsibility for his own life. And she couldn't ruin hers trying to run his. Of course, she would always try to look out for him. That was part of what it meant to love somebody. But she would never again spend so much time focusing on him that she put her own life in danger.

Vickie also convinced Sharday to tell Frank about her experience with drugs. "He's your father, honey. I think he deserves to know. And if it'll make it easier, I'll be right here when you tell him."

So, Sharday called her father and asked him to come over. And just as Vickie hoped he would, after he learned of his daughter's recent addiction, he hugged and squeezed her and told her over and over that he loved her so much. He said that he needed Sharday to take care of herself because he didn't know what he'd do without her. Vickie knew Sharday needed to hear that from her father and she was grateful that Frank had stepped up to the plate. But then, to her surprise, Frank took the conversation even further by telling Sharday about the various musicians he knew who were never able to reach their potential because they had gotten sidetracked by their addictions to drugs. He told Sharday that she had more than enough talent to make it and that she was already well on her way – much farther along than he'd ever gotten, but if she really wanted to succeed in the music industry, she would have to stay away from drugs.

Sharday nodded her head as her father spoke, soaking up every word he said. She knew he had been a musician for longer than she had been alive. He had spent years on the road. He had seen it all. And by the time he left, she had renewed her vow to stay away from all drugs, even weed.

* * * * *

Donnell had been happy to give Sharday the space she needed to relax and chill, just as long as she did it at home. Even if that meant putting up with her mother visiting every day. He had handled their first Wednesday phone check-in with Maya on his own because Sharday had been holed up in Mitchellville at the time. But other than that, he hadn't been able to get anything done while she was gone. He couldn't focus because he had convinced himself that Vickie was up to her usual trick of trying to turn Sharday against him. He was worried that once her mother was done, she would never want to come back home.

But after he went over there and brought Sharday back, everything began to fall into place for him. He had lots of free time on his hands and he used every bit of it to get back in with the local branch of the gang and talk his way into a job with them. They were into everything down here, from slinging drugs and carjacking to owning laundry mats and car washes as fronts. And Donnell was willing to do whatever it took to earn his piece of the pie.

By the time Sharday's second weekend back at the apartment rolled around, she was starting to go stir crazy and wanted to go out -- she had only left the apartment once to go to church with Vickie, Bruce and April the weekend before -- and Donnell had a pocket full of gang-related money that he was eager to flaunt.

He took her to an expensive champagne brunch. Left the "Nav," as he now called their rented Lincoln Navigator, with valet parking. Once they had been seated and the waiter came to take their orders, Donnell said, "We don't want any of that cheap, free champagne. Bring us a bottle of Moet. Better yet, make it Dom." When the waiter said that would cost extra, Donnell said it didn't matter and told Sharday to order whatever she wanted, whether it was on the brunch menu or not. Then, when it was time to pay the bill, he pulled out a thick wad of money and peeled off two hundreds. "Keep the change, dog," he told the waiter, who was so thrilled by the king-sized tip that he personally escorted them to the front door.

After they got back in the Nav and pulled off, Sharday said, "Whew! That was fun! Thank you, Boo!" And then, a heartbeat later, "But where you get all that money from? You went to the bank again?" She had enjoyed his extravagance after two whole weeks of being shut in. But now that they were paying their own bills, they needed to make their advance last as long as they could.

"Nah, Day-Day. That's from my tips at the car wash," he said. "Them niggas be rolling up in they Benzes, Ranges, Lexuses, and BMWs and they can't wait to break a brother off just to show how much they balling. I told you how it work. Everybody wanna be known as the biggest tipper." In reality, Donnell had reconnected with Boyd, who'd really come up since the last time Donnell had seen him and was now running two car washes and a couple of crack houses for the gang. Boyd gave Donnell a job at his busiest car wash, which also did a healthy behind-the-scenes drug business. And since all they pushed was weight -- no tens or twenties changed hands there, Donnell's cut was at least three to four hundred dollars each day even though he wasn't actually dealing drugs.

"For real, Boo?" she said as she leaned back against the headrest. This new job of his was starting to sound too good to be true. She'd never heard of anybody making the kind of money he was flashing at a car wash. But she was still struggling to get back to a place of normalcy, and she was determined to make that her first priority. So she sighed heavily and closed her eyes. Donnell knew how much they had at stake; she'd just have to trust that he wouldn't do anything to jeopardize that.

Donnell didn't bother answering her since it was clear that she didn't want to talk anymore. Instead, he lowered his window a little and inhaled the fresh air. He was too pleased with himself for words. Hadn't been back home a month and was already making enough money to keep himself and Sharday in good style until they went back to Jersey. And he didn't have to deal drugs to do it! He thought his sweet setup at the car wash was his payoff for doing hard time without snitching, but the truth was that word to look out for him had been sent down the line to Boyd from Big Slim up in Jersey. Still, the end result for Donnell was the same.

Sharday dozed on and off for the rest of the ride. And when they got back to the apartment and Donnell headed for the studio, she headed for the bedroom, changed into her nightgown and climbed right into bed. She wasn't exactly sleepy, but she still didn't feel ready to get back to making music, and she didn't feel up to doing anything else either. So, she laid in bed flipping through the channels on the television for a while. But she wouldn't dare to turn on a religious show while Donnell was in the house and nothing else was on.

She turned off the television and lay back against the pillows as she stared up at the ceiling. Sooner or later, she was going to have to tell Tyesha and Kayla about the pills -- preferably sooner. Because like her mother was always telling her, the more people she told her secret to the less power it would have over her. She would tell Tyesha first, and then she'd decide when to tell Kayla. Because Tyesha was her best friend, which meant that she deserved to know first. Plus, keeping this secret from Tyesha was causing a slight separation between them. And she missed her girl.

She picked up the phone and called Tyesha, who quickly agreed to hit the National Harbor with Sharday the next day just to hang out.

"It's about time you're ready to start going out again!" Tyesha said. "I thought I was going to have to come over there and drag you out of the house!"

Sharday laughed. "Girl, stop tripping. I just needed a little time to relax and unwind."

"Yeah, right!" Tyesha said. "You know you and Don--"

The phone beeped, briefly cutting Tyesha off. Sharday looked at the caller ID and saw that it said Belinda Wallace. "Hey, Tyesha. That's my father and them on the other line. Let me call you right back."

"Okay," Tyesha said. "Hit me back."

Sharday clicked over to the other line and said, "Hey Daddy or Belinda! What's going on?"

It turned out to be Belinda, and she was calling to invite Sharday and Donnell over for Sunday dinner the next day. "Well, Donnell has to work tomorrow," Sharday said. "His off days are Friday and Saturday. And I just promised Tyesha I would hang out with her down at the Harbor tomorrow. I was talking to her on the other line when you called."

"Well, why don't you bring Tyesha with you for an early dinner? And then the two of you can head on over to the Harbor afterwards." Belinda chuckled. "We don't mind if you eat and run."

"Okay," Sharday said. "That girl's always up for a good meal, so I'm sure she'll be happy to come." Which also meant that Sharday would definitely have to tell Tyesha about the pills before they got there. Because Belinda and Frank both knew, so it was possible that the topic might come up at dinner.

"Great," Belinda said. "Now, what's this about Donnell having a job?" Donnell was an ex-convict, just like her son would be once he finally came home at the end of the year -- her baby had been gone for five long years on a repeat drug offense. But if Donnell could get a job after being in prison for the same kind of charges, then there was probably hope for her boy, too

Sharday told Belinda about Donnell's job at the car wash, and then Belinda started talking about Frank's new career as a business manager for a couple of local singing groups.

"Daddy's managing groups now?" Sharday asked in surprise.

"He hasn't told you yet?" Belinda said. "Daggone me and my big mouth. He's probably planning to tell you tomorrow at dinner. Act surprised if he does, okay?"

"Okay, Belinda, I'll do that. And I'll see you tomorrow, okay?"

As soon as she hung up from Belinda, Sharday called Tyesha back to tell her about the change in plans, then she clicked off the phone and climbed out of bed in search of the jean capris she'd worn to brunch. It was strange, but all of a sudden she felt like joining Donnell in the studio. Maybe it was the fact that she was finally going to share her big secret with Tyesha. Or maybe it was the fact that she had just learned her father was planning to manage other groups. But whatever it was, something had her hoping that Donnell had a new track for her to listen to. And that was a good thing! With a big smile on her face, she quickly slipped off her nightgown and put her shirt back on. She was finally ready to get back to her music!

SEVENTY-TWO

IT IS NOW SIX-THIRTY A.M.! PLEASE WAKE UP! PLEASE WA-- Sharday sat up and quickly shut off her alarm clock so it wouldn't wake Donnell, then she climbed out of bed and headed for the shower to get ready for church.

Donnell lay still until she left the bedroom, then he rolled over and opened his eyes. He remembered the days when she used to write to him about how much she hated getting up early on Sunday mornings to go to church when she lived in Mitchellville and had no choice, but now here she was popping out of bed like she just couldn't wait to go when she didn't even have to. And what was up with her wearing that cross under her clothes all the time now? She was always changing. First it was the proper speaking and the college thing. Now it was the religious thing and not wanting to smoke weed anymore. And who knew what would be next? He didn't know whether this was just part of what it took for her to grow into a woman or whether she would always be this way, changing from one thing to another. But either way, he really didn't care. Because he was the nigga who always remained the same -- through prison, through Jersey, and through whatever else might come their way. And deep down inside, she was always gonna be his Day-Day regardless. Donnell and Day-Day to the end, no matter what. And as far as he was concerned, that was all that mattered.

When she came back into the room wearing her robe and looking sexy and damp, he suppressed the urge to pull her back in bed and instead said, "You gonna be back in time to drop me off at work?" Sundays were his longest day -- from ten in the morning to eight at night, so he wanted her to drop him off and keep the Nav until she came back to pick him up.

"I don't think so, Boo. Why don't you just take the truck with you? I'm cool with the Cougar."

He sat up and looked at her. "You can't be driving around in that old shit, Day-Day. We don't flow like that no more."

She laughed and said, “Come on, Boo. It ain’t even that deep.”

But he was dead set against her using the Cougar and wanted to rent something else for her to drive. She refused, said it would be a waste since she’d have the Altima to herself once April went back to college the following week. And anyway, she was planning to go back to work at *Old Navy* starting the next day, so whatever car she had would mostly just be sitting in the parking lot all the time anyway.

Donnell had forgotten all about the Altima. It wasn’t exactly what he had in mind for Sharday, but it would do -- if she still wanted to drive it after she got used to the sporty little Cadillac he planned to rent for her. “Well, we can just rent something for a couple days then,” he said. “Until April go back to school.”

“We’ll see,” Sharday said, knowing she had no intention of letting him rent a car for her. As far as she was concerned, he was already spending way too much money as it was. “Why don’t I just have April bring me to the car wash to pick up the Nav later on today, and then we can figure out the rest of it tomorrow.”

“Deal,” Donnell said. He was going to start calling around as soon as she left to see which company had one of those Cadillacs for rent.

* * * * *

Sharday was seated on the fourth pew in church with her family, fingering her cross pendant and listening intently to Pastor Barnett’s sermon about the victory Jesus purchased for us thousands of years ago when He died on the cross and was resurrected three days later. The pastor explained that Jesus took on sin, and sickness, and poverty, and all the other ills of the world so that we could live free of the effects of those things. And when Jesus said He came to Earth so that we could have life and have it more abundantly, that did away with any notion that we are here to just get through and get by and hang on and wait for the good life in heaven. Of course, there are going to be challenges -- the enemy is busy. The Bible says Satan is constantly seeking to kill, steal and destroy. But Satan has already been defeated for those of us who are in Christ. And to claim the victory, all we have to do is accept Jesus Christ as our savior and make him the Lord of our lives.

Sharday felt that the pastor was speaking directly to her throughout the entire sermon. Especially when he talked about Jesus taking on the ills of the world so that we could live free of them, because she knew deep in her heart that it was the Almighty God who had freed her from her addiction to pills. He had released her from it in a matter of mere days without any hospital detox or rehab program or any of the other things most people have to go through to get free of drugs. And in her mind, the reason she qualified for this divine help wasn't anything she had done but the constant prayers of her mother and Bruce, and the Bible passages they had read over her every day, and the Christian television shows they left playing in the background day in and day out.

So when the pastor issued the altar call and invited those who wanted to accept Jesus Christ as their Lord and Savior to come forward, Sharday glanced down the pew at her mother, Bruce, and April, who had already established their personal relationships with Jesus, and she decided that today was the day she was going to begin establishing hers too.

She took a deep breath, leaned over to April and said, "Excuse me. I need to get out." Then, with April staring wide-eyed in shock, and Vickie reaching up to squeeze her hand and whisper "I'm so proud of you, honey," and Bruce beaming like the proud papa, Sharday slid out of the pew and walked down to the front of the church.

She shook the pastor's hand, bowed her head as he prayed over her and the others who had come forward, and followed the pastor's assistants down the hall to a room that had been set up for just this purpose. Once they reached the room, Sharday was paired off with one of the pastor's assistants, who counseled her, led her through the prayer of salvation and gave her a Bible. Then Sharday exchanged telephone numbers with the pastor's assistant and agreed to call the assistant anytime she needed to talk. The whole process took no more than thirty minutes in total, but Sharday felt like a brand new person when she left the room clutching her new Bible.

She found her family waiting in the lobby of the church, where her mother hugged and squeezed her for so long she finally had to say, "Okay, Ma. That's enough."

"I'm sorry, honey," Vickie said, releasing her. "But I'm just so proud of you!"

"So, am I," Bruce said as he leaned over to embrace Sharday in a warm hug. "I knew you'd finally come around!" He laughed to keep the mood light, but it had been his hope all along that if they planted the seed by exposing Sharday to the Word the Lord would do the rest. And now that it had finally happened he felt grateful and totally awed by the power of the Lord.

"Yeah, yeah, yeah!" Sharday said, laughing too. "Now, are we going out to eat or what?"

"I know, right!" April chimed in. "I'm starving." She linked arms with Sharday as they followed Bruce and Vickie to the car and said, "You look great today. Much better than last Sunday. Do you feel like you're back to normal now?"

Sharday had allowed Bruce and Vickie to tell April about the pills because April was family and it would have been too hard to try to hide it from her. Plus, she wanted April to know what happened to her so that April wouldn't make the same mistake, especially since it all started with the same No Doze pills that a lot of college kids were taking these days.

Now she shrugged lightly and said, "Pretty much. But my main thing now is to just keep my head on straight and make sure I don't fall back into the old patterns. No weed and no champagne. No stressing over things I really can't control. You know what I mean?"

April shrugged too. She didn't fully understand what Sharday meant because she wasn't exactly clear on how Sharday moved from taking No Doze pills to taking uppers and sleeping pills. And they hadn't really had a chance to talk much or hang out because Sharday had been recuperating ever since April returned home for Spring Break. So April simply said, "I guess." But then, because of her own faith, she added, "But whatever you need to do to stay on course, Sharday, I know God will help you do it."

Sharday smiled and squeezed April's arm. "Me too, April," she said. "I'm counting on it."

Bruce took them to the Annapolis harbor for brunch, and they sat outside on a deck overlooking the water as they feasted on seafood with their omelets and waffles. As they were nearing the end of brunch, Vickie said, "So what are you girls planning to do for the rest of the day? Bruce and I are thinking about going to a movie, and we'd love to have you join us if you don't have any other plans."

Sharday shook her head as she swallowed her last shrimp. "I wish I could, Ma. But I promised Tyesha I would hang out with her today. I haven't spent any time at all with her since I've been back, so we're going to go down to the National Harbor." She lowered her voice. "Plus, I haven't told her about the pills. And I think it's time."

Vickie nodded her head and said, "I agree."

"Well, when are we going to hang out together?" April couldn't resist saying. "I'm going back to school next weekend and we haven't had a chance to spend any time together yet either."

Bruce and Vickie glanced at each other in surprise but didn't say anything.

Sharday looked up at April, surprise written all over her face too. "Well . . . I . . . I . . . you know, April. I've been recovering."

"I know," April said sympathetically. "But now that you're starting to get out again, I just don't want you to forget about me."

Sharday was so touched to hear that spending time with her meant this much to April that she couldn't help grinning. She laughed and said, "Forget about you? Stop playing April. You don't know it, but I've already volunteered you to drive me over to the car wash after we leave here so I can pick up the truck from Donnell." And then, after a brief pause, "And I'm going back to work tomorrow, but my days off this week are Tuesday and Wednesday and I don't have any other plans and Donnell will be at work. So, there you go! We'll have plenty of time to spend together before you leave!"

April laughed too and said, "That's all I'm saying! Sisters have to make each other a priority!"

Bruce squeezed Vickie's hand under the table, then he said, "And on that note, it's time for us to leave."

Once they got back to the house in Mitchellville, April and Sharday headed for the Altima, while Bruce and Vickie went inside to wait for April to get back and go to the movies with them.

On the way to the carwash, April told Sharday that she was planning to break up with Isaiah before she went back to school because she wanted to be free to date some of the guys up there who were interested in her. "I mean, I still care about Isaiah," she said. "But I'm starting to feel confined by our relationship. I'm too young to be tied down like this. I want to explore my options."

"Then that's exactly what you should do," Sharday said. She explained to April how her own preoccupation with keeping tabs on Donnell up in New Jersey had ultimately led to her addiction. And then they promised each other that they would never let their interest in a man take precedence over their responsibility to look out for themselves, and they vowed to speak up if either of them ever saw the other doing that.

"I've already done it once with disastrous results, so I know better now," Sharday said. "And you can learn from my experience without having to go through it yourself."

April nodded thoughtfully. Then she said, "You know, I bet that never would've happened to you if you had stuck with Malcolm instead of taking Donnell back."

"I know," Sharday said before she realized it. She promptly clapped her hand over her mouth as if that could take back her words. It had been a very long time since she'd allowed herself the luxury of remembering her relationship with Malcolm, and it still pained her to think of him now. So she pushed her memories away and said, "But on the other hand, if I had stuck with Malcolm I never would've made it to New Jersey in the first place. I'd still be in college sweating my way through every exam instead of getting ready to release my first album."

"Well, that's a point," April said as she pulled to a stop in front of the car wash. She still thought Sharday would've been better off with Malcolm than Donnell. And she also knew that Malcolm was just as talented as Donnell, even though Sharday never seemed to want to acknowledge that. But Malcolm was an opportunity that had already come and gone, and there was nothing to be gained by dwelling on him now. So she leaned across the front seat to hug her big sister and watched as Sharday climbed out of the car, walked over to the Navigator, and used her key to open the door and get in.

Sharday started up the Nav and clicked on her cell phone to call Donnell. "Hey Boo, I'm out front. I got the truck," she said when he answered.

"Alright Day-Day. See you at eight," he said.

"Okay, Boo. See you later." She clicked over to call April and said, "I'm all set, April. Why don't you pull out first and I'll follow. Have fun at the movies."

"Will do," April said as she pulled out of her parking space and headed down the street. She looked in the rearview mirror to make sure Sharday had pulled out too, then she said, "Have fun at the harbor with

Tyesha. Tell her I said hi, and I'll see you tomorrow night." She had agreed to pick Sharday up from work on Monday night so that they could hang out together until Donnell got home and he wouldn't have to rent a car for Sharday.

"Thanks April. See you tomorrow." Sharday disconnected the call and drove straight back to the apartment, where she decided to lie down on the sofa for an hour before she left to pick up Tyesha.

The next thing Sharday knew, she was being awakened by the incessant ringing of the telephone. She forced herself up and leaned over to grab the handset. "Hello," she croaked.

"Girl, where are you?" Tyesha said. "It's almost four o'clock. We're going to be late for dinner if you don't come on."

Sharday yawned and said, "Hmm, I fell asleep."

"Apparently. So, are you going to get up and get it together or what? Your father and Belinda are expecting us. And I'm ready to smash!"

Sharday was still groggy, but she couldn't help but laugh. "Girl, you are too greedy. Always have been."

"Whatever. Are you coming or what?"

Sharday rubbed her eyes and yawned again. "Yeah, I'll be there," she said. "Give me fifteen minutes."

She got up from the sofa and went into the bathroom to brush her teeth and wash her face. Exactly twelve minutes later, she was unlocking the doors of the Nav so that Tyesha could get in.

"Day-Day! What up, girl!" Tyesha shouted as she climbed into the truck. "Dang, it feels like I haven't seen you in ages!"

Sharday laughed. "Hey Tyesha. I have to admit it's been a minute." And then, "Girl, you're looking good! Love the skinny jeans. You have the perfect body for them."

"Thanks, Day-Day."

Sharday nodded and turned to look through the rear windshield before backing out of the parking space. Although she seemed to be focused on her driving, she was actually trying to figure out how and where to talk to Tyesha. The initial plan had been to take Tyesha back to the apartment and talk to her there before they went to dinner, but thanks to Sharday's extra long nap, that wasn't going to work now. She needed a new plan.

"So, what's Belinda cooking for dinner?" Tyesha asked. "Do you think your dad will let us have a glass of champagne like he usually does? Some bubbly would be great right about now."

Sharday shook her head and said, "I'm not in the mood for champagne tonight, Tyesha. I'm not drinking anymore. Or smoking either."

Tyesha looked at her in surprise. "What? Since when did all this start, Day-Day? And why?"

Sharday had just turned out of the parking lot to their apartment complex, so she parked at the curb on the street and turned the radio off. Then she looked at Tyesha and said, "We need to talk."

"Clearly," Tyesha said. "What's going on with you?"

Sharday took a deep breath and said, "Oh my God, Tyesha. Where do I start? It's such a long story."

"Start at the beginning. Like we always do." Tyesha unbuckled her seat belt so that she could get comfortable. "And if we have to call your dad and Belinda and tell them we're going to be late, or even that we're not coming at all, then so be it."

Sharday unbuckled her seat belt too and she switched her cell phone to vibrate. Then she laid her head back against the headrest and started from the beginning. Tyesha already knew quite a bit about the circumstances Sharday had dealt with up in Jersey. But now Sharday filled in the details about the posse, and Donnell's outrageous behavior when he was around the posse, and the No Doze pills, and Candy's colored amphetamines, and the sleeping pills and champagne Sharday used to balance the effect of the amphetamines, and her attempt to kick the habit on her own, and her stay at Mitchellville so that Bruce and Vickie could help her get the drugs out of her system, and her recuperation period at the apartment, and finally, her vow to stay away from all drugs and alcohol.

Tyesha was so astonished by the words coming out of Sharday's mouth that she didn't say a single word the whole time Sharday was speaking. And even after Sharday had finished, all Tyesha could manage to say was "wow" a couple of times. She couldn't believe that the street smart Day-Day she knew had allowed herself to get sucked into the world of hard drugs. But then again, the whole situation boiled down to Sharday trying to keep up with Donnell, and Sharday had proven over and over again that she would do pretty much anything where Donnell was concerned.

Finally, Tyesha said, "Girl, I really don't even know what to say. I just . . . I mean, really . . . I just . . . I just can't believe all this."

"I know. If it didn't actually happen to me, I wouldn't believe it either."

"Well . . . I guess all I really can say is that I'm glad you're over it now. Hopefully, you learned your lesson and that will be the end of it."

"That's it?" Sharday said. "No insightful advice about staying drug free? No nasty comments about Donnell and how I would be better off without him? Now I'm the one who can't believe it. You must be falling off your game."

Tyesha laughed. "Get a grip, Day-Day. 'Just say no!' That's my advice for right now. Even though after I look up amphetamines on the internet tonight, I'll probably have some more advice for you."

"I knew it!" Sharday said, laughing too.

"And as far as Donnell goes, what can I say that I haven't already said? And what difference would it make anyway? But I do have a question for you."

"What?"

"Why in the hell did you hide this whole thing from me for so long?" Tyesha was starting to get angry now. "You should've told me about it when you were still in up Jersey! Or at least once you got back here!"

"I know," Sharday said. "But I was too ashamed. I felt like I had become a junkie and--"

"Ashamed! Girl, we go way too far back for that! We're supposed to be closer than close. Best friends forever and all that! Did you forget?"

"I know, Tyesha. I--"

"Look Day-Day, shit happens in this life. And since we're just getting started with our lives it stands to reason that a lot more shit will be happening to both of us before its all said and done. My plan has always been for us to lean on each other to get through whatever comes our way. Because that's what best friends are for. But it's not going to work if you're too ashamed to tell me what's going on with you."

"I know, Tyesha, and I'm sorry. I made the wrong choice."

Tyesha looked at her. "Uh huh. Well, I just want you to know that you can tell me anything because I'm always going to have your back – even when you're wrong. Of course, I'll tell you that you're wrong, but then I'm going to do whatever I can to help you make things right. And I'm pretty sure you would do the same for me."

"And you know it," Sharday said, tears welling up in her eyes. "You know I've got you. Always."

Tyesha noticed the tears and decided that her point had been made. "So, what are you going to do about Donnell?" she asked, changing the subject.

"I'm not going to do anything about him." Sharday told Tyesha how Vickie had helped her to see that she had to make herself her top priority and leave it to Donnell to take care of himself.

"And you're going to be able to do that?" Tyesha asked skeptically.

"What choice do I have?"

"But what are you going to do when you get back to Jersey and he starts wilding out again?"

"Well, I'm going to talk to him about that before we go back. And once we get up there, if I see that he's starting to get out of control, I'll talk to him about it again. But other than that, there's nothing I really can do. So, I'm just going to focus on taking care of myself."

"Hmmm," Tyesha said. "That doesn't sound like a realistic plan to me."

"I know," Sharday said. And then she burst into tears. "Oh my God, Tyesha! It was so hard being up there because it seemed like I was the only one who wasn't totally over the top. I mean really! And knowing that I'm going to have to go through all that again just blows me!"

Tyesha leaned over and hugged her friend, let her cry out some of the pent up frustration. Once the flow of tears slowed, Tyesha leaned back and said, "Maybe you shouldn't go back up there, Day-Day. Not if it's going to be like that. The album's already finished anyway, so why do you have to be there?"

Sharday wiped her face again with the napkins she'd pulled from the console between the two seats and said, "Because Tank wants us there. So we don't have a choice." She sniffed. "I mean, don't get me wrong. It wasn't all bad. In some ways, it was actually really nice. But having the posse around all the time ruined it for me."

"Then we're going to have to come up with some ways for you to deal with the posse and not let them get to you," Tyesha said.

"We can try," Sharday said doubtfully. Then she wiped her eyes one last time and turned to Tyesha with a look of steely determination on her face. "But for real, no matter what they do when I get back up there, there's no way I'm going to let a bunch of low life thugs like the posse come between me and my music career. And I'm not going to let them, or Donnell, or anybody else stress me out so much that I turn back to taking pills. And I mean that, Tyesha."

"I heard that!" Tyesha said, hoping with everything in her that Sharday would never turn back to the pills again.

Sharday started up the truck and put her seatbelt back on. "Oh my God, it's ten after five! Check my cell, Tyesha. I bet Belinda has been blowing it up." And with that, she pulled away from the curb and headed for the highway.

Tyesha buckled up her own seatbelt and leaned over to pick up Sharday's cell phone. She hated that Sharday had gone through all of this on her own with nobody to lean on. But when she went back to Jersey this time around, Tyesha was going to call her every single day and maybe even go up for a few weekend visits. And if it seemed necessary, she would also insist that Sharday come home from time to time to take a break from it all. As a matter of fact, she was going to stay in close contact with Vickie and Bruce once Sharday left so that they could coordinate their efforts. And if it took calling Donnell to harass him into helping Sharday get some down time she would do that too. Whatever it took, that was going to be her attitude about it. Because she never wanted her girl to feel so alone and overwhelmed again that she felt she had to turn to hard drugs just to get through.

SEVENTY-THREE

Sharday went back to her job at *Old Navy* the next day. She had chosen the noon to eight shift again, and this time around they had given her every other weekend off and Tuesdays and Wednesdays on the alternating weeks. Nothing had changed since she'd left besides some of the employees, so the job was a breeze. Just something to do to keep her occupied and put a few extra dollars in her pocket.

She spent most of her free time that first week with April and Tyesha, who were both still on Spring Break. April volunteered to pick Sharday up from work all week since Donnell worked the three to eleven thirty shift at the car wash Mondays through Thursdays, and Tyesha made a habit of riding with April each night. Once they picked Sharday up, they would either go out to eat or get a carryout order and take it back to Sharday's apartment, where they would hang out laughing and talking until about midnight – just before Donnell came back home.

On Sharday's two days off that week, they shopped, went to see a movie each day, drove up to Baltimore to hang out at the harbor, and even rode through Sharday and Tyesha's old neighborhood in southeast so that Tyesha could show Sharday the things that had changed since she'd been gone. They tried to convince Kayla to come hang out with them for a few hours on Thursday evening, but with her full-time job and her baby, and her husband still at work on the evening shift of his job, Kayla simply wasn't able to get away on such short notice.

Once Spring Break ended, April went back to Northwestern, Tyesha returned to her normal routine of college, work, raising Jolean and trying to spend time with Howard, and Sharday quickly developed a pattern of her own as well. She spent her Tuesdays off at the gym with Vickie, her Wednesdays off with Frank and Belinda, and she went to church with Vickie and Bruce every Sunday morning. Plus, she saw Tyesha at least briefly almost every day and she stayed in touch with Kayla by phone.

Sharday also began spending more and more of her free time in the studio. Of course, she and Donnell worked together in the studio on his music every weekend she was off. And initially, she spent her time alone in the studio working on lyrics for his latest tracks. But as time went on, she began searching through his album crates for samples she could use to make songs of her own. She found that she enjoyed having the freedom to work on her own music in secret, even though she was sure she'd eventually get around to sharing some of it with Donnell once she got it to a level that she felt was up to his standards.

The highlights of each week for her were on Friday and Saturday nights, because she and Donnell always went out on those nights, regardless of whether or not she had to work over the weekend, and Donnell always did it up big. Expensive meals and big tips; a steady supply of the best champagne at the hottest clubs. She couldn't help it, she loved the special treatment they received everywhere they went these days. And although she had her suspicions about what he might be doing to stay so flush with money, she figured they wouldn't be around long enough for him to do any real damage.

But on the Friday night exactly one week before they were scheduled to go back to Jersey, they were eating seafood at a restaurant on the southwest DC waterfront when Donnell received a cell phone call he said he had to take. "Yeah, it's me," he said into the phone. And then, "Nah! What the . . . ?" He motioned to Sharday to give him a few minutes, then he quickly got up and headed away from the table.

As Sharday sat in the dining area savoring her lobster tails, Donnell stood in a distant corner of the spacious lobby listening to a fellow gang member tell him that there had been a shooting at the car wash. An attempted robbery that one of their own lieutenants had stopped by emptying both of his guns. Turns out a rival gang was responsible and the lieutenant had killed one of the leaders. So now, they would most likely be involved in a gang war. And the word from Boyd was for Donnell to go back to Jersey early and stay out of it.

Donnell hung up the phone a few seconds later and slowly headed back towards Sharday. He knew she wouldn't be willing to leave before Sunday because her mother was throwing them a big going away party tomorrow night and had already invited her family from Philly to come down. But he'd have to at least convince her to lay low until the party and leave as soon as possible after it was over.

As he sat back down at the table, he noticed that she'd finished her meal. He pushed his own plate away and signaled the waiter to bring the check. His appetite was gone and all he wanted to do was get back to the apartment. "Let's skip dessert and get out of here, Day-Day," he said.

She looked at him. "Okay. But what's wrong, Boo?"

"I'll tell you when we get back to the Nav," he said.

Once they were back in the truck and on their way, Donnell said, "Bad news, Day-Day. Some niggas tried to rob the car wash tonight and security ended up shooting one of them."

"Oh, my God. What?" she said. "So, nobody else got hurt? All your coworkers okay?"

"So far," he said.

"What you mean by that?"

He knew he had to tell her at least part of the truth about the gangs because that was the only way he could make her realize it was too dangerous for them to stay here. He briefly turned to look at her. "They saying a gang was behind it, Day-Day," he said before returning his eyes to the road. "Which mean security killed a gang member and they gonna want revenge for that."

"Oh," she said, too surprised to say anything else. But in her mind, it was all finally starting to come together. He had come down here and joined a gang. That's how he was making so much money. And now, the shit was about to get raw. She could feel herself becoming angry that he had kept her in the dark the whole time. But then she remembered that she'd kept her drug problem from him, too. He still didn't know about it. And anyway, she'd known all along he was up to something, but she was too busy enjoying the perks to do anything about it. She sighed heavily, turned to look at him, and said, "So, now what?"

He exhaled heavily, too. "Well, first, I was thinking we should just lay low until next weekend," he said. "But you know what, Day-Day? The more I think about this shit, the more I think we should just leave. Just go back to Jersey a week early."

She nodded in agreement and turned to look out the window. "Okay, Donnell. But can we stay for the party? Or do we have to leave tonight?" she asked. She would follow his lead on this, regardless of how much she'd been looking forward to the party and having another week at home. Because Donnell was pretty fearless. And if he was telling her that he would rather run than stay and deal with whatever was getting ready to go down, she wasn't about to second guess him.

He said they could stay in and pack tomorrow, load the car before they left for the party tomorrow night, then hit the road straight from there. "You can follow me to drop the Nav off and we'll take the Cougar out to Mitchellville," he said. "Ain't nobody seen me driving that since we been back, so we should be alright."

"Okay, Donnell," she said again, still staring out the window.

Neither of them said anything after that. They were each too absorbed in their own thoughts. Donnell was wondering how many homies he would lose in the days and months to come, hoping his niggas didn't take too many hits. He was also grateful Boyd had given him a pass and had sent it through the chain of command so everybody in the gang down here and up in Jersey, too, would know he wasn't running from the fight – he was being sent away. Shit, they all knew he had a chance to make it big with Sharday. And thanks to *Urban Legend's* strong ties to the gang, everybody stood to benefit.

For her part, Sharday was trying to figure out what to tell her parents about why she wanted to go back to Jersey a week early. But then she realized that the car wash would probably make the morning news. Which meant she'd have to come up with a version of the truth to tell everyone tonight. After some thought, she decided to keep it simple. She would just tell them about the shooting and say there were rumors of gangs being involved. Then she'd say Donnell didn't want any part of that, so he'd decided they should go back to Jersey tomorrow night after the party.

As soon as they got back to the apartment, she picked up the phone and started dialing. Her mother and Bruce were first on the list, and Vickie was so freaked out she wanted to come pick up Sharday right away. She said Donnell had gone too far this time and Sharday needed to get away from him until he left the DC area. "Those gangs shoot everyone in sight to get to the person they want, and you know it, Sharday," she said. "As a matter of fact, I really don't think it's a good idea for him to come over here tomorrow night and put the rest of our lives at risk either."

Sharday protested, but Vickie wouldn't change her mind. Donnell wasn't welcome at the party. When Sharday asked Bruce to referee, he agreed with Vickie. He said it would be best for them to leave town immediately. "It's too dangerous here for the two of you right now," he said. "You need to give things a chance to cool off."

Sharday could hear the fear in their voices, so she wasn't exactly angry at them. But she felt frustrated and disappointed. "Maybe we should just pack tonight and leave in the morning," she said.

Vickie said, "I think you should leave tonight, honey. Don't worry about packing. I'll come over there next week and get everything together and ship it up to you." She was afraid for her daughter's life. And she would much rather miss Sharday, knowing she was safe in New Jersey, than worry about her while she was here.

"You and Donnell need to head back to Jersey as soon as possible, Sharday," Bruce said into his cordless handset. And then, in an attempt to lighten the mood, "And don't worry about missing the party. We'll plan an even bigger and better one after the album comes out."

Sharday gave the obligatory chuckle, but it sounded hollow. She was sad that it had come to this, with her and Donnell having to sneak out of town. What was wrong with them? The closer they got to their dreams, the more they seemed to self-destruct. She said goodbye to her mother and Bruce. Told them she would call from Jersey and would also miss them until she saw them again.

Vickie promised that she and Bruce would fly up for a visit in a couple of weeks. Maybe they would even fly April in for the visit, too. She managed to maintain her composure until the call ended, then she buried her face in Bruce's chest and cried for her daughter.

After Sharday hung up the phone on her end, she made her way to the studio and found Donnell bent over his keyboard bringing a new melody to life. "You know what, Boo?" she said. "My mother and them got all scared on me after I told them about the shooting and everything. They said we should just skip the party and get out of here tonight. And I'm thinking they might be right."

Donnell exhaled inaudibly. He hadn't realized he'd been holding his breath while she was speaking. But he had really screwed up this time and given Vickie some strong ammunition to use against him. So, he was grateful to hear that Sharday was sticking by him anyway. "Skipping the party ain't a bad idea, Day-Day," he said. "But we ain't gotta panic and shit. Let's just pack tomorrow like we planned to and leave at around the time of the party." And then, "But now that I think about it, I do think we should go drop the Nav off tonight. That truck draw a lot of attention, and the sooner we get rid of it the better."

She nodded. "Okay. That sounds like a plan."

She followed him to the rental car company's lot in the Cougar and waited for him to put the truck keys in the night drop-off box. Once they got back to the apartment, they cooked dinner and ate, he hit a blunt and they made love, then they bathed and climbed in bed together. This would be their last night home, and it was bittersweet because they were leaving on the low and didn't know when they'd be back. But at least they had a music career waiting for them up in Jersey. So, although they were clearly running away from something, they were also running toward something, too. And once Sharday pointed that out, they both relaxed enough to finally fall asleep.

The "gang shooting" at the car wash made the local news shows the next day, and since Sharday hadn't called anyone besides her mother and Bruce the night before, her and Donnell's phones rang off the hook all day. Everyone called. Frank and Belinda, Andre and Nanette, Tyesha and Jolean, Kayla and John, Donnell's mother and youngest sister, Miss Gloria and Walter, Donnell's oldest sister, Lynette, even his next younger brother who was on lockdown in Jessup, Maryland. Sharday and Donnell stuck to their story -- he only worked at the car wash, and now that he knew the gang rumors were true, he was driving them back to Jersey tonight. Everybody except Andre bought it, because he was the only one who knew the true extent of Donnell's involvement with the gang and he hadn't even let on to Nanette.

Vickie called Sharday's cell at noon and was distraught to learn that they were still in town. "Sharday, honey, this is serious!" she said. "You have to get out of there! You should already be in Jersey by now!"

"Calm down, Ma," Sharday said. "I know how serious the situation is. And Donnell does, too. We're leaving today, as soon as the sun goes down. I promise."

"Well, make sure you do," Vickie said. "And call me as soon as you get on the road to let me know you're gone."

At dusk, Donnell started loading the Cougar. He didn't notice the black car parked five spaces over or the two rival gang members dressed in all black inside of it. He had no way of knowing they'd been on the verge of him leaving, convinced that he'd already skipped town because the Nav had been missing all day, when they saw him emerging from the apartment building loaded down with luggage.

As Donnell and Sharday pulled off in the Cougar forty-five minutes later, neither of them spotted the black car following them with no headlights. It caught them both off guard when Donnell turned out of the complex and stopped at the sign at the corner, and his enemies rolled up to the left of them and let loose with a hail of bullets before speeding away.

Donnell took a hit in his neck and three in his upper torso. He instinctively floored the gas pedal, even as he let go of the steering wheel to clamp his hands over the spurting wound at his neck. Sharday had started screaming the moment the first shot was fired. But now, her scream abruptly ended when the car slammed head-on into a nearby street light pole and she was knocked unconscious.

Two Years Later

EPILOGUE

Sharday stood in the wings of the stage at *The Cellar*, her heart beating in overdrive and palms sweating while Clyde introduced her as, "Lady Day, the Grammy Award winning, triple-platinum selling superstar."

This would be her first live performance since the tragedy that took Donnell away from her two years ago. He lost his life on the scene and all she suffered were a few bullet grazes, a broken tibia, some bruising, and a brief coma. Her psyche had been deeply scarred, but her body would recover quickly.

The doctors approved her release from the hospital after a mere week and a half. But the morning before she was scheduled to leave, Vickie, Bruce, Frank and Belinda sat down to talk to her. They said the television newscasters were reporting that the car wash had been a known gang hangout, that Donnell was reputed to be a member of the gang, and that even Urban Legend was strongly suspected of having ties to the New Jersey branch of the gang. The national print media had also picked up the story and were sensationalizing it: Two young black kids from the ghetto who almost made it out through music but were cut down by senseless gang violence. Her parents said they had shielded her from the frenzy of reporters and photographers for as long as they could, but now that she was going home, she needed to be prepared to deal with it.

Sharday listened quietly at first and then started crying, which she'd been doing sporadically every day since she awoke from the coma. But this time her tears were accompanied by wails of agony, because it just broke her heart that her Boo had left this Earth trying to deal with all that stress and pressure on his own. Why hadn't he confided in her? Was it the same reason she had never confided in him about the pills? Because he was ashamed of what he had gotten involved in? Or was it because he wanted her to see him as a better and more perfect person than he actually was? And he was afraid that if she saw the true cracks in his armor she wouldn't want to be with him anymore? The same stupid way she used to be with Malcolm? Well, whatever the reason, look where it had gotten them! And now, they would never have the chance to fix it!

Vickie leaned over to envelop her daughter in a warm hug. Frank, Belinda and Bruce crowded around the hospital bed and laid hands on Sharday, too. They were all saying things like, "You'll make it through this," "God doesn't give you anymore than you can handle," and "In time, it'll get easier."

Sharday tried to take comfort in their words but couldn't because her mind was suddenly burning with the thought that she should've realized what was going on while they were up in Jersey. The posse members! Those low-life thugs! They were always curling up their fingers and saying something that sounded like, "Oh Gee!" in a weird fraternity-type voice. She'd just written it off as a party thing at the time, but now that she thought about it, she should've known better. Snoop Dogg and his cohorts from the West Coast were famous for throwing up gang signs. So, why hadn't she recognized it when the posse was doing it? Apparently she had been so desperate to become a star back then that she blocked out anything that didn't fit with her plan. Which was probably why she'd turned to speed and let that take over her mind -- to avoid seeing what had been staring her right in the face all along.

Oh, my God! I could've saved Donnell if I had just paid attention, but now he's gone forever, she began to think over and over. She eventually became so agitated that the nurse had to be called in to give her a sedative.

The doctors decided to keep her an extra night for observation. And when they released her the next morning, her parents and the hospital personnel snuck her out through the emergency room to avoid the media circus at the main entrance. One lone cameraman from the *Washington Post* snapped several shots of her from his perch at the top of a tree. The following day, her picture appeared on the front page of the *Metro* section along with a hastily put together article filled with speculation and innuendo.

She spent the next ten and a half months holed up in the apartment grieving, turning down repeated offers to move in with Vickie and Bruce, Frank and Belinda, even Tyesha and Jolean. In the meantime, Tank had released Double D-Day's self-titled debut album within weeks of Donnell's highly publicized death and it quickly climbed the charts. The fact that

Donnell had been killed in a gang-related drive-by and Sharday was now a recluse who refused to give interviews only fueled the public's obsession with them. The album went platinum, then double and eventually triple platinum. They won the Grammy for Best Rap Album, two Billboard awards, and awards from the NAACP, BET, MTV, VH1 and Soul Train. Tank and Jeff accepted the awards on her behalf because, through it all, Sharday was hiding out in the apartment, praying, listening to gospel music and trying to hang on to her mental health.

Then winter slowly began to turn to spring, and sorrow's grip on her gradually loosened its hold. She no longer felt guilty about failing to save Donnell because she finally understood that had never been within her power. She was still struggling with some major issues -- for example, her mother and Tyesha's theories that she had chosen Donnell over Malcolm because of her own insecurities and she had chosen drugs over sobriety to dull the pain that came from knowing she had made the wrong choice, as well as her own nagging suspicion that maybe Donnell would've turned his life around if she had shared her relationship with the Lord with him. Yet, the one thing she knew for sure was that it was time to come out of hiding and reclaim the music career Donnell had died trying to give her. But not with *Urban Legend*. She would never work with them again, no matter what.

The royalties from *Double D-Day* had started trickling in by this time. And according to Quentin, despite the mediocre contract, Sharday and Donnell's mother, who was his next of kin, were both going to be very wealthy women. Quentin negotiated Sharday's release from *Urban Legend* by arguing that Double D-Day technically no longer existed and by agreeing to let the label release two "posthumous" albums -- Donnell had recorded so many songs with Sharday in his short lifespan that two albums' worth wouldn't even make a dent. And once that deal had been finalized, Quentin secured Sharday a sweetheart deal with Sony Records that included a million dollar signing bonus.

Sharday used some of her bonus to put a down payment on a two-acre estate in a gated community in Mitchellville and buy a Mercedes Benz coupe. Donnell would've expected no less. She also withdrew enough money from her royalties account to give each of her parents fifty thousand dollars. She knew Bruce was covering all of her mother's expenses. And despite Frank's bragging to the contrary, she had long since realized that Belinda was doing the same for him. So now that she had money, she wanted her parents to have some finances to bring to the table, too.

She sent her grandparents in Philly twenty thousand dollars because they were living on fixed incomes and the money would be a big help. She also gave Tyesha, Kayla and April ten thousand dollars each out of her royalties. Tyesha could use the funds to help ease her transition into the real world now that she was doing her last year at Maryland and she had gotten Jolean off to Spellman College. Kayla and John would probably add their ten grand to the money they'd started saving for a house now that John had finally made it into the DC Fire Department after failing the entrance exam twice. April was the only one who didn't need the money. Bruce and Cathy were paying her college tuition and she had a healthy bank account they'd started for her back when she was a newborn. But she'd been there for Sharday when life was at its darkest and proven herself a true sister to the end, so Sharday wanted her to have the money anyway.

Sharday spent a week and a half furnishing her master bedroom and buying new equipment for her basement studio, then she turned the rest of the decorating over to Vickie and left for New York to record her first solo album. Sony had leased a two-bedroom suite at the Trump Towers for the duration of her stay, but she didn't spend much time there because she was in the studio ten to twelve hours each day during the week, and every Friday night she caught a flight back to Maryland so she could spend the weekend at home.

In New York, she was working with the hottest hip-hop producing duo on Sony's roster. But at home, she dug out the songs she'd created in secret back when Donnell was still alive, spent a couple weekends trying to polish some of those up, then tossed them all aside and created five more tracks in a streak of inspiration that later kept her up at night in New York composing verses and rhymes. Her new music was much better because her samples were more obscure and her lyrics were a lot deeper given everything she'd been through. And her production team at Sony was so impressed that three of the songs ended up on her solo debut. Sony's lawyers also cleared the way for her to record her cover version of a gospel song, *Never Would Have Made It* by Marvin Sapp, for the album, which was very important to her. She decided to entitle her new album, "I'm Still Me." And even as she was finishing the last few recording sessions, Sony was revving up it's massive publicity machine. They lined up radio and magazine interviews for her, a mini-tour of performances at nightclubs in the top twelve cities in the country, even a number of television appearances. She'd convinced them to make *The Cellar* the first stop on her tour because it was the only place she'd ever performed solo before. But now that the time had come, she was so nervous it was all she could do to paste a smile on her face and head onstage.

Clyde gestured toward her and said, "Ladies and gentleman! I give you Lady Day!" He knew she was nervous, understood that it took a lot of guts for her to do this after all she'd been through. But she had always been a tough little cookie. That was what he liked about her. And the fact that she'd picked his club to make her comeback only endeared her to him more, because with that one act of loyalty, she had literally put *The Cellar* on the map. Now, as she approached, he leaned over to kiss her cheek and whispered, "Show them what you're made of, Sharday. You were born for this."

The encouraging words from Clyde were so unexpected they brought a genuine smile to her face. She hugged him tightly and whispered back, "Thanks, Clyde. For everything." Then she accepted the mic from him and turned to face her audience.

By this time, much of the crowd was already on its feet giving her a standing ovation. She looked out beyond the bright, hot lights and saw that her family and friends had been placed front and center at an extra-long reserved table with her production team and several head honchos from Sony. Vickie and Bruce, Frank and Belinda, her grandparents, April, Tyesha and Howard, Kayla and John, Jolean and Rome, Gloria and Walter, Andre and Nanette. They were all there, and they were clapping wildly and calling out to her. She also knew from the publicity folks at Sony that the rest of the audience was mostly made up of celebrities and the media – almost everybody who was anybody had called in favors to get tickets.

"Thank you! Thank you all so much for coming out tonight!" she said. The audience roared back in approval and she felt the familiar rush of adrenaline course through her body. From that point forward, it was on. She sang the first two singles from her album, which were both catchy hip-hop anthems that would surely rule the clubs this summer. Then she hit the audience with one of her own creations, a haunting ballad about true love found and lost. Finally, as an encore, she left them with the remix of her first single, using the pre-recorded voices of Lil' Wayne and Drake as she sang and rapped her parts live. All the tracks she and Donnell had recorded together were off limits to her until Urban Legend made its final selections, but nobody could stop her from shouting out her Boo. "Rest in peace, Donnell Dickerson!" she said. "Always and forever, Boo! You'll never be forgotten!"

The audience erupted in crazy applause and she took her final bow, leaving the stage for good. But instead of making the quick escape through the back door she had contemplated earlier while standing in the wings, she confidently headed for the reserved table to greet her family, friends and new colleagues from Sony. She reveled in their congratulations and confirmed that her inner circle still planned to meet at her estate for an after-party. Then, on her way out through the front, she stopped at a number of the tables to meet her fans. There were prominent figures in the music industry, A-list actors, comedians and athletes. People she had only dreamed of meeting back when she was growing up in the hood and hoping to make it big. She was so hyped by the time she finally left *The Cellar* that she held an impromptu press conference on the sidewalk before climbing into her waiting limousine.

Once the chauffeur pulled off and they left the noise and the crowd behind, Sharday slipped off her heels and sank back into the luxurious leather seat. Tonight officially marked the beginning of her new career as a solo artist. And it had gone so well that she was confident she could be just as successful on her own as she and Donnell had been together. Of course, she still missed him. Probably always would. But at least she had God to lean on now, and He had already proven more than once that He could and would bring her through anything.

This time around though, she was going to handle her music career much differently. For one thing, she was with Sony now, which meant that she was in a much more professional working environment. No blunt smoking at important meetings, no gang bangers hanging around ruining everything with their thug mentality. And she would never tolerate that kind of madness again. Plus, one of the most important things she'd learned from recording *"I'm Still Me"* was that she needed to go home periodically to stay grounded. So, from now on, she would make sure she touched home base at least once a month, regardless of what was happening with her career. And she would also rely on the other coping mechanisms she had discovered, such as going to church whenever she could and watching at least one TV sermon each week to help keep her connection with the Lord strong. Because she didn't intend to ever let her life spin out of control again the way it had when she was up in New Jersey with *Urban Legend*.

She turned to look out the window and found herself reliving tonight's performance. Couldn't help but smile as she remembered how enthralled the audience had been from the moment she walked onstage until the moment she left. All four songs had been hits! Even her ballad! The dance floor stayed packed the entire time!

Her smile morphed into a happy grin and she leaned forward to help herself to the chilled bottle of sparkling water the chauffeur had already opened and left in the built-in ice bucket for her. This solo thing was going to work for her; she could feel it in her soul. And she was looking forward to everything her future held in store.

THE END

Made in the USA
Charleston, SC
09 March 2017